Acclaim

36 Argu   od

"Goldstein can make Spinoza sing and Godel comprehensible, and in her cerebral fiction she dances across disciplines with delight. . . . *36 Arguments* radiates all the humor and erudition we've come to expect from Goldstein, and despite the novel's attention to the oldest questions, it has arrived at exactly the right moment. . . . One of the funniest [academic satires] ever written. . . . Goldstein doesn't want to shake your faith or confirm it, but she'll make you a believer in the power of fiction."   —*The Washington Post*

"When Rebecca Goldstein, the American philosopher-novelist who looks like Rapunzel but thinks like Wittgenstein, was awarded the prestigious MacArthur Award (commonly known as the 'genius award') in 1996, she was praised for her ability to 'dramatize the concerns of philosophy without sacrificing the demands of imaginative storytelling.' That is putting her achievements lightly. Her most recent book, *36 Arguments for the Existence of God*, is a vast, rambling fiction . . . which is nonetheless possessed of a steely intellectual coherence that is frighteningly impressive to behold."
                                                —*The Times* (London)

"*36 Arguments for the Existence of God* affirms Ms. Goldstein's rare ability to explore the quotidian and the cosmological with equal ease. . . . The novel's bracing intellectual energy never flags. . . . It affirms Ms. Goldstein's position as a satirist and a seeker of real moral questions at a time when silly ones prevail."
                                                —*The New York Times*

"Hilariously irreverent. . . . The draw of transcendental longings, Seltzer discovers, is not to be found in logical proofs but in the accumulated wonder of all that can be encountered in this life: love, family, the sheer privilege of being alive."   —*Financial Times*

"Four hundred pages of smarts. . . . [*36 Arguments*] lays out a great range of witticisms, echoes and allusions."
                                                —*London Review of Books*

"Like an answer to a fevered prayer. . . . Part academic farce, part metaphysical romance, all novel of ideas, *36 Arguments for the Existence of God* may not settle the question of whether God exists but it does affirm the phenomenon of literary miracles."

—Maureen Corrigan, NPR

"A looping tale [with] affectionate irony about academic life, culture wars, and relationships in turn-of-the-millennium America. . . . The same engaging cocktail of philosophy, roman à clef fun, and scholarly soap opera that marked her earlier books. . . . She shows off all her considerable smarts. . . . Playful, humane."

—*The Globe and Mail* (Toronto)

"The best Jewish woman writing in America today. . . . Her latest, *36 Arguments for the Existence of God,* is flat out the most gratifying novel—woman's, Jewish, American, whatever—this reviewer has read in many a long reading season. *36* triumphs in a whole bunch of literary subgenres. . . . [It is] a novel whose manifold delights can only be hinted at in a review. *36 Arguments for the Existence of God* is brimming with richly realized characters, brimming with ideas, brimming with life."

—*The Jerusalem Report*

"[Goldstein] has taken on some of the deepest philosophical questions of human existence and shaped them into a page-turner at once funny and heartbreaking and challenging and—yes—proves that there's no such thing as 'too smart' to write a terrifically engaging novel."

—*Moment* magazine

"When a writer is as clever as Goldstein, it does not seem fair that she should also write with charm, humour and emotional acuity. But that is the package on offer in this ingenious and heartwarming novel. . . . A delightful novel, which could be one of the literary hits of the year."

—*Mail on Sunday* (London)

"A remarkable novel—as entertaining as it is illuminating—savagely funny in its characterizations, brilliant in its contemplation of the self and the sublime. This is a timely and timeless book, and definitive proof of Rebecca Newberger Goldstein's protean intellect and engaging talent."

—Jess Walter, author of *The Zero*

"An enjoyable feast of ideas that also serves as a very funny satire on the politics of campus life."
—*The Times Literary Supplement* (London)

"Thoughtful, witty, and—I cannot stress enough—really entertaining, 36 Arguments is part campus comedy, part romantic farce, part philosophical treatise. It is also, without question, the smartest kid in class. . . . Not since *The Tao of Pooh* has philosophy been so much fun."
—*The Christian Science Monitor*

"Rebecca Newberger Goldstein does it all. She has written a hilarious novel about people's existential agonies, a page-turner about the intellectual mysteries that obsess them. The characters in 36 *Arguments for the Existence of God* explore the great moral issues of our day in a novel that is deeply moving and a joy to read."
—Jonathan Safran Foer, author of *Everything Is Illuminated*

"A tour de force showcasing Goldstein's intent intellect and vast knowledge."
—*The Daily Beast*

"Goldstein's glorious novel celebrates the perils, pitfalls and profound joys of a life of the mind and spirit."
—*The Jewish Chronicle*

"Goldstein is a brilliant exponent of her subject, and she has crafted a story that is caustically irreverent, yet provocative and informative without being completely didactic. And . . . by the end, 36 *Arguments* is also deeply touching."
—*The Boston Globe*

"Satire with a soul."
—*The Chronicle of Higher Education*

"Triumphant. . . . With wicked comic genius, the book masterfully manipulates philosophers and their principles, kabbalistic literature and its acolytes, and a whole series of paradoxical ideas that live, breathe, and take on lives of their own."
—*The Jewish Week*

"[36 *Arguments*] proves that you can be both smart and funny, that Albert Einstein and Albert Brooks have a lot more in common than their first names. . . . The payoff is sublime."
—*Chicago Tribune*

"In elegant and often hysterical prose . . . [Goldstein] leaves us with a way to think about what having a soul might actually mean."
—*The American Prospect*

REBECCA NEWBERGER GOLDSTEIN

36 Arguments for the Existence of God

Rebecca Newberger Goldstein received her doctorate
in philosophy from Princeton University. Her award-
winning books include the novels *The Mind-Body Problem*, *Properties of Light*, and *Mazel* and nonfiction studies
of Kurt Gödel and Baruch Spinoza. She has received a
MacArthur Foundation Fellowship and Guggenheim
and Radcliffe fellowships, and she was elected to the
American Academy of Arts and Sciences in 2005. She
lives in Massachusetts.

www.rebeccagoldstein.com

Rebecca Newberger Goldstein is available for select
readings and lectures. To inquire about a possible appearance, please contact the Random House Speakers
Bureau at rhspeakers@randomhouse.com.

36 Arguments for the Existence of God

A WORK OF FICTION

36 Arguments
for the
Existence of God

A WORK OF FICTION

Rebecca Newberger Goldstein

VINTAGE CONTEMPORARIES

VINTAGE BOOKS

A DIVISION OF RANDOM HOUSE, INC.

NEW YORK

FIRST VINTAGE CONTEMPORARIES EDITION, FEBRUARY 2011

The Library of Congress has cataloged the Pantheon edition as follows:
Goldstein, Rebecca.
36 arguments for the existence of God : a work of fiction /
Rebecca Newberger Goldstein.
p. cm.
I. Faith and reason—Fiction. I. Title
II. Title: 36 arguments for the existence of God.
PS3557.0398T47 2010
813'.54—dc22   2009017022

Vintage ISBN: 978-0-307-45671-7

www.vintagebooks.com

Printed in the United States of America
10 9 8 7 6 5 4 3

For Danielle
Beloved skeptic and poet

CONTENTS

36 Arguments for the Existence of God

A WORK OF FICTION

I

The Argument from the Improbable Self

Something shifted, something so immense you could call it the world.

Call it the world.

The world shifted, catching lots of smart people off guard, churning up issues you had thought had settled forever beneath the earth's crust. The more sophisticated you are, the more annotated your mental life, the more taken aback you're likely to feel, seeing what the world's lurch has brought to light, thrusting up beliefs and desires you had assumed belonged to an earlier stage of human development.

What is this stuff, you ask one another, and how can it still be kicking around, given how much we already know? It looks like the kind of relics that archaeologists dig up and dust off, speculating about the beliefs that once had animated them, to the best that they can be reconstructed, gone as they are now, those thrashings of proto-rationality and mythico-magical hypothesizing, and nearly forgotten.

Now it's all gone unforgotten, and minds that have better things to think about have to divert precious neuronal resources to figuring out how to knock some sense back into the species. It's a tiresome proposition, having to take up the work of the Enlightenment all over again, but it's happened on your watch. You ought to have sent up a balloon now and then to get a read on the prevailing cognitive conditions, the Thinks watching out for the Think-Nots. Now you've gone and let the stockpiling of fallacies reach dangerous levels, and the massed weapons of illogic are threatening the survivability of the globe.

None of this is particularly good for the world, but it has been good for Cass Seltzer. That's what he's thinking at this moment, gazing down at the frozen river and regarding the improbable swerve his life has lately taken. He's thinking his life has gotten better because the world has gone bonkers. He's thinking zealots proliferate and Seltzer prospers.

It's 4 a.m., and Cass Seltzer is standing on Weeks Bridge, the graceful arc that spans the Charles River near Harvard University, staring down at the river below, which is in the rigor mortis of late February in New England. The whole vista is deserted beyond vacancy, deserted in the way of being inhospitable to human life. There's not a car passing on Memorial Drive, and the elegant river dorms are darkened to silent hulks, the most hyperkinetic of undergraduates sedated to purring girls and boys.

It's not like Cass Seltzer to be out in the middle of an icy night, lost in thought while losing sensation in his extremities. Excitement had gotten the better of him. He had lain in his bed for hours, mind racing, until he gave up and crawled out from under the luxe comforter that his girlfriend, Lucinda Mandelbaum, had brought with her when she moved in with him at the end of June. This comforter has pockets for the hands and feet and a softness that's the result of impregnation with aloe vera. As a man, Cass had been skeptical, but he's become a begrudging believer in Lucinda's comforter, and in her Tempur-Pedic pillow, too, suffused with the fragrance of her coconut shampoo, making it all the more remarkable that he'd forsake his bed for this no-man's stretch of frigid night.

Rummaging in the front closet for some extra protection, he had pulled out, with a smile he couldn't have interpreted for himself, a long-forgotten item, the tricolor scarf that his ex-wife, Pascale, had learned to knit for him during the four months when she was recovering from aphasia, four months that had produced, among other shockers, an excessively long French flag of a wool scarf, which he wound seven and a half times around his neck before heading out into the dark to deal with the rush in his head.

Lucinda's away tonight, away for the entire bleak week to come. Cass is missing Lucinda in his bones, missing her in the marrow that's presently crystallizing into ice. She's in warmer climes, at a conference in Santa Barbara on "Non-Nash Equilibria in Zero-Sum Games." Among these equilibria is one that's called the Mandelbaum Equilibrium, and it's Cass's ambition to have the Mandelbaum Equilibrium mastered by the time he picks her up from the airport Friday night.

Technically, Lucinda's a psychologist, like Cass, only not like Cass at all. Her work is so mathematical that almost no one would suspect it has anything to do with mental life. Cass, on the other hand, is about as far away on the continuum as you can get and still be in the same field. He's so far away that he is knee-deep in the swampy humanities. Until recently, Cass had felt almost apologetic explaining that his interest is in the whole wide range of religious experience—a bloated category on anyone's account, but especially on Cass's, who sees religious frames of mind lurking everywhere, masking themselves in the most secular of settings, in politics and scholarship and art and even in personal relationships.

For close to two decades, Cass Seltzer has all but owned the psychology of religion, but only because nobody else wanted it, not anyone with the smarts to do academic research in psychology and the ambition to follow through. It had been impossible to get grants, and the prestigious journals would return his manuscripts without sending them out for peer review. The undergraduates crowded his courses, but that counted, if anything, as a strike against him in his department. The graduate students stayed away in droves. The sexy psychological research was all in neural-network modeling and cognitive neuroscience. The mind is a neural computer, and the folks with the algorithms ruled.

But now things had happened—fundamental and fundamentalist things—and religion as a phenomenon is on everybody's mind. And among all the changes that religion's new towering profile has wrought in the world, which are mostly alarming if not downright terrifying, is the transformation in the life of one Cass Seltzer.

First had come the book, which he had entitled *The Varieties of Religious Illusion,* a nod to both William James's *The Varieties of Religious Experience* and to Sigmund Freud's *The Future of an Illusion.* The book had brought Cass an indecent amount of attention. *Time* magazine, in a cover story on the so-called new atheists, had singled him out as the only one among them who seems to have any idea of what it feels like to be a believer—"to write of religious illusions from the standpoint of the regretfully disillusioned"—and had ended by dubbing him "the atheist with a soul." When the magazine came out, Cass's literary agent, Sy Auerbach, called to congratulate him. "Now that you're famous, even I might have to take you seriously."

Next had come the girl, although that designation hardly does justice to the situation, not when the situation stands for the likes of Lucinda Mandelbaum, known in her world as "the Goddess of Game Theory." Lucinda is, pure and simple, a wondrous creature, with adoration her due and Cass's avocation.

And now, only today, as if his cup weren't already gushing over, had come a letter from Harvard, laying out its intention of luring him away from Frankfurter University, located in nearby Weedham, Massachusetts, about twelve miles upriver from where Cass is standing right now. Cass has spent the last two decades at Frankfurter, having first arrived to study under the legendary Jonas Elijah Klapper, the larger-than-life figure who had been Cass's mentor and Cass's tormentor.

After all that has happened to Cass over the course of this past year, he's surprised at the degree of awed elation he feels at the letter bearing the insignia of *Veritas*. But he's an academic, his sense of success and failure ultimately determined by the academy's utilities (to use the language of Lucinda's science), and Harvard counts as the maximum utility. Cass has the letter on him right now, zippered into an inside pocket of his parka, insulating him against the cold.

It will be a treat to tell Lucinda about Harvard's offer. He can see the celebratory clinking of flutes, her head thrown back in that way she has, exposing the tender vulnerability of her throat, and that's why he's decided to wait out the week until she comes home to tell her. There's no one in all the world in a better position than she to appreciate what this offer means to Cass, and no one who will exult more for him. Lucinda herself has known such dazzling success, from the very beginning of her career, and she has taught him never to make apologies for ambition. Ambition doesn't have to be small and self-regarding. It can be a way of glorying in existence, of sharing oneself with the world and its offerings, of stretching oneself just as wide to the full spread of its possibilities as one can go. That's how Lucinda goes about her life.

It's 1 a.m. now for Lucinda. She's taken the little amber bottle of Ambien with her—he'd checked their medicine cabinet round about 2 a.m.—so she's down for seven and a half hours. She'll be sleeping in T-shirt and shorts, her muscled legs—Lucinda competes in triathlons—probably already having fought their way clear of the bedclothes. Lucinda begins each night neatly tucked within her comforter, carefully placing her cold feet in the pockets, but no sooner is she asleep then the long struggle for freedom begins, and her legs are nightly manumitted.

For thirty-five weeks now, Cass has had the privilege of acquiring this intimacy of information regarding Lucinda Mandelbaum: her rituals of brushing and flossing and exfoliating and lotioning; the facts that she gets hiccoughs if she eats hard-boiled eggs too quickly and that her cold hands and feet are the result of Raynaud's syndrome; that she had spent her junior year of college at Oxford and had acquired a taste for certain British products that she orders from a Web site called British Delights; that as a girl she had wanted to be either a concert pianist or Nancy Drew; that she sometimes makes a whole dinner of a product called Sticky Toffee Pudding, is mildly libertarian in her politics, and gasps always with the same sound of astonishment in lovemaking.

How is it that Cass Seltzer is intimate with the texture of Lucinda Mandelbaum's life? His election—in that old crazy

Calvinist sense, about which Cass knows more than a little—
is absolute.

Suspended here above the ice-stilled Charles, he pictures
Lucinda asleep, her mouth slightly open and her delicate eyelids fluttering in dreams—oh, make them happy!

She usually falls asleep before him, and the sight of her
sleeping always wrenches his heart. All that mental power
temporally suspended, her lashes reclining on the delicate
curve of her high cheekbone, her fluffy ash-blond hair
released from its daytime restraints and spread fragrant and
soft on her Tempur-Pedic pillow. He sees the little girl she
must have been. He sees the phantom child yet to be, materi-
alizing before his mind with her mother's incandescent skin
and hair, her gray eyes outlined in blue and lit with points of
fierce intelligence. Watching Lucinda sleeping or absent-
mindedly playing with a strand of hair while she scratches out
the esoteric symbols of her science, or leaving their front
gate—with its sign left over from the previous owners,
"Please close the gate, remember our children"—the force of
the fantasy catches him off guard.

Nobody out there is keeping the books, of course, but
maybe he's earned the right to such happiness? Maybe the
years he'd given up to mourning Pascale have paid out a retributive dividend? No. He knows better than to believe in
such hocus-pocus, nothing else but more spilled religion.

Pascale's absurd scarf mummying him up to his rimless
glasses, he hadn't thought much about where he would go at
this hour and had headed straight for Harvard Square and
then down to the river, and then up onto Weeks Bridge, dead
center, which seems to be the spot that he'd been seeking.

The night is so cold that everything seems to have been
stripped bare of superfluous existence, reduced to the purity

of abstraction. Cass has the distinct impression that he can see better in the sharpened air, that the cold is counteracting the nearsightedness that has had him wearing glasses since he was twelve. He takes them off and, of course, can't see a thing, can barely see past the nimbus phantom of his own breath.

But then he stares harder and it seems that he *can* see better, that the world has slid into sharper focus. It's only now, with his glasses off, that he catches sight of the spectacle that the extreme cold has created in the river below, frozen solid except where it's forced through the three arches of the bridge's substructure, creating an effect that could reasonably be called sublime, and in the Kantian sense: not cozily beautiful, but touched by a metaphysical chill. The quickened water has sculpted three immense and perfect arches into the solid ice, soaring fifty or sixty feet to their apices, sublime almost as if by design. The surface of the water in the carved-out breaches is polished to obsidian, lustered to transparency against the white-blue gleam of the frozen encasement, and, perspective askew, the whole of it looks like a cathedral rising endlessly, the arches becoming windows opening out onto vistas of black.

Standing dead center on Weeks Bridge, in the dead of winter in the dead of night, staring down at the sublime formation, Cass is contemplating the strange thing that his life has become.

To him. His life has become strange to him. He feels as if he's wearing somebody else's coat, grabbed in a hurry from the bed in the spare bedroom after a boozy party. He's walking around in someone else's bespoke cashmere while that guy's got Cass's hooded parka, and only Cass seems to have noticed the switch.

What has happened is that Cass Seltzer has become an intellectual celebrity. He's become famous for his abstract ideas. And not just any old abstract ideas, but *atheist* abstract ideas, which makes him, according to some of the latest polls, a spokesperson for the most distrusted minority in America, the one that most Americans are least willing to allow their children to marry.

This is a fact. Studies have found that a large proportion of Americans rate atheists below Muslims, recent immigrants, gays, and communists, in "sharing their vision of American society." Atheists, the researchers reported, seem to be playing the pariah role once assigned to Catholics, Jews, and communists, seen as harboring alien and subversive values, or, more likely, as having no inner values at all, and therefore likely to be criminals, rapists, and wild-eyed drug addicts.

"As if," as Cass often finds himself saying into microphones, "the only reason to live morally is fear of getting caught and being spanked by the heavenly father."

Cass Seltzer has become the unlikely poster boy for this misunderstood group. His is a good face for counteracting the fallacy of equating godlessness with vice. Handsome, but not in a way to make the squeamish consider indeterminate sexual orientation, Cass has a fundamental niceness written all over him. He's got a strong jaw, a high ovoid forehead from which his floppy auburn hair is only just slightly receding, and the sweetest, most earnest smile this side of Oral Roberts University. Is this a man who could possibly go out and commit murder and mayhem, rape our virgin daughters, and shoot controlled substances into his veins?

His life has been largely commandeered not only by Sy Auerbach, the literary agent–cum–cultural impresario who represents him, but by a speakers' agent, publicists, media escorts, and other attendants who two years ago were as alien to him as atheists remain (despite Cass's best efforts) to the majority of Americans.

No wonder, then, that Cass undergoes moments when he feels he's lost the *feel* of his own life, its narrative continuity, the very essence of which was insignificance and an obscure yearning in many directions. The loss hardly matters, since he likes this new narrative so much better, likes it too much to own it fully as his own.

For the most part, fame is agreeable to Cass. For one thing, people treat him more nicely. It's a revelation to learn what a nice bunch of upright mammals we're capable of being. Everybody happily, gratefully, applies the Golden Rule when it comes to interacting with the famous. Thou must treat the famous as thou wouldst wish to be treated thyself. Easy! If only everybody could be famous, we would all be effortlessly altruistic.

Of course, notoriety presents its own challenges. Last week, a girl had shown up after one of his lectures with a copy of his book and asked him if he "signed body parts." Before he could find his voice or gain control over the blush spreading beyond his high hairline, she rolled up her sweater and offered him the heartbreaking baby innocence of her tender inner arm. Not knowing what else to do, wishing the present moment to become the past as quickly as possible, he had mutilated the butterfly softness in the tiniest spider scrawl he could manage.

"It must be that Seltzer boyishness I keep reading about," Auerbach had said, laughing, when Cass had told him about it, wanting his reassurance that this sort of thing was within the bounds of the normal, that it didn't transgress an academic's sacred trust to the impressionable young. "Stop worrying and start enjoying. Anyway, why isn't it a good thing if a guy like Cass Seltzer becomes a cult figure? Why not you rather than a Scientologist moron like Tom Cruise? Think about it, Seltzer."

Seltzer is still thinking.

This boyishness of his: before this year, that quality listed awkwardly in the direction of a handicap, socially and professionally, not to speak of romantically. Not that there had been any romances to speak of during that long cold February of the soul that had arced from the day six years ago when Pascale regained her speech and announced the end of their marriage until that day two and a half years ago, when Lucinda Mandelbaum had sat down next to him at the first Friday-afternoon Psychology Outside Speaker lecture of the new fall semester. But now, under the transfiguration of his fame, even his boyishness has become charmed. He's no boy (forty-two), but he has got boyish looks and boyish ways, of which he used to be boyishly unaware, until he read himself described as "boyish" in several newspapers, magazines, and blogs too many. So now when he goes bounding across some stage, his hair flapping a bit round his ears in time with his eager strides, somewhere in the recesses of his mind he knows that this is boyish, and that this is good.

He knows now, too, from the profiles, that though he's a tall and lanky man—well, of course, that he knew—he carries himself as if he weren't, as if, as one of the features had put it, "he's almost apologetic to be taking up so much vertical space." It's actually less embarrassing to read these personal descriptions of himself than he would have imagined. It's hard to take the person featured in these articles seriously as the Cass Seltzer that he's known all his life.

Cass is still trying to assimilate the fact that his book has become an international sensation, translated into twenty-seven languages, including Latvian. He understands that it's not just a matter of what he's written—as much as he'd like to believe it is—but also a matter of the rare intersection of the preoccupations of his lifetime with the turmoil of the age. When Cass, in all the safety of his obscurity, set about writing a book that would explain how irrelevant the belief in God can be to religious experience—so irrelevant that the emotional structure of religious experiences can be transplanted to completely godless contexts with little of the impact lost—and when he had also, almost as an afterthought, included as an appendix thirty-six arguments for the existence of God, with rebuttals, his claim being that the most thorough demolition of these arguments would make little difference to the felt qualities of religious experience, he'd had no idea of the massive response his efforts would provoke.

He would never have dubbed himself an atheist in the first place, not because he believes—he certainly doesn't—but because he believes that belief is beside the point. It's the Appendix that's pushed him into the role of atheism's spokesperson, a literary afterthought that has remade his life.

Tomorrow morning, he will meet with Shimmy Baumzer, the president of Frankfurter University, who will affect his I'm-just-a-hick-from-a-kibbutz demeanor, the better to cover up just how masterful an operator he is.

"What do I have to offer you to keep you from deserting us for those shmendriks up the river?" Cass knows that Baumzer will say to him, because that's what he had said to Cass's former colleague Marty Huffer, now at Harvard, three years ago, when Huffer's research on the psychology of happiness had hit the big time in a book that a mainstream publisher had brought out to a sizable audience and which had been Huffer's ticket out of Frankfurter.

It was Huffer's editor to whom Cass had originally sent the manuscript of *The Varieties of Religious Illusion*. Cass knew his name from Huffer's endless regaling of his former colleagues with tales from the life now lived far above their heads. The editor had called six weeks after Cass had sent the manuscript to him, just at the point when Cass was considering which university press to send it to next, and had invited him to lunch in New York. Over grilled branzini, he had allowed that Cass's approach was interesting, "especially the Appendix. I liked it. It's more provocative than the rest of the book. I don't suppose you could switch it around and make the Appendix the book and the book the Appendix, could you?" While Cass was still gaping, the editor had named his figure.

"This is the absolute upper limit of what I can offer," he had said, the slightest seizure distorting his upper lip.

Going back on the Acela Express—this was the first time Cass had ever taken the expensive high-speed train rather than the slower regional or, more often, the Chinatown bus, which makes the run from New York's Chinatown to Boston's for fifteen dollars and only occasionally catches fire—the fumes of his euphoria making him so giddy that he had laughed aloud twice and sufficiently startled the starchy matron next to him so that she had changed places well before she detrained at New Haven, Cass had suddenly thought back to the editor's oddly defensive words and the equally odd look on his face while he had said them, a suppressed smile of some sort making merry with his upper lip.

René Descartes identified the seat of the soul as the pineal gland, but in Cass's experience it's the upper lip that reflects the true state of the soul, giving accurate tells on the self-regarding emotions. Self-doubt and self-satisfaction will both betray themselves there. And if there is an egotist lurking within, the upper lip is the place that will give him away.

Flashed by the backside of New London, Connecticut, Cass thought back to the editor's self-congratulatory upper lip and felt the touch of a misgiving tugging at the edge of his elation. Back in Cambridge, he called Marty Huffer, asking him what he thought of the offer. Ninety seconds after he had hung up with Huffer, Cass's phone had rung, with Huffer's agent, Sy Auerbach, on the line.

"You can't possibly accept a contract for a book like that without representation," Auerbach had informed—or flattered or rebuked—him.

"But I already all but said yes to him," Cass tried to explain. "I think I may have verbally committed myself to him."

"No such thing. From now on, I'm the one he deals with. I'm your representative. Do you get it?"

"I'm not entirely sure."

"Well, here's something that might help you process it. If I can't get you more than that offer, then I'll forgo my commission."

"But he was so nice to me."

The agent laughed, a mirthless noise.

"What did he do that was so nice?"

"Well, for one thing, he took me out to an expensive restaurant."

"Which restaurant?"

"Balthazar."

The agent laughed again.

"Listen, if you let that junket to Balthazar persuade you to accept that offer, then that will be the most expensive lunch you've ever had. That lunch will cost you hundreds of thousands of dollars."

Auerbach had held an auction for *The Varieties of Religious Illusion*, and not only had the Balthazar editor made a bid five times his "absolute upper limit," but he had been roundly outbid.

Cass has certainly had his moments of doubt about his agent, wondering whether beneath the cynical exterior there was an even more cynical interior. Is he showman or shaman? A little of both, Cass has come to think, but a force for good for all that. Sy Auerbach has an agenda that goes beyond putting the "antic" back in "pedantic" and the "earning" back in "learning." His idea is that the time has come for a different kind of public intellectual. The old-time intellectuals, who were mostly scientifically illiterate, not knowing their asses from their amygdalas, have been rendered worse than dead; they've been rendered irrelevant by the scientists and techno-innovators, who are the only ones now offering ideas with the power and sweep to change the culture at large.

Auerbach harbors such impatience for the glib literati—the "gliberati," as one of his own digerati had christened them—that Cass has wondered whether there might not be some personal history. In particular, Cass has wondered whether Auerbach might not have known Jonas Elijah Klapper, the man of letters who had once reigned unopposed over vast stretches of the humanities, including Cass Seltzer's. Certainly, Auerbach must have known *of* Klapper. There was a time when Jonas Elijah Klapper had been revered by scholars the world over—with the notable exception of the British, whom Klapper had been forced to despise en masse, observing that "they seem to have lost, with their empire, the possibility of understanding me." The only thing that Klapper, born on the Lower East Side, must have admired about the English was their accent, since he had successfully acquired it. When Sy Auerbach describes the kind of thinker he detests, obscure references rendered in dead languages falling from their lips like flecks of food off a messy eater, it always sounds to Cass as if he's holding Frankfurter's former Extreme Distinguished Professor of Faith, Literature, and Values up to his mind's eye and ticking off his attributes one by one.

For months, Auerbach had only existed as a disembodied voice on the phone, always answering the "hello" with the announcement "Auerbach." The image that the voice had conjured had been surprisingly on the mark, as Cass learned when he finally met the man at a packed reading Cass had given at the 92nd Street Y. This was almost a year after Auerbach had held the auction for *Illusion* that would make an unlikely millionaire and celebrity out of Cass Seltzer. Auerbach is a large and showily handsome man, with a petulant mouth and fine white hair, looking like milkweed that has burst its pod. He wore a dramatic white fedora and a flashy white suit. It was early summer and hot, but he looked the sort who might easily don a billowing Victorian cape when the weather turned cooler, and brandish a silver-tipped walking stick.

Auerbach, with his uncanny nose for intellectual property, hadn't hesitated in accepting Cass as a client, unconcerned that there was already a glut of godlessness on the market. Atheist books were selling well, sometimes edging out cookbooks and memoirs written by household pets to rise to the top of the best-seller list. Though he never argues with success, his agent would probably be just as happy if the atheist with a soul went lighter on the soul.

The atheist with a soul. Cass always smiles at the absurdity of the phrase. But which is the more absurd element? The truth is—and what's the good of a man contemplating an inhumanly frozen world at 4 a.m. if no truth-telling ensues?—that Cass is somewhat at a loss to account for what he has done. How to explain those Thirty-Six Arguments for the Existence of God (see Appendix), all of them formally constructed in the preferred analytic style, premises parading with military precision, and every shirking presupposition and sketchy implication forced out into the open and subjected to rigorous inspection?

Cass had started out with all the standard arguments for God's existence, the ones discussed in philosophy classes and textbooks: The Cosmological Argument (#1), The Ontological Argument (#2), The Classical Teleological Argument (#3A), the arguments from Miracles, Moral Truth, and Mysticism (#'s 11, 16, and 22, respectively), Pascal's Wager (#31), and William James's Argument from Pragmatism (#32). He had also analyzed the new batch of arguments recently whipped up by the Intelligent Design crowd—to wit, The Argument from Irreducible Complexity (#3B), The Argument from the Paucity of Benign Mutations (#3C), The Argument from the Original Replicator (#3D), The Argument from the Big Bang (#4), The Argument from the Fine-Tuning of the Physical Constants (#5), and The Argument from the Hard Problem of Consciousness (#12). But then he had gone beyond these, too, attempting to polish up into genuine arguments those religious intuitions and emotions that are often powerfully evocative but too sub-syllogistic to be regarded as actual arguments. He had tried to capture under the net of analytic reason those fleeting shadows cast by unseen winged things darting through the thick foliage of the religious sensibility.

So Cass had formulated The Argument from Cosmic Coin-cidences (#7), appealing to such facts as these: that the diam-eter of the moon as seen from the earth is the same as the diameter of the sun as seen from the earth, which is why we can have those spectacular eclipses when the corona of the sun is revealed in all its glory. He had formulated The Argu-ment from Sublimity (#34), trying to capture the line of rea-soning lurking behind, for example, the recent testament of one evangelical scientist who had felt his doubts falling away from him when he was hiking in the mountains and came upon a frozen waterfall—in fact a trinity of a frozen waterfall, with three parts to it. "At that moment, I felt my resistance leave me. And it was a great sense of relief. The next morn-ing, in the dewy grass in the shadow of the Cascades, I fell on my knees and accepted this truth—that God is God, that Christ is his son and that I am giving my life to that belief."

For the right observer, Cass supposed, the sublime trinity of arches etched out in the ice below might yield a similar epiphany.

Cass had named the twenty-eighth in his list "The Argu-ment from Prodigious Genius," though privately he thinks of it as "The Argument from Azarya." The astonishment of beholding genius, especially when it shows up in child prodi-gies, is so profound that it can feel almost like violence, as if a behavioral firestorm has devastated the laws of psychology, leaving us with no principles for explaining what we're seeing and hearing. "There are children who are born as if knowing" are words that Cass had heard twenty years ago, inspired by a child who could see the numbers and thought that they were angels.

And then there's The Argument from the Improbable Self (#13), another one that engages Cass in a personal way. He had struggled to squeeze precision into the sense of paradox he knows too well, the flailing attempt to calm the inside-outside vertigo to which he's given, trying to construct something semi-coherent beneath that vertiginous step outside himself that would result from his staring too long at the improbable fact of his being identical with . . . himself.

If somebody hasn't experienced this particular kind of metaphysical seizure for himself, then it's hard to find the words to give a sense of what it's like. Cass had experienced it as a boy, lying in bed and thinking his way into the sense of the strangeness of being *just this*.

Cass had had the lower bunk bed. Both he and Jesse, his younger brother, had wanted the higher bunk, but, as usual, Jesse had wanted what he wanted so much more than Cass had wanted it, with a fury of need that was exhausting just to watch, that Cass had let it go. Lying there awake on his lower bunk, Cass would think about being himself rather than being Jesse. *There* was Jesse, and *here* was Cass. But if someone were looking at the two of them, Jesse *there*, Cass *here*, how could that observer tell that he, Cass, was Cass *here* and not Jesse *there*? If it got switched on them, everything the same about them, the body and memories and sense of self and everything else, only now he was Jesse *here* and there was Cass *there*, how would anybody know? How would he know, how would Jesse? Maybe a switch had already happened, maybe it happened again and again, and how could anybody tell?

The longer he tried to get a fix on the fact of being *Cass here*, the more the whole idea of it just got away from him. If he tried long enough to grasp it, then he could get the fact of being *Cass here* to blank out of existence and then come dribbling weakly back in, like a fluorescent fixture flickering on and off toward death. He would get the sense of having been shot outside himself, and now was someone who was regarding his being Cass Seltzer as something like his being in the sixth grade, just something about him that happened to be true. Who was that Other that he was who was regarding his being Cass Seltzer as if he didn't *have* to be Cass Seltzer? The sense of giddiness induced by these exercises could be a bit too overwhelming for a kid in a lower bunk bed.

It could be a bit overwhelming still.

"Here I am," Cass is saying, standing on Weeks Bridge and talking aloud into the sublimely indifferent night.

Cass knows he needs to tamp down his tendencies toward the transcendental. It isn't becoming in America's favorite atheist, who is, at this moment, Cass Seltzer, who is, somehow or other, *just this here.*

"Here I am."

How can it be that, of all things, one is *this* thing, so that one can say, astonishingly—in the right frame of mind, it *is* astonishing, with the metaphysical chill blowing in from afar—"here I am"?

"Here I am."

When you didn't force yourself to think in formal reconstructions, when you didn't catch these moments of ravishments under the lens of premises and conclusions, when you didn't impale them and label them, like so many splayed butterflies, bleeding the transcendental glow right out of them, then . . . what?

It's even hard at a time like this to resist the shameful narcissistic appeal of reasonings like The Argument from Personal Coincidences (#8) and The Argument from Answered Prayers (#9) and The Argument from a Wonderful Life (#10). William James had rebuked the "scoundrel logic" that calculates divine provenance from one's own goody bag of gains, and Cass couldn't agree more with the spirit of James, but here it is, his bulging goody bag, and call him a scoundrel for feeling personally grateful to the universe when, at this same moment that he is standing on Weeks Bridge and tossing hosannas out into the infinite universe, there are multitudes of others whose lives are painfully constricting with misfortunes that are just as arbitrary and undeserved as his own expansive good luck, but Cass Seltzer does feel grateful.

At moments like this, could Cass altogether withstand the sense that—hard to put it into words—the sense that the universe is *personal*, that there is something *personal* that grounds existence and order and value and purpose and meaning—and that the grandeur of that personal universe has somehow infiltrated and is expanding his own small person, bringing his littleness more into line with its grandeur, that the personal universe has been personally kind to him, gracious and forgiving, to Cass Seltzer, gratuitously, exorbitantly, *divinely* kind, and this despite Cass's having, with callowness and shallowness aforethought, thrown spitballs at the whole idea of cosmic intentionality?

No, no, that doesn't capture it either. Those words are far too narrowed by Cass's own particular life, when what it is he could feel, has felt, might even be feeling now, has nothing to do with the contents of Cass's existence but, rather, with existence itself, Itself, this, This, THIS . . . what?

This expansion out into the world, which is a kind of love, he supposes, a love for the whole of existence, that could so easily well up in Cass Seltzer at this moment, standing here in the pure abstractions of this night and contemplating the strange thisness of his life when viewed *sub specie aeternitatis*—that is to say, from the vantage point of eternity, which comes so highly recommended to us by Spinoza.

Here it is, then: the sense that existence is just such a *tremendous* thing, one comes into it, astonishingly, here one is, formed by biology and history, genes and culture, in the midst of the contingency of the world, here one is, one doesn't know how, one doesn't know why, and suddenly one doesn't know where one is either or who or what one is either, and all that one knows is that one is a part of it, a considered and conscious part of it, generated and sustained in existence in ways one can hardly comprehend, all the time conscious of it, though, of existence, the fullness of it, the reaching expanse and pulsing intricacy of it, and one wants to live in a way that at least begins to do justice to it, one wants to expand one's reach of it as far as expansion is possible and even beyond that, to live one's life in a way commensurate with the privilege of being a part of and conscious of the whole reeling glorious infinite sweep, a sweep that includes, so improbably, a psychologist of religion named Cass Seltzer, who, moved by powers beyond himself, did something more improbable than all the improbabilities constituting his improbable existence could have entailed, did something that won him someone else's life, a better life, a more brilliant life, a life beyond all the ones he had wished for in the pounding obscurity of all his yearnings, because all of this, this, *this*, THIS couldn't belong to him, to the man who stands on Weeks Bridge, wrapped round in a scarf his once-beloved ex-wife Pascale had knit for him for some necessary reason that he would never know, perhaps to offer him some protection against the desolation she knew would soon be his, and was, but is no longer, suspended here above sublimity, his cheeks aflame with either euphoria or frostbite, a letter in his zippered pocket with the imprimatur of *Veritas* and a Lucinda Mandelbaum with whom to share it all.

II

The Argument from Lucinda

to: GR613@gmail.com
from: Seltzer@psych.Frankfurter.edu
date: Feb. 26 2008 5:37 a.m.
subject: possible argument #37

You awake?

to: Seltzer@psych.Frankfurter.edu
from: GR613@gmail.com
date: Feb. 26 2008 5:38 a.m.
subject: re: possible argument #37

Awake.

to: GR613@gmail.com
from: Seltzer@psych.Frankfurter.edu
date: Feb. 26 2008 5:39 a.m.
subject: re: re: possible argument #37

I think I may have come up with another
argument. A really good one. Tell me I'm
crazy but I think this one might be it. Tell
me I'm crazy but I think this one is
different.

to: Seltzer@psych.Frankfurter.edu
from: GR613@gmail.com
date: Feb. 26 2008 5:40 a.m.
subject: re: re: re: possible argument #37

All right, you're crazy.

to: Seltzer@psych.Frankfurter.edu
from: GR613@gmail.com
date: Feb. 26 2008 6:00 a.m.
subject: re: re: re: re: possible argument #37

But I still want to hear it.

to: GR613@gmail.com
from: Seltzer@psych.Frankfurter.edu
date: Feb. 26 2008 6:01 a.m.
subject: re: re: re: re: re: possible argument #37

It went away. I tried to formulate it and it completely went away. I think I miss Lucinda.

to: Seltzer@psych.Frankfurter.edu
from: GR613@gmail.com
date: Feb. 26 2008 6:08 a.m.
subject: the argument from Lucinda

Of course you do. But that's no reason to believe in God.

to: GR613@gmail.com
from: Seltzer@psych.Frankfurter.edu
date: Feb. 26 2008 6:10 a.m.
subject: re: the argument from Lucinda

:-) Good night.

to: Seltzer@psych.Frankfurter.edu
from: GR613@gmail.com
date: Feb. 26 2008 6:13 a.m.
subject: re: re: the argument from Lucinda

Good morning.

III

The Argument from Dappled Things

When Lucinda Mandelbaum entered the crowded auditorium of the Katzenbaum Brain and Cognitive Sciences Center at Frankfurter University for the inaugural Friday-afternoon Psychology Outside Speaker lecture of the new semester and rejected an aisle seat, instead clambering lithely over the legs, laps, and laptops of the assorted faculty members and graduate students, all of whom had been impatiently awaiting her maiden entrance, even though it was not she but, rather, Harold Lipkin of Rutgers University who was the invited speaker; and when she then slipped into the empty seat next to Cass Seltzer, bestowing on him a sweet little shrug of coy chagrin at coming in late and making a bit of a commotion in getting to him; and when she then proceeded, all through Lipkin's lecture, entitled "The Myth of Moral Reason," to address her running commentary on Lipkin's efforts exclusively to Cass, so that Cass, who had in fact been looking forward to Lipkin's lecture, seeing how the psychology of morality dovetailed with his own research on the psychology of religion, ended up missing a good part of it, instead chuckling appreciatively at Lucinda's zingers and even managing to launch one himself that had made Lucinda snigger so enthusiastically that his good friend and colleague Mona Ganz, sitting several rows in front of them, her well-groomed girth just able to settle itself into the seat she always claimed for herself, front and center, swiveled her head around and then, determining the identity of the sniggerer, reversed the motion just as sharply—"like that kid in *The Exorcist*," Lucinda observed, making Cass give vent to a chortle so disloyal that it certainly ought to have been swiftly followed by a stab of guilt, considering Mona's devoted mindfulness toward him, especially during the ravaged weeks and months that had followed the post-aphasic Pascale's first words to him from her hospital bed, which, in their percussive rhythm and impeccable precision, "I must of necessity break your heart," were as reflective of the poet that Pascale was (*La Sauvagerie et la certitude,* Prix Femina, 1987) as they were effective in dampening the desire of her husband to live out any and all possible forms of his future—it had been entirely by mistake.

Lucinda had thought that Cass Seltzer was someone else entirely. To be precise, she had thought that Cass Seltzer was their mutual colleague Sebastian Held, to whom she had been introduced last week at the welcome party that she thought the university had thrown for her. (Actually, she had been wrong. The party had been in honor of all the newly arrived faculty.)

Lipkin, a small man with a booming, pedantic, overenunciating style, was an excitable lecturer, who rose onto his well-shod tiny tiptoes as he hammered home his points. He was already launched at full steam in his oratorical trajectory, irrigating the first row with his spittle, speed-clicking his way through the PowerPoint presentation that swerved abruptly from brain scans of sophomores, neuroimaged in the throes of moral deliberation over whether they should, in theory, toss a hapless fat man onto the tracks in order to use his bulk to save five other men from an oncoming trolley, to sweeping conclusions that claimed to deliver final justice to John Rawls, not to speak of categorically laying to rest the imperative-rattling ghost of Immanuel Kant.

"He Kant possibly mean that" had been the quip of Cass's that had been anointed by Lucinda's titter.

Cass had never been good at this sort of thing, making fun and making light, but Lucinda's proximity, or, more to the point, her having so deliberately chosen proximity to him, had revved up his wit. The Katzenbaum auditorium was sub-terranean and windowless, but it seemed to have become ungloomed ever since Lucinda claimed her seat, as if some of the dazzle from outdoors had been tracked in on the bottom of her shoes.

It was one of those September days, the sky looking like an inverted swimming pool, and the white-gold liquor of after-noon light drizzling through the leaf-heavy trees and pooling on lawns and walkways and the gleaming crowns of Frank-furter's youth. Cass had quoted the line "Glory be to God for dappled things" to himself, which was from a favorite poem by Gerard Manley Hopkins, as he made his way across the stippled campus. "Glory be to God for dappled things— / For skies of couple-colour as a brinded cow; / For rose-moles all in stipple upon trout that swim; / Fresh-firecoal chestnut-falls; finches' wings." And then that stunning second stanza, beginning, "All things counter, original, spare, strange; / Whatever is fickle, freckled (who knows how?) . . ."

How was Cass to know that Lucinda Mandelbaum was slightly prosopagnosic, "prosopagnosia" being the technical term for an inability to recognize faces? Arguably, Lucinda's prosopagnosia had nothing to do with any malfunctioning in her fusiform gyrus. Arguably, prosopagnosia, in the case of Lucinda, was more a matter of mental efficiency than deficiency. Lucinda tended, largely unconsciously, to group faces into kinds, and then was likely to exchange one of a kind for another of the same kind. She could often, when her mistake was discovered, reconstruct the logic of her unconscious taxonomy. Her confusions sometimes led to awkwardnesses, but Lucinda generally knew how to cover herself, and her errors more often amused than alarmed her.

"Did he say brain scans or brain scams?" Lucinda whispered now into Cass's tingling pinna.

"Do Lipkins recognize the difference?" Cass had returned with breathtaking celerity.

Cass had never been quick on the verbal draw, and the years he had lived with Pascale had buried him deeper beneath his reticence. Pascale went after statements with ferocity, ripping them into phonetic shreds. It was her poetic technique. At least several of her poems had been the result of her free-verse attack on some phrase he had uttered, including the prize-winning *"Je ne peux pas te nier ça"*: "I can't deny you that."

There had been something lupine about Pascale Puissant, and, as much as he had loved her, it had turned him cautious. Her beauty—her pointed features, hollowed cheeks, burning black eyes—had always reminded him of a starved wolf. Even the gash across her mouth of her deep-red lipstick, often a bit smeared, suggested bloodstains from a wild meal of still-quivering flesh that had left her just as starved.

Narrow as a boy of twelve, her tiny derrière able to fit into Cass's large palm, her voice, heavily accented, dissolving like smoke into thin air, Pascale was nonetheless a force with which to be reckoned. Her father, a mathematician at the

Institut des Hautes Etudes Scientifiques, in Bures-sur-Yvette, twenty kilometers outside of Paris, had chosen her name in honor of Blaise Pascal, who had founded mathematical probability theory when a gambler asked him for some rules to govern rational game-tabling.

After her parents divorced, when she was nine, Pascale had chosen to live with her father. It was pleasant for her at Bures-sur-Yvette, all the distracted mathematicians living together in housing owned by the Institut on parklike grounds, a playground in the middle with a jungle gym from which she had liked to hang upside down, "for the images and the vertigo." All the children she played with were the offspring of mathematicians, which made them less annoying, in general, than typical children. Also, her father left her alone far more than her mother would have. So she chose to live with her father, therefore not with her mother, and therefore refused to see her mother anymore.

"Refused to see her? That seems extreme. Had she mistreated you?"

"No, not at all. What do you mean? I just told you that I had to *make* the decision. I had to fabricate it out of my will. If she had been a bad mother, then I wouldn't have had to make the decision. The *situation*"—she pronounced it as a French word—"would have decided."

"But why wouldn't you see her anymore, just to visit, now and then?"

"*Now and then.*" She paused for a few moments, and Cass wondered whether she was going to go to work on that expression, but she let it go. "No, there could be no *now and then*. If I had chosen to live with Marie-France, then it would have been exactly the same, then I would have refused to see Papa."

"Marie-France? That's your mother?"

"But of *course!* Who else?"

She glared. He wasn't paying attention. She often glared, thinking that he was lacking in attention. She was wrong. When it came to Pascale, whatever it was Cass was lacking, it wasn't attention.

"So it was more or less random, whether to live with your mother or father. It was more or less symmetrical. But then, once you decided, it was completely asymmetrical. He got all of you, and she got none."

"It was still symmetrical, absolutely, but in the abstract. The symmetry was preserved, *absolument,* but in the abstract."

She was annoyed with him. Her infinite eyes were darkening with impatience. Her scowl brought her brows together in one continuous line over her delicate but imperious nose. He was being slow, deliberately obtuse. He was very sweet, her Cass, and tried very hard to make her life easier. He believed that in doing all the household chores, the paying of the bills and the shopping and the cooking, and the dealing with the computer, and even doing her research in the Edna and Edgar Lipschitz Library at the Frankfurter University, where he taught, he could put himself, in his own small way, in sacred service to her muses. But occasionally, for reasons that eluded her, he was determined not to understand the simplest of things. It was a mystery to her. Also extremely annoying.

Sometimes, in order to show her that he really was following her, or to test his own comprehension, he would try to finish her sentences as she groped for the right English words, and if she smiled her red-toothed smile and said *"Exactement!"* his day was made. But there were times, too, when he chose the coward's way and only pretended to know what she was going on about.

For example, her views on probability. Though she was named after the founder of probability theory, she thought the entire concept a perversion of reason. An event that happens happens. Its non-occurrence, therefore, cannot happen. Never, when something happens, can its not happening also happen. It is happening 100 percent, and it is 0 percent that it is not happening. And since a thing either happens or not, there is only 100 percent or 0 percent of the probability. *C'est logique!* Therefore, what is the probable but the confused? And what is the confused but the cowardly? And what is the cowardly but the immoral? And what is the immoral but the probable? It is full circle! Therefore—she always said this word with a special emphasis, equal accent on both syllables, and blowing a bit of air into the *f,* so that the aspirated phoneme seemed to ascend on the smoky fragrance of her voice—there is only the absolutely impossible, what they rightly call the thing with 0 probability, and the absolutely necessary, which they say has probability 1, Papa had informed her, but she had vehemently countered that, no, it must be measured as 100, or, better yet, as infinite, since certitude is infinite. There*fore*—maybe she had inherited the love of the adverb of consequence from mathematical Papa, or maybe, as Cass enjoyed picturing, all the children of Bures-sur-Yvette, hanging upside down on the jungle gym, solemnly sprinkled their sentences with *donc*—there is only, in the calculus of probability, the numbers zero and infinity.

"And do you know, Cass—Papa, he did not argue with me."

Cass could well believe that Papa, he did not argue with her. What Pascale believed, she knew, and what she knew, she knew with savage certitude. *La Sauvagerie et la certitude.*

"Basically, she's full of shit" was the way that Mona had put it, which Cass thought hardly did the situation justice. Mona, with her high-school-level French, couldn't even read Pascale's poetry in the original. Cass had translated as best he could, but clearly it wasn't good enough.

"Her poetry is a crock, too. That relentless keening. It hurts my ears just reading it. She's the Yoko Fucking Ono of poetry. She's *anti*-art."

"How is she anti-art, Mona?" Cass felt compelled to ask, even as he acknowledged to himself that Mona's Yoko Ono comparison had something to it. "Say what you will about her, Pascale is a brilliant poet. How can her poetry be anti-art?"

"I'll tell you exactly how. Art is supposed to increase our *mindfulness*. Pascale wouldn't know mindfulness if it bit her on her skinny French ass."

This last phrase, which might easily be perceived as not only anti-Gallic but, even more egregiously, intolerant of a woman's right to choose the shape of her own body, was a testament to just how angry Mona felt, on Cass's behalf, or how hard she was trying to get Cass to feel some anger on his own behalf. (She never succeeded.) But her assertion about the mindfulness function of art was straight out of her textbook. Mona had done her doctoral work with Arlene Unger, who makes the concept of mindfulness central to her existentialist psychology. The concept was central to Mona as well. She worked it in whenever she reasonably— or even unreasonably—could. Mona, who was quick to ask the first question at lectures, always began her query with the phrase "As an Ungerian, I'm wondering." You could tease Mona about almost everything—her bisexually frustrating love life, her Omaha, Nebraska, upbringing, even her weight—but mindfulness was off limits. Mindfulness was Mona's religion.

And Mona had indeed been mindfully present to Cass during the long ordeal with, and without, Pascale; mindfully eager for every blood-smeared detail, which she had picked clean with raptor-zeal; mindfully condemnatory of the mindlessness that had left Cass so battle-of-the-sexes-scarred—"I hate to say it, Cass, but you've been pussy-whipped. So have I, if it's any consolation"—that she, Mona, repeatedly wondered whether he'd ever be able to love a woman again.

Mona was facing stoically forward now, but Cass knew her well enough to read the silent reproach in her back. He knew what it must be costing Mona not to give way to temptation and swivel around backward to see what was going on *now*, and he felt remorse in a highly theoretical sort of way, which is to say that he supposed that somewhere, in whatever part of the brain was supposed to be involved in moral reactions—did Lipkin say it was the right orbitofrontal cortex or the left?—his neurons must be making desultory guilty gestures, and perhaps eventually he would register the muted activity.

Lipkin was now affirming the unthinkability of the unsayable, which prompted Lucinda to tickle Cass's ear with a whispered "Ah, the all-too-common Wittgenstein Fallacy. "

It was as if she were prescient. The next words out of Lipkin's mouth were "as we have learned from Wittgenstein."

"Ah, the all-too-common As-We-Have-Learned-from-Wittgenstein Fallacy," Cass shot back, winning from Lucinda a smile of such splendor, along with a playful elbow dig in his side, that he might have died happy at that moment, asking nothing more out of life than this.

When the unthinkable had happened, when everything

had become unsayable for Pascale, she had clutched at Cass, her beautiful and terrible eyes gone even more terrible. One moment she was complaining that her right arm felt like "a little sharp-teeths bête, bite, bite," and the next she was staring at him wildly, unable to utter a word, a soundless howling in her eyes.

The doctors had argued back and forth over whether the clot should be removed. Poor Pascale, with her repudiation of probability, was now caught in a deadly matrix of risks. Dr. Micah McSweeney, the neurologist with a love of literature—whose scruples about mixed metaphors had caused him to allow the loss of his right leg in a kite-surfing accident to determine his entire piratical presentation—had alone stood firm against surgery. McSweeney stood on a peg leg and wore a kerchief knotted over the top part of his head. Was the neurologist bald underneath? Was the jaunty kerchief another prosthetic? Cass would never know. The important point was that McSweeney had read Pascale's poetry, and he knew that to operate was impossible. He, too, knew what he knew with savage certainty.

During the long days of sitting beside Pascale, her wild poetry silenced within her and her convulsively tragic eyes trying so hard to communicate some essential message to him, her icy child-sized hands clutching and unclutching his large warm palm, Cass had felt himself achieving a new and revelatory penetration into the nature of love. His adoration of the afflicted darling of his life, his own tormented wife, sank so deeply into his being that he felt it must be transforming him on the cellular level.

He had first laid eyes on her on a cold December evening at a reading she had given at the crowded Grolier Poetry Book Shop in Harvard Square. The Grolier had been crowded with books, not with people. He had been one of only three attending the reading of her newly translated book, and he was pretty certain that the other two, a man and a woman, had come in to get out of the cold. The man kept loudly blowing his nose into what looked like a torn scrap of a brown paper bag, and the woman noisily unpacked a sandwich, the aluminum foil making a racket. Cass had wished that he could reach out his enormous hands to ward off these insults from the eyes and ears of the poet, her smoky voice struggling beneath the foreign tongue and barbarities.

But though he had fallen in love with Pascale because of her words, it was only now, in her writhing wordlessness, that he knew how entwined their two souls were. They inhabited this silence with an intimacy so complete it all but matched a person's own intimacy with himself. The two of them were alone together inside this silence, with all the world outside. Her brilliant words, counter, original, spare, and strange, had entranced him, but also distracted him, distanced him even as they pulled him in. Perhaps words always do. We depend on them to read each other's souls—what else do we normally have?—but it's only in cases like this, when the other is simply given to one, soul to soul laid out before one like a scene before the eyes, that one really knows who the other is.

He had spoken of all this and more to his stricken wife, sometimes in words, but more often in the soundless communion to which they had been both reduced and elevated.

And then, one evening, after the supper tray—loaded with the home-cooked food he brought her—had been removed, she had spoken, vindicating McSweeney, who alone had known what Pascale's own passionate desire was in regard to the question of whether to operate or not, while Cass had wandered lost in the matrix of risks.

"I must of necessity break your heart."

Meaning: I have lain here in my silence and I have fallen in love, as you, too, have fallen in love in my silence. It is symmetrical, *absolument*, in the abstract.

Meaning: There*fore*, it is necessary to love Micah McSweeney.

Meaning: There*fore*, it is impossible to love you. *A tout à l'heure*, devoted Cass. You have served the muses well, in your time.

For all these years, it had been impossible for Cass to think of Pascale, her starved-wolf eyes and the long coarse black hair that always held an intoxicating fragrance that he had thought of as the scent of ethereality itself, without a gasping contraction round the ventricles of his heart.

Lipkin must have miscalculated the length of his talk. It was nearing the end of the hour, and he obviously still had a lot more material to get through. He was powering through his PowerPoint at a maniacal clip.

"Oh dear, don't tell me he's going to throw in the Milgram experiment now, too? Lipkin, Lipkin, where will this end?" Lucinda was laughing deliciously in Cass's ear.

Lipkin had clicked up onto the screen the famous picture of Adolf Eichmann in his bulletproof glass booth, the three Israeli judges, in their heavy black robes, sitting above him like buzzards. The top of the screen was labeled "Only following orders."

And, sure enough, remarkable Lucinda had been right that Lipkin was using Eichmann as a segue into the famous Milgram experiment about following orders that had been conducted at Yale in 1961, a few weeks after the Nazi SS-man, who had been hiding out for ten years in balmy Argentina, was kidnapped by the agents of the Mossad and smuggled

back to Jerusalem to go on trial for his enthusiasm and efficiency in loading Europe's Jews into trains.

"I think," Cass whispered back to Lucinda, "that Lipkin's
performing his own psychological torture on us."

Cass was perhaps getting just a bit punch-drunk. This gibe
fell a little flat and, if you thought about it, didn't really make
that much sense.

"It's amazing, the sputum that passes for science in these
parts," Lucinda responded. This witticism was all the wittier
given that Lipkin was a spitter, but it had made Cass's grin go
a little shaky around the corners, since it touched a sore spot.
Did Lucinda know what his own specialty was? Was she aim-
ing a gibe at him as well? Given her camaraderie, it was hard
to believe, but his experience had been that those occupying
the more technical reaches of the field could be pretty dismis-
sive of people like him. Sebastian Held, for example, who was
a Mandelbaum wannabe, was downright rude. Did the
enchantress beside him have similar tendencies? There was
nobody who went further in the direction of the technical
than Lucinda Mandelbaum.

Her first book, *Mathematical Foundations of Game Theory
with Applications to the Behavioral Sciences,* based on her doctoral dissertation, had formulated the famous Mandelbaum
Equilibrium, and she had been trailblazing ever since. After
receiving her Ph.D. from Stanford, she had spent the next
three years at Harvard's dauntingly elite Society of Fellows,
had garnered the Distinguished Award for an Early Career
Contribution to Psychology from the American Psychological
Association, and the Troland Award in cognitive psychology
from the National Academy of Sciences, awarded to an under-
forty scientist.

By the time Lucinda went on the job market, post-Society,

she received offers from every top department in the world that had an opening, which had been her goal. She had accepted Princeton's offer. All the other job candidates in the field that year who got hired elsewhere were aware that they were employed only because Lucinda Mandelbaum hadn't wanted their jobs. That was three years ago, and her productivity had not suffered since. Only last year, *Newsweek* had included her in their cover story of "Thirty-Five Scientists Under Thirty-Five Who Are Remaking Their Fields." She had stared out of the pages, one of only six women, and the single representative of the "soft sciences" among the cosmologists, molecular biologists, and computer scientists. Of the thirty-five who had been featured, it had been, unsurprisingly, Lucinda's striking face that had been reserved for the blowup photo on the first page of the article, her pale-gray eyes staring straight at the reader as if daring him to be the one to look away first, her measured mouth only hinting at her victory smile.

Game theory is the attempt to use mathematics to capture the relative rationality of different strategies in various situations, where how well a person fares isn't just a matter of his own decisions but of the decisions of the other players. It's a theory that analyzes behavior in terms of rational agency, meaning the theory assumes that each agent wants the biggest payoff, or utility, for himself. Each agent wants to balance a minimum of expected loss with a maximum of expected gain. Lucinda Mandelbaum is famous for having found applications for game theory everywhere, not just in economics and statesmanship and warfare, which are the most obvious places to look, but in areas that don't seem to involve rational agency at all. All living things, down to the level of the so-called selfish gene, are following strategies that people like Lucinda are elucidating.

Given Lucinda's area of expertise, it was ironic that she should be sitting here in the auditorium of the Katzenbaum Brain and Cognitive Sciences Center, chatting up Cass Seltzer under the illusion that he was someone else entirely. Even Lucinda could—wincingly—admit that she was here only because she, of all people, had let her enemies outplay her.

Of course, Lucinda had her share of enemies. Everybody does, since life, as she can demonstrate, is often a zero-sum game, where one person's win is another person's loss. But a person like Lucinda attracted not only more enemies, but enemies of a different kind, namely griefers: people who wished her grief for no other reason than to wish her grief. Lucinda was unabashedly ambitious, she was unapologetically successful, she had always played hard, and . . . she was a woman. A beautiful woman. The imbalanced distribution of natural gifts seems unfair because it is; and people will always try to make things fairer by giving grief to the gifted. Griefers present one of the complications in the rational-agency model.

The trouble for Lucinda had begun when Shimmy Baumzer, the president of Frankfurter, wanting to restore the university to those refulgent days when it had been able to boast on its faculty such international figures as Jonas Elijah Klapper, had used that article in *Newsweek* as a strategic plan. He made fabulous offers to each and every one of those Thirty-Five Scientists Under Thirty-Five Who Are Remaking Their Fields, from Aashi Alswaan, computer scientist, to Simon Zee, cosmologist.

Lucinda had only intended to use the generous terms—

not only a whopping salary but a minimal teaching load—
to improve her situation at Princeton, playing one institution off against another. This was standard academic strategy. Instead, it was Lucinda who had been played, and she
couldn't believe that her being a woman wasn't relevant.

David Prentiss Cuthbert, who was the chairman of the
Princeton Psychology Department, had frankly had enough
of Lucinda Mandelbaum, whose aggressive intellectual style
had always been off-putting to him, and most especially after
the *Newsweek* article had appeared. Lucinda hadn't even tried
to pretend to be embarrassed by the hype. If she could have
had that damn article shrunk down and laminated to wear
around her tyrannical throat, then she would have. So, while
Cuthbert had encouraged her to press her demands and to
threaten to leave if Princeton failed to match Frankfurter's
offer, he had also gone to the dean and told him that,
"between the two of us, Bill, I wouldn't be sorry to see her go.
Her demands are infinite. I spend more time trying to keep
her happy than I do the rest of my department put together. If
I'm going to run this department, I have to assume that no
one is indispensable."

The Goddess of Game Theory had been knocked off her
game, and it had been a chastening experience. She had spent
the summer doing what someone like Cass might have called
searching her soul. The depth of the animosity against her—
she had learned of Cuthbert's treachery—astounded and
wounded her. He apparently resented her so much that he
was willing to act against the interests of his department just
to damage her, for surely it couldn't be good for Princeton to
lose her to Frankfurter.

She had only tried to game the system, and now here she
was, within retching distance of the stink of failure, packing

up her office in Green Hall and nobody stopping by to help her or offer her even a token word of insincere regret. She didn't doubt for a moment why this punishment was being inflicted on her. It was the combination of her mother's beauty with her father's brains, which he had used to become an extremely successful doctor-lawyer specializing in malpractice. Caught in the summer's swampy misery, she almost felt aggrieved with her parents for bequeathing her the singular genetic sum.

Perhaps the nagging sense that her parents had somehow done her wrong explained why she ended up sticking out the summer in Princeton instead of returning to the home in the Philadelphia Main Line that the Mandelbaums had bought from the estate of the late Eugene Ormandy, the conductor of the Philadelphia Orchestra. That summer made her hate New Jersey so much that she wondered how she could have lasted in Princeton for the three years she'd been there. Nevertheless, she stayed the summer, though there was no place she would rather have placed herself than supine on a chaise lounge, Tanqueray and tonic in hand, in the middle of the rose garden that lay just outside the french doors of the room that the Mandelbaums called "the conservatory." Philippa, her mother, had planted the rose garden herself and did much of the tending with her own delicate hands, although Hy Hua, their Vietnamese gardener of twenty years (he'd been a boat person), did the heavy lifting.

Philippa had once used the beloved rose garden as the setting to try to draw her little daughter into a fantasy of the sort that Philippa herself had loved when she was a child of seven. Standing under a folly smothered with Rambling Rector, Paprika, and a few other climbers, she had smiled at her little towheaded daughter in her corduroy Oshkosh and said:

"Someday, you're going to stand here in your flowing white dress and your white tulle veil, with some strong, good, handsome man beside you, and he'll be thinking that, of all the beautiful roses in this garden, he has picked the loveliest one of all."

"Which one did he pick? The Alchymist?"

This was their favorite rose, not only because of its beauty—it changes shade day by day, deepening from cream into orange—but also because Philippa had been able to grow it herself from division, a fascinating process which little Lucinda had avidly followed.

"No, you silly! You! You'll be the rose he picks."

"I'm not a flower. And, anyway, picking flowers only makes them wilt, even if you put sugar in the water to give them energy. Don't let that man pick me, Mommy."

But here was a complication: If her father adored her mother so much, as he self-evidently did, then why had he wanted Lucinda to be so different from Philippa? Why had he so extravagantly cultivated Lucinda's intellectual pride and derived such pleasure from his little baby's taking on everyone and whupping them upside the head? Why did he continue to tell that punch line, "Don't let that man pick me, Mommy," with undiminished relish?

It was the first time she had asked herself such questions, and it made her unsteady. She didn't know how to describe the feeling, and she didn't know how to explain it away.

It was a setback, of course, for Lucinda, to take up the post, lucrative as it was, at Frankfurter. The department was a bit of a joke, stocked with all sorts of flakes. Sebastian Held seemed the only one who did what Lucinda considered real science. But, still, the very laid-backness of the place was a welcoming change for the time being. She could regroup and come back stronger than ever.

Lucinda took a rather implacable attitude toward the softer and more addled areas of psychology. She had to. Psychology, like Lucinda herself, couldn't afford to indulge in softness. In some sense, she and psychology were similar, their fortunes joined, both of them with a lot to prove, with a presumption of softness to overcome. In the case of Lucinda, the presumption was the result simply of her being a woman, especially a woman who looked the way she did. She had had to put up with a lot to get where she was, and the putting up never really stopped. Look how precipitously she had been toppled from her perch at Princeton. A woman who thinks for her living always has to be on her guard, always has to cultivate her implacability.

Deep down, she still thought of herself as shy. She had been pathetically shy as a girl. But at a certain point, while still an undergraduate, she had realized that shyness was a luxury she could ill afford, and had found that the best way of overcoming it was, whenever possible, to go on the attack. She herself had coined the verb "to fang" when she was an undergraduate at Harvard, where she had begun to hone her aggressive style of questioning. To fang is to pose a question from which the questioned can't recover. You could see the stun, the realization of helplessness setting in.

Lipkin was already quite a bit past the one-hour time limit and was foaming like a mad dog. For all his bombast throughout the talk, he ended rather limply, hurriedly restating his claim that moral reason is a myth. Perhaps his mouth had run dry.

Lucinda's running patter all through Lipkin's talk had

seemed to indicate that she was listening to Lipkin as superficially as Cass himself had been. But when the call for questions came, hers was the first hand to shoot up—or maybe it was tied with Mona's—but in any case, Lucinda Mandelbaum was the one who was recognized. Just about everybody in the auditorium had been waiting for this moment. Would they be witness to the first fanging at Frankfurter? She stood up. The gesture itself was uncommon in these parts, and it seemed to raise the proceedings to a new level.

"Thank you, Harold, for that provocative talk. I think I speak for everyone here in saying how much we admire both your erudition and your ability to speak so quickly."

The laughter was good-natured. Lipkin's smile was grim.

"You've packed so much in that it's hard to know where to begin. I'm going to restrict myself to the last point you made. I want to challenge your claim that the Milgram experiment shows that there's no moral reasoning going on. And my objection to your interpretation of the Milgram experiment is an objection to your entire thesis that reasoning isn't functioning in our moral calculations, that it's all just gut reactions.

"Milgram's results are astonishing, but no more astonishing than the result we get in game theory in what we call escalation games. What I'd like to suggest is that Milgram's experiment is an escalation game, and the playing of an escalation game certainly involves reasoning.

"Take the simplest escalation game, the dollar auction. Two or more people can bid on a dollar. Each bid has to be higher than the last, and the highest bid gets the dollar—just like in a regular auction—but, crucially, the lower bidders have to pay whatever their last bid was, even though they get nothing. Given these rules, the bidding will quickly go up to a dollar,

with the last bidder having bid ninety-nine cents. Will it stop
there? No, because then the ninety-nine-cent bidder will have
to pay ninety-nine cents and get nothing for it. So he ration-
ally bids a dollar and a cent, so he'll lose only a cent rather
than a dollar, which is outbid by a dollar and two cents, and so
on. What happens in the dollar auction is that people will bid
five dollars, ten, fifteen dollars, just to get a dollar in return. In
fact, once you get a dollar auction started, there's no rational
way for it to end, since the cost to either player of bowing out
will be high, and the marginal cost of raising his bid is just a
penny. So it's rational to keep bidding, a penny at a time, even
though this leads to an irrational result.

"Anyway, the Milgram experiment is an escalation game.
Once a participant takes the first step, he's already paid a certain price—he's inflicted discomfort, and he's feeling bad
about it—but if he stops he'll get nothing for his pain. He
won't have successfully completed a psychological experiment and contributed something to science, and that authority figure running the experiment is going to be displeased
with him. So, once he's made his first bid, and the experimenter escalates by telling him he has to give an even
stronger shock at the next mistake or he will not have completed the experiment like a good subject, he's more than
likely to escalate by complying. Just like the dollar auction,
once you start there's no natural place to end until the experimenter calls a halt to it. It's all perfectly rational, step by step,
even if it leads to a bizarre result. In fact, given that the experiment is, in fact, an escalation game, the outcome is completely predictable.

"And here's how to empirically test what I'm proposing.
Run the experiment with the participants instructed, with no
matter how much authority, to administer a deadly voltage on

the first trial, without any incremental escalation, and see what happens. I predict that not a single subject will do it."

Lucinda Mandelbaum had, on the spot, not only devised an alternative explanation that undermined the claims of the presenter, but, in the best scientific tradition, had also conceived a way of testing the two alternative hypotheses. And it had all come out so smooth and polished—frankly, a lot more coherent than the delivered lecture itself. Cass thought there might have been a scattering of applause following her rejoinder, although he couldn't be sure that he hadn't projected his own silent ovation onto the external world.

Cass, ravished, followed the ensuing dialogue between the astonishing Lucinda and the atomizing Lipkin. There was no doubt in Cass's mind, as he was sure that there was no doubt in anyone's mind, including Lipkin's, that Lucinda got the better of the man, whom Cass now actively disliked for keeping up his increasingly whining refusal to accept Lucinda's brilliant counter-explanation.

Pavel Yarnau, the smarmy chair of the Psychology Department, finally called a halt to the heated Q & A, thanking "our speaker for providing us all with such a lively time and much food for thought. And now let's continue the discussion over more mundane fare, not to speak of drink. I ask you all to join me upstairs in the Leah and Marty Feingold Room for the reception in honor of Professor Lipkin."

"Well, this *has* been fun," Lucinda said to Cass as they were both standing, waiting for their row to clear out so that they could proceed. Did she mean merely Lipkin's talk or the communion between them? Her eyes were scanning the crowd. "Are you going to that dinner for Lipkin?" she asked without really looking at him.

"No, I didn't sign up."

Cass rarely put his name on the sign-up sheets that had slots for ten faculty members and four graduate students to entertain the speaker at one of the local restaurants that had sprouted up along the formerly decrepit and now almost hip Maudlin Street. With the inflated property values of Cambridge and Boston driving chefs to outlying areas, Weedham, Massachusetts, was enjoying a restaurant renaissance, trendy little spots blossoming amid the blight.

"Well, then, I guess I'll see you soon," and she turned away, apologetically squeezing past the colleagues over whom she'd just recently stepped. Cass stood there watching her as she strode up to the podium. She and Lipkin shook hands cordially, even enthusiastically. Lucinda was smiling broadly as she spoke to him, and he was laughing as he answered her. There were obviously no hard feelings between these MVPs.

Cass watched for a while, his head cocked and his crooked smile in place, until everybody started heading out to the reception, lining up behind Lipkin and Lucinda like retinue behind royalty. Cass skipped the reception, and went home happy, chewing over it all. It wasn't so much food for thought. It was ambrosia.

He saw Lucinda Mandelbaum two days later, at a university building where faculty meetings were held. She was standing next to Sebastian Held, both of them tanking up on caffeine in the few minutes before the meeting began.

Cass hated faculty meetings and skipped as many as he could get away with. Watching his colleagues' intense engagement in the proceedings, the eloquence and pedantry slathered on points too minute for any but the best-trained minds to discern, he would be overtaken by his own failure to grasp human nature. But today he had looked forward to coming.

Lucinda, dressed in a pair of tailored black slacks and a pale-gray sweater matching the color of her eyes, seemed deep in conversation with Sebastian Held, but Cass strode right over and greeted them both enthusiastically.

"Hello," Lucinda had said, smiling back at him with formally polite blankness, reaching out her hand to shake his with a briskly firm shake. "Lucinda Mandelbaum."

"Yes, of course. I'm Cass. Cass Seltzer."

"Nice to meet you, Cass."

"Oh, we've already met," he said, stopping himself before he could wail out his dismay: Don't you remember? Don't you remember how we laughed together like careless gods?

"Oh, sorry. I'm terrible with faces. Remind me of what you do?"

"Psychology of religion."

"Psychology of religion?" Her thin upper lip curled slightly, not quite achieving a smile. "As a branch of abnormal psychology? Or are you one of those people who try to offer an evolutionary explanation for group madness?"

"Well, not exactly. What interests me more is the phenomenology of religion in all its varieties. What does it feel like from the inside? What sorts of terrors does it address, and what sorts of emotional growth does it both block and enhance? And how does the religious response manifest itself, even in ways that may not seem religious?"

Her lip curled a bit more, and it was a smile, and she lifted her chin so that her throat was exposed.

"It must be frustrating to deal with irrationality."

"How can one be a psychologist and not deal with irrationality?"

"If I thought that were true, I'd never have gone near the field."

"Well, I guess it's a good thing for the field, then, that you don't think it's true."

"But is it a good thing for the field that you do?"

Cass studied her face, which seemed both serious and friendly. He couldn't tell from it, or from her serious and friendly voice, whether her question was ingenuous or sarcastic. Either way, he didn't know how to respond. Lucinda held his gaze for several more ambiguous moments and then turned back to Held to resume their interrupted conversation.

He didn't say more than ten words to Lucinda, nor she to him, for the rest of the semester.

Autumn and winter had gone by without his taking much notice. He must have shown up and taught his classes; he had his students' class evaluations to prove it. And they were pretty good evaluations, too, considering he couldn't remember a thing about the classes, neither preparing for them, nor giving them, nor reading the papers and grading the exams he had apparently assigned and administered. He had done it all sleepwalking with his eyes open, instructing the youth by day and writing, writing, writing by night.

Lucinda's question to him, so direct and so undecipherable, had stunned him, and he needed to answer her. He needed to extract some answer out of the questions that had been roiling in him for the past two decades, the questions that he had lived out with Jonas Elijah Klapper and the questions he had lived out with Azarya. He had never cashed in that experience for hard insight.

Had he tried out any of his new thoughts on his students? He couldn't remember, but a few of the more perceptive class evaluations had spoken of how it was cool to watch Professor Seltzer arguing with himself. "Sometimes it could get a little weird, like that dude at the end of *Psycho*. But in a good way."

No doubt he had been distracted. It had been all he could do just to keep up with his classes and his fantasies. He never skimped on his fantasies, no matter how busy he was. He didn't need to, since they blended with all he saw and thought and wrote and said. It was the love of the impossible that made everything possible. He was battered by the beating wings of unlimited desire, but they lifted him, too. Battered, emboldened, and exalted, and all at once.

Mona was convinced, despite his disclaimers, that he had stopped attending the Psychology Outside Speaker lectures because he couldn't stand the circus they had become—"what with that Mandelbaum creature performing in all three rings at once, juggler, lion-tamer, tightrope walker, bareback horse-back rider, lady on the flying trapeze . . ."

"That's five rings, Mona."

"And counting. She's such an insufferable showoff. She's destroyed the whole atmosphere of our department. Do you know, that pig Pavel doesn't even go through the motions of asking for questions anymore? He just turns to her with an obscene leer and squeals, 'Lucinda?' and the whole place cracks up, including the star—by which I don't mean the out-side speaker. It's revolting. The whole display is revolting. Everybody bows down to that creature, and only because she's a bully."

"Surely there's more to it than that."

"You mean the fucking Mandelbaum Equilibrium? Cass, you think anybody here understands it better than you and me? They don't know the Mandelbaum Equilibrium from e = fucking mc². For all they know, it's got as much to do with psychology as my grandmother's blintzes. It's not like mind-fulness. Just because everybody can understand mindfulness, and can't understand what the Mandelbaum Equilibrium is even *about*, they let her get away with carrying on as if the rest of us are just her movable props. Do you know, people have told me that they have to keep introducing themselves to her over and over again, because she's just not mindful enough to remember who anyone here is? For some reason, she always seems to remember me, though. I'm one of the few whose names she actually knows, although for some reason she seems to think I'm Hungarian."

Cass had been surprised by Mona's severity toward Lucinda, especially since he had heard Mona complaining that people don't let women academics get away with the kind of high-handedness that their male counterparts habitually employ. He would have thought Mona would be the first to applaud Lucinda for her ballsiness.

Cass had barely been on campus fall semester. He'd taken a leave of absence because of the extensive book tour the publisher had set up for him: twenty-one cities in two months, and then another month spent in England, Scotland, and Ireland. He'd kept in touch through sporadic e-mail with Mona, who tried mindfully to keep the communications focused on him, "who, after all, is the only one of the two of us who's suddenly leading the life of Cindefuckingrella."

He had returned from London only a few days before. He was coming to campus now to gather any mail that might have accumulated. It was the Wednesday before Thanksgiving, and it was already evening, and the campus was deserted except for a few foreign students forlornly clumping here and there, their footsteps echoing with melancholia on the abandoned Frankfurter concrete. The moodiness of an early evening in late November softened the hard outlines of the aggressive architecture. The bluing air was crisped and smoke-sweetened, and the leaves crunched gratifyingly under his feet as he walked up the dirt path from the faculty parking lot that was closest to the Katzenbaum Brain and Cognitive Sciences Center.

The Katzenbaum Center was built in the style that prevailed on Frankfurter's campus, meaning that it was a rectilinear, flat-roofed building, made of red brick with an exposed steel structure, a large show of glass, and a generous helping of concrete, which was stained red to match the bricks. The campus went heavy on the concrete. This, Cass had been told, was the International Style of architecture, which had been considered boldly cutting-edge after the Second World War, when Frankfurter had been established, its Master Building Plan embarked upon. To Cass it looked like the style of architecture favored by the wealthy Reform temples and Jewish community centers of northern New Jersey, where he had grown up. He associated this architecture less with Le Corbusier than with Hadassah. The founders of the school, together with the money they had raised, had been Jewish, and the school, though non-denominational, still attracted a disproportionate number of Jewish students.

Cass was just opening the heavy glass door when Lucinda materialized on the other side of it. She had taken the stairs down from her sixth-floor office rather than using the elevator. He saw the dark figure swiftly descending, almost a blur of motion, though he hadn't realized that it was she. Why would he have realized, when a hundred times a day he had seen her superimposed on his surroundings?

The vision of Lucinda was always whisper-close, her phantom elbow ready to poke him playfully in the ribs. She had stood beside him on a sidewalk in Portland, Oregon, staring up at his illuminated name on the marquee of a big old opera house that he would be speaking in that night, both of them shaking their heads at the incongruity. She had walked the moonlit fog in London, floated by his side in fabled Oxford, teased him about his debate with Sir Jonathan Sacks, the Chief Rabbi of Great Britain, at London's Jewish Book Festival, on reason and faith. So why wouldn't he see her now, approaching him across the sterile vestibule of Katzenbaum, as he stood there holding the door wide open for whoever it really was?

She must have felt the cool, crisp air sweeping in. She looked up at the man standing there holding the door for her, his head tilted to one side and a loopy smile wobbling about on his pleasantly discomfited face.

He expected that she wouldn't recognize him. He would simply smile at her without saying a word, as he held the door so that she could pass him by and disappear into the darkening world.

Lucinda looked up into his face, did a double take, and then burst out laughing.

"What?" he said. He could feel his embarrassingly responsive complexion beginning a slow burn. He had said nothing, and already she was laughing at him.

Without a word, she reached into her satchel and pulled out the familiar book, with its laminated foil jacket. It was a jolt of intimacy to see his progeny emerging from out of her bag.

"I'm not very good with faces, but I'd be willing to bet good money that you're the author of this book. Wait a minute." She opened the back flap and held the picture side by side against the original, the soft cuff of her winter coat slightly caressing his blazing cheek. "Yes. Don't deny it. You penned this tome. You're Cass Seltzer!"

"You're reading it."

"Not really. I've simply incorporated it into my weight-lifting regimen."

"That's why I added all those extra arguments for God's existence. The publisher was supposed to mention its physical-training possibilities on the back cover."

"I find it makes a rather good stepladder, too. Easily transported from room to room. Had you intended that as well?"

"As a stepladder to enlightenment!"

Lucinda laughed, throwing back her head. She had a brave and sweeping peregrine of a laugh. And just like that it was back, reconstituted, the sense of blessed ease they had shared inside that dappled afternoon. Cass felt the way her whispering breath had warmed his ear.

"Aren't you going to ask me whether I like your book? Or are all other opinions beside the point now that the *New York Times* has found it 'invariably engaging and provocative,' and *The New York Review of Books* has described you as 'the William James for the twenty-first century'?"

He couldn't believe it. She had actually memorized the choice bits from his reviews that were used in the ads for the book. Not even his mother had memorized the quotes.

"I'm afraid to ask you what you think of it. I'm afraid you're going to fang me."

"You don't have to worry about that. The fanger of my fangee is my friend."

"Funny, I don't think of myself as a fanger."

"Oh, but you are, my friend, a fanger of no mean talent. You fanged God!"

"Can I have them quote that on the cover of the paperback? 'A *fanger of no mean talent:* Lucinda Mandelbaum, author of the Mandelbaum Equilibrium.'"

She quickly cast her eyes downward, so that her long

lashes rested on the ridge of her cheekbones for a few seconds, and when she raised her eyes again it was with a different expression altogether.

Lucinda's lips were thin, and if there was any imperfection in her face, it was in her stiff upper lip. But now her upper lip quivered slightly, and the transformation was complete. It was a thing counter, original, spare, and strange, what had happened to her face. He could imagine no face more beautiful in all the world, no face more touching in its exposure. He could never go back and recover the face that had been there only moments before.

"Thank you," she whispered.

"For what?" he whispered back.

"For saying that that's who I am. That that's who I still am, even if I'm here."

Cass could have taken offense, but he didn't. With that strong sense of gazing directly into another, soul to soul, of seeing it all and all at once, as if it were an endless vista laid out before his eyes, he grasped the sorrows behind Lucinda.

Her move to Frankfurter had obviously cost her dearly, but she never let on. She could have just bided her time here instead of giving it—giving *them*—everything she had. There was nobody at Frankfurter she needed to impress. But she carried on as she always had, performing at peak, a prizefighting champ. And just for the sheer sport of the thing, for the reasons sustained in her own ardent heart. She wasn't competing against anyone but herself. That's what people like Mona didn't get. He hadn't altogether gotten it himself until this moment of seeing straight through to the soul of her.

Lucinda Mandelbaum, of the famous Mandelbaum Equilibrium, just kept playing the game with her heart and soul, making everybody here feel that by her very presence they had all been admitted into the insider game, when all the while she was aware that that insider game was transpiring elsewhere, away from Frankfurter and away from Lucinda Mandelbaum, and maybe she would never get herself back into it the way she had been, the way she had been born to be.

That transformed face of hers that she was holding out to him told him everything. It was astounding that she would trust him with the sight of it. What had he done to earn the trust of Lucinda Mandelbaum?

He saw the fragility within the fanger, the willed boldness and gumption of this brave and wonderful girl.

He saw the dappledness of her.

Glory be to God for dappled things, he silently quoted his second-favorite poet.

IV

The Argument from the Irrepressible Past

Despite the metaphysical exertions of his night, suspended over sublimity on Weeks Bridge, Cass remembers that he has a meeting with Shimmy Baumzer at eleven in the morning. So, before settling down again beneath the luxury of Lucinda's comforter, he sets his alarm for 9 a.m., and then, just to be safe, he sets the second alarm clock, on Lucinda's side. It's already after six, the bedroom on the top floor of the duplex brightening, and he wonders whether he'll be able to fall asleep at all, hugging the last tattered bits of epiphany and Lucinda's fragrant pillow . . . and is awakened into terrifying confusion, the awful ringing setting his frantic heart to pounding, while he is desperately trying to make it stop, scuttling back and forth across the mattress, fumbling with the two alarm clocks—which one the hell *is* it?—until he finally realizes it isn't an alarm clock at all.

It's the telephone.

"Hello?"

"It's me!"

"Lucinda?"

"Lucinda? Who the hell is Lucinda? It's me! Roz!"

"Roz Margolis?"

"Is there another?"

"Roz. My God. Roz. My God."

"For a famous atheist, you sure call out to the deity often enough there, sweetie."

Roz is laughing, girlish peals that contrast with her husky voice. It brings her home to him as nothing else could. Say what you will about Roz Margolis, she certainly knows how to laugh.

"Roz," he repeats. There's still some small chance he's dreaming.

Roslyn Margolis had been Cass's girlfriend years ago, when he had first come to Frankfurter to study with Jonas Elijah Klapper. She had spent ten months at Harvard, and that's how long she and Cass had been together. Still, those ten months had been something. They had been so packed with drama that they had left the impression of being ten years, ten decades, ten eternities.

They had never lost touch. Over the years, he had been wakened often enough in the middle of the night to answer the phone and hear Roz on the other end, always calling from some remote time zone, miscalculating the hour that it was for Cass, apologizing profusely in between her laughter and questions and unbelievable news. News from Roz always came filed under "Unbelievable."

"Cass, I can't believe how famous you've suddenly gotten yourself. It's incredible! I've heard you on NPR at least a hundred times. And I read that feature in *Time* magazine. The atheist with a soul! Since when are you an atheist? I remember when you were contemplating the Kabbalistic meaning of potato kugel!"

"Where are you calling from, Roz? Are you still studying the fearsome people of the Amazon rain forest?"

"No. I'm *here!*"

"Where 'here'?"

"Cambridge! I'm studying the fearsome people of *Cambridge!*"

"What are you doing here?"

"It's a good thing I'm not the sensitive type, Cass. You're supposed to be shouting out, '*Yippee! Glory be! Hallelujah!*' Or whatever you atheists with souls call out in your ecstasy!"

Cass moves the phone receiver slightly away from his rattled ear. He's becoming increasingly convinced that this is no dream.

"Well, contain your excitement, because I'm going to be in your Roz-starved arms in a few minutes! I'm calling from my car! I'm just passing Porter Square now. What do I do, make a right or a left?"

"Neither! Listen Roz, I can't wait to see you, but I'm not even dressed and . . ."

"Not dressed? Okay, I just went through a red light!"

"And I've got an important meeting this morning."

"I'll drive you! I'm already in the car."

"Roz, you can't come now."

"But I'm here, Cass! I'm literally here! You can't stop me."

How literally true Cass knows this to be.

The doorbell is ringing.

"Guess who-oo!" She's laughing into the telephone. "You know, I thought of giving you some advance warning, but I know how much you love spontaneity and—Well, will you look at that? Here you are! Cass! Sweetie!"

Cass has opened the door in his blue terry-cloth bathrobe and slippers, and Roz has thrown her arms around him in a viselike grip, nuzzling him on the neck so that her last words come out muffled.

"Roz," Cass is saying as he tries to loose himself from Roz's amazing clutch. Or not so amazing. Roz has to be in tip-top shape for her fieldwork. Her sheer physical presence has certainly helped her to gain the respect of some serious hunter-gatherers, who had named her Suwäayaiwä, which translates, at least according to Roz, as "a whole lot of woman."

"Roz." Cass can't help himself, he's laughing along with her. "Come on, let go of me. You're hurting. Let me get a good look at you."

Those last are the magic words. Obediently, Roz drops her arms from around Cass's neck and takes a giant step back on his front porch. She wafts her arms out into the air and executes a little pirouette, something you would think would make a woman of her height look silly, but Roz brings it off with panache. She's always been quite the dancer. She had certainly led Cass a wild dance in their day.

"Roz, you look fantastic!"

"Don't I?" She puts her two hands together in a fist and shakes them above her head from right to left, a champion's gesture.

"No, really, Roz. No joke. You look . . . you look just amazing."

Of course, there have been significant changes in her appearance since Cass has seen her last, but, remarkably, the changes seem to be all for the better.

Roz has to be forty-six, forty-seven, . . . no, Roz is nearing fifty. When they broke up, Cass had been twenty-two, stranded on the shoals of a graduate-school debacle, and Roz had just completed her Ph.D., had gotten herself a contract to turn the dissertation into a book, and had nabbed herself a plum tenure-track job in the Anthropology Department at Berkeley.

In the interim, she's become a blonde of various artfully alternating and blended tones, and it suits her. Everything about her appearance suits her.

The Roz whom Cass had loved wore disintegrating jeans or long hippie skirts and preferred to go barefoot, as she had in the rain forest. She could never get the bottoms of her feet entirely clean.

There's nothing remotely hippie about the woman on Cass's front porch, except that she still has hair that reaches midway down her back, full and glossy and conspicuously expensive in its shaping and shading. It's a much sexier head of hair than she had tossed around at the age of twenty-nine. She had always had good skin, glowing with natural color, and she's still glowing, though it could be from the cold, or maybe the *ars obscura* concocted by the cosmetics industry. There are laugh lines lightly traced around her laughing green eyes, but that seems only right for Roz, considering how much laughter must have seized her in these passing years. She's wearing a short, swingy red wool coat, beautifully cut, with fur round the collar and cuffs that looks undeniably authentic. What would it be? Sable? Seal? Mynx? Or is he conflating mink and lynx? Mynx, if there is such a thing, would definitely suit her. She's in high-heeled black boots that put her almost nose-to-nose with Cass, and she's carrying a large black quilted purse whose tasteful gold trim has "Chanel" embossed on it. The only remote reminder of the old hippie attire is the long gold-and-ebony earrings dangling out from under her lustrous hair.

Smiling seductively, she slips off her black gloves and

unbuttons her coat to reveal a swanky red wool suit underneath, with great shiny thick buttons down the jacket front. There's an ebony-and-gold choker around her throat to match the earrings. The suit skirt is cut short, and the long span of leg above the boots is spectacular. Them's some gams, as Roz herself had once observed to Cass, and them's still are.

The smile above the choker is vintage Roz, halfway between a grin and a leer. She looks, as Shimmy Baumzer might put it, like the fox in the cathouse that swallowed the canary.

"I'm reversing the clock. I've taken control of my biochemistry."

The mention of the clock pressingly reminds Cass that he's going to be late for his appointment with Shimmy.

"I have a matching mink hat, too, only I didn't want you to see me with hat-head. It's in the car." She tosses her unhatted head in the direction of the red Mercedes she's parked haphazardly on the street. If she doesn't get a ticket for parking without a Cambridge-resident sticker, she'll get one for having her backside sticking out far enough to obstruct traffic.

"I'm impressed. I'm more than impressed. I'm speechless with admiration. But, Roz, I wasn't kidding about that appointment."

"Who you going to see who could possibly be more important than your best girl, whom you haven't seen in at least a hundred years?"

"I've got an appointment with the president of Frankfurter. I have to be there in about half an hour."

"Frankfurter? That's perfect, sweetheart! I'd love to see the old place. Get some clothes on! We're going to be late!"

So Cass skips his shower and heads upstairs to throw on some clothes, leaving Roz in the living room below. Roz is never shy about poking around and has an anthropologist's instinct for fieldwork, so it wouldn't surprise Cass if, by the time he's loping down the stairs, she's more familiar with his present life than she was a few minutes before.

"If you want, I'll take the wheel, since, as you might remember, I drive like a maniac."

Now that she mentions it, he does remember.

"No, we'll take my car. I've got a faculty parking sticker. You might want to move your car into the driveway, though. You'll probably get a ticket."

"But we'll be late for your appointment! I'll just take my chances. Life's a thrill! Wait a minute, I just want to get my hat. You can't leave mink lying around in Cambridge. Some PETA nut will break in and douse it with fake blood."

He waits for her to get back into the car and backs carefully out of the icy driveway.

"You sure you don't want me to drive? I could get us to Frankfurter faster than it's taking you to get out of this driveway."

"It's fine, Roz. I'll drive and you'll talk."

"Okay, but don't think I'm not going to get everything out of you. For starters, I want to know who this Lu*cin*da is. I hope she's an improvement on that last woman of yours. What was her name? That batty poet with the red lipstick smeared across her teeth?"

"Pascale Puissant."

"Pascale, right. Boy, that was a man-eater if ever there was one. Anyone ever told you you're a philogynist?"

"Is there such a word?"

"Probably not, due to lack of demand. I remember you said her beauty reminded you of a wolverine."

"A wolf, Roz, not a wolverine."

"Same difference. Red in tooth and claw. Where's that from?"

"Tennyson."

"Did she stick it out with that doctor?"

"They lasted less than a year."

Roz reaches over and ruffles Cass's hair, letting her hand drift down the back of his neck. He wishes it didn't give him the thrill it does. Men's bodies are cads. Still, the sensation reminds him of Lucinda, if that's any redemption.

"You're better off without her. You should be grateful to that brain doctor—what was his name again?—for luring her away from you."

"Micah McSweeney, and I am."

"Sometimes I think your mate-selection module got knocked out of whack in the commotion you went through with me."

"You may be right."

"Remember when you begged me to marry you?"

"Did I? Sure you're not mixing me up with some other bloke?"

They're both grinning.

"Did you? On your *knees,* did you!"

"And what did you say? Did you by any chance say, 'I need a life of maximal options'?"

"You still remember!"

Her voice is rich and husky, though the vibrating veins of animation that run through it make it sound as if it belongs to a higher range. It's exactly the voice Cass remembers from twenty years ago. If Cass doesn't glance over at her, he'd swear it's the twenty-nine-year-old woman. Then again, even when he does give her a quick sidelong glance, she looks not much older than when they had been lovers. The biggest difference is, she looks a lot tidier and more expensive—though he wonders about the bottoms of her feet.

"So tell me what you're doing in these parts. You're still at Berkeley?"

"No, I'm not. I'm *retired*!"

"Retired? You're too young."

"That's the beauty of it! The University of California is bankrupt! The only money they have is in their pension funds. They're broke, and can't pay our salaries, but they're flush with pension cash! So they offered early retirement to any senior faculty that wanted it! They're paying me a yearly stipend that just about matches my salary, only I don't have to go to work! How sweet is that? I hit the jackpot!"

"Are you staying in California?"

"I'm keeping all options open. With a little encouragement, I'd dislodge that Lu*cin*da person. I noticed you're living with her." He'd been right that she had devoted those five minutes to research.

"I am."

She gives a melodramatic sigh.

"I thought so. A girl takes her eyes off a guy for two or three measly decades, and the next thing she knows, he's two-timing her." This last is delivered, to perfection, in her Mae West impersonation. "You haven't gotten married again, have you?"

"No, we're not married."

"I'd be hurt if you had gotten married and hadn't told me."

"You know I wouldn't do that."

They're on the Larz Anderson Bridge, crossing the frozen Charles. Cass glances left and sees Weeks Bridge gleaming in the brilliant wintry light. As they make a left on the far side of the Charles onto Storrow Drive, Cass gestures and says, "Look over there, Roz. Do you see the way the rushing water has carved out a cathedral in the ice? It's sublime, isn't it?"

"Sublime? Cathedral?" She's craning her neck to see what he's talking about, but they're already making the turn that will get them onto the turnpike, and she turns back to him, shrugging. "So this is how the atheist with the soul carries on. Sounds like there's a whole lot more soul than atheism going on in there. How'd you come to write a book like that anyway?"

"We can talk about my book later. Let's concentrate on you first."

"You always know the right thing to say!" She laughs. "Okay. So you want to know what I'm doing now that I'm retired from academia? You won't believe it! Cass, this is the most exciting adventure of my life."

"I hope this one doesn't involve international lawyers and investigators from the State Department."

"I'm sorry, but I'd smuggle those papers out again in order to help Absalom." Absalom Garibaldi had been her dissertation adviser and field supervisor in the Amazon. "I had to defend him against those outrageous charges his enemies were making! Accusing him of intentionally infecting people for experimentation, like a Nazi doctor, when we were trying so desperately to inoculate everyone! You remember what we went through!"

"I just sometimes wish you wouldn't take the risks you do."

"Well, this is one you're going to love! This one is unbelievable! I've started my own non-profit! It's called the Immortality Foundation! We're going to conquer aging! It's ironic. I *retire* so that I can devote myself to wiping out old age! You have no idea how close to our goal we really are! Anybody who can just hold on long enough is going to make it. We don't have to accept aging! Think of it! We don't have to accept decline and decay and diminution! Aging is simply barbaric. It's like bubonic plague."

"You don't literally mean immortality, do you?"

Roz breaks out into her peals of laughter.

"You think I'm going off the deep end, right? You think I'm going to end up like the Klap, Yahweh rest his bogus soul!"

"'Rest his soul'! My God, Roz! Is he dead? My God! I hadn't heard anything!"

"Calm down, Cass, calm down! You're going to kill us both! No, I haven't heard he'd died! I just assumed it!"

"Don't do that to me!"

"I'm sorry, Cass! I should have thought before I spoke!"

"That'll be the day," Cass mutters. He's seriously rattled, his hands gripping hard on the steering wheel to stop their trembling.

"The Klap" refers to Jonas Elijah Klapper. This was how Roz had invariably referred to the man who had been Cass's idol.

"I'm sorry," she repeats. "My God, I didn't know he still has that kind of hold on you. I'm really sorry."

"It's okay, Roz. I'm okay. And who knows, maybe Klapper *has* died."

"I honestly had taken it for granted. I haven't heard a word about him in years. So I just naturally assumed he was dead. What else could have shut him up for this long?"

"It's true that it's been decades since he's published anything."

"It's like he disappeared off the face of the earth. That guy was always publishing. He'd excuse himself to go the bathroom and come out holding his latest. It's like he *shat* magnum opi—is that the plural?"

"Opera."

"Really?"

"The plural of 'opus' is 'opera.'"

"I love the way you know these things. How do you know these things?"

"Klapper."

"Which brings me back to the question: how could he have deprived the world for so long of his erudition? That is, if he's still alive."

"But surely there would have been an obituary in the *Times*. He was too important in his day for his passing to go unremarked."

"Well, I could easily have missed it. I spend a lot of time in places that don't have the *New York Times* home delivery."

"Even your hunter-gatherers will know when Jonas Elijah Klapper dies."

"If you think that, then you're still delusional. I know he loomed larger than life itself for you and his other hierophants, but that was collective lunacy."

"Granted. But he was still a monumental figure. He'll get a major obituary in the *Times*."

"There was nothing monumental about him besides his ego."

"That's not true. His memory was phenomenal."

"Okay, the guy had memorized a lot of stuff. I think that's what convinced you he was a genius."

"Well, it certainly convinced him."

"I once called him Gertrude Stein in drag, on account of

his major project being to convince everyone else of his genius. It wounded you deeply."

"You were always wounding me deeply when it came to Jonas Elijah Klapper."

"Just so long as I never wounded you about anything important. What about that magnum opus he was working on? The magnum opus to top all magnum opera? Did it ever appear?"

"No."

"On messianism, right? That was supposed to be his latest thunderklap, right?"

"*The Messianic Ideal in the Course of World History: 1750 B.C.E. to 1988 C.E.*"

"He makes an earth-shattering discovery, so big he can't even share it with his elected ones, and then he just shuts up about it? I think the only rational conclusion is that he's dead."

"Maybe he discovered his discovery wasn't so great, after all."

"Oh, come on, Cass. You know he wasn't capable of self-criticism. The only proof that any one of his thoughts ever required was that *he* had thought it. So you never tried to get in touch with him over all these years?"

"Lord, no."

"You were cosmically furious."

"Was I? I don't remember that. I just remember being cosmically confused."

"You've never been great about getting in touch with your anger. You were furious, all right, more on account of the others, especially Gideon Raven. You in touch with him?"

"Now and then. Who would have guessed what he'd make of himself after that disaster?"

"He's certainly been productive, producing his pearls. I hope he's happy as a clam."

"Oyster."

"What?"

"If he's producing pearls, he's an oyster, not a clam."

"Are oysters happy?"

"Probably less happy than clams."

"Who don't have to produce any pearls for *The New Yorker* on deadline. Gideon's always publishing there."

"He's one of the main horses in their stable."

"He never got his doctorate, did he?"

"Not after putting in thirteen years with Klapper. He wasn't going to start all over again."

"It's impressive, the niche he's made for himself. What would you call him?"

"An intellectual-at-large. Klapper's leaving him in the lurch was the best thing that could have happened to him, as it turned out."

"Best thing that could have happened to you, too, as it turned out."

"It was hard to see that at the time. Of course, he did offer to take me with him. I was the chosen one."

"You had sense enough not to go."

"I couldn't very well do that to Gideon. He should have been the one. And, anyway, by that time I was pretty disillusioned."

"'Disillusioned' doesn't begin to capture it. You were devastated, desolated, devoured by the dentures of despair."

"Not as devastated, desolated, and devoured as Gideon."

"And then Lizzie left him, on top of it all. What a colossal mess that guru-with-the-kuru of yours created."

"Kuru?"

"The human equivalent of mad-cow disease. You get it from eating the brains of your dead ancestors."

He laughs, shaking his head at her deadly aim. "I've got to say, you're the one who sounds furious."

"I was back then, the whole time we were together."

"Really? It's amazing we had all the fun that we did."

"Just think of the fun we could have now, with the Klap no longer in your life. Oh yeah. Now there's Lucinda."

"You know, I don't think I ever really held Klapper responsible. He was in the grip of something inexorable."

"No excuse. Some mental diseases are moral diseases, too. You can be insane and a mean, selfish bastard simultaneously."

"I know you think so."

"He was obscene."

"I thought it was against the anthropologist code of ethics to call anything obscene."

"Even among the Onuma"—these were her Amazonian people—"who don't even have the concept of privacy, what with the guys running around with just a string holding up their foreskins and the women wearing just these little ruffly waistbands that don't hide a *thing,* nobody would ever publicly masturbate the way Klapper did."

"I assume you're speaking metaphorically? That's metaphorical masturbation?"

"With that tumescent ego standing in for the prize." She looks at Cass's face and laughs. "Okay, I'll stop. Let me just say that I'm proud that I was never taken in by him. I never could believe how he took you in."

"He took in a lot of better minds than mine."

"All except the British!"

"Who seem to have lost, together with their empire, the ability to appreciate Jonas Elijah Klapper!"

Cass can barely get out the words from the laughter that's choking him. Only Roz can get him choking on laughter.

"I'm glad to see that you can laugh about him now. That's healthy!"

"It's taken me long enough."

Roz doesn't answer, and Cass, glancing over, sees that she's got him under a scrutinizing stare.

"What is it?"

"I'm taking to heart your implied admonition that I should think before I speak."

"You're an old retired dame. You're not about to change your ways now. Go on and say it."

"Well, I was just thinking what a deeply personal book *The Varieties of Religious Illusion*—which by the way I loved—actually is. Every one of us is in it, in a way. Klapper and Azarya and Gideon and me. You've worked us all into what everybody thinks is a psychologist's learned discussion of religion."

They're pulling off onto the road that leads to Frankfurter's campus, making the sharp right that will bring them up the steep hill on which the university is laid out, and Cass is considering the surprising thing that Roz has just said, trying to judge if there's any truth in it, and feeling the queasiness of suspecting that there is, and wondering why that should induce queasiness, when Roz gives a yell.

"What's that?" She's pointing out her window. "Wait a minute! It can't be! It's a genuine protester! *Whooohoo!* The sixties live!"

Sure enough, there's a kid with a hand-lettered placard on the side of the plowed road.

"What does his sign say? I couldn't make it out with all the glare from the snow. Let's go back, Cass! Let's see what kind of action's going down in good old Frankfurter."

"Are you kidding, Roz? I'm late. And anyway, this road is one-way and slippery as hell."

"Oh, Cass, you're no fun at all! Just slow down and I'll bail!"

And so he does, and so she does, which is no mean athletic feat in those high-heeled boots. His eyes on the rearview mirror, he watches her slip-sliding away, and he can't help laughing out loud as she plops her fur hat down on her head, imagining that he can actually hear her muttering, "The hell with hat-head!"—which is, in fact, exactly what she's muttering.

V

The Argument from Reversal of Fortune

There had always been the hothouse atmosphere of a mystery religion enclosing Jonas Elijah Klapper and his band of disciples. Entrance into his circle had the feel of an initiation. "I sense the aura of election upon you," he would pronounce in a hushed voice to some severely young person, who, unsurprisingly, rarely disagreed. Cass had not disagreed when confided the news about himself.

Cass had first arrived at Frankfurter as a graduate student in order to study with Jonas Elijah Klapper, who himself was then only newly arrived on campus, the single professor composing the Department of Faith, Literature, and Values that Frankfurter had constructed around him in order to lure him away from the English Department at Columbia University, which is where Cass had first come under his sway.

As a pre-med, intending to be a doctor like his father (though not necessarily a gastroenterologist), Cass had had little time to take courses outside his requirements. It was his last semester of college when he attended Jonas Elijah Klapper's oversubscribed course, "The Manic, the Mantic, and the Mimetic," and his life has never been the same.

Rumpled as he came shambling into the lecture room, a

Jewish walrus in a shabby tweed jacket, by the time Jonas Elijah Klapper was fifteen minutes into the hour he looked in need of a tranquilizer dart, the few wisps of his frizzed gray hair sticking out in every direction as he mussed it in his inspired distraction, his eyes rolling around in daemonic frenzy, tears trailing his declivitous jowls as he brought forth the riches of his prodigious memory. With his eyes staring off to just above the head of the tallest student in the class—that would be Cass—it was as if the words were imprinted on the drifting dust motes of Hamilton Hall, and he had simply to read them off from midair, great long paragraphs ranging from Augustine confessing to Zarathustra thus spaking.

This is what it is to be a mind, a real mind, a cultivated mind. This is what it is to lay claim to the entire intellectual corpus, all of it filed within the capacious precincts of one's own inviolably sacred inner life.

An inner life! That's what Cass wanted! A self! Professor Klapper's asides, which sometimes expanded to the size of the hour, were often variations on the theme of "get thyself a self." Cass hadn't even known before this semester that he didn't have a self to call his own.

"Thinkers treat theories like fashionable women treat clothes. They must always have one, and it has to be sufficiently avant-garde so that the lower orders have not yet acquired it, are not buying cheap knockoffs at Macy's and Gimbels. So, if you are taking this course to find out what the well-dressed theoretician is wearing this year, then I shall have to disappoint you. There is only one theory, and it is the theory you shall pull bloody from the afterbirth of your own self."

This was heady stuff. This was disruptive, destabilizing, and absolutely necessary stuff.

"We are no more born into the self than we are born into the truth. Both must be acquired with a labor and a love that call forth powers few possess, with the consequence that the earth is populated by veritable zombies, whose inner emptiness would elicit a chorus of execration if exposed to the eyes of the few carriers of consciousness among us."

Cass had almost gotten through college, had all but wasted irretrievable years of his life, without having realized that he was about to take the next step having never embarked on the first. He had done nothing toward acquiring a unique and inviolable being. That is what he was being shown that he wanted—only everything!—as he sat in that classroom wandering breathless in the rarefied landscape that opened up within the sculpted syllables of Jonas Elijah Klapper's lectures, which were rendered in the very voice of Western civilization, sweeping in a matter of mere sentences from frolicking disquisitions to stentorious exhortations to whispering tremolos, a voice that astonished even itself with its impartings, moving the speaker to tears that traced their torturous way down the pleated jowls of ageless genius.

Listening to the immensity which was Jonas Elijah Klapper grappling with the immensities of Goethe and Nietzsche and Swedenborg and Blake, not to speak of Yahweh Himself, had induced the out-of-person giddiness of his childhood lower bunk bed: *Jesse there, Cass here.* What transpired in Room 201 of Hamilton Hall also veered vertiginously toward disempersonment, at least for Cass Seltzer, beholding for the very first time the world-spurning, worlds-spawning nature of pure genius, and something even—yes, something even *beyond genius.* That was the greatest astonishment that Cass had taken away from Jonas Elijah Klapper's class on "The Manic, the Mantic, and the Mimetic." Professor Klapper himself

implied that genius, exalted as it is, can amount to a derelic-
tion of duty. Goethe had *settled* for being a genius, the professor had whispered, and Cass's spine had tingled, as it always
tingled when the professor's voice dropped down to a quaver-
ing hush, even when Cass had no idea what Professor Klapper meant, as he so often had no idea what Professor Klapper
meant.

Cass had gone to speak with Professor Klapper during
office hours, and he had been made privy to an enthralling
exposition on the evolution of Professor Klapper's thinking
through the successive developments that he called "paradox
shifts," and at the end of the two-hour private session, the
great man had murmured to him, "I sense the aura of election upon you."

Arriving in Frankfurter as a graduate student of Jonas Elijah Klapper, Cass felt stunningly ill-prepared to take on faith
and literature, not to speak of values. He had learned on his
acceptance that he was one of only twelve students sharing
the honor, and the other eleven were all far more advanced
than he. Gideon Raven was the number-one student among
them. He had already been a graduate student for twelve
years.

Cass had spent the summer at his parents' home in Persnippity, New Jersey, sitting on the back deck and reading his
way through the professor's extensive corpus, some twenty-
eight tomes in all. His parents had taken the news calmly. His
mother, who tended toward strong views, was constrained in
this case by her strong views on personal autonomy. She was
also a bit distracted by Jesse's decision to move out of the
NYU dorms into an apartment that she couldn't figure out
how he could afford. His father had only once raised the subject of Cass's giving up his plan to go to medical school. It had

to be somewhat of a disappointment for Ben Seltzer. He had loved to talk over Cass's pre-med courses with him, and was himself a happy gastroenterologist, as he was a happy husband, a happy father, a happy weekend squash player. His wife, Deb, was more the intellectual—a "culture vulture," as Ben fondly called her—and he was always more than happy to accompany her to operas and symphonies, lectures, art exhibits. "More than happy to . . ." more often than not characterized Ben Seltzer's attitude. It was from him that Cass had gotten his height, as well as the implicit apology in his bearing for taking up too much space. When his father asked him whether he was sure about giving up on medical school, it sounded almost as if the man knew that it was written in the handbook of Jewish parents that he was required to ask, and he was just trying to get it over with. Cass was accommodating. He wanted to get it over with, too. He held up his current book, which happened to be Jonas Elijah Klapper's *The Perversity of Persuasion,* and said, "This is sheer genius, Dad." His father's response, after a considerable pause, was to say that maybe he'd give it a read, "or, better yet, your mother can read it and then explain it to me."

Cass had started at the beginning, with the transparent brilliance of the early works, including the groundbreaking *Goethedämmerung,* proceeded steadfastly onto the undisputed genius of the middle works, most notably *The Perversity of Persuasion,* and groped his way as best he could through the opaque splendor of the latter works, including *Wandering Between Two Worlds,* the last volume that Professor Klapper had published to date. Cass had conscientiously read it through to its very last sentence, even though the only thing he had truly understood had been the quote from Matthew Arnold, a poet whom Jonas Elijah Klapper did *not* revere—the professor gave out grades and Matthew Arnold had received an ignominious B-minus—but whose "Stanzas from the Grande Chartreuse" had supplied him his title:

Wandering between two worlds, one dead,
The other powerless to be born,
With nowhere yet to rest my head,
Like these, on earth I wait forlorn.

Cass's mother did read *The Perversity of Persuasion*, though whether she ever explained it to his father Cass didn't know.

"What do you think?" Cass had asked her, as she sat beside him on the deck, midway into the book.

"He's quite oracular," she had answered.

Cass had nodded and then smiled, pleased with her answer.

After a few more minutes of reading had passed for both of them, he looked up and asked, "When you say 'oracular,' do you mean that in a good way or a bad way?"

She had yielded one of her more inscrutable smiles.

"I couldn't really say. I guess you'll find out for yourself when you get to Frankfurter."

Jonas Elijah Klapper's sole course offering during this first year at Frankfurter was to be the two-semestered "The Sublime, the Subliminal, and the Self," a seminar that had a pre-registration of twenty-three students, which was high for a graduate seminar. There were the professor's own graduate students, now down to seven. The departed five had ultimately decided, after passing through Kübler-Ross's five stages of grief, not to move to Massachusetts, which Klapper had made a non-negotiable condition for their continuing to be supervised by him. "The Sublime, the Subliminal, and the

Self" also had six graduate students from Frankfurter's English Department, another six from Religion, one from Philosophy, and three undergraduates who had managed to garner the elusive permission of the instructor.

The three were all, Cass couldn't help noticing, extremely comely girls, who entered the room that first day in a clutch of bosomy frolicsomeness. But even they soon fell into the nervous silence that was de rigueur among the professor's chosen students.

The tone was set by Gideon Raven, whose brilliance and intensity were disguised within the mien of a hyper-alert baby. His head was round, his face—especially in relation to his fleshless body—full. His eyes were circular as well, their shape enforcing an impression of innocence, no matter the conflagrations raging behind them. It was the gaunt jitteriness— the fingers gnawed to the quick, the dissent pooling in his philtrum—that gave him away. Although Gideon had been studying with Jonas Elijah Klapper for an apostolic twelve years, and was teaching his own courses at Frankfurter this semester on the metaphysical poets, still, here he was in attendance, just as he had attended every one of the professor's Columbia classes, graduate and undergraduate, since becoming his student.

Jonas Elijah Klapper shuffled in and settled his heft into the chair with a soft sigh, while plopping his bulging satchel onto the gleaming oval of the table. Gathering himself together, he proceeded to go round the table, starting from his immediate left, to stare each of the twenty-three students full in the face, an excruciating exercise for the subjects. One girl, Asian, got up in the middle of her turn and wordlessly left. The professor, taking no notice, had simply let his eyes proceed to the next.

This first item of business concluded, Jonas Elijah Klapper cleared his throat and began to recite, from memory, in his beautiful Anglicized voice, Matthew Arnold's "Dover Beach," which had been assigned for this first meeting.

The sea is calm to-night.
The tide is full, the moon lies fair
Upon the straits;——on the French coast the light
Gleams and is gone; the cliffs of England stand,
Glimmering and vast, out in the tranquil bay.

Professor Klapper's voice, his smile, his entire being, embodied the becalmed stasis of the first stanza.

Come to the window, sweet is the night-air!

Klapper was personifying youthful vigor, a reckless bounding into hope. His shoulders even gave a bit of a jump.

Only, from the long line of spray
Where the sea meets the moon-blanch'd land . . .

An ominous warning was being sounded, the slightest shiver of the sinister disturbing the surface of sonority.

Listen! You hear the grating roar
Of pebbles which the waves draw back, and fling,
At their return, up the high strand,
Begin, and cease, and then again begin,
With tremulous cadence slow, and bring
The eternal note of sadness in.

And the promise of joy that had flickered only a moment before in Klapper's voice and playful shoulders, withdrew itself.

> *Sophocles long ago*
> *Heard it on the Aegean, and it brought*
> *Into his mind the turbid ebb and flow*
> *Of human misery; we*
> *Find also in the sound a thought,*
> *Hearing it by this distant northern sea.*

> *The Sea of Faith*

He whispered in that charged hush that could rise to the rafters of a crowded undergraduate lecture hall, and had no difficulty now projecting to the farthest reaches of the seminar room.

> *Was once, too, at the full, and round earth's shore*
> *Lay like the folds of a bright girdle furl'd.*
> *But now I only hear*
> *Its melancholy, long, withdrawing roar,*
> *Retreating, to the breath*
> *Of the night-wind, down the vast edges drear*
> *And naked shingles of the world.*

> *Ah, love, let us be true*
> *To one another! for the world, which seems*
> *To lie before us like a land of dreams,*
> *So various, so beautiful, so new,*
> *Hath really neither joy, nor love, nor light,*
> *Nor certitude, nor peace, nor help for pain;*

And we are here as on a darkling plain
Swept with confused alarms of struggle and flight,
Where ignorant armies clash by night.

It was such an astounding rendition, the last stanza recited at an accelerated pace, quickened with a kind of arcing, aching desperation. Just as the eternal note of sonorous sadness had always been there in the waves' pounding, even before the poet had heard it, so, too, the rhetorical urgency of that last stanza had been in the poem, only Cass had been deaf until this moment.

Jonas Elijah Klapper himself seemed unspeakably moved, to the point of prostration, by his own performance. He placed his right elbow, swathed in the brown suede patch ornamenting the dusky tweed, onto the table and buried his furrowed brow into his fleshy open palm.

And from that forlorn posture, his face hidden from sight, he sent forth a query.

"'Its melancholy, long, withdrawing roar.' Why the 'melancholy'? Why the 'long'? Why the 'withdrawing roar'?"

His voice was so weakened that he could barely muster the rolling *r*'s that he had elocuted to perfection moments before.

A sustained and uneasy silence followed the withdrawing roar. The lack of a response stretched itself out, until the silence itself seemed like a metaphysical presence that had quietly crept in and taken a seat at the seminar table. Even Gideon Raven stared down at the gnawed fingers of his left hand, which were playing keyboard on the left thigh of his crossed legs.

Cass was amazed by the vacancy that had suddenly invaded the room. Though Cass's understanding of the poem had been immeasurably deepened by the professor's recitation, no great insight was required to answer the question on the table. Obviously, Professor Klapper had thrown it out just to get the ball rolling.

And there sat Jonas Elijah Klapper, his outspread palm still cushioning his mighty brow. The very sunbeams splattering on the grainy wooden table seemed to tremble with the tension. They were all, even the sunbeams, letting Jonas Elijah Klapper down; and in letting Jonas Elijah Klapper down, they were doing nothing less than disappointing the whole of Western civilization, its faith, its literature, its values.

Could Cass, callow as he was, allow this to happen? He knew that, among all the people in that breathlessly strained room, he was, without a doubt, the least qualified to speak. He included here the toothsome undergraduates, who had probably been studying poetry longer than he, who was, after all, only an importunate petitioner from pre-med.

Cass felt physically incapable of maintaining his silence, not only because of Jonas Elijah Klapper, and all he stood for, but also because of how "Dover Beach" had laid its palpating finger on the something soft and inchoate inside him, the thing he hardly dared to call his soul. Just like the lyrical narrator, he, too, had been paddling around oblivious on the surface of a sea of faith that he had presumed was infinitely benign, only to submerge his ears below the waves and hear the eternal note of sadness, like the mermaids singing each to each that Alfred Prufrock says he had heard once—no, maybe not like Prufrock's mermaids—and to wonder, along with the poet, *what's left to believe in?* and to grasp at the same answer that the poet had seized on: love and love alone. Love is the only solace. Not just any love, of course, not an easy, superficial love, but the love of the like-minded, the like-souled, the one who hears the eternal note of sadness in the same key and register as you. Together with such a love, clasping each other tightly round for dear life, you can gaze out the window at the dream-stripped harshness and bear the awful sight of it.

Jonas Elijah Klapper, sunk in his blinded pose, didn't see the lone hand raised aloft. And so, in service to the poet, to the seminar, to Faith and Literature and Values, but, first and foremost, to Jonas Elijah Klapper himself, Cass tentatively began to speak into the void, of how the absolute faith of the childhood of man, in both the individual and the species, "which I guess would be the Middle Ages, when belief in an ultimate divine presence was full and calm and sweet, was wrenched away in a long, withdrawing roar, as we grow up and discover the way the world really is, through science and most especially the theory of evolution.

"Darwin's fingerprints are all over this poem. The *Origin of Species* had been published just a few years before 'Dover Beach' was published."

Cass had done his homework, not only perusing the poem at least thirty times—he himself had it memorized by the eighth or ninth read—but going to the Lipschitz Library and reading everything about the poem he could get his hands on.

"The central metaphor in 'Dover Beach' is the ocean, and the poem itself is like a bridge passing from lush Romanticism to the brave new world of Modernism, where we aren't shaded from the hard truths of the natural world, and we have to create what meaning we can get from our relations with one another. That's all we have, in the end. The sublime has abandoned us, and what sublimity we have remaining we have to make for ourselves, subliminally, from the material of our own self."

Cass had been surprised by the surge of his own insights.

That thing about the sublime, the subliminal, and the self—what this whole seminar was about!—had just hit him like a wallop between the eyes while he was talking.

Professor Klapper's eyes, which were shaped to the contours of sadness, slanting downward like two arrows taking aim at his lower face, had kept themselves unseen, obscured in the iconic thinker's pose.

There was silence in the classroom, the fraught silence of billions of agitated neurons soundlessly firing, until, at last, Jonas Elijah Klapper lifted his brow from off of his palm and revealed his face, which was contorted in silent-film fashion with the unmistakable mien of unmitigated aghastment and dismay. His lips were twisted, and his nose, a fleshy mound piled high on his face, was crinkled up as if some gaggingly offensive smell had entered the room.

"*No, no, no!* That's not what I was talking about at all!" He held up his two hands in an apotropaic gesture. "Not at all, not at all! Spare me, spare us all, such bromides. And above all keep the bad fictions of Charles Darwin out of my classroom. Darwin's fingerprints are all over this poem, indeed! I will not have such infantile slobberings upon the sacred body of literature"—he pronounced it, as always, "lit-er-a-toor"—"not even upon a poem of Matthew Arnold's. And since, Mr. Seltzer, you are a committed Darwinist"—the word came pushed out of his lips as if by peristalsis—"let me inform you that, though Arnold may have published 'Dover Beach' in 1867, he had actually written it sometime between 1849 and 1852. The *Origin of Species* was published in 1859. If you want to point to such precursors and influences, then do at least check the dates. You'd have been better off citing the *Vestiges of the Natural History of Creation*, published anonymously in 1844, by Robert Chambers, a radical journalist. But do, please, have a care for my suffering sensibilities! Now it is Darwinism with which I must contend." He turned his head away so that his mournful countenance fell upon the non-Darwinians in the room. "As I have oft warned those of you who have any proclivity to receive my instruction, most of what passes for science is merest scientism."

The moments while Klapper spoke had at first borne the true marker of a nightmare: too perfect a realization of one's worst fears not to be a dream delivered sizzling from hell. Horrible disbelief was followed by far more horrible belief, and for the remaining hours of this first meeting of "The Sublime, the Subliminal, and the Self," as Jonas Elijah Klapper's voice continued without interruption, not even Gideon Raven hazarding a comment, Cass sat unmoving, unhearing, almost unexisting, deliquescing into a numbness that approached the state of being nothing at all.

The two-and-a-half-hour seminar was drawing to a close. Professor Klapper was speaking of next week's assignment, Aristotle's *Poetics*.

". . . answering the challenge that his discarded teacher, Plato, issued after he had symbolically, if not diabolically, banished the poet from his city of reason. As Plato wrote in his *Republic*"—Klapper was staring off into the inscribed distance—"'Let us, then, conclude our return to the topic of poetry and affirm that we really had good grounds then for dismissing her from our city, . . . for reason constrained us. And let us further say to her, lest she condemn us for harshness and rusticity, that there is from of old a quarrel between philosophy and poetry.' I skip over a few lines here, not from lack of recall but lack of relevance, and proceed: 'But nevertheless let it be declared that, if the mimetic and dulcet poetry can show any reason for her existence in a well-governed state, we would gladly admit her, since we ourselves are very conscious of her spell.'

"Now, my creatures of sweetness and light"—this was one of his endearments for his students—"it is in the context of this gauntlet flung down by Plato that Aristotle's *Poetics* must be read. Aristotle is answering the older philosopher's challenge by pragmatically—I use the word in the sense of William James, which is my own as well—connecting it to psychopoiesis."

Cass recognized the word from his summer studies of the twenty-eight tomes. Psychopoiesis. Soul-making. The coinage was, so far as Cass knew, Klapper's own, struck out of the ancient Greek.

"Poetry is in the business of psychopoiesis at least as much as philosophy is. And if I might be permitted, humbly, to stand between Plato and Aristotle and offer my emendation, you will hear me fervently whispering 'oh more, far more!'"

Cass was suddenly called back into himself by the pain squeezing his heart as he contemplated that all but he and the girl who had voluntarily departed under the professor's gaze would be returning next week to hear the dialogue between Plato, Aristotle, and Jonas Elijah Klapper. Even those three undergraduate lovelies, who had managed, over the course of the seminar, to progress from chattering neophytes to wide-eyed acolytes, would be allowed to attend. He alone was to be cast out for the sin of his unclothed ignorance and arrogance.

And then, suddenly, Jonas Elijah Klapper was addressing him again, all vestiges of vexation vanished.

"Mr. Seltzer, I would like you most especially to pay keen attention to Aristotle's concept of peripeteia. Would you, by blind chance or happy happenstance, happen to know what peripeteia means?"

"Reversal of fortune." Cass's hoarse voice sounded unfamiliar to him. It sounded older, the voice of an ancient knowing that the best has been and will be no more.

"Excellent! Peripeteia! Reversal of fortune! Exceedingly excellent! It's a most un-Darwinian concept, wouldn't you say, my dear boy? Now you are thinking! Yes, until next week's peripeteia, my creatures, my delights!"

And Jonas Elijah Klapper, still beaming, gathered up his books and papers and shambled out the door.

Cass looked up from the table to see forty-two eyes fastened upon him. The three girls looked away so quickly they may have lost a few eyelashes. Only Gideon Raven continued to hold his stare, blankly and noncommittally. He pushed back his chair and came over to Cass's side, tossing something onto the table right in front of him.

Cass's first thought was that Gideon Raven was so outraged with him, either for upsetting Jonas Elijah Klapper or, more probably, for the original sin itself, that he wanted to pelt him with a spitball and his aim wasn't good. Cass looked up questioningly, and Raven gave him a little twitch of a smile and then exited from the room, the rest of the seminar silently filing out after him.

Cass looked at the missile. It was a piece of paper that had been folded over many times, until it was the volume of a sugar cube. Cass unfolded it to find a flyer for something called "Sex Week at Frankfurter":

Our goal is to promote an open discussion of love, sex, intimacy, and relationships. All sexualities, no matter how alternative, and all individuals, of whatever sexual experience, are welcome. If you would like to get involved contact Shoshy Wasserman at 555-4256 or Hillel Schlessinger at 555-7861.

What did this mean? Could Gideon Raven be so offended that he was insinuating that Cass was of an alternative sexuality? The fire in Cass's face and under his scalp, which had begun to subside, re-flared.

After a few minutes of sitting there alone, it occurred to him to turn the paper over. There, scribbled in chicken scratch, were the words:

meet me midnight, view from nowhere

Cass had not the hint of a clue as to what these words could mean. Was it a line from a poem? These people were all so formidably well read. Whatever it meant, it must have been given to him because of what had befallen him during the seminar. Did it contain a hint as to what was the nature of the peripeteia that he had just undergone? Was it what he needed to know in order to survive as a student of Jonas Elijah Klapper's?

He trotted over to the Lipschitz Library and up to the reference librarian on duty. She was a woman of about sixty, thin-lipped and spare. The nameplate identified her as Aviva Landesmann.

"Would you have any idea how I could go about finding out what this means?" Cass asked Aviva Landesmann.

She read it aloud, scowled at Cass, and then read it aloud again.

Aviva Landesmann looked familiar somehow. She reminded him of someone, someone who stirred up forgotten love and confusion.

Did psychologists have a word for this sort of thing, a reminding that consists in nothing but a mute emotion that can't name its own object? Was he having a Proustian moment? He wouldn't know. Wherever he turned, he was confronted by the vast ignorance that made him unentitled to be a student of Faith, Literature, and Values.

Aviva Landesmann was staring at the slip of paper. She turned it over and saw the announcement for Sex Week at Frankfurter, and her expression, which was none too encouraging to begin with, curdled with distaste.

"Feh!"

That's when it hit Cass. Aviva Landesmann reminded him of his beloved bubbe, his mother's mother.

His mother always kept the details of her stormy relations with her mother from Cass and Jesse when they were little, but he remembered the unsettling voice from behind the closed door of his mother's bedroom when she phoned his bubbe, terrifying bursts of fury that his mother emitted with no one else. When she emerged, her face white and strained, she could only say that his bubbe had "done it again." He later learned that what Bubbe had done again was what people with borderline personality disorder always do with their intimates: get their goats, push their buttons, pick at their vulnerable spots, draw them into destructive dramas that don't let up until the borderline tastes blood. Then, finally, Bubbe had stepped over some invisible line and had gone too far, even for her. All that Cass knew was that the support group that his mother belonged to, Borderline Offspring Injured Lifelong (BOIL), backed Deb up in her decision. One of the rules in the BOIL handbook was: set the limits of your own tolerance. Deb had reached her limits.

Cass had nevertheless loved his bubbe. He couldn't help himself. She used to sing a special song about a rooster,

"Cookooreekoo," just for him. She had spoken in a special cooing voice, just for him, her oldest grandson, whom she called Chaim, his Hebrew name.

"Oy, such a boychik, so *shoen*"—which means "beautiful"—"so *klig*"—which means "smart," though it tore up her heart that he was being brought up like a *vilda chaya*, a wild animal.

Deb always blamed inbreeding for her mother's personality disorder. Deb blamed inbreeding for a great deal. Deb—who was originally Devorah Gittel Sheiner—came from a family that belonged to a sect of Hasidim, the Valdeners, who had originated in a town called Valden, in Hungary. Almost all the Hasidic sects are named after the towns where their first Grand Rabbi, the founder of his dynastic lineage, had originated, or where he had established his rabbinical court. So there are the Satmars, from Szatmárnémeti, Hungary (now Satu Mare, Romania), the Lubavitchers from Lubavitch, Lithuania, the Breslovers, from Breslov, Ukraine, and at least a dozen sects still surviving from the dozens more there had been before the Second World War. And all of them are crystallized around a charismatic Rebbe, the term that means "my rabbi," with the position of Rebbe passed down through family lines, from father to son or to another male relative, though occasionally there are controversies, splits, factions. Only the Breslovers never saw fit to have any Rebbe but their first, Rabbi Nachman of Breslov: a mysterious figure with messianic aspirations, known for his collection of allegorical tales, and himself the great-grandson of the eighteenth century's founder of Hasidism itself, Rabbi Israel ben Eliezer, known as the Ba'al Shem Tov, the Master of the Good Name.

The current Rebbe of the Valdeners, Rav Bezalel Sheiner, also claimed a lineage that could be traced back to the Ba'al

Shem Tov. Deb was related, on both her maternal and paternal sides, to the Valdener rabbinic dynasty, though according
to her that was nothing to brag about. Valdeners tend to
marry each other, so just about everybody was related to
everybody.

"And then they wonder about the genetic diseases."

Cass's father, Ben Seltzer, had also come from a fairly
observant family, but it was standard modern Orthodox, so
Deb's family was exotic to him, too. Both Deb and Ben had
wandered far from the religiosity they had each been born
into, but Deb had had to travel a lot farther to get to where
they were, the non-kosher and non-Sabbath-observing house
in which Cass and Jesse had been raised. After Jesse's Bar
Mitzvah, his parents had let their membership in the synagogue lapse.

The Valdeners lived in a self-contained village, tucked into
the folds near the rocky Palisades edging the Hudson River. It
wasn't a gated community, but it might as well have been.
Nobody but Valdeners lived in New Walden, except for a few
sons-in-law and daughters-in-law who had come over from
some other Hasidic sect.

The other sects lived in urban areas—in Jerusalem, or
Montreal, or Brooklyn—always in some well-defined section.
In Brooklyn it was in Williamsburg and Boro Park, where the
Valdeners, too, had settled when they had first come to America. The previous Valdener Rebbe, Reb Yisroel Sheiner, who
in the 1930s had shepherded some portion of his flock out of
Europe and into safety in the nick of time, had decided in the
1950s, that Brooklyn, too, was getting *tzu heiss*—too hot—
what with the increasing crime rate and the deteriorating
relations between the Hasidim and the blacks and Puerto
Ricans, not to speak of the high rents that made it difficult for

the large Valdener families—average number of children, 6.9—to afford decent housing. The Rebbe had quietly, so as not, God forbid, to raise the fears of the Gentile farmers in the area, purchased a large chicken farm not far from where Rip Van Winkle had snored, and built a self-contained shtetl, the first village in New York State to be completely governed by a religious authority, with the town's mayor being none other than the Grand Rabbi himself, and the aldermen his closest disciples.

The village was to have been called New Valden, but through a county clerk's typing error it had been Americanized to New Walden. The Valdeners had no idea that the spelling mistake brought them into nominal intimacy with the ghost of Henry David Thoreau, sounding the chord of American transcendentalism—visionary, romantic, self-reliantly impractical. The Valdeners knew from Thoreau like they knew from clam chowder.

Cass had only visited New Walden a few times, since his mother hated the village and would go unusually quiet for days before a visit. It was a strange place, where he and Jesse were made to feel outlandish because they didn't dress in short black pants and large black felt hats, didn't have long side curls and speak the language of the place, which was Yiddish. Cass remembered some little boy, maybe a cousin— there were throngs of them, many of them with Cass's and Jesse's red hair—laughing with scorn when they were introduced, some kid named Shloimy or Moishy or Yankel finding the name "Cass" hilarious.

Even though his mother went strange around her, Cass had loved his widowed bubbe. Another thing that was hard to ignore was that his bubbe didn't treat Jesse as nicely as she treated him. It wasn't even clear that Bubbe knew Jesse's name. She called him "little boy." If Jesse came over and tried to climb onto her lap—a space freely offered to Cass—Bubbe would push him away.

"Feh, here he is again. The second *tog*"—day—"of *yom tov*"—a holiday—"always schlepping after the first. Why don't you go find your mommy, little boy, and let your older brother enjoy in peace a little?"

Jesse was so shocked by Bubbe's behavior that he would go off without a word of protest, an unusual response for Cass's brother, who could fly off the handle if Cass or his mother or father failed to read his mind concerning something he wanted. Cass always saved for Jesse at least half the babka that Bubbe gave him, even though she would impress upon him that she had made the delicious yeast cake for him "special," as if she had foreseen he might want to share it with the little boy, his brother.

He wasn't allowed to taste the babka, or anything else, until he had made the right blessing, the *bracha*. If he ever forgot, which he rarely did, his bubbe would purse her lips and say, "Feh! Like an animal, a *vilda chaya*, he's being brought up. *A shanda fur da Yidden*." A disgrace for the Jews.

His bubbe had taught him all the *brachas* that had to be made before eating. There was one for fruit, but another one specifically for grapes, and one for vegetables and one for bread and one that was for a grab bag of things. And, of course, there was a *bracha* for baked goods, *mazoynos,* including Bubbe's babka. Bubbe would quiz him closely every time he visited. It wasn't as straightforward as just knowing the general types, since foods could be mixtures, and some of the categories trumped the others. The *bracha* also depended on how much of something there was and also whether something had been done to the food to make it change its type: the apples in apple juice didn't count as fruit. It was complicated. What if there were raisins in the babka that Bubbe had baked for her little Hasid, her little pious one? Should Chaim make the *bracha* for the baked good or for the fruit? (The baked good!) And what about cereal? If it was corn flakes, then you have to make the one for vegetables, *ha-adama,* for things that grow in the ground. But it it was Cheerios, then you said *mazoynos.*

You also had to be careful about silverware and dishes, never mixing up the dairy with the meat. It had been poor Jesse's fate to have mixed some Bosco into his milk with a teaspoon from the wrong drawer, and Bubbe's wrath had been biblical. She had taken both boys out to the backyard and shown them how now she had to stick the spoon in the dirt to clean it. Dirt to clean? When they had asked their mother, she had answered in a way uncharacteristically terse: "If it seems crazy to you, you understand it perfectly."

Cass could have asked his mother to review the *brachas* with him. She still knew everything, including Yiddish. But he could tell that she would rather he didn't master his *brachas* too well.

Funny that he could still miss his bubbe, even though by now he understood a lot more about the personality disorder that had made her decide that Chaim was *git*—good—and the "little boy" who was his brother was *nish git.* She had died when Cass was a junior in college, but she had been banished from their lives long before then, with the full approval of BOIL.

When he came back after the interval that Aviva Landesmann had specified to him, she had something better to offer him than babka. It was *The View from Nowhere,* by the philosopher Thomas Nagel. Cass thanked Aviva much more than she was probably used to being thanked and went off to his carrel, three flights below ground level in the Lipschitz Library.

The basic idea in *The View from Nowhere* is that we humans have the unique capacity to detach ourselves from our own particular point of view, achieving degrees of objectivity, all the way up to and including the view of how things are in themselves, from no particular viewpoint at all. This is what Nagel calls the View from Nowhere, and he analyzes all sorts of philosophical problems by showing how they arise out of the clash of the subjective point of view with the View from Nowhere.

The View from Nowhere was hard going, but Cass kept plugging along, at first motivated simply by his burning desire to get to the bottom of Gideon Raven's gnomic message. But then Cass got to a section that made him forget all about gleaning any clues to his afternoon's ordeal.

BEING SOMEONE

One acute problem of subjectivity remains even after points of view and subjective experience are admitted to the real world—after the world is conceded to be full of people with minds, having thoughts, feelings, and perceptions that cannot be completely subdued by the physical conception of objectivity. The general admission still leaves us with an unsolved problem of particular subjectivity. The world so conceived, though extremely various in the types of things and perspectives it contains, is still centerless. It contains us all, and none of us occupies a metaphysically privileged position. Yet each of us, reflecting on this centerless world, must admit that one large fact seems to have been omitted from its description: the fact that a particular person in it is himself.

What kind of fact is that? What kind of fact is it—if it is a fact—that I am Thomas Nagel? How *can* I be a particular person?

Cass only realized he had been holding his breath when he let it out. Here was the bedtime metaphysics that used to exercise him to the point of hyperventilation being described with precision by a prominent philosopher. (Thomas Nagel sounded prominent from the book jacket.) *Cass here, Jesse there.* The ritual used to send him hurtling so far outside himself that, night after night, he had become frightened that he might never find his way back in again, might never be able to take for granted that he was who he was. Cass had never hoped to find another person who could understand the strange state he used to induce in himself, and he had certainly never guessed that it might be shared by a philosopher.

It can seem that as far as what I really am is concerned, any relation I may have to TN or any other objectively specified person must be accidental and arbitrary. I may occupy TN or see the world through the eyes of TN, but I can't *be* TN. *I* can't be a mere *person*. From this point of view it can appear that "I am TN," insofar as it is true, is not an identity but a subject-predicate proposition. Unless you have had this thought yourself, it will probably seem obscure, but I hope to make it clearer.

He became so caught up in *The View from Nowhere,* the dense mass of its distinctions parting for him like the sea, that he forgot the whole point of why he was reading it.

He wasn't sure whether Professor Klapper would approve of Thomas Nagel. The style of *The View from Nowhere* was of the sort to send Jonas Elijah Klapper fleeing for protection from "the talismanic attachment of certain philosophers to logic. No thinker worth our contemplation is going to be held back by the Law of Non-Contradiction, which I do not recall being ratified with my approval."

Cass heard the gong of the ten-minute warning and crash-landed back into *Cass here*. He thought he understood the reason why Gideon Raven had tossed him a spitball commending *The View from Nowhere*. It was precisely so that what had happened to him over the course of the last few hours would happen. Somehow or other, maybe even because Gideon Raven had gone through a similar baptism by fire, he'd known the right salve. Nothing but extra-strength objectivity could help.

Cass emerged from his narrow cell a minute or two before the library was going to close at midnight. The rows of carrels lining the walls down here in the bowels of the library were disgorging a thin stream of pale and brooding graduate students. Just a few carrels down from Cass was Gideon Raven, sliding his door shut behind him, giving the combination lock an extra, paranoid twist.

Raven spotted him and came over, taking the book out of Cass's hand and reading the title with raised eyebrows.

"Might as well just walk over there together" is what he said as he handed Nagel back to Cass.

"The View from Nowhere," it turned out, referred to a working-class bar in downtown Weedham that had a certain cachet with the graduate students. Its given name, at least as it was represented on the dimmed blue neon sign that had given out a long time ago, was "The View," for no discernible reason, since it was just a dive on one of the side streets off moribund Maudlin Street, a wooden shanty no different from any on the decaying block. Some student wag had dubbed it "The View from Nowhere," and the name had stuck among the cognoscenti.

There was a slight rain falling as they descended the steep hill that led out of the Frankfurter campus and headed into the down-at-the-heels center of Weedham, the sidewalk glinting whenever they passed a streetlight.

Cass had never spoken with Gideon before, and so he was surprised at the confidential tone that Gideon assumed from the very beginning, as if they had already gotten over the preliminaries.

"Lizzie, that's my wife, is giving me hell. She didn't want to move to Weedham. She hates it here. It's hard enough for her to be the wife of a permanent graduate student, but at least in Manhattan she had the museums and movie theaters and her friends from Barnard. Here pretty much all she has is me. She works at the Edna and Edgar Lipschitz Library, but that's not as exciting as it sounds."

Cass had never before been the recipient of marital confidences, and he had no idea how to respond. It was the kind of mature activity he hadn't imagined for himself. It must mean he was getting on in years, that he could be walking side by side with someone who was not only married but unhappily married.

"Yeah, I can see that" is all that he managed.

"In a sense, I can't blame her. When we got married, I'd already been working with Jonas for four years, so it was safe to assume I was nearing the end. I told her I'd have my degree and a tenure-track assistant professorship, preferably on one of the coasts, in a year or two. I said it in good faith. Although maybe, in retrospect, I shouldn't have been so confident. Maybe I should have taken the grim statistics into account."

Gideon's intimations were putting the finishing touches to the day's discombobulations. It was after midnight, they were sliding into yet another day, and exhaustion fell on Cass with a perceptible thud.

"What do you mean, the grim statistics?"

"Nobody's ever completed a dissertation under Klapper."

"What do you mean? What happens to them? Does he ask them to leave?"

"No, I've never known him to ask someone to leave—once, that is, he's chosen you. He subjects us to tests of his own devising. You may not even realize you're being tested until it's over. He's got his own pedagogical methods. You have to submit to them. It's not easy. Believe me, I've been with him twelve years, and I still don't find it easy. But if you pass, then Jonas will always be forbearing with you. I wouldn't say that he's slow to anger—well, you witnessed that for yourself— but that sort of grace that you also witnessed is characteristic of Jonas. If he takes you back in, you're one of us."

Cass absorbed this information as best he could, knowing that more was being given to him than he could understand at the moment.

"I've been with Jonas for longer than anyone, and you can always come to me when you're in doubt, although you'll find that Jonas is relatively accessible. But there are times when he isn't, especially when the next phase in his thinking is being worked out, which can be cataclysmic—the paradox shifts."

"What happens to his students, if they never get their doctorates?"

"They leave, for one reason or another. It's always a terrible ordeal for Jonas."

"But you're not planning to be a graduate student for the rest of your life, are you?"

Gideon laughed. He had a surprising laugh. There were recessed places in him where the infantile had pooled, and his laugh was yet another of them. It was a high-pitched giggle, gleeful and a little slurpy.

"Certainly not! I'm not lying to Lizzie when I tell her that I'm not leaving without my degree! I've sunk twelve years into this. I intend to leave Jonas with his imprimatur stamped on my accursed forehead!"

Gideon Raven was at least half a foot shorter than Cass, and he took strides disproportionately long compared with his height. This gave him a bobbling locomotion, his round head springing like a pigeon's.

They walked down a few steps to enter the bar. There appeared to be no windows, and the gloom was lying heavy on everything. As Cass's eyes adjusted, he saw a long free-standing bar up front, a few authentic working-class types sitting immobile and silent, and booths toward the back. Behind the bar there were yellowing posters of 1950s pin-up girls. The bartender looked as if he must have hung them up himself decades ago, when he would already have been an old lech.

Gideon went to get a pitcher, and Cass sank down at a sticky booth. Rousing from his mind any bits that were still rousable, he tried to sort out the items of information he had gathered today. They added up to ten:

1. The next assigned book for the seminar was Aristotle's *Poetics*.
2. His long experience with *Cass here, Jesse there* may have had something to do with The View from Nowhere.
3. Gideon Raven was a hell of a nice guy.
4. Gideon's marriage to Lizzie had problems.

5. Jonas Elijah Klapper did not like Darwin's theory of evolution.

6. Jonas Elijah Klapper believed that much of what passes for science is scientism.

7. None of Jonas Elijah Klapper's graduate students had completed their doctorates.

8. When Jonas Elijah Klapper was testing a graduate student, one didn't necessarily know it until it was over (if then).

9. Once one was chosen by Jonas Elijah Klapper, one would not be exiled.

10. He, Cass Seltzer, would not be exiled.

Gideon came back with a pitcher of beer, two mugs, and several shots of tequila, and when he had sorted them out and sat down, Cass asked him, "What exactly is scientism?"

Gideon drained his mug and chased it with a tequila before he answered.

"Scientism is the dogma of our day. It's the sacred superstition of the smart set that savors its skepticism. It's the product of the deification of the stolid men of science, so that the arrogance of the illiterati knows no bounds. More particularly, it's the view that science is the final arbiter on all questions, on even the question of what *are* the questions. Science has wrested the questions of the deepest meaning of humanity out of the humanities and is delivering pat little answers to all our quandaries."

"And much of what passes for science is scientism."

"Exactly."

"But a lot of what passes for science really is science."

"No doubt. But I wouldn't go emphasizing that point in front of Jonas if I were you."

"What's he got against science?"

"The same thing that he's got against Great Britain."

"What's wrong with Great Britain?"

"They don't get Jonas Elijah Klapper."

"The whole country?"

Gideon might have considered the question rhetorical, since he didn't let it interrupt his drinking. He drank with an extraordinary thirst. Cass tried to keep up, which brought him quickly to the point of wondering what would happen if, theoretically, he tried to stand.

When Gideon decided again to speak, he launched back into the theme of his marital difficulties as if that's what they had been discussing this whole time.

"Jonas warned me not to marry Lizzie. 'She is in her victorious prime, the pinnacle of her prothalamic prowess.'" His impersonation was uncanny. It wasn't for nothing that he was reputed to be the foremost expert on Jonas Elijah Klapper. Cass had heard, when he was back at Columbia, that Gideon had already published half a dozen articles analyzing Jonas Elijah Klapper's paradox shifts. "'The bloom of youth has painted her vividly with the war stripes required for victory on the battlefields of sex. She stands before you, a Maori warrior, only armed with mighty cleavage. She shall go downhill on that front, have no doubt. Heed me well, young pup! That woman will run to fat before the first five years are out, and by the tenth she'll have a lap wide enough to hold the heap of mewling babes she shall wrest from your besieged manhood.'"

Cass was shocked by what Gideon was saying. He didn't want to rush to any interpretations, but, at least on the surface, the words sounded misogynistic.

"So I take it Professor Klapper's never married?"

"The only woman Jonas ever talks about with real longing is Olga the cheesemonger at Zabar's. And, of course, good old Hannah."

"Hannah?"

"You really are a novice, aren't you? You mean to tell me you don't know about the sainted Hannah? Sophocles' Antigone, Dante's Beatrice, Quixote's Dulcinea of El Toboso, and Luke's Madonna all rolled up in one."

Cass couldn't tell whether Gideon was being ironic or not. The more they drank, the less possible it became to tell. Gideon Raven seemed to be undergoing his own paradox shifts, and all in one sitting.

Cass shrugged, so weary he had to exert himself to lift his shoulders.

"She's the one with the crazy eyes he keeps framed on his desk."

Cass had seen the photograph in Professor Klapper's Columbia office.

"Ah, so that's Hannah. I wondered who that was."

"Of course you wondered. Who can help wondering at those haunted eyes, lit by the unmistakable lambency of lunacy? Hannah Klepfish, the extraordinary woman to whom Jonas Elijah Klapper owes it all."

"Why's that?"

"It's his mama, Mr. Seltzer, that's why. Hannah Klepfish is our very own Jonas's mother, which makes her, in some sense, the mother of us all. And as one of the last of the thinkers who take Freud seriously enough to allow their own psychology to be dictated by him, Jonas is required to have a chronic case of mother fixation. Of course, she was no common mother. She had the gift of prophecy. While she was carrying Jonas, she was vouchsafed the divination—the *mantikê* in ancient Greek, the *nevua* in ancient Hebrew—sorry, you develop these tics when you've been with Jonas as long as I have—that she was destined to die in childbirth, but that she was carrying a boy child who would survive and be a great light unto the nations. As Jonas tells it, she heard a great voice declaring that it had been decreed."

"So she died in childbirth?"

"Oh, I'm sorry, had I implied that? No, the old girl pulled through. Jonas is the youngest, but all his siblings—there are four or five of them—are girls, and Hannah had been a bit long in the tooth when she at long last gave birth to the prophesied son, just like the matriarch Sarah, a comparison of which Jonas himself is quite fond. So the divination had been two-thirds accurate. And to Hannah was born a son, and the child was unlike any other, growing in knowledge from one day to the next, from one hour to the next, so that what he did not know upon waking he could teach to others upon going to sleep."

"Meaning he was exceptionally smart?"

"Did you have any doubt?"

"No, of course not."

"No, of course not," Gideon Raven repeated. "As for poor old Hannah, not even the late-life glories of such a son as hers were able to save her from the howling hounds of madness."

"What?"

"Rumor has it she was as gaga as she looks."

"So what you're saying is that she was actually crazy."

"Certifiable. Jonas, being the proverbial doting son, refused to send her away. He was forced to keep her locked up in the attic with a caretaker named Grace Poole."

"You're kidding, right?"

"I'm not capable of making this stuff up. They had a big

estate called Thornyfield on the banks of the East River, and one night Grace got stinking drunk—unfortunately, she was often what they call 'in her spirits'—and Hannah escaped the attic stronghold and set fire to Cornyfield, plunging to her death amidst the flames. The *Daily News* headline was 'Hindenburg Mom Lights Up New York Skyline.' You can well imagine the effect on a soul like Jonas's. He's never quite recovered his senses, which is why he's apt to fly into a homicidal rage if you answer one of his bloody obvious questions in the bloody obvious way, instead of somehow retrieving the mess of oblique associations he'd had in mind. 'No, no, no, that's not what I was thinking of at all! I'd meant how would Matthew Arnold have responded to Sophocles' intimations of eternal sorrow had he read Schopenhauer's response to Hegel, as he anticipated Adorno's necessary observation that there is no poetry after Auschwitz? That's what I'd meant by querying the "long, withdrawing roar."'"

"I see," Cass said quietly. Now he wasn't sure whether Gideon Raven was taunting him or consoling him. Both, he suspected. He had already decided that, whatever his motive, Thomas Nagel's *The View from Nowhere* had no part in it. "So it isn't true about Hannah being crazy."

"Well, I wouldn't go that far."

"But she didn't burn down the house."

"I'm not capable of making that stuff up, but Charlotte Brontë was. *Jane Eyre*. Sorry. I thought you'd get the reference right away. Grace Poole and all."

"I was pre-med."

"You were pre-med?"

"Yes."

"Permit me to be vulgar, but *wow*. How did you end up working with Jonas?"

"My senior year, I took 'The Manic, the Mantic, and the Mimetic.' It changed my life."

"As you no doubt told Jonas? Not in so many words, of course. Or maybe yes, in so many words?"

"Yeah, I guess."

"Cass, I don't really know why I'm telling you this, since there's really nothing in it for me. But just because there really is nothing in it for me, you should take what I'm saying extremely seriously. I want you to concentrate hard and try to understand what I'm going to tell you. It's been a long, hard day, you look like you're ready to collapse, but I want you to listen closely. Are you listening?"

"Yes."

"Go back to pre-med."

Cass was silent for a while.

"I guess what you're saying is that I can't make the grade, that I'm just not good enough to work with Jonas Elijah Klapper."

"You're not getting it, Mr. Seltzer. The un-Adorno-ed truth: if I had any chance to go to medical school, I'd be out of here so fast the back draft would blow the foam off this beer. I've sunk twelve years into Jonas Elijah Klapper. You haven't lost anything yet. Just walk out of here and never look back, Billy Budd."

Yet another classic Cass had never read.

"Baby Budd, Jimmy Legs is *down* on you." Gideon was again impersonating someone or other.

"I don't know what you're referring to."

"You've never read that either? Well, no matter. You won't need Melville in medical school. Medical school! God, what I wouldn't give for the chance to go to medical school! The humanities are finished, dead so long they're long past stinking. Jonas is the Shakespearean gravedigging clown. Medical school! Could you imagine the joy and jubilation on the part of Lady Lizzie! To have a real doctor as a husband, instead of a gravedigging clown-in-training whose only acquired skills are appeasing and impersonating Jonas Elijah Klapper."

Gideon fell into a gloomy silence, and Cass had no inclination to disturb it. At some point, Gideon had replaced the pitcher with another, and they were nearing the bottom of that one, too.

"You had any dinner tonight?" Gideon asked, and on being told that Cass hadn't, he went to get some sustenance, bringing back "the house special," a saucer plate with some tubules of beef jerky.

Cass thought about getting up and leaving—he'd probably be doing Lizzie a favor—but he was pretty sure that he no longer had access to the muscles controlling his limbs. If you have to think about it, it's not a good sign. He wasn't altogether certain either whether he could find his way back to his bleak room on Canal Street. He was dissolving into oblivion for the third time that day, and only the middle time had been edifying.

From some unlit level of his mind, a submerged question, vaguely menacing, swam to the surface. A slippery, eel-like thing, with a long poisonous ray—he struggled to get a grip on it.

"Why isn't he Klepfish?"

"Hmm. What's that, young Billy?"

"Klapper, not Klepfish, why?"

"He changed his name."

"Another book, or for real?"

"For real, Baby Budd."

"Klepfish." Cass was staring down at the table, shaking his

head, unable to assimilate the enormity of the fact, repeating the name softly.

"Time to get you home, Billy boy. Come on. Upsy-daisy." And Gideon Raven, all five feet eight of him, helped the towering Cass to his feet with surprisingly tender solicitousness, which is how he delivered him to his room. Cass couldn't quite remember, but he had a vague memory of Gideon's actually helping him get his shoes off and into bed, murmuring, "Fated boy. What have you done?"

Next week, Cass was back at the less-crowded seminar table—the three undergraduates had jumped ship, as well as the philosophy graduate student and a few of the English students.

In addition to Aristotle's *Poetics,* Cass had brought to class the reassuring knowledge of the culminating fact on the list that he had assembled last week. Cass had been chosen, and he would not be exiled.

VI

The Argument from
Intimations of Immortality

to: Seltzer@psych.Frankfurter.edu
from: GR613@gmail.com
date: Feb. 27 2008 1:15 a.m.
subject: the missing proof

Are you awake? Any new proofs tonight?

to: GR613@gmail.com
from: Seltzer@psych.Frankfurter.edu
date: Feb. 27 2008 1:20 a.m.
subject: re: the missing proof

In a manner of speaking, yes. You'll never
guess who breezed into town today. Roz!

to: Seltzer@psych.Frankfurter.edu
from: GR613@gmail.com
date: Feb. 27 2008 1:23 a.m.
subject: re: re: the missing proof

Has she really been downgraded to a breeze?
How is she? What's she up to?

to: GR613@gmail.com
from: Seltzer@psych.Frankfurter.edu
date: Feb. 27 2008 1:35 a.m.
subject: re: re: re: the missing proof

Pretty much the typical. She rode along with
me to Frankfurter, and I dropped her off
while I went to see Shimmy Baumzer (who
stood me up). By the time I got back, Roz
had organized a campus protest. The
president's wife, Deedee Baumzer, is a
sorority girl from the University of Texas,
and she's long been pushing for less geek
and more Greek at Frankfurter. Either Shimmy
finally caved, or he's feeling sufficiently
sure of himself these days. It's been a good
year for Shimmy. He's got some glitter on
his faculty, and the trustees and the donors
have been happy. Shimmy moved to revoke the
ban on the Greeks, and there was a backlash.
When Roz and I got to the campus, we passed
one student with a hand-lettered sign: "Say
NO to Greeks." Roz jumped out of the car to
investigate, and by the time I'd gotten back
she'd joined the counter-campaign on the
pagan side. She'd rallied a group of
students who were chanting "Go Greek" and
there were a few more kids on the other
side, also chanting. And right in the middle
was Roz holding a placard saying "Maccabees
= Taliban."

to: Seltzer@psych.Frankfurter.edu
from: GR613@gmail.com
date: Feb. 27 2008 1:36 a.m.
subject: Hanukkah redux

It does my heart good to hear.

```
to: GR613@gmail.com
from: Seltzer@psych.Frankfurter.edu
date: Feb. 27 2008 1:41 a.m.
subject: re: Hanukkah redux
```

There's more. She intends to live forever.
She's started something called the
Immortality Foundation. Here's a link to her
web site: www.immortality.org.

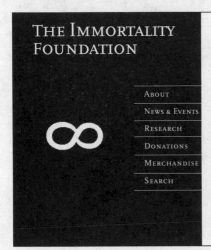

THE IMMORTALITY FOUNDATION

ABOUT

NEWS & EVENTS

RESEARCH

DONATIONS

MERCHANDISE

SEARCH

The Immortality Foundation is dedicated to vanquishing aging. What could make greater claims on our resources, our sympathies, our moral sensibilities? Humankind is universally being subjected to gratuitous torture, in the form of debilitating old age and premature deaths (anyone dying younger than five hundred years old is dying prematurely!).

Not to dedicate ourselves to eliminating torture amounts to callous indifference! Not to dedicate ourselves to eliminating needless deaths amounts to colluding with murder!

Do Not Go Gentle!

```
to: Seltzer@psych.Frankfurter.edu
from: GR613@gmail.com
date: Feb. 27 2008 1:53 a.m.
subject: immortal Roz
```

I made a donation.

to: GR613@gmail.com
from: Seltzer@psych.Frankfurter.edu
date: Feb. 27 2008 1:55 a.m.
subject: re: immortal Roz

You want to live five hundred years?

to: Seltzer@psych.Frankfurter.edu
from: GR613@gmail.com
date: Feb. 27 2008 1:58 a.m.
subject: re: re: immortal Roz

I want Roz to live five hundred years.

to: GR613@gmail.com
from: Seltzer@psych.Frankfurter.edu
date: Feb. 27 2008 2:00 a.m.
subject: re: re: re: immortal Roz

:-) Good night.

to: Seltzer@psych.Frankfurter.edu
from: GR613@gmail.com
date: Feb. 27 2008 2:01 a.m.
subject: re: re: re: re: immortal Roz

Good morning.

VII

The Argument from Soul-Gazing

Cass steps onto his front porch to retrieve his newspaper and is startled by the gentleness of the day. He sniffs exultantly. The air carries the fragrance of ethereality that Cass still associates with Pascale's billowing dark tresses. Now he can inhale that mysterious essence without the familiar clutch around his heart. Love for Lucinda has finally lifted mourning for Pascale.

He had spoken with Lucinda last night, and New England's overnight thaw seems an appropriate response. He'd think he was dreaming if not for the persuasive detail of a sodden *New York Times* that he pulls out of an ankle-deep puddle of melted snow.

Their connection hadn't been long, but it had been wonderful. He reached her as she was walking back to her hotel, and it had been like walking beside her. She was coming from a small Italian restaurant where she'd dined with some game theorists, who had all gone silly on choice bottles of 1997 Mondavi Cabernet Sauvignon Reserve, compliments of Apostolos Pappadopoulos, whom everyone calls Pappa. Pappa is the organizer of Lucinda's conference, and he's famous for his expansive good spirits. Everybody wants to get invited to the conferences that Pappa runs.

"Only it's such a bore to be the only sober head at a table," Lucinda had remarked good-naturedly. "I was the only one who could tell that the jokes weren't really all that funny." She hadn't been able to indulge like the others, since she still wanted to get in some work, polishing up her talk. Lucinda hasn't wanted to talk about the contents of her talk, only telling Cass that she'll be presenting some new ideas. Cass can sense how much she has riding on the reception.

They'd spoken mostly about the conference, as she walked back from the restaurant in balmy Santa Barbara—"Poor you," she had sympathized, "freezing in Cambridge!"— Lucinda rattling off names that didn't mean anything to him and reporting on how good or bad she judged their delivered papers to have been. "And did you fang any of them?"

She had laughed.

"I think I might have left bicuspid imprints on a few. You know, these game theorists are a tough crowd. They're not wussy psychologists. Wussologists!" She'd laughed in that adorable way she has of relishing her own humor. "I hope Pappa celebrates again in the same style after my talk. Then I can get silly on hundred-dollar bottles and laugh uproariously at bad jokes. I want to knock some major socks off these people."

"You will, Lucinda. I get happy just thinking of all those argyles flying in the air, the game theorists scrambling to pair up their mixed-up garters after the Q & A."

She laughed with almost as much enjoyment as if she had made the joke, but then her mood quickly modulated.

"Rishi's giving the keynote," she said evenly.

Rishi Chandrakar had been her colleague at Princeton,

where Lucinda had far outshone him. She doesn't understand, she had told Cass repeatedly, why Pappa would ask Rishi rather than her to deliver the keynote.

"Rishi won't deliver the keynote. He'll deliver the anticlimax." And Cass had meant it, too. He doesn't know the first thing about Rishi Chandrakar, but he knows Lucinda Mandelbaum.

"That's sweet of you to say," she said. "Cass, you're sweet. Tell me what's going on at your end. Anything new?"

"An old friend from way back when showed up in Cambridge, an incredible character. I'll tell you all about it when you get home. It would take me too long to describe over the phone."

"One of those crazies from those cults you study?"

"Cults like Judaism, Christianity, and Islam?" He laughed.

"Yeah, like that." She laughed back. "Did I ever tell you that when I first got to Harvard as an undergraduate I just couldn't understand how there could be a Department of Religion? Why not departments of astrology and alchemy and chiromancy and necromancy? And then I found out Harvard actually had a Divinity School. How could they live with that and still claim *Veritas* as their motto?"

"I'll never achieve your level of tough-mindedness," he said. William James had distinguished between minds that are tough and tender. Their tone had returned to breezy.

"That's because you're the atheist with a soul. I don't come so burdened."

"But I've gazed into your soul, Lucinda."

"That would make you the first to do that, including me. May I ask what you saw in there?"

"That would also take me too long to describe over the phone."

The conversation, so sweet and silly, made him feel guilty for holding out on her about the Harvard offer, especially since the topic of Harvard had come up, and especially since he had spilled the beans earlier that evening over dinner with Roz, who had extravagantly congratulated him, leaning across the little candlelit table they were sharing, making sure to keep her hair from getting singed in the flames, and placing both her palms on his cheeks to draw him in for a smooch. Roz had never learned how to kiss halfway.

They had been sitting in a darkened romantic nook in the Spanish restaurant Dalí. The eccentric little restaurant was a post-kitsch composition of romantic grottoes, arched doorways, beaded curtains, golden tiles, embossed copper ceilings, mosaics, sunflowers, hanging hams, and other Spanish tchotchkes. It had been Roz's favorite restaurant back when they'd been together, though they had rarely been able to afford it. She had certainly dressed up for the occasion. Cambridge was in deep-freeze, but she was showing a lot of skin in a slinky sleeveless black silk dress that had a red ruffle-flower at the right shoulder and another at the left hip. She was looking good, so good that Cass kept his eyes steadily away from her décolletage, out of loyalty to Lucinda. When he'd complimented her on the dress, remarking on its Dalí-esque appropriateness, she grinned in a way that made him wonder whether she'd known all along she was going to get him to bring her here.

He hadn't really wanted to go out to dinner, since he has a lot of homework if he's going to surprise Lucinda with his mastery of the Mandelbaum Equilibrium when she returns on Friday night, but Roz had wheedled him into it.

After some expert flirting with their waiter, Roz got down

to business, asking Cass for names of people she could approach as potential donors to the Immortality Foundation.

"As a matter of fact, I do happen to know some people who might be interested. Do you know Luke Nanovitch?"

Cass had met Nanovitch at one of Sy Auerbach's high-powered dinners, held at the Rialto in Cambridge, where Nanovitch had held forth to the assembled scientists and techies. Nanovitch, an inventor and futurist, has been proved right so many times when announcing what impossible thing he planned to invent next that he's given up noticing when people don't buy his prophecies. "Improvements to our genetic decoding will be downloaded via the Internet," he had announced, his tone of voice the same as if he were predicting that the waiter would soon appear to take their orders. "We won't even need a heart. The trick is to keep yourself alive for two decades more. It would be beyond ironic to die just short of the singularity that's just around the corner." Cass would have thought Nanovitch was mad if he hadn't met him at an Auerbach-orchestrated dinner. He has faith in his agent's shrewdness.

"Only by reputation, but I'd love to meet him!" Roz exclaimed now. "Nanovitch is one of my heroes!"

"Yes, I can see why. I heard him talking about your very own cause. Before that, the only thing I'd ever heard along these lines was the idea of flash-freezing corpses. . . ."

"Cryogenics, the human Popsicle! Cryogenics is for crackpots!"

"Ah yes."

"Don't give me that smile, Cass. I'm not a crackpot! And if you don't accept that on faith—though I'm a bit miffed that you don't—then consider Nanovitch, one of the visionaries of our day. You're not going to call Nanovitch a crackpot. More like the pot of gold at the end of the rainbow."

"Contemplation of one's mortality can addle even the clearest of thinkers. It's a bit like religion in that way. In fact, it *is* religion."

When Cass had dared to suggest something along similar lines to Nanovitch, the man had serenely smiled and said, "It's not religion. It's molecular biology."

"By which you mean," said Roz now, "that fear of death gives a lot of wishful oomph to the God hypothesis."

"Exactly."

"All the more reason to try and cure our mortality with scientific advances. If we succeed, we'll deprive the heavenmongers of their cruel false promises."

"The afterlife of the skeptics," Cass said, smiling.

"Which is all the afterlife that we need! This!" And she threw her glass of Rioja back like a pro, taking the opportunity to remind Cass, after she swallowed, to "drink plenty of red wine. The resveratrol promotes longevity. Which reminds me."

She reached into her purse and pulled out a baggy bursting with pills and capsules: gelatin globules filled with yellow viscous fluid or reddish oils, shiny black pellets and lozenges of mahogany brown, and then some homemade-looking capsules with powders ranging from white to sandy tan to mocha brown. There must have been twenty-five in all.

"You swallow all that?"

She answered by getting them all down with amazing dispatch, using her water, and then taking a long swig of resveratrol as a chaser.

"This is nothing! You should see what I swallow in the morning!"

"Do you know what you're doing?"

"Do any of us?"

"But you're doing something extreme here. You could be doing yourself more harm than good."

"Look, we all know what's going to happen if nature is allowed to take its course. This is what strong intervention looks like. That's what I'm interested in. Strong intervention."

"You take even more than that in the morning?"

"I take vitamins, antioxidants, and hormones three times a day. The biggest dose is in the morning. The smallest dose is what you just saw."

"What are you trying to do to yourself, Roz?"

"Live a very long time."

"You could be killing yourself."

"Have a little faith. I'm not doing this blindly. I consult with molecular biologists and gerontologists."

"Do they know what they're doing? How much real science is this based on?"

"The science is incomplete, sure. It always is. If we wait around to get it, we'll never live to see it gotten. The best we can do is experiment with ourselves."

"I don't like the sound of that."

"Life isn't a randomized, double-blind, peer-reviewed clinical trial. Big gains require big risks, and we're after the biggest gain of all."

Cass decided to say no more about Roz's experiments on her body. She always was a risk-taker and she always will be one.

"Have you thought about the other high-tech way to cheat death?" Cass was thinking of the position advocated by another participant at Auerbach's Rialto dinner, a philosopher

named Nicholas Duffy. Duffy had been the only one to challenge Nanovitch at all, though he was more or less on the
same wavelength. "If you could reverse-engineer the neural
program that constitutes a person's mind, you could upload it
to a less-vulnerable physical medium," Cass said to Roz.
"There could even be multiple backups, in case of a power
failure or a nuclear attack."

"You mean just backing up our software, and throwing
away this beautiful hardware platform we call my body? Are
you *kidding,* Cass? I don't want to look into the mirror and see
a rectangular screen! I don't want to run my virtual fingers
across your shivering keyboard or have you uploading into
me for a virtual roll in the hay! Give me my body or give me
death!"

This was turning into one of the conversations with Roz
when Cass wasn't sure whether she wanted him to be laughing quite as much as he was. Meanwhile, the tapas had
started to arrive, with their waiter theatrically reciting the
names of the nine dishes as he balanced them expertly
around the candlelit table.

"This question of preserving our software or our hardware
reminds me of those ancient Judeo-Christian debates on
whether an immaterial soul survives the death of the body, or
the body itself is resurrected when the Messiah comes," Cass
said, watching Roz tuck into the tapas as if there were no
tomorrow, even though she was betting on several centuries'
worth of them.

"What did the ancient rabbis say?"

"They're pretty much on your side on this one. They
choose the body over the disembodied soul."

"Glad to hear it. Anyway, Cass," she continued, washing
down a green-lipped mussel with some more Rioja, "the

sooner you get me in touch with Nanovitch while I'm here in Cambridge, the better. And what about that agent of yours?"

"Sy Auerbach? What do you want with Sy Auerbach?" It occurred to Cass that maybe Roz had a book she had written or was planning to write. Everybody has written or is planning to write a book.

"Auerbach strikes me as the kind who'd want in on immortality. I read that blog of his. He's our kind of guy!"

"Okay, I'll give you his coordinates. He's in New York, of course."

"I'm on my way to New York! Maybe he'd want to meet me personally! I'd love to be one of the regulars on his blog."

"I'll see what I can do."

"Thanks, Cass. You know, it's wonderful that you've come up so much in the world, and it's wonderful that you're willing to be so generous and help me with connections, and it would be wonderful, too, if *you* became a friend of the Immortality Foundation. Even if you didn't want to be a *major* financial donor, but just enough to indicate that you support what I do."

"Well, actually, Roz, I'm not sure that I do."

"You think it's unrealistic, right? You think it's science on selective serotonin reuptake inhibitors! But it's not! Some of the biologists that my foundation is supporting have results that are going to make the possibility of radically extending life a reality. I'm talking *radically* radically!"

"Well, I'll tell you, Roz, I'm just not altogether convinced that radically radically is such a good idea."

"Huh?"

"Well, obviously, adding a few years or even decades to our normal life spans would be terrific; nobody would want to go back to the days when forty was considered a ripe old age. . . ."

"Forty! For the first few hundred thousand years of human history, half of the population died in infancy and childhood! A third of young men died in warfare before they were twenty. A woman's marriage ceremony was rape, and she had a good chance of dying if a pregnancy came from it. Talk about nasty, brutish, and short! But did our species give in to this barbarism? Of course not! And we're the lucky results of the Glorious Refusal, which means we have the obligation to keep on refusing the barbarities that nature is constantly trying to force on us!"

"Right," Cass said, smiling. She had delivered her last lines to an imaginary audience of potential donors. "Obviously, the move toward four score and ten has been good. But what I'm not convinced would be so good is extending life so much that the whole meaning of what it is to live a human life would change. And that's the sort of thing you're talking about, right? That's what you mean by radically radically? Radically radically would mean reframing all the basic existential questions. And it's not clear that we have the wherewithal to think that through. We have a hard enough time with the old set of questions."

Roz had carefully laid down her fork, which had been on its way to her mouth loaded up with *pollo al ajillo.*

"I never know how to respond when people say things like that to me. I'm at a loss. It's like someone saying that they don't know whether suffering is a bad thing."

"Well, people say that, too, you know, that it's necessary that there be some amount of suffering in the world to create the opportunity for certain virtues to develop, virtues like forbearance and compassion. . . ."

"Courage, charity, forgiveness, empathy—even true love, which don't mean a thing if it ain't got that sting." Roz finished his sentence for him. "Suffering provides us wonderful opportunities for character-building. Yes, I'm familiar with this line of reasoning. The only people who push it are the God-apologists, who are trying to make excuses for what an insufferable world this is, even though there's supposed to be an omnipotent, omniscient, and well-intentioned Big Boy running the show. Any suffering the apologists can't rationalize away as a product of our having the ennobling capacity for free will, including the free will to inflict unspeakable atrocities on one another, they try to explain with this character-building song and dance. I find the song pornographic and the dance macabre. A grieving mother whose child was senselessly lost has the chance-in-a-lifetime opportunity to develop her soul toward tranquil acceptance. And what of that dying child himself, who doesn't have the psychological and spiritual equipment to transcend what's happening to him and is never going to get it because he's going to be *dead*? Wouldn't this theodicy require, at the least, that all humans— I'm not even going to bring up the suffering of animals— have an equal opportunity to develop their capacities for nobility? Cass, this is obscene. I don't have to tell you any of this. I learned it all from *The Varieties of Religious Illusion*. That's where I learned the bloody word 'theodicy' in the first place."

A change had come over Roz, a modulation into a lower key. She had been hyper, even for her, since she'd landed on his doorstep yesterday morning. But now her voice had lost its manic edge, her face its clowning slant. She looked, if anything, even younger, flushed and earnest.

"You're right, of course. I wasn't actually pushing that argument about suffering, just making the point that it's not a tautology to say, 'Suffering is bad.'"

"I think it is. I think that 'Suffering is bad' is as obvious as it gets. And even if people don't think it's so obvious in the generic case, they catch on fast enough when the suffering is *theirs*. '*My* suffering is bad' is a tautology to anyone who says it. I'd like to see someone in the throes of agony still pushing this treacle called theodicy. Sure, the transcendent possibilities afforded by suffering make this a better world. But only when it's the other guy doing the suffering."

Cass nodded. He wasn't going to argue with her. And she was right to bring up the children who never get the chance to theodicize their suffering, just as Dostoevsky had been right: "If the suffering of children goes to swell the sum of sufferings which was necessary to pay for truth, then I protest that the truth is not worth such a price." Cass had quoted that in his book.

"I loved your book," she said suddenly, out of the blue. "I haven't told you yet, have I, how much I loved it? It made me proud."

"Thank you," he said, dumbfounded.

Roz, too, seemed a bit unsteady, her pacing slowed.

"You're doing something important, Cass."

"Oh, come on, Roz. You used to be able to hold your alcohol better."

"No, I mean it. I kept thinking that only you could have written *The Varieties of Religious Illusion*. You've spent years trying to understand what happened back then, all the drama with the Klap and Azarya and even me, and this book is the outcome, and the world's the better for it."

"I don't know what to say. Thank you. It means the world to me to hear you speak like this. I had no idea."

"I guess you know now how I feel about what you've been doing with your life. So—why don't you tell me your objections to what I'm doing?" She was smiling again. "What have you got against immortality?"

"I just wonder whether coming to terms with one's own mortality isn't a necessary part of seeing oneself with the proper objectivity. Understanding that you have your time here on Earth, as the others that came before you had theirs, and as those who will come after will have theirs. You weren't for ages and ages, you are now, and soon enough you won't be anymore. There's nothing special about you just because you happen to be you. There's nothing special about your time just because it happens to be your time."

"We'll still have mortality enough to try our souls, Cass. Living forever isn't on the table. Death will come. It's simply mathematics. I'm just talking about curing our senescence, our biologically running down. There's nothing we can do to prevent accidents like falling down the stairs and breaking your neck, or being caught in the crossfire of some pointless feud, or getting hit by a runaway trolley. There's no way to bring the probability of life's slings and arrows down to zero, which means that, by the laws of probability, something's going to get you, sooner or later. Five hundred years is actually a bit of an exaggeration. It's probably more like two hundred years on average that we can expect to live, once we've wiped out senescence. Every morning, you play Russian roulette, and the gun has no memory. Sooner or later, your bullet will come. No one is literally immortal. So *carpe diem*! In fact, *carpe diem* all the more, because if you die today—and you know, if you compute which is the most likely day that you'll die, then mathematically the answer is always today— then you'll be losing out on all the more, an eternity of more."

"So what you're saying is that death will be even more terrifying, since we'll have so much more to lose. And the life we'll be losing will be that sweet life of undiminished poten-tiality, with all our powers still intact. You're making death even more alarming. Death is going to be just as inevitable, if your mathematics is right, but we've got that much more to lose. So remind me again of what we gain?"

"You don't think that eliminating the horror of watching yourself run down, getting more debilitated and diminished and pathetic with every year you live past seventy, isn't a gain? You don't think that the probability of your getting, on aver-age, two hundred years to explore all of life's possibilities isn't a gain?"

"You don't think our pleasure in life will be diminished if we have more than double a normal life span? The ability to savor life does tend to diminish as one gets older, doesn't it, once the freshness and newness has worn off?"

"Does it? I haven't noticed."

"After you've seen it all and done it all, several times over, doesn't the pleasure pall?"

"You can never see and do it all! And I think the capacity for pleasure is something that needs to be cultivated, like an appreciation for music or wine. The more experience you have, the more profound the pleasure. Memories add depth."

Cass didn't answer. He held his glass of Rioja up before the candle flame, staring into its rich ruby color as it caught the light. It was a good bottle, a Muga Reserva 2003—"very ele-gant and suggestive" is the way the menu had put it.

"What is it?" she asked.

"Well, it's a funny thing, Roz. I've missed you."

"That's funny?"

"I have to confess that I hadn't exactly realized it until now."

"I hadn't realized how much I'd missed you either, until I read your book. It brought me running."

"Running? Where?"

"Why, here. Right here."

He shook his head, agape at the irony. He'd written *The Varieties of Religious Illusion* in order to answer the question Lucinda had posed to him. He didn't know at the time whether the question was sarcastic or sincere. He only knew that to answer it he had to write an entire book, working out his conviction that the religious sensibility comes in many varieties and isn't exclusively confined to explicitly religious contexts. He hadn't expected Lucinda to read his book, much less to be carrying it in her shoulder bag as she materialized out of his fantasies in the autumn twilight. And as a consequence of his writing the book, all sorts of other things had followed—not least of all, Roz.

"Now, Roz. We're old enough friends to speak perfectly honestly, aren't we?"

"*Perfectly* honestly? I don't know whether we'll ever be old enough for that, not even if my crack team of researchers come through for me. But proceed."

"You're not actually saying that you're interested in me romantically? Not after all these years. We're in such different places from where we were back then."

"I'd say that's probably all for the good. We weren't even old enough to be too young for each other."

"Part of my being in a different place now is that I'm with Lucinda. It's a wonderful place for me to be."

Cass had kept his gaze fastened on the jeweled depths of the Rioja. Roz waited for him to look her in the eye before she spoke.

"Do you want to be in that same place for two hundred years?"

"Not a day less."

"Well, then, the least you could do, Cass Seltzer, would be to become a friend of the Immortality Foundation!"

He burst out laughing, as much in relief as anything else. Roz had had him going there. The rest of the meal continued with more Rioja and laughter, and they'd even splurged on a dessert: *besos de amor*, dates stuffed with marzipan and drizzled with tamarind sauce. Marco, their waiter, had bent low to kiss Roz's hand in farewell, and Roz had patted him tenderly on the cheek.

VIII

The Argument from the Existence of the Poem

Gideon Raven had always had a rigorous bent to his mind. He'd come to identify this as his major problem. It made him panicky to step from one thought to the next without some connective scaffolding, even if slippery and narrow. It was a form of cognitive acrophobia, and he was acrophobic to begin with.

He'd close his eyes and picture himself stepping tentatively out into midair, his jumpy foot nervously feeling for something solid before advancing. Even in his imagination he was an earth-crawler, eyes filled with dirt, unable to fling himself forward an inch, much less streak like a shooting star.

Step! he'd urge his dangling doppelgänger. Step and be saved! Cling and be damned! O ye of little freaking faith.

It was why his poetry had never been worth a damn, why it had progressed from middling to mute. It was why, after a full dozen years, he was still a graduate student, which was to be something a little less than human, the determination of his life for someone else to decide. He railed against Jonas, but he knew he deserved no better than to spend his life paralyzed in this purgatory of pedantry.

He could, of course, make a decisive move. It was theoretically in his power. He could call it quits and leave academia, dip his arms up to his elbows in the river of cash flowing from trickle-down economics. Three of the five original Klapper defectors who had decided not to move to Weedham were already learning how to program computers, and the other two had applied to law schools.

But that was the thing about purgatory. It voided volition. Obsessed with genius, he had never been further from it. Genius was a matter of incantatory intuitions and phosphorescent blasts into the dark. Genius was a matter of thunderclap reasons, of which reason knew nothing. Genius was oracular, overweening, and severe. It left it to others to grub around in dusty doubts and cavil in insect voices.

All of Klapper's students obsessed unhealthily on the nature of genius, its signs and *siphirot*, the Kabbalistic term for emanations—Jonas had been introducing Kabbalistic terms more and more frequently—though in obsession, as in all things, Gideon outstripped Klapper's other students. They recognized the unwholesomeness of their preoccupation, its self-destructive futility and navel-gazing focus, but that was hardly a deterrent. Genius itself is diseased and self-destructive, antisocial and ill-mannered. It's also the only thing that redeems us.

In the metaphor of the Great Chain of Being, man is assigned a place between the angels and the animals, but that isn't exactly right. Between man and the angels there's another ontological stratum, vanishingly slim and eternally endangered, occupied by the men and the women of genius. As the angels communicate only with the angels, and the animals with the animals, so the geniuses speak each to each, sometimes overhearing phrases fallen from the angels up above them, as we, in turn, overhear them.

I do not think they will speak to me.

There you go again, schmuck. That's the whole problem. You can't even talk to yourself without sounding like someone else.

Nothing came to Gideon pure and unblemished. He was sophisticated, in the original meaning, defiled and desecrated. If he didn't love Lizzie so much, he'd have offed himself last week.

And he'd never write poetry again. He'd never get out an original line again. Every line he heard could be traced back to someone. The perversity of persuasion had slimed everything.

The more Cass got to know Gideon, the more aware he grew of the man's tunneling despair. It was strange, since Cass admired Gideon so much. Aside from Jonas Elijah Klapper—who inhabited another category of being altogether—Gideon was the most extraordinary person Cass knew.

"I know this is going to sound naïve to you, from your point of view and all, but I don't want to be a genius," Cass confessed to Gideon one night after a few pitchers. "All I really want is to be able to understand the geniuses. Understand a little bit of what they say when they talk back and forth across the millennia to each other. I'd be happy if I could just follow the ideas of men like Hegel and Goethe and Jonas Elijah Klapper."

They were in The View from Nowhere, just Gideon and Cass, though some of the others were supposed to join them after midnight. The seminar had closed ranks now. All of the outsiders from the other departments had dropped out, so it was just Klapper's seven. In addition to Gideon and Cass, there were Nathan Suarez, Miriam Chan, Ezra Lull, Zack Kreiser, and Joel Lebow. The mean number of years they'd spent as graduate students, averaging in Gideon's 12 and Cass's 0, was 7.2. But attendance at any seminar taught by Jonas Elijah Klapper was a tacit requirement that nobody had ever thought to challenge. After all, why would one? Miriam had shown up at the seminar last week with a raging fever, which hadn't surprised anyone, though Professor Klapper had firmly ordered her home, reminding her that there was no need for her to expose others to her misbehaving microbes.

"To bed, Miss Ching, with pots of tea, and no reading to overly tax your strength. A little Robert Frost perhaps. Whitman, in moderation, when you're feeling more robust."

Cass had reacted to the preoccupation with genius in his own way. He had taken out books on famous minds, as interested in their lives as in their ideas (maybe even a little more). Right now he was reading E. T. Bell's *Men of Mathematics*, which was the best yet, even though it had real mathematics to slow him down. Some of these people sounded as if they had to be changelings, non-human visitors from some other sphere, with powers so prodigious they burst the boundaries of developmental psychology, lisping out profundities while other children were playing with their toes. Gauss, for example, who struck Cass as the most amazing one yet, which was no wonder, since, according to Bell, Carl Friedrich Gauss was one of the three greatest mathematicians of all recorded history, the other two being Archimedes of Syracuse and Sir Isaac Newton.

Gauss was German, born in 1777, and the stories that Bell told about him defied belief. His father couldn't appreciate what his son was, and if he'd had his way the prodigy would have become a gardener or a bricklayer like him. His mother, though semi-literate, had been his protector when he was young and vulnerable, making sure that he was able to get schooling. Gauss's genius had shown itself when he was barely out of infancy.

"People who witnessed it said it was like something otherworldly," Cass said, quoting Bell.

Gideon had patiently heard out Cass about the child Gauss, including the story involving the stern schoolmaster who, out of mean-spirited spite, had given his pupils the exercise of adding up all the integers from 1 to 100. Within seconds Gauss had returned the answer, seeing, in a flash, that adding pairs from opposite ends of the list gave the same sum: $1 + 100 = 101$, and $2 + 99 = 101$, and $3 + 98 = 101$, so all he had to do was take 101 fifty times and he had the answer.

"The children were supposed to work out the solution on a slate and then put it on the teacher's desk, piled one on top of the other. Gauss, who was ten, wrote it down as soon as the teacher got the words out and said in his peasant dialect, '*Ligget se,*' 'There it lies.' Of course, the teacher thought the kid was a lazy lout. After all the slates got piled on top, hours later, all of the answers wrong, the teacher found Gauss's with just the number 5,050. And then he realized what he had."

Gideon nodded. "I see why you find these stories interesting, from the point of view of psychological curiosities, but they just don't engage me the way literary genius does. It's not even genius in the same sense. These computational tricks don't indicate a special order of soul. They're like machines, these kids. Sometimes they're even functionally retarded."

"Gauss wasn't an idiot savant. These aren't little computing tricks. Gauss was comparable to Goethe."

"I don't accept that. Gauss's talents were from the brain, not the soul. I'm not saying he was an asshole—I don't know anything about the guy—but theoretically he could have been, and that's the point. He could have been a total asshole when it came to all human concerns and just had some single part of his brain overdeveloped. Isaac Newton was simple-minded to the point of semi-retarded when it came to spiritual matters. He used his cerebral calculating machine to calculate the date of the end of days. They're the Gump Worsleys of thinking."

"Who's Gump Worsley?"

"He was a goalie for the Canadiens." Gideon was from Montreal, and if the names he bandied didn't come from the canon, chances were they came from the Canadiens. "He was this short, pudgy guy, looked like he'd keel over if you asked him to drop down and do twenty, with a hanging beer belly and a goofy mug of a face. He never played with a mask. He said his face was his mask. And he threw up before every game, his good-luck ritual. But he was a great goalie. At his height, in 1968, he went undefeated in the playoffs with eleven straight wins."

"Gauss wasn't a Gump."

"Coulda been. But Goethe? No way a Gump."

"I don't know how you can be so sure."

"Here's how: literature works the whole soul, and mathematics doesn't. It's as easy as that. That's why Gauss could be a prodigy at two, before he'd even acquired a self."

The need to acquire a self had been a sustained theme in the thought of Jonas Elijah Klapper, surviving every paradox shift. All of Klapper's students understood that education is a desperate business, psychopoiesis, the making of the soul of which they would have been otherwise bereft. Psychopoiesis requires that one be in the right place at the right time, one of the hot spots, occasionally located at our better universities, where the overhang is porous, and scraps from the higher conversation rain down. Thus we acquire an education; thus the species lurches on.

There were of course the exceptions, upon whom Jonas thought much, but of whom he seldom spoke: potential progenitors of a greatness that made mere genius seem jejune. Goethe, for example, had settled for genius, announcing to the world that, although he had been present at the creation, he would not lay claim to the final knowledge of the world, a revelation that had provided the subtext of Jonas's first work, *Goethedämmerung*.

The sad truth was that almost nobody had a self. None of Professor Klapper's students were certain they had one, not even Gideon Raven. The only people they were certain had selves were the writers whom Professor Klapper assigned them to read, and even here there was room for debate. And then, of course, there was Jonas Elijah Klapper himself.

"Gauss wasn't a full-fledged mathematician at two. He wasn't creating mathematics yet, just demonstrating the enormous capacity for doing so. There's creative genius in mathematics, too."

"I don't dispute the existence of mathematical genius."

Cass laughed.

"Why are you laughing?"

"It just struck me as funny, I couldn't really say why."

"Could be the beer laughing, Baby Budd," Gideon had replied good-naturedly.

"'We do not prove the existence of the poem,'" Cass had quoted from Wallace Stevens.

"Not bad, Baby Budd. Not bad at all." Gideon lifted the near-empty pitcher in a toast.

There was a large and raucous group of graduate-student

types at the next table, with a lot of punning going on, mostly around philosophers' names, to judge from the comments that got lifted airborne and floated over to where Gideon and Cass were sitting.

"When my mistake was pointed out to me, I felt like a complete buber," they heard, followed by shouts of laughter. And: "It's buried so deep we'll have to use a heidegger." And: "He went into a bertrand and began to babble about the class of all classes that aren't members of themselves." There were more, judging from the shouts of laughter, but those were the ones that Cass had caught.

One of the punsters got up to get another pitcher and, on his way to the bar, paused and greeted Cass and Gideon.

"You probably don't recognize me, right?"

"Who could recognize anybody in this light?" Gideon had returned pleasantly.

"Yeah. You know, I once saw Jed over there"—the kid indicated the bartender with a backward toss of his head—"outside, in so-called natural light, and it was scary. Anyway, I'm Jordan Block. I'm a grad student in philosophy. I was in that Klapper seminar the first day, and I think I recognize you two. You guys were there, right?"

"Yeah."

"Sure."

"Did you ever hope in your wildest dreams to witness such a farce? The whole scene was out of *Monty Python*. That bit when he went into his trance and intoned, '*Wovon man nicht sprechen kann, darüber muss man schweigen,*' and then, in the same breath, lumped it with the Private Language Argument, with no inkling that there's a distinction between early and later Wittgenstein. What about '*wovon man nicht* knows the first fucking thing, *darüber muss man schweigen?*' I was almost tempted to come back the next week just to hear the hash he was going to make out of Aristotle. You think anyone showed up?"

Cass glanced at Gideon, who was listening to Jordan with an insouciant smile. He shrugged at the question, and then added an affable "Your guess is as good as mine."

Jordan laughed. "Yeah, I recognized you." He nodded at Cass. "You were the one he started shrieking bloody murder at because he didn't like what you said about a poem. What a douche bag. Well, see you around."

"Yeah," Gideon returned with his imperturbable smile, which was removed as soon as Jordan left them.

"That's typical."

"Is it?"

"Of course. Jonas gets that all the time from the so-called philosophers. He's the only one who's doing real philosophy these days, ever since the logical positivists set out to hunt down and exterminate any genuine philosophical insights. These are the guys who run around calling out 'meaningless' wherever they find something difficult and profound. It's like skeet shooters shouting 'pull.' If they can't bag it in some trivial empirical test, they blast it out of the skies with 'meaningless.' Look, according to these guys, even Nietzsche isn't a real philosopher, and that—to use one of their own favorite ploys—is a *reductio ad absurdum* if ever there was one."

"Why didn't we set the guy straight? Shouldn't we have defended Professor Klapper?"

"There's no point. These guys are ideologues. Their worldviews would crumble if you got them to give up their positivistic, nihilistic scientism. The English departments are mired in political ideology, and the philosophers are buried in scientistic ideology. Jonas is the sole defender of the faith."

"I still think we should have defended him. It doesn't seem honorable. I feel like we've let Professor Klapper down. It just isn't right to let him be smeared that way. It's like letting truth be smeared."

"It's okay." Gideon laughed. He laughed for a while, and he laughed hard, and Cass figured it was, as Gideon was likely to say, the beer that was laughing. "We don't need to set guys like that straight," he finally said. "What we need is a new pitcher. You look like you could use a little protein, too. I'll wait a few minutes—I don't want to run into that Blockhead again—and then I'll go get you a nice nourishing plate of jerky."

It was reassuring to Cass that Gideon wasn't ruffled by the philosophy student's riff. Cass had felt a cold, numbing shock of disbelief go through him as Jordan Block defamed Jonas Elijah Klapper. But Gideon's explanation made sense. Of course, if Professor Klapper had picked up the lit taper of philosophy after the professional philosophers had tried to stamp it out with scorn and scientism, they would resent him and try to make him a laughingstock. Jonas Elijah Klapper often remarked that professionalism was the last refuge of the scoundrel.

IX

The Argument from the Eternity of Irony

Though the Blockheads might scoff, the undeniable truth was that Klapper's standing in the world was as high as, if not higher than, it had ever been. As proof, he had been invited to deliver one of the most prestigious endowed lectureships in the civilized world, the Prufrock Lecture in the Humanities and Human Values at Harvard University.

Cass had gone over to Cambridge by himself, taking the two-car commuter train to Porter Square. He hadn't yet seen Harvard, and he'd wanted to get there early to wander around the iconic institution of higher learning.

Cass had loved the whole feel of the place. The self-enclosed Yard, with the homey iron fence around it as if to protect grazing cattle; the freshman dormitories framing the green in brotherly, and now sisterly, communion; the understated Puritan architecture, the prim red brick with white trim, content to be as it is without ostentation; and then, in another frame of self-containment, side by side with the communing dormitories, there was another open expanse, anchored at one end by the neoclassical grandeur of the Widener Library and at the other by the nobility of the Memorial Church, the simplicity of the red-brick-and-white-trim theme taking on an inspired transcendence with that soaring white spire. This scene, this Yard, this fenced oasis of American genius, is where Jonas Elijah Klapper belonged.

Professor Klapper had touched on this circumstance himself, toward the end of last week's seminar—devoted to *On the Genealogy of Morals,* Nietzsche's most incandescent work, Klapper had said, and he himself had burned with a rare flame, prolonging the seminar by twenty minutes, which happened seldom, since teaching was, for him, an all-consuming fire in which he was, as he put it, the *korban,* the burnt offering, so that by the end of the two-and-a-half-hour seminar he would be utterly spent, instantaneously passing from inferno to ash. But for Nietzsche there had been an extra twenty minutes of divine afflatus, which had carried Jonas Elijah Klapper to an inspired recitation of the famous words from *Götzen-Dämmerung,* or *Twilight of the Idols:* "Our true experiences are not at all garrulous. They could not communicate themselves even if they tried. Whatever we have words for, that is already dead in our hearts. In all talk there is a grain of contempt." He had, appropriately, gone silent, staring off beyond the head of the tallest person, who was, of course, Cass, and then, all at once, Jonas Elijah Klapper had crumpled, the bulk of his upper body slumping, his massive head's precipitous descent fortuitously broken by his open palm, into which his face was then buried, and he had sat prostrate and immobile, which could be alarming if one hadn't seen it before, but they all had, and they waited until he would recover himself and would, with the weariness of the woe-besotted world, gather up his papers and books and shuffle out, only this time he had bestirred himself to remind the class of the upcoming Prufrock Lecture and, more specifically, of the literary illustriousness of the hall where the lecture would take place, "since, my cherubim"—his endearments to the class had grown ever fonder as the semester had progressed—"the masterful Henry James had chosen that precise stage for the pivotal scene in *The Bostonians*.

"I thought for your amusement I would provide you with a snippet of James's rendering of Memorial Hall to deepen your own apperception when you attend on Tuesday coming. I shall recite, as is my wont, from memory:

" " "Now there is one place where perhaps it would be indelicate to take a Mississippian," Verena said, after this episode. "I mean the great place that towers above the others—that big building with the beautiful pinnacles which you see from every point." But Basil Ransom had heard of the great Memorial Hall; he knew what memories it enshrined, and the worst that he should have to suffer there; and the ornate, overtopping structure, which was the finest piece of architecture he had ever seen, had moreover solicited his enlarged curiosity for the last half hour. He thought there was rather too much brick about it, but it was buttressed, cloistered, turreted, dedicated, superscribed, as he had never seen anything; though it didn't look old, it looked significant, it covered a large area, and it sprang majestic into the winter air. It was detached from the rest of the collegiate groups, and it stood in a grassy triangle of its own.' I skip a few paragraphs now, for I have taught long and must wonder myself at how I am managing to persevere. I shall conclude with this: 'The effect of the place is singularly noble and solemn, and it is impossible to feel it without a lifting of the heart.' The expatriated Henry James, who, returning to his native shores, finds much to strike him as tawdry, inferior, and small, is being ironical, of course. But the Jamesian irony negates the negation into contrapuntal affirmation. You, too, shall, I rather think, find contrapuntal

affirmation within the bombastic Ruskinian Gothic extravaganza of Memorial Hall, as, too, within the quieter interior of
its Sanders Theatre."

After hearing Memorial Hall so brilliantly described, Cass
felt stupid that he hadn't been able to find it. He kept passing
it by, thinking it was a church. He was misled, too, by its
no longer sitting on a grassy triangle, separated from the collegiate groups. The university had grown up around it. By
the time he finally figured out what a bombastic Ruskinian Gothic extravaganza looked like, and located Sanders Theatre within it, there were no more seats to be had in the vast
interior.

The theater fanned out from the stage, and he was just able
to squeeze himself onto a cold stone bench that was inside
the entrance and up against a wall. A couple of moments
later, a tall girl in dreadlocks entered and asked if she could
squeeze in beside him. Somehow they managed.

"Did I miss anything?" she whispered.

"I don't think so. I just got here myself," he whispered
back.

There was a chain of introducers, a Harvard faculty member introducing a Harvard dean who introduced another Harvard faculty member who finally introduced Jonas Elijah
Klapper.

"Big fleas have little fleas upon their backs to bite them,
and little fleas have lesser fleas, and so on ad infinitum,"
Cass's neighbor whispered.

He was worried that she was going to be a problem. First of
all, she was almost in his lap, which was distracting. Second,
she was one of those people who consider attendance at a lecture a participatory sport. Cass preferred, under any circum-

stances, less activist lecture neighbors. And this was Jonas Elijah Klapper's Prufrock Lecture! He needed to concentrate.

"Professor Klapper was for many years referred to as the 'Sage of Morningside Heights.' New York's loss is our gain, and I take this opportunity to formally rechristen him the 'Wise Man of Weedham.' And now, without any further ado, I give you the Extreme Distinguished Professor of Faith, Literature, and Values at Frankfurter University, Jonas Elijah Klapper, who will enlighten us all tonight on the subject of 'The Eternity of Irony: The Messianic Ideal, 750 B.C.E. to 1987 C.E.'"

Cass gasped aloud, so that the girl sitting next to him gave him a quizzical look.

"It's 'The Irony of Eternity,'" he told her, because that was the correct title of Professor Klapper's talk. But the girl thought Cass was making a joke and dissolved into giggles, which were fortunately drowned out by applause as Professor Klapper mounted the stage. Klapper kept his eyes cast down, his expression inscrutable, as if determined to let the acclaim make its way around him unheeded. A great man, thought Cass, swelling with an overpowering emotion, a joy splanchnic (that is from one's inner parts, from the Greek for "organ"; Cass's vocabulary had been undergoing a rapid expansion, *pari passu* with his soul's—*"pari passu"* was new, too).

"I thank you for that introduction. I shall indeed essay to live up to the sobriquet of the Wise Man of Weedham, so eloquently bestowed upon me by Professor Knudsen, who is our premier guide through the thickets of Norwegian folk tales.

"I must, embarrassingly enough, begin with an emendation in regard to the title of my lecture tonight," and Cass turned to the girl beside him and gave her a vigorous nod. "I must add to the span of years I shall traverse a full millennium. Should I have said that we must travel backward in time to 1750 B.C.E. I feared you might have thought the task too daunting."

Cass figured that Professor Klapper hadn't wanted to embarrass Professor Knudsen with the more substantive emendation. As for Cass's too-near neighbor, she was muttering, "Fasten your seat belts. It's going to be a bumpy night."

Cass's fears regarding his bench-mate were realized. She never let up. His desire to shush her struggled with his deeply ingrained sense of politeness. As usual, the latter prevailed. He lost the thread at 1750 B.C.E., with that "figure shrouded in legend whom we call by the Greek name Zoroaster, though 'Zarathustra' was the name much preferred by Nietzsche," unable to follow the labyrinthine trail as it wound its way to the "omen-encrusted moment of the chosen now, when it is becoming awkward for even the most scientistic non-seers of the hardened Materialist Mafia, with their stranglehold on our great institutions of learning, to deny the liminal sublime before us."

"Well, were you able to follow that?" the dreadful girl asked him when it was all over. She was grinning.

Cass shook his head no.

"Where you headed now?"

"To the reception for Professor Klapper at the Faculty Club."

"You are? Me, too!"

It was a private reception with various big shots invited, but Jonas Elijah Klapper had secured invitations for the seven graduate students of his own department.

"We might as well head on over," the girl announced. "Do you know the way?"

"No, not really."

"You're not Harvard?"

"No, I'm Frankfurter."

"No kidding! I went there as an undergraduate! What are you there?"

"Graduate student."

"What department?"

"Faith, Literature, and Values."

"That's a department?"

"That's Jonas Elijah Klapper's department."

"I don't think they had it when I was there."

"No, they didn't. They just created it this year in order to get him to come." He knew he was bragging.

"So he's the first professor in the Department of Faith, Religion, and whatsit?"

"Faith, Literature, and Values. That's right. He's the whole department."

"Well, I know he loves his colleagues."

The girl laughed at her own joke, and Cass smiled politely.

"What did you major in at Frankfurter?" he asked.

"Anthropology."

"How was that?"

"Total bullshit."

"I'm sorry to hear that."

"No, it worked out great. I needed to detox from all that verbiage, so what do you think I did?"

"What did you do?"

"I went to the Amazon to study the Onuma. That was as far away as I could get from bullshit and still remain in academia."

"Who are the Onuma?"

"They live in the rain forest, and they're often described as the last of the hunter-gatherers, although, technically speaking, that's not exactly right, since they garden. They're one of the last cultures to come in contact with modern civilization."

"But now they've come in contact with you."

"And they'll never be the same!"

"Isn't that a problem?"

"You mean like Heisenberg's Uncertainty Principle, but with bigger particles?"

"Yeah, like that."

"Well, actually, Absalom has thought about that quite a lot."

"Absalom?"

"Absalom Garibaldi. I work under him. He started studying the Onuma in 1964. He walks a fine line between a hands-off policy and humanitarian intervention. Just think about sickness. Their view is that disease is caused by the curses of their enemies and the only way to combat the curses is to blow ebene up their nostrils, which is one hell of a hallucinogenic drug, and go into a trance where you can undo the curse, and that view is not anything that we're going to try and talk them out of. But if Absalom sees a child dying of a bacterial infection, he's going to slip the kid some antibiotic to go along with the ebene and the witch doctor's charms. Obviously, our being there leaves a footprint, but that isn't really an argument against our studying them, especially since it can shed so much light on our evolutionary past."

"I didn't mean to suggest otherwise. I was just being facile."

"It's nice that you can admit that. I assume you haven't been an academic for long."

"No. I'm a first-year grad student."

"What made you decide to go to Frankfurter?"

"Jonas Elijah Klapper."

"Yeah, like me. I just went where Absalom was."

"To the Amazon."

"Yes, but I meant my institutional affiliation."

"Which is here?"

"Harvard? No. I'm at Berkeley. When I first started working with Absalom he was at Tulane, but I just switched when he did."

"Yeah, some of Professor Klapper's grad students did the same when he came from Columbia to Frankfurter."

"Were you a Frankfurter undergrad?"

"No, Columbia."

"So basically neither of us knows where the hell we're going right now."

They had walked determinedly across Harvard Yard, each following the other, and now exited onto a street, which they crossed.

"That looks like the right place," the girl announced, pointing to a redbrick building not noticeably different from any of the others around it. "Excuse me, is that the Faculty Club?" the girl asked a woman passing by.

"Yes, it is."

"I always find my way," she said, turning back to Cass, "even when I have no idea where I'm going. It's inexplicable."

"It must come in handy in the rain forest. What country do the Onuma live in?"

"The borderlands between Brazil and Venezuela. I'm mostly in Venezuela. I lived in a village called Meesa-teri. *Teri* just means 'village.'"

"Do you speak . . . what's the language they speak?"

"They speak Onuma. That's what we call it. They don't have a name for themselves. 'Onuma' is a name from the Kentubas, another tribe, and it means 'dirty feet.' Is this the reception for Klapper?" she asked a woman inside the Faculty Club who was sitting behind a table.

"Yes, it is." She smiled in a transparently perfunctory way. "Your name, please?"

The girl turned to Cass with a flourish, gesturing for him to go first.

"Um, yes, I'm Cass Seltzer."

"I have it, Cass," the woman said, her traveling finger stopping at a name on her list. She handed him a name tag. "And your name, miss?"

"I'm with him," the girl said.

"I still need your name." The perfunctory smile was growing rigid round the corners. The woman had an upper lip so stiff it looked as if it could make puncture wounds.

"Roslyn Margolis."

"I don't seem to have you on the list, Ms. Margolis."

"Are you sure? Didn't you inform them I was coming, Cass?"

"I don't know."

Roslyn Margolis smiled at the gatekeeper.

"Absentminded professors!"

"Oh, are you a professor, Professor Cass, I mean, Professor Seltzer? Excuse me. I hadn't realized. You look so young."

"He is young! He's a prodigy! That's why he's so absentminded! Cass, how could you have forgotten to let the club know I was coming with you?"

"Oh well, not to worry. This can be remedied lickety-split," said the gatekeeper, producing a magic marker and the fixings for a name tag. "You know," she said to Roslyn in a confidential tone, "we have quite a few professors who forget to mention their significant others."

"Oh, thanks. I appreciate it. We could have used your help the last time this happened. I was almost kept out of seeing him inducted into the American Academy of Arts and Sciences," said Roslyn Margolis, pinning on her name tag.

"Oh my! The Academy! And so young! Well, wonderful to have met you both!"

Cass stared at Roslyn Margolis. He had begun to doubt everything she had said up until this moment, not excluding that her name was Roslyn Margolis.

"Anyway," the girl continued, as they headed into the reception area, "so far as my speaking Onuma, I do speak some. There are lots of dialects. Sometimes people from one village can't understand the people from another village. They can be pretty isolated from each other. There are still lots of villages that haven't had any contact with outsiders."

"Are they noble savages?"

"Noble savages?"

"You know, uncorrupted by society's venality."

"Frolicking like bunnies in Rousseau's Never-Never Land? Funny you should ask. When I first applied to be Absalom's student—he was wary of me, since I was coming from studying the kind of anthropology he doesn't have much use for, but, then, I didn't either, so it worked out great—but when I first met him, I asked him what they were really like, the Onuma, and he said, 'They're assholes.'"

She laughed. She had a wonderfully lusty laugh. Cass couldn't hear it without grinning himself.

"And are they?"

"Assholes? It's against the anthropologist religion to say anything judgmental, so if it strikes you as judgmental then don't repeat it, or Absalom or I will have to kill you, which we're capable of, but, yeah, basically they're assholes. They're not noble-savage pretty. The Onuma are about as good a counterexample as you're going to find for a universal moral instinct. They don't seem to have any compunctions about lying or stealing, the men can beat their wives whenever they feel the need to, they're constantly raiding each other's women, which is how their wars start, it's always about kidnapping women, and then the raided go raiding to get them back, preferably taking a few extra women with them as long as they're going to the trouble, and they have an unquenchable thirst for revenge."

"It sounds like a dangerous place to be a woman."

"It's a dangerous place to be a human."

"And what do they make of you?"

Roslyn Margolis, if that was indeed her name, was a tall, slender girl, only a few inches shorter than Cass, but she looked, despite her slenderness, as if she would never have to ask a man to remove any twist-off top for her. Her face looked strong, too. There was something bold and arresting. Once you really looked at her, it was hard to look away. She had a high-bridged nose and clear blue eyes, and her upper lip looked sweetened by all the laughter it had laughed, it looked generous to share that laughter with others, and it looked, despite all its fun, noble. Her whole bearing had something noble about it. But, even with the height and obvious physical strength and the suggestion of nobility, she was feminine.

She was certainly dressed feminine, in a long peacock-blue skirt of crinkly velvet and a silky blouse in the same color that was shot through with gold embroidery. She was one of those women that could qualify as beautiful without being pretty. It was something about the sheer quantity of life that seemed compressed into her.

"Well, first they thought I was a dead person who had come back from the sky country. They kept asking me how I had died, what it was like to be dead. They have a pretty complicated mythology, mostly derived from their heavy use of hallucinogens. The men get high every day, and believe me, that stuff is powerful. It also makes them drip long grotesque strands of green snot, which would be enough to get Jean-Jacques to rethink that noble-savage shtick. They finally accepted that I'd never died when I came down with a head cold. Dead people don't sneeze. But they were never completely convinced that I was a woman. Their name for me is Suwäayaiwä, which roughly translates as 'a whole lot of woman.'"

She laughed again. The words she had pronounced—her name, the word "Onuma" itself—were heavily nasalized, almost a snort. If she was making this all up, she was really good, better even than Gideon, who also had a way with extended put-ons, and whom Cass spotted just as Jonas Elijah Klapper was entering the room.

"Frankly, I like it a lot better than 'Roz.'" She'd nasalized "Roz," too.

Jonas Elijah Klapper was flanked by the three men who had introduced him at Sanders Theatre, and the crowd immediately shifted to swarm around them like worker bees around the queen. Gideon was there in the attending circle, and, almost instantaneously, all five of the other Klapper students materialized. Now Cass seriously wanted the girl in dreadlocks to go away. It was enough that she had made him miss the thrust of the Prufrock Lecture. He didn't want to miss hearing what was going on now around Jonas Elijah Klapper.

"Well, Suwäayaiwä," he said, putting out his hand to shake hers, "it's been a pleasure meeting you. Good luck here in Cambridge-teri."

She laughed, and again he couldn't resist her laughter's invitation to come along for the ride and laugh along with her. She shook Cass's hand, and he gracefully abandoned her, hurrying to be in Klapper's proximity.

But Roz found him again before the reception was over. Cass and Gideon and Miriam and Nathan and Ezra and Zack and Joel were standing in a huddle. The group of seven had supped on canapés and spreads and sipped from Harvard's excellent sherry. None had felt this good since transplanting from New York.

"Are you going to the dinner?" Roz asked Cass. He had forgotten all about the girl in dreadlocks who might or might not have been christened "a whole lot of woman" by a tribe that might or might not exist.

"What dinner?"

"The dinner for Klapper at Robert Harris Chapman's house."

"Are we?" Cass asked Gideon.

"Un-uh." He shook his head no. "That's not for us."

"I just got invited," said Roz.

"By whom?" Gideon asked.

"By Robert Harris Chapman. He's a perfectly wonderful man, funny as hell in an urbane kind of way. You'll love him. He teaches drama and English here, and he's the head of the Loeb Drama Center. I heard from Doris Turner over there"— Roz motioned with her head toward a woman of formidable amplitude and mien, who was a Shakespearean scholar at

Harvard and had indeed been cited by Professor Klapper as "the premier authority on the Sonnets 101 to 116"—"that his home is decorated like a Moroccan sultan's and that he mixes the meanest drinks in town. Do you want to come?" she asked Cass. "It seems only fair. After all, I got myself into this shindig by pretending I was with you!"

Cass laughed along with her. Suwäayaiwä was a force of nature not to be withstood.

"No thanks," he said, withstanding nevertheless.

"Why not? When are you going to get an opportunity like this again? You can see how your adviser comports himself with his peers. You can peer behind the seven veils at the heavenly hosts and see what goes on when you aren't looking."

"It's not my style to finagle my way into a place I don't belong."

"Okay, I can understand that. No, on second thought, I can't. I'll just go tell Robert that I'm not going to be able to make it after all, and then you and I can go off and you can explain to me what exactly *is* your style."

They went to the 1369 Jazz Club. Roz had been in Cambridge for a couple of months. She was here to pick up some evolutionary biology, she said, attending what everyone called the Simian Seminar, which was given in the living room of a biological anthropologist. Cass and Roz walked the several blocks to the jazz club—Roz had been here once before but had been driven, so she wasn't exactly sure how to find her way, but she did—and she had talked a lot about Absalom and about the Onuma and about how strange it was for her to be in "Cambridge-teri." She loved that Cass had called it that. "It puts it into perspective for me."

Roz was a self-described jazz-junkie. She asked the man at

the door, "Who's on?" and when she heard that Raphé Malik was putting in an appearance, she let out a war cry she must have picked up in Onuma-land. Cass was surprised to discover he wasn't embarrassed. Roz's resistance to the emotion communicated something of itself to those she was with. This was the first sign of what Cass would come to think of as the Margolis magic, waffling on the question of whether it was black or not.

It was Malik on trumpet, and Frank Wright on the tenor sax and vocals, and William Parker on bass, and Syd Smart, who was a Cambridge native, on the drums. Cass didn't know much about jazz, but apparently, judging from the reaction of the audience and Roz, this was a night of miracles.

And it was, too. It was all new to Cass: Cambridge and jazz and a woman like Roz. He was swept off his feet. Even though she was older than he and far more experienced, having lived at the ends of the world for months on end, she made him feel as comfortable with himself as he had ever felt. He had the sense that whatever it was that he most liked about himself was what she liked, too.

He had gallantly walked her back to her place, a little apartment that was reached by way of a creaky outside flight of stairs and was attached to the second floor of a grand house on Francis Avenue, owned by what she called an "embalmed" couple.

"He used to be a Harvard English professor, and she was a Harvard professor's wife, if you know what I mean. They're straight from Central Casting. It was the wife who interviewed me. She's so frail that I just wanted to pick her up and carry her up these stairs. She said her husband would have to meet me to approve me as a tenant. He greeted me with 'I'm a Wilde man,' and it took me a few beats to figure out he was talking about Oscar. I don't know why he thought my knowing this about him was relevant to my renting the place. Maybe he got confused and thought I was a prospective graduate student. I've never seen him since, though she comes around to check on things once in a while. They built this addition to keep their daughter from running away from home during her stormy adolescence. Sometimes I get the creepy feeling that they'd had monitors installed, like in the spy movies, and that the old couple still tune in now and then, hoping for some kinky action. What do you say we make them happy?"

The brazen act came off with her clothes. Cass was startled by the tenderness of Roz. She was able to be tender, sexy, and hilarious all at once. They stayed up all night. Roz declared herself famished—"Orgasms burn calories!"—and jumped up and came back with a pint of Cherry Garcia and two spoons, which they ate facing one another cross-legged in bed. Any questions Cass might still have had about how women are anatomically put together were conclusively answered. Living among the Onuma, she'd told him, had cured her of the cult of female modesty. By morning, he had stopped being alarmed by her. She was more Roz Margolis, a Jewish girl who had grown up on the Upper West Side and been sent to the Ethical Culture school before going off to Frankfurter, than she was Suwäayaiwä, warrior anthropologist. By noon, he still didn't know exactly how much of her to believe, but he did believe himself in love. The strange thing was, so did Roz.

"I'm crazy about you," she announced as they drank coffee in her kitchen. She'd made them some toast, too, and scrambled up a mess of eggs with butter and cumin.

"You sure you're not just crazy?"

"Me? No, I'm the sanest person I've ever met. You'll see when you get to know me better, Cass. I'm the sanest person you've ever met, too. We're both sane. That's what's so crazy about us."

"So I'm sane, too. How do you know?"

"Our type can always recognize each other. We're like werewolves able to sniff each other out."

They fell into couplehood with relative ease. The only topic, and it was hardly an insignificant one, on which Cass and Roz agreed to disagree was Jonas Elijah Klapper. Roz didn't view the Extreme Distinguished Professor of Faith, Literature, and Values in quite the same way as Cass did:

"*What?*" Roz bolted up in bed so abruptly that her womanly breasts bounced with a soft little plop.

Cass immediately regretted the words out of his mouth even as he heard them.

"What did you say he said to you?"

It was too late. He had told her the story of how he had gone, with an undergraduate's fear and trembling, to the posted office hour of Columbia's pre-eminent professor, the one who stood before his crowded undergraduate course without any notes, leaping from personal reminiscences to quoted stanzas to revelations of the ontological scaffolding that underlies genius, and that at the end of the two-hour private session the great man had murmured, "I sense the aura of election upon you."

Cass had let the fire of Roz mix with the fire of Jonas Elijah Klapper, and, mixing his fires, he had transgressed.

"What did you say he said to you?" she repeated.

He closed his eyes and pronounced the words with which Jonas Elijah Klapper had anointed him.

Roz had burst into laughter, collapsing backward on the bed and writhing. When she finally found her voice, she rasped out, "I'm sorry! I'm so sorry! But I thought you had said that he sensed the odor of luckshen on you—and, frankly, I don't know which line is funnier!"

"Luckshen" is the Yiddish word for noodles, and it was the first time Cass didn't find Roz's laughter irresistible.

X

The Argument from the
Purer Self

Cass can't believe his eyes as he makes the right onto the drive leading up onto Frankfurter's hilltop campus. The overnight thaw has brought out the protesters, many of them pushing their luck in baggy shorts and flip-flops. If the fragrance in the air intoxicates Cass, the students are even more susceptible. The atmosphere of exulting giddiness is all over campus.

There are tables with flyers, and kids with armbands holding up hand-lettered signs. It looks like the era of be-ins and walkouts, which Cass had been a bit too young to experience firsthand. In those days, too, springlike weather always enhanced the chances for student activism. Richard Nixon had made a fatal error in ignoring the politico-meteorological dimension when he announced the expansion of the Vietnam War into Cambodia on April 30, 1970. The invasion of Laos, on the other hand, happened in February 1971, and the campuses were quiet. Who wants to stage a walkout in February?

Cass drives up the hill and passes the Ida and Howard Lowenstern Dorm, which, he notices, has paint-splattered banners hanging from some of the windows. One, in Hebrew, reads "מכבים! לך, Go Maccabees!"

Cass flashes back to Roz's hand-held sign yesterday, "Maccabees = Taliban." Talk about taking on a sacred historical mythology! The Maccabees are the heroes of the Hanukkah story, the stirring tale told to Diaspora Jewish kids so they don't feel so deprived missing out on Christmas. "Maccabiah" is the name given to countless color wars in Jewish summer camps and day schools, not to speak of the Olympic-type international sporting event held every four years in the state of Israel. "Maccabees = Taliban" are fighting words!

The Maccabees were the Jewish liberation army that had fought against the Hellenistic Seleucid Dynasty of Antiochus IV in the second century B.C., a dynasty that had brought a Hellenized lifestyle to Palestine, including Greek philosophy, art, worship of the body, and a pantheon of raunchy gods.

At the center of the ancient revolt had been a family of the priestly caste, the father, Mattathias, a rural religious leader with five sons. The entire armed resistance movement, the uniquely successful one in Jewish history until 1948, had taken on the name Maccabee. The word's origin is a matter of scholarly dispute. Some thought it might be an acronym taken from the words of the Torah verse *"Mi kamocha ba'elim Adonoi"*: "Who is like unto you among the gods, O Lord!"— the battle cry of those anti-Greek Judaeans, and the slogan painted in blue on a bedroom sheet hanging between two windows of the Sophie and Hyman Dorfman Dormitory.

There's another sheet hanging almost directly under that one: *"Τογα Παρτι!"* It takes Cass a few moments to figure it out: "Toga Party!"

Cass parks in the lot closest to the Katzenbaum Brain and Cognitive Sciences Center and walks across campus to the Nussbaum Administration Building. The campus has an air of festivity about it. Cass had never given it any thought before now, but the so-called Greek system does have elements harking back to ancient Greece, with its worship of physical beauty and athleticism, even the higher calling of Dionysian madness. The Greeks had loved their secret societies, too, not to speak of initiation rites.

Now that Cass considers it, Roz's equation of the Maccabees with the Taliban isn't entirely off the mark. The Maccabees, in opposing Hellenism, were opposing cosmopolitanism. They were religious fundamentalists who might well have sympathized with the Taliban's dynamiting of the Buddhas of Bamyan in Afghanistan, classics of Indo-Greek art that the religious purists decreed must go, since they had once been used as idols. Religious purity is at the heart of the Maccabee story, too, as symbolized by the central miracle of the Hanukkah story. When the Jews, having vanquished their enemies after three years of fighting, went to rededicate their holy temple, destroying the Greek statues and inscriptions, they sought some "undefiled" oil to light the lamp known as the N'er Tamid, the eternal light. They found enough for only one night, but it burned for eight days, which was just the time needed to purify a new batch, which is why Hanukkah is celebrated with a candelabra, the menorah, for eight days.

As a psychologist of religion, Cass has given much thought to the longing for spiritual purity, its source in the primitive emotion of disgust.

Disgust is so fundamental that it's one of the six universal facial expressions (happiness, sadness, fear, surprise, anger, disgust), all of them manifested on a baby's face during the first few months of its life. The best theory is that disgust is a response evolved to protect the body from harmful ingestants, such as putrefying substances—often odious-smelling to us—as well as substances that are prime carriers of disease, like bodily excreta and parasitic insects and worms.

The primitive emotion was adapted, by an almost metaphorical extension, to help out in solving the problems that are inherent in being a large-brained social animal. Other people can potentially harm us and so are perceived as potential defilers, and their practices or values are viewed as contaminated. And they—sometimes judged as individuals, and sometimes in swarming aggregate—can become elicitors of disgust. This went hand in hand with the evolution of the sense of our selves as immaterial souls distinct from our bodies—a purer self avoiding contamination by ever-more metaphorical defilers. So disgust is also triggered by upsetting reminders of our own embodiment—for example, contact with the decay of death, or with deviating sexual practices (so often described as animalistic), or with violations of the envelope of our bodies.

So many of the taboos of the various religions can be traced back to the psychology of disgust, and to the antithetical notion, staking out the opposite neurobiological pole to the disgust response, of spiritual purity: the self's removal from all of the disgusting aspects of the world.

Cass thinks he sees the guy from yesterday, the protest-of-one that Roz had spotted at the side of the road. He's no longer in his parka with his hood up, as he had been yesterday, and Cass sees that he's wearing a yarmulke. He's also no longer alone—there are three similarly headgeared young men with him, as well as two girls in ankle-length jean skirts, standing behind a table and giving out leaflets. The sign that's draped over the table repeats his slogan of yesterday: *"Nais gadol haya sham,"* "A great miracle happened there." The miracle of the oil. The beaker of purity.

The Maccabees had cleared the holy temple of the defilement of alien values, of all signs of the pagan Greeks with their glorification of the human body as a thing of beauty. As Cass's bubbe would have said, "Feh!"

"Feh," Cass suddenly realizes, is an expression of central significance in understanding the etiology of religion. "Feh" says a lot.

In the president's office there is a subdued air, or at least Bunny Bernstein, the president's executive secretary, seems subdued. Bunny is usually a happy lark of a person, but she's looking pinched today, the Botoxed space between her brows straining toward a frown.

It occurs to Cass that this brouhaha must have been brewing even yesterday and was the reason for Shimmy's having to skip their meeting. Bunny had apologized for Shimmy's absence, telling Cass that they couldn't be sure, but it looked as if there might be an unexpected event that the president had to make sure about.

"Ah," Cass had said, smiling, "unexpected events are always the hardest to make sure about."

"Isn't that the truth," Bunny had returned, her smile as wide as it could be in her largely immobilized face.

Cass knows—everybody knows these sorts of things at Frankfurter, where personal privacy is about as easy to maintain as among the Onuma—that Bunny is one of Deedee Baumzer's oldest friends, her sorority sister from Gamma Gamma Gamma, and over the years—perhaps because they frequent the same plastic surgeon—the two have come to look like honest-to-God sisters.

Now that Cass has been on *The Daily Show,* Bunny always greets him with "Hey, Cass, have they invited you on *The Col-*

bert Report yet?" But since she had just asked him that yesterday, she only asks him if she can get him some coffee as she shows him to a seat in the president's well-appointed waiting room.

Shimmy doesn't keep Cass waiting more than three minutes, an unusual courtesy toward a faculty member. Even Bunny looks taken aback.

As usual, Shimmy is dressed in an elegant suit that seems too tight in the shoulders and legs. Shimmy is a former Israeli paratrooper, and though the constant fêting of potential donors has thickened him around his middle, he still gives the impression that it's pure muscle that's bulging the suit. The suggestion of brute force he projects is almost as useful to him as his polished self-deprecatory charm, the paratrooper instincts he keeps out of sight until they're required.

As powerful as his image is, it never occludes Deedee's. References to "Shimmy" are almost reflexively followed by "and Deedee," and there is a sophomoric joke on campus that is not confined to the undergraduates:

Question: You think Shimmy has been anyplace interesting recently?

Response: Yes indeedee!

Deedee is bodacious, blonde, and buxom, her teeth capped and her breasts implanted to perfection—the last a birthday present she gave herself when she turned forty. Her accent is the charming lilt of her native Texas. If she goes overboard in her armor-heavy jewelry, her manner is always gossamer-winged. Some had worried, when Shimmy was announced as the new president of Frankfurter eight years ago, that Deedee's background might not altogether suit her to Frankfurter's campus, but Shimmy and Deedee have worked together splendidly as Frankfurter's first couple, and the fund-raising campaign has enjoyed unprecedented success.

"Cass, Cass," Shimmy greets him now, shaking his hand solemnly. This gesture, like the facial expression that accompanies it, is highly formal for Shimmy Baumzer, and Cass worries whether he's going to be roughed up for his intention of defecting. Cass knows that Shimmy knows there's no way he's not going to accept Harvard's offer. He's not going to finesse Harvard's offer into a sweeter situation here at Frankfurter, and he's all but certain that Shimmy understands.

Still, protocol requires that Shimmy flex those muscles underneath the bulging suit. He probably thinks that Cass would be insulted if he were to do anything less. Cass wishes that this entire procedure could have been dispatched by way of e-mail.

"Hold all calls," Shimmy commands Bunny.

Shimmy's accent, a harsh gurgle in the back of his throat, subtracts from the sense of elegance he projects. He ushers Cass into his huge beige office. There's a table already laid out with a linen tablecloth, china plates, crystal goblets. Domes of steel are keeping the food warm.

"I thought we'd have our lunch in here instead of going to the Faculty Club."

"That's fine," says Cass. "Perfect."

The whole outer wall of Shimmy's ground-floor office is glass, looking out on the Plotnik Quad. Shimmy goes to the window and stands quietly, his arms awkwardly behind him, as if manacled in cuffs.

"You saw the situation we have out there?" He casts his eyes at Cass. It's extraordinary, but their color seems to have changed. They're no longer those cold marbles of blue, but have muddied into brown and are rimmed with shadows that make them appear bruised. His jaw looks slacker, too, and there seems to be more room in the shoulders of his suit.

Cass nods at Shimmy's question.

"So what do you think?" Shimmy asks lugubriously.

"I can't imagine it's anything to take too seriously."

"No?"

"I wouldn't think so. The kids are just having a good time. It's a beautiful day, and they're using this as an excuse to play outside."

"They were playing outside, too, in May of 1970, when they broke down the door of this very building and occupied the president's office for three weeks. They smoked his Havanas, and then wrote a letter to the *Weedham Town Crier* claiming that he was a secret Castro supporter."

"With all due respect, Shimmy, I don't think today's protests have attained quite that level of seriousness. This is hardly the Vietnam War that they're protesting."

"Larry Summers thought he had tsuris? Believe me, I have bigger tsuris."

Shimmy lets the venetian blind fall with a clatter, blocking out the sunlight that had been streaming in. He indicates a seat at the table for Cass and then sits down himself. Bunny appears as if by telepathy and soundlessly removes the domes from the serving platters. There's poached salmon, asparagus, wild rice. The wine is chilled and white and from the Golan Heights. Shimmy indicates that Cass should begin, though he himself just stares gloomily at the salmon on the serving plate.

"It's a volatile situation. A powder box. A tinder keg. It can get ugly fast."

"I don't know, Shimmy. I just walked across the campus,

and I didn't pick up anything ugly. If anything, it's impressive that the kids are putting the issue into some sort of historical context. You can look at it as a triumph of our educational policies."

Shimmy's reaction is baffling. At nineteen, he'd been among the legendary paratroopers who had made their way into the Jordanian-held section of East Jerusalem in 1967 and had fought their way to the Wailing Wall. In 1973, Shimmy had led a battalion of soldiers across the Suez Canal and established a bridgehead that had allowed the Israelis to push on toward Cairo. And in 1976, he had helped plan the daring raid (it was always called "a daring raid") at Entebbe in Uganda that freed one hundred hostages from a hijacked jetliner that had been on its way to Israel. What were a few frolicking students to a warrior like Shimmy Baumzer?

Still, Cass is feeling increasingly uneasy about Shimmy's distress. The president's face seems gaunter, and an elegiac line in his upper lip is emerging. His accent no longer sounds incongruous. Instead, it's the custom-tailored suit that seems the anomaly.

"Deedee feels strongly about bringing the Greek system to Frankfurter. What can I say? Deedee feels strongly."

Cass nods. If Shimmy doesn't know what to say, then he, Cass, certainly doesn't know what to say either.

"I'm being squeezed. Do you know what I'm saying, my friend? Squeezed between a hard place and a firing squad. I can talk to you like this. You're an ally."

Cass nods.

"You know, we have in common a good mutual friend. Mona Ganz."

Again, Cass nods. The truth is, he and Mona are no longer as close as they used to be. There's been a cooling off since

Lucinda and he have been together. Mona's attitude toward Lucinda hasn't softened. It's one of those mysteries that Cass is content to leave unsolved.

"I wouldn't say that Mona has ever been indiscreet. Such a mindful friend would always be mindful of the loyalties of friendship. But from the little she's told me, I think you understand the situation I've got here."

Now, what's that supposed to mean? Better not to think about Mona's exact words.

"Do I think, my friend, that Frankfurter needs fraternities and sororities in order to be a real college, like, say, the University of Texas? Not necessarily."

Shimmy sighs, while raising his two hands, the palms open and upward, and his shoulders rising in a shrug: the eternal gesture of the existential resignation of the Yid.

"To have first-rate faculty, faculty that can hold its own against any in the world, including in snooty Cambridge, Massachusetts, that has been my dream, waking, sleeping, day come, day go, morning, night, and noon. Nobody is going to set up tables and hand out flyers demanding that the administration explain itself if we are trying to make here a first-class faculty, with the Jew in the crown—no, what's the expression? the *jewel* in the crown, the internationally celebrated author of *The Illusion of the Varieties of Religion,* a book which, I am not embarrassed to say, I quote at every opportunity, such an impression it has personally made on my way of thinking. And now, when I am squeezed—I know you'll understand me, with someone like you I don't have to spell it out—with my own visions for Frankfurter on one side and other considerations on the other, what do I learn but that the jewel is in danger of being snatched up by the grasping hands of Harvard University? What's the matter, they don't have enough big shots there, they have to try to take away the little that we have?"

The transformation that has come over Shimmy is extraordinary. He looks fragile, vulnerable, like someone whose childhood was spent dodging Cossacks in Poland rather than picking oranges and carrying an Uzi in a kibbutz outside of Jerusalem.

"So tell me, my friend, what do I have to do to keep you from going over to those shmendriks up the river?"

XI

The Argument from Transcendental Signifiers

The large suite of offices assigned to the Department of Faith, Literature, and Values had been part of Frankfurter's enticement package to Jonas Elijah Klapper and were intended to be used for the international scholars he was authorized to invite with the generous discretionary funds the university had provided him. Jonas had used these offices for storage rooms, having Miriam Chan file the massive amounts of written matter that he had accumulated over the years. Jonas had saved everything for posterity, an inestimable boon for the future generations of scholars who would study him. His *Nachlass* reached all the way back to the wide-ruled *machberet,* the notebook in which he had formed his first Hebrew letters.

Miriam was a methodical and efficient young woman, but the task was daunting, especially since Professor Klapper tended to snatch whatever she was about to file out of her hands, so that he could peruse it and share the background with her, such as the fact that when he arrived as a first-grader at P.S. 2 on Henry Street, on the Lower East Side (named the Meyer London School, after one of the founders of the Socialist Party of America and the first elected socialist congressman: there had followed a digression), he knew how to read, although nobody had taught him, certainly not his mother, who remained a stranger to the English language.

"How I came by the knowledge remains to this day shrouded in mystery," he whispered to Miriam.

Also mysterious was how everything about his cramped Columbia office had been preserved, right down to the spiky plant on the windowsill, which had been dead for years. The very arrangement of the clutter on Professor Klapper's desk was duplicated, with space cleared for the photograph of his mother in its ornate silver frame. The wooden-slatted chair into which he was poured was either an exact replica of what he'd had at Columbia or had been transported along with the desiccated crown of thorns.

There were times when a student, sequestered with the professor, would encounter him in a rare mood of confidentiality, as if Jonas Elijah Klapper were suddenly made aware of the loneliness of his loftiness, grown weary of the constant burden of delivering himself ex cathedra. The realization would leave him eager to talk as others do, personally and intimately. The identity of the student was inconsequential. One simply had to be there when the mood struck, and today was Cass's lucky day.

"I am not a preterist—that is, one whose chief interest and delight are in the past. As must anyone who regards with seriousness the eschatological idea that scaffolds the strata of the greater metaphysics, I point my face resolutely toward the future. And yet the past—I speak here of the personal past— has a power over the present. The past haunts the present with the taunt of what is gone. As Tennyson so irrefutably put it, 'And Time, a maniac scattering dust, / And Life, a Fury slinging flame.' "

The last line was whispered in a voice so tremulous and faint that Cass wasn't certain whether the last word was "flame" or "fame."

Cass was here, by appointment, to plot the course of his study for the next few years. Professor Klapper was insistent that his graduate students not be required to take any of their courses in other Frankfurter departments. Indeed, he strongly warned against it. But since he was the solitary professor in the Department of Faith, Literature, and Values, and since he taught only one seminar a semester, the professor's position had presented the dean of graduate students with a technical problem—to wit, how are the students in this department to fulfill the course requirements for the Ph.D.? The problem for now related only to Cass Seltzer, since the other Klapper students had long ago fulfilled their course requirements. The plan arrived at was that there would be an extensive syllabus, still to be constructed, that would cover all the best that had been written regarding faith, literature, and values. Cass had already embarked on faith. Professor Klapper had assigned him *The Book of Mormon* by Joseph Smith. Cass had no idea why.

But today the snow was falling on the campus outside and making all seem hushed and transformed, eerily reminding one, as in the distortions of dreams, of something that turns out to be simply itself; and Jonas Elijah Klapper had forgotten all about matters of syllabi. He was in a reminiscent frame of mind, full of mourning for all the lost paradises, which are, as Proust has so indispensably reminded us, the only paradises that there are.

It was a Friday, and the haunting taunt was of the many years of congenial Fridays that Jonas Elijah Klapper had passed among the select society that would meet in the hidden mews near Washington Square Park, behind the heavy green door of NYU's Deutsches Haus. This was where the elected members of the New York Institute of the Humanities attended talks by the crème de la creamy New York intelligentsia, preceded by greasy food and even greasier gossip. How he had loved to dish with Susan Sontag.

"Did you know that she was born Susan Rosenblatt?" Jonas Elijah Klapper had confided, mashing his chin down toward his chest, so that his jowls fanned out like an Elizabethan ruff. "Yes, Susan Rosenblatt," he continued. "'Sontag' was the name of her mother's second husband. She did not like the new dad on the scene, but even at the tender age of twelve she was exquisitely attuned to the tyrannical demands of literary ambition."

Cass nodded.

"Which brings to mind another fearless female riding bareback on the bucking beast of ambition, the estimable Laura Reichenthal. Oh, do not look so stricken, Mr. Seltzer! I do not expect you to be familiar with *that* name. However, I would be very much surprised to learn that you'd not heard of Laura Riding"—Cass hadn't—"the poetess paramour of the superior poet Robert Graves, and enmeshed in the conception of his authentically brilliant *White Goddess,* in which he wrote these words, which I quote from Appendix B: 'Do I think that poets are literally inspired by the White Goddess? That is an improper question. What would you think should I ask you if, in your opinion, the Hebrew prophets were literally inspired by God? Whether God is a metaphor or a fact cannot be reasonably argued. Let us likewise be discreet on the subject of the Goddess,' a subtle point which has not, alas, been influential. Well, let us be discreet, too, regarding the physical description of the Goddess, 'a lovely slender woman with a hooked nose, deathly pale face, lips red as rowanberries, startlingly blue eyes and long fair hair.' That hooked-nose damsel is Laura Reichenthal, whose first marriage was to a man named, I believe, Gottschalk, which hardly suited, and she simply plucked the name 'Riding' from thin air, though I suspect there was metaphor behind it."

As far as Cass could tell, Professor Klapper was saying that a poet named Laura Reichenthal had changed her name to Laura Riding.

"I adduce one more example to bring it up to the magic three of poetic enchantment: the sad-eyed bon vivant and haut wit of the fabled Algonquin Round Table of the New York literary scene of several decades past. I refer, of course, to Dorothy Parker, who was born Dorothy Rothschild, no relation in the least to the banking-and-finance dynasty, which established branches across Europe and was ennobled by both the Austrians and the British. Dorothy's family were sans 'von.' She married a stockbroker named Edwin Pond Parker II and kept him on for barely two years, explaining that she had married him to escape her name."

There was no escaping the suggestion that Professor Klapper's chosen subject, for the moment, seemed to be name-changing.

"It is not ethnicity per se, you understand," Professor Klapper said, as if reading Cass's mind. "Consider, for example, the writer, both original and soporific, Gertrude Stein. Hers is a name that requires no more. It is, in its own way, perfect, as is that of the mustachioed Alice B. Toklas. But this is not always so, and there is no shame in availing oneself of remedial renaming. If a motion-picture hussy, whose vocabulary ceased developing long before her bosom, can avail herself of cognominal improvements, why not we who are the very stuff of words? That avatar of self that bears the full weight of one's reputation, that transcendental signifier by which one sallies forth into the world even when one's self is not present, is none other than one's name. Would you permit me to be rather more direct?"

Cass nodded.

"Your name."

"My name?"

"Yes, I wonder if it isn't too . . . effervescent."

"Effervescent?"

"Indeed. I have to confess that I myself had a good chuckle when I first came upon it on the class roster."

Something odd was happening to Jonas Elijah Klapper's face. His muscles were seizing up in violent spasms, his contorted cheeks were stained with tears. Cass became frightened until the sounds escaping from his everted mouth revealed that Jonas Elijah Klapper was laughing.

"Oh, I *am* sorry! I have a wicked sense of humor! But you do catch the gist of what it is I am saying? If even I cannot contain my merriment at your fizzing appellation, then what can we expect of others? Have you considered, Mr. Seltzer, the possibility of adapting it?"

"No." Cass didn't know what his precise emotion was, but he could feel the fire under his skin.

"I submit you think upon it. You might, for example, take Cass as your last name."

"Then what would my first name be?"

"Do you have, perchance, a Hebrew name?"

"Chaim."

Jonas Elijah Klapper opened his eyes very wide.

"Were you aware of its meaning?"

"Life, isn't it?"

"'Lives.' Its gematria value is thirty-six, which is twice eighteen, which is the gematriac value for 'life.' Thirty-six is of a hiddenness that sustains existence."

Cass knew that the letters in the Hebrew word *chai,* meaning "life," could also be read as the number eighteen, which is why Jews often write Bar Mitzvah gift checks in multiples of eighteen. But beyond that he didn't know what Professor Klapper was talking about. He would ask Gideon.

"And yet, for all that, 'Chaim Cass' is not quite right. What, might I ask, was your mother's maiden name?"

"Sheiner."

"Better, but not much."

Klapper leaned back into his slatted chair. It had a thick green cushion on it. Cass stole a glance at the photograph of the professor's mother, who had been named, Cass now had every reason to believe, Hannah Klepfish.

"I have it!" Klapper announced. Was his adviser about to baptize him? "I know where it was that I've heard that name Sheiner before. The name of Sheiner is ablaze with majestic luster. It is the dynastic name of the Chief Rabbi of the Valdener Hasidim, a small sect whose leader can trace his lineage back to the inflamed visionary who channeled the Kabbalism of Isaac Luria, the sixteenth-century lion of esoteric Judaism also known as the Arizal, into a more accessible populist venue, and who became the founder of the single most important religious revision in Judaism, by which I mean Hasidism. Hasidism grew into a mass reaction against the abuses of the Pharisaic normative tradition. There are a plurality of Hasidic sects, each led by its own charismatic Grand

Rabbi—or Rebbe, as he is wont to be called. I refer, of course, to Rabbi Israel ben Eliezer, the holy Ba'al Shem Tov or Master of the Good Name, also abbreviated into the appellation the Besht, back to whom all Hasidic sects trace themselves. The Ba'al Shem Tov's past is shrouded in legend, as befits a legendary figure of his proportions, but he was most likely born in 1700, and in the small Ukrainian village of Okop. He was an orphan, who dressed and comported himself like an ignorant peasant while he went off to the forests to commune with cosmic forces. Nobody guessed his singular holiness. He finally revealed himself to the world when he was thirty-six. Had you any idea?"

Of which aspect of the preceding sequence was his adviser asking had he any idea? Cass opted for the concrete.

"Well, yes. My mother was born into a Valdener family. She's related to the Valdener Rebbe. I used to visit New Walden as a child."

Jonas Elijah Klapper shot forward in his chair so that he was half hanging off it. His facial expressions sometimes mimicked a silent-film actor. At this moment, you could almost hear Cecil B. DeMille shouting through his horn, "Show us amazement!"

"So, then, you, too, can trace your lineage back to the holy Ba'al Shem Tov?"

"Well, yes, I guess I can. I never really thought about it."

"Never really thought about it?"

Jonas Elijah Klapper collapsed back into his chair, his outburst knocking the stuffing out of him.

But he soon recovered. He sat up and, turning his back to Cass, put his elbows on his desk and buried his face in his palms. Cass sat there in an agony of uncertainty. Anything at all could be happening now. One guess was as good as the next. Minutes passed. Should he quietly exit? Had Jonas Elijah Klapper already excused him and gone back to work? Cass knew from the others that this sometimes happened.

"Well, this is extraordinary," Professor Klapper finally said, turning around in his revolving chair and again facing Cass. "This is something I could never have foreseen."

Jonas Elijah Klapper was gazing at Cass with discomfiting intensity, as if searching in Cass Seltzer's amiable though distressed visage for signs of the Ba'al Shem Tov's lingering presence. Cass was forced to stare straight back into the professor's face, and at close range.

It was, for some obscure reason, excruciatingly uncomfortable to be this physically close to Jonas Elijah Klapper. Not even he was Pure Spirit. The soaring sentences were punctuated by panting intakes of air. The thighs, encased in gray broadcloth, seemed like items better described in the vocabulary of architecture than of anatomy. His face, too, was markedly corporeal—heavy and fleshy. The cultivated elegance of his mind had done what it could, but when he spoke of "the divine pathos," "the inconsolable solitude," "the fraught distance between the poet and reader," he never managed to look more pathetic, inconsolable, or fraught than the man behind the deli counter. But his eyes were sad. There was a depth of sadness in his eyes.

"I have a great interest in meeting the Valdener Rebbe, a man who I suspect confounds that prejudice which sees no worldly knowledge in the Hasidim. As you, of course, are intimately aware, my dear Mr. Seltzer—or may I call you Reb Chaim?—the Grand Rabbi of the Valdeners named the seat of his New World rabbinical court New Walden, presumably alluding to the American transcendentalism of our own homegrown seers Ralph Waldo Emerson and Henry David Thoreau."

That wasn't the way Cass's mother told the story, but Cass wasn't about to argue with Professor Klapper's superior erudition.

"We shall seize this extraordinary expedient posthaste! Reb Chaim, I count on you to make the necessary arrangements!"

XII

The Argument from Prime Numbers

They rode to New Walden in a Lincoln Continental.

It had been Roz who had gone to the streamered lot in Somerville and rented the car on Klapper's—or, rather, Frankfurter's—dime. Jonas Elijah Klapper had never learned to drive, so a chauffeur was needed, or so Roz kept insisting to Cass.

"But I know how to drive."

"Tell him your license has expired! I'm not missing this!"

Professor Klapper had seemed a bit put out to learn that an unknown female would be accompanying them, but his attitude toward Cass had undergone so steep an upgrade since he'd learned of Cass's Valdener connections that he had refrained from too vigorous a protest.

After Professor Klapper had settled himself into the front passenger seat, he turned and examined the driver at length, peering at her over the top of his bifocals.

"I presume from your coiffure that you are an adherent of Rastafarianism. I can assure you that I accord your belief system the same respect I do all religions. I believe it to be a prejudice of temporalism, akin to racism and sexism, when a religion is dismissed on the grounds that it has been established at a time too near the present. Indeed, all religions emerged at some present or other. So let me hasten to declare that you will find nothing but deference on my part for your faith that Haile Selassie is the Messiah."

Cass braced himself for Roz's reaction, which, if they were lucky, would be confined to peals of laughter, but Roz stared straight ahead and remained silent.

Jonas Elijah Klapper, satisfied that he had made his point of view known, turned himself to the activity of getting the seat belt around him and inserted into its buckle. He was struggling with the contraption, and Roz, under normal circumstances, would have offered to help, but she couldn't risk an utterance that would unblock the swell of laughter that she was forcefully resisting for poor Cass's sake. At last they heard the click, and Roz wordlessly put the car into gear.

Before they'd gotten very far on the Massachusetts Turnpike, Jonas Elijah Klapper decided that he did, vehemently, object to the Rastafarian's driving. Either Roz normally drove like this, or she was enjoying getting a rise out of their passenger. From the back, Cass could see that Professor Klapper was gripping the sides of his seat.

"Which of these contraptions indicates the speed at which we are recklessly hurtling, young lady?"

"Gee, I don't know. Is there any way to tell our speed, Cass?"

"Now, see here, they have helpfully posted the speed limit at regular intervals— There! There! We just passed another sign with '55' emblazoned upon it! There must be some way to determine the rate at which you are hastening us toward our death."

He leaned over to try to get a look at the dials.

"Don't do that, Jonas! Never crowd the driver, especially at the rate we're going!"

"So you admit we are exceeding the limit! I demand that you pull over immediately and cede the steering wheel to Mr. Seltzer!"

"His license is expired! It's against the law!"

"So is the reckless endangerment of one's mortally afrighted passengers! I shall defray all costs should Mr. Seltzer be issued a summons."

"What about the points on his record? What about the hike in his insurance premiums?"

"Gladly shall I compensate for all, young lady! Premiums, tickets, a hush-hush bribe to the stalwart officer in blue if he can be induced to take it! It shall all be worth it to live to see another morrow!"

The professor prevailed. Cass and Roz switched places.

It was a cold but piercingly bright Sunday afternoon in late February. As they crossed the Hudson River on the Tappan Zee Bridge, the skyline of Manhattan rose up in all its glory.

"It isn't far now," Cass announced. He found himself excited to be returning after all these years.

His mother had been amazed when he'd told her about the field trip he was taking. He had called her, at Professor Klapper's urging, to find out how they should get in touch with the Rebbe to arrange for a personal visit.

"My cousin Henoch," Deb had answered. "He's the Rebbe's *gabbai,* or personal assistant. It all goes through Cousin Henoch."

"Do you have Cousin Henoch's phone number?"

"I'll get it from Shaindy." Shaindy, another of Deb's countless cousins, was the only one in the family with whom Deb remained in contact. Deb's family had been unusual in New Walden, since Deb had no brothers and sisters, prompting her to fantasize that whatever had prevented her parents from being maximally fruitful had prevented them from having any children at all. The fact that she looked so much like her father, Mendel Sheiner, who had been a bookkeeper in a jewelry exchange in Manhattan's Diamond District, didn't count conclusively against her fantasy. A lot of the Valdeners resembled each other. The Rebbe may have decided to redistribute the wealth, taking from a family with lots of children to give to a sterile couple. Anyway, it was a fantasy.

"It's not going to be traumatic for you to go back there?"

"No, not at all. I didn't have to grow up there the way you did. I don't have any trauma associated with the place."

"Well, that's good. I guess." They both laughed. "Wait till I tell Jesse. He won't believe you're going with Klapper to New Walden."

"How's he doing?"

"Pretty well, I think. He's got a job at the library. And he's enrolled as a non-matric at Fairleigh Dickinson. I think the quiet time might be doing him some good. I'm hoping he's reflecting."

Jesse was living at home for the year, on a forced leave of absence from NYU for having been involved in a ring that sold term papers to other students.

"That's good. Is he around now?"

"No, he's out. I never ask him where. After all, if he were still at school, I wouldn't know."

"That seems right," Cass said, though sometimes he wondered. His mother had strong scruples in regard to autonomy and self-determination. She had had to overcome so much external pressure—her parents, her community, the Valdener

Rebbe—in choosing her own way through life that she was loath to exert pressure on anyone else. When it came to Jesse, pressure probably wouldn't have made any difference anyway.

"I'll give you a report on New Walden when I get back."

"It won't have changed much, that's for sure. It's a point of pride that if the Besht were resurrected and he made his way to New Walden . . ."

"Because, let's face it, what else would he want to do with himself?"

"That goes without saying. Anyway, he'd get to New Walden and he'd speak to the Valdeners, ask them what they thought, what they knew, and he wouldn't realize that a day had gone by since he'd walked the earth in the early eighteenth century. Nothing would have changed."

"Better sanitation, though."

"Marginally."

His mother hated the place. But not Cass. As soon as they got across the bridge, he started looking out for landmarks.

They turned onto the Palisades Parkway toward Bear Mountain.

"This is it, this is the exit," Cass said when he saw the sign for New Town.

They drove through New Town, down Main Street, and when they got to the T-junction where it ended, Cass surprised himself by knowing exactly which way to turn, the left—the other left, and then the right that brought the Lincoln Continental right there to the parking lot with the heap of buses that marked the entrance to New Walden.

The buses were the property of the New Walden Kosher Bus Company, owned by a Valdener Hasid who lived in New Walden. The bus company was the town's biggest business, and the man who owned the company, Alter Luckstein, was

New Walden's richest man. None of the buses matched any of the others. They were different models, different sizes. Alter read the classified ads in the trade papers for any bus that had been in an accident or had caught fire. Then he bought it, fixed it up, and put it back on the road. Luckstein's buses not only took the Valdeners back and forth between New Walden and Brooklyn or Manhattan, where many of them worked in the Diamond District or the large electronics-and-camera stores, but also were rented out across the wider metropolitan area by Orthodox Jewish day schools and other Jewish organizations. They even had some regular public routes from New York to nearby towns, competing well with Greyhound.

Just past the buses there was a sign: "Welcome to New Walden, America's only shtetl. Please observe the custom of our ways and dress modestly. No women in shorts or pants or sleeveless tops."

Otherwise, the place looked extraordinarily ordinary, at least at first blush, a nondescript tract of roads, little more than wending country lanes, that were lined with modest two-story houses, their front lawns strewn with plastic tricycles, slides, and toys.

They had an appointment to meet with the Grand Rabbi at four o'clock, and they were early.

"Let's park and walk," Roz suggested from the backseat. "Mingle with the natives, find some informants. You can't do fieldwork from a car."

"We are not here to do your fieldwork, young lady. If you want to get out and walk, please don't restrain yourself. Mr. Seltzer and I shall console ourselves over the loss of your company."

"Come on, don't you want to stretch your legs after that

long ride? And, Cass, you must want to check out your old haunts. Do you remember where your grandmother lived?"

"No, I do not wish to, as you say, *'stretch my legs.'* " Jonas Elijah Klapper shuddered.

It was too cold for children to be outside playing with the toys. They passed a few women pushing baby carriages, shepherding very young children, almost all of them seemingly girls, with long hair escaping from their hooded coats.

"The older kids are in school," Cass said, as he drove around the neighborhood. "Sunday's just a regular day for them."

"So they go to school six days a week?" Roz asked.

"They get out early on Fridays. Especially in the winter, when the days are short, so the Sabbath, which starts at sundown, comes early. The Sabbath, Shabbes, is something to see. That's when the men deck themselves out in these amazing fur hats called *shtreimels* and these long satin caftans, called *kaputas*. And they all wear high leather boots, almost like jackboots, with their pants tucked in."

"Do the women get to wear amazing fur hats?" Roz asked.

"No, the women just dress dowdy, in a way guaranteed to call no attention to themselves."

"I wonder if I'll pass," Roz said. She was wearing the same long crushed-velvet skirt that she'd been wearing when Cass had first met her. He'd warned her about the laws of modesty. She didn't have to wear her hair covered, since she wasn't married, but Cass and she had decided that the dreadlocks had best be concealed, so she'd bought a peacock-blue kerchief, and in a restroom at their last pit stop had looped her hair up in it in a sort of turban. For their part, Cass and Klapper had come supplied with white satin skullcaps in their pockets that Jonas Elijah Klapper had supplied, "Ronald's Bar Mitzvah June 12 1977" embossed in gold on the inside.

"I think the goal is just not to offend them. At best, they'll think you're a stray that the Lubavitchers have converted."

"The Lubavitchers. They're the ones with the mitzvah-mobile, right? They used to come to Frankfurter when I was an undergraduate, lassoing boys to put on phylacteries and girls to light the Sabbath candles."

Cass had driven past his bubbe's house without announcing it, slowing down slightly—they were going less than fifteen miles an hour anyway—and trying to take it in. He'd always known it as his bubbe's house. His grandfather had died before he was born. It was a modest tract house, and it made him happy to see the number of toys crammed into its front yard now. He hoped the children who owned these toys were enjoying better childhoods than his mother had in that house. He felt a stab of love for that unhappy woman, his bubbe, who had had such a fine eye for discerning the flaws in others, the slights to herself, reacting with gleeful contempt for the former and unstanchable rage toward the latter, but who had, for some mysterious reason, loved and always forgiven her little Chaim. One of his earliest memories—it might have been his first—was his bubbe's collapsing at the sight of him when they'd come for a visit after he'd had his first haircut. She had shrieked as if slashed by an assassin's blade, clutching at her chest, berating his mother. He'd never forget it, it had scared him so badly.

"Something else I remember from when I used to visit here as a kid is that they don't cut the boys' hair until a certain age, I think maybe three or four."

"Is that a Samson-and-Delilah thing?"

"No," said Klapper. "The ceremony of the first haircut is

called an *upsheering,* and it is celebrated when the male child turns three, as one of life's passages, like the Bar Mitzvah, which is celebrated almost universally among Jews, even the most secular, though its materialistic trappings have made it a parodical spectacle far from its original intent of signaling the Jewish male's full attainment of selfhood, with all of its attending moral and spiritual responsibilities."

An interlude of silence followed. Jonas was recalling his own modest Bar Mitzvah on the Lower East Side. His father had deserted them that year. The man had been so insignificant that it had taken Jonas several days to realize what was different in the household and to ask, "Where's Pop?" Jonas's Bar Mitzvah had been celebrated with a bottle of schnapps in their shul on Eldridge Street, a plate of his mother's delectable sponge cake, and some store-bought *eier kichel*—egg cookies. But Jonas had sung his haftorah faultlessly from memory. His *d'var Torah,* the traditional Shabbes speech in which moral lessons are drawn from the weekly portion of the Torah, had also been delivered without notes, and, according to his mother and older sisters, grown men had wept.

"According to Yehuda Ickel, the leading secular authority on Kabbala, with whom I have often discussed such matters, the Hasidic custom can be traced back to the sixteenth-century Kabbalists who inhabited the mystical city of Safed, in northern Palestine, or S'fat, as it is called in Hebrew, long one of the spiritual hot zones, receiving a disproportionate radiation of the Elevated Mysteries from the Seminar from On High. The dominant figures were Moses Cordovero, the tireless taxonomizer of Kabbala, and his student Isaac Luria, known also as the Ari, meaning literally 'the Lion' and derived from the acronym for 'Ashkenazi Rabbi Isaac.' You will also see him referred to as Arizal. Arizal was the most fecund visionary to appear in Jewish mysticism, with all that would emerge from the inspired city of S'fat forever after bearing his imprimatur, though he had written, in his lifetime, but a few poems, and his oral teachings were . . ."

"What are all those signs?" Roz cut him off.

Nobody answered her. Though Cass was grateful to Roz for choking back her laughter at Professor Klapper's mistaking her for a Rastafarian—he knew her well enough to know that that was the only explanation for her silence—he hated the casual tone she had adopted toward him. She was treating him as if he were anyone else. She was even addressing him by his first name. Cass could feel Professor Klapper, in the passenger seat in front, bristling. But, remarkably, he kept his temper, which might have been due to the exaggerated respect he seemed to have developed for Cass recently, taking delight in calling him Reb Chaim when they were alone. Or maybe he didn't want to mess with a Rastafarian.

Professor Klapper had, however, lectured Roz briefly but sternly on their way here on restraining herself in their audience with the Valdener Rebbe.

"Try to make yourself as inconspicuous as you possibly can, young lady. The Hasidim have a refined sensibility regarding the desirable trait of modesty, or *tzniyus,* in a woman. Recall the Bard's words regarding the virtuous Cordelia: 'Her voice was ever soft, gentle and low, an excellent thing in woman.'"

"Don't you guys see?" Roz was saying now. "Every few feet there are signs nailed onto the trees. Cass, park the car a minute. I want to see what it says."

"Indeed, do park the vehicle, Mr. Seltzer, and let the young lady alight and investigate to her heart's content. We shall go straight to the Rebbe. We shall find you soon enough, or you us, of that I am certain."

Roz climbed out onto the sidewalk, and the Lincoln Continental pulled away. Roz gave way to laughter, and it wasn't soft, gentle, and low.

A woman walked by pushing a carriage, with two toddlers clinging to her skirt on either side of her; she was trying to maneuver her charges to make as wide a circle as possible around the woman staring at a tree.

"Hello," Roz said to her, turning with a smile.

"Hello." She didn't smile back, but she didn't turn tail and run either. Compared with the typical first contact with an unknown tribe, this was like being visited by a Welcome Wagon lady giving out free coupons to local businesses.

"I'm new in town, and I'm trying to figure out what these signs mean."

"*Menner seit. Froyen seit.* Men's side, women's side. Men and women don't walk on the same side of the street." She had a slight European intonation, more a suggestion of foreign birth than a genuine accent.

"At least I ended up on the right side," Roz said, with a small demure smile.

"Yes. There is the *menner seit.*" She pointed across the street. "Not for you," she added, just in case there could still be any remaining question.

"Well, thanks. Those are beautiful children you have."

The woman's response was to turn her head slightly away from Roz. Was it forbidden to compliment the kids here? The mother was delicate-featured and little more than a girl herself. Roz thought, trying to peer beneath the rigid expression, that she was probably eighteen or nineteen. Her pale, delicate skin was not touched by makeup, and it was hard to believe it ever had been. She was a natural redhead, too, judging by her pale-reddish eyelashes and eyebrows. Her hair was hidden beneath a scarf, tied with less pizzazz than Roz's.

"I have an appointment with the Rebbe."

"Yes." This babe was impossible to impress. She had a teenager's sullenness mixed with a matron's severity.

"Could you tell me the best way to get to his office?"

"His office is in his home. If you keep going straight down this street, you'll see the shul, the synagogue. The shul you won't be able to miss. Across the street from the shul, there is the Rebbe's house."

"Hello, sweetie." Roz squatted down before the redheaded child nearer her. "And what's your name?"

The child—Roz couldn't tell if it was a girl or a boy—spun around and burrowed into its mother's brown woolen coat. Roz had observed that this was common behavior for children, though not universal. The Onuma children weren't timid or bashful. They'd march right up to you and start to explore your clothes, your hair, the contents of your pockets, just as their parents did. Roz stood back up.

"Shy, huh?"

"With outsiders."

"Probably doesn't get to see them that often?"

"No, we're lucky that way."

Roz wandered around for a while. The only people she saw were women hurrying with small children. The *menner seit* was deserted. It reminded her of an Onuma village when the men were off on a raid to replenish their supply of brides.

She walked down the road that led to the synagogue. Her informant had been right: there was no missing it. It was a huge rectangular white stucco mess of a building, with arches and castellated cornices. Despite the grandiose architectural touches, the sheer bulk of the building gave it the look of one of those giant stores where people wheel out a year's supply of pet food and toilet paper. It was like a Costco that had found God. All of its windows, including two big ones in the front, were arched in a shape that Roz knew had some sort of religious significance. Oh yeah. Those tablets Moses schlepped down from the mountain.

Roz's family was the assimilated sort, New York City vintage. For her family, one of the ten commandments might as well have been to eat at a Chinese restaurant on Friday nights. She'd had a college boyfriend, Len Solo, who sometimes used to spend vacations with Roz's family. Once, Roz's mother, Alicia, had been talking with Len, and he'd pronounced some Yiddish word wrong—"kibbitz" with the accent on the second syllable, like "the bits"—and Roz's mother had corrected him, saying, "You sound like a goy." To which Len had responded, "Alicia, I *am* a goy!" And Alicia had burst into laughter—Roz had inherited her mother's laugh—saying, "I don't know why I'd assumed you were Jewish!" That was where Roz's family stood when it came to their own tribe. It was a curiosity to them that sophisticated people could continue to care, most especially when it came to dating and marriage.

Roz had given a lot of work to figuring out the kinship relations of the various Onuma villages. Kinship was at the center of their social organization, determining the two most important aspects of their social relations—namely, which men they went to war with and which women they could marry. There were complicated incest prohibitions, as there would have to be in villages in which just about everybody was related to everybody else, though sometimes the men would do some fancy kinship reclassifying so that they could get women they wanted for themselves or their sons. This could lead to big fights between the reclassifier and others who had also wanted the women for themselves or their own sons.

Cass had told Roz about how his mother had blamed inbreeding—what anthropologists called endogamy—for a host of the Valdeners' problems. Deb jokingly told her sons— only Cass wasn't so sure whether it was a joke—to marry women from as far away from their own group as possible— what anthropologists call exogamy—to "dilute those concentrated Valdener genes."

Finding the synagogue, and the Rebbe's house, had solved one mystery. The streets of New Walden were emptied of men because all of them were here, dressed identically in long black wool coats and large-brimmed black felt hats. The young boys were wearing these hats, too. Almost all of the men had beards, and all of them, young and old, had magnificent side locks, shaped like corkscrews and reaching down to their shoulders. There were a lot of blonds and redheads. You could see it with the men, since they didn't cover their hair the way women did.

Wait a minute. Hadn't Cass told her that in this sect the women actually shaved off their hair right after their weddings, and that any hair you saw on their heads, peeking out from their kerchiefs, was a wig? That rated right up there on the bizarro scale with almost anything she'd seen among the Onuma. It made the large families the Hasidim produced a minor miracle. These men were bedding bald women.

The men, on the other hand, were splendidly coiffed. It had to take some doing to get their side locks to curl like that. Did they use rollers? There were dozens of men swarming in the streets outside the shul, and dozens more outside the

Rebbe's house, which was twice as large as any of the other houses, redbrick with black shutters.

She looked for a sign indicating the *froyen seit*. Any town that segregated the sidewalks was going to segregate the entrance to the Rebbe's house. She didn't see Cass or the Klap anywhere, and she wondered how she was going to get herself inside for the powwow with the Rebbe. She didn't want to miss it. It was probably unsafe to approach any of the men to ask them for instructions. There were clearly female-contamination taboos in place here.

She walked down the paved driveway, keeping far to her right to avoid passing too close to the men, and was rewarded by the sight of two women standing outside a side door. She walked up to them and, before she opened her mouth, they pointed her to the open side door.

She walked a few steps in and saw an empty room to her right. She looked back at the women questioningly. *"Gei, gei"*—"Go, go"—the older woman urged, flicking her wrist in a motion bespeaking "be gone." Roz turned back to the room. There were a few wooden slatted chairs, and no windows. It looked like a converted pantry. Was she just supposed to sit here and wait?

She walked back down the hall to the women at the door. One was about sixty and one was about eighteen, but they were dressed almost identically, with kerchiefs wrapping their heads as a diaper does a baby's bottom, and a little fringe of synthetic bangs sticking out in front, looking as natural as the bristles from a plastic whisk broom.

"I'm supposed to see the Rebbe."

"Yes," the younger woman responded. "We showed you. There. There."

"I came here with two friends. *Menner.* I think they're already in with the Rebbe. Our appointment was for four o'clock. I drove all the way from Boston to see the Rebbe."

"Yes. There. There. *Froyen tsimmer.*"

"I'd like to speak to the person in charge."

Now the older woman stepped in.

"There." She pointed back inside.

Roz went back inside. These gender taboos were inconvenient. She should have dressed up as a man, like Barbra Streisand in *Yentl.* Roz could be convincing. She had done it before. If someone didn't come and get her soon, she'd just go and insert her big contaminated female self into that crowd of homeboys in the front yard. That ought to get their attention.

She should have stuck with the men. Klapper had written to the Rebbe on his professional stationery, embossed with his full title: "Extreme Distinguished Professor of Faith, Literature, and Values, Frankfurter University, Weedham, Massachusetts." Cass and the Klap were probably lounging like pashas on tufted settees, being served herring in cream sauce.

But they weren't. They were sitting, like Roz, on wooden folding chairs, although the room they were in was larger and had windows, and there were quite a few other men, all Hasidim, waiting along with them. But the stationery must have done the trick, since they had hardly sat down before a Hasid came for them and ushered them into the Rebbe's office.

It was a spacious room lined floor-to-ceiling with leather-bound Hebrew books. The Rebbe himself was sitting behind a large handsome desk flanked on either side by two middle-aged Hasidim, both wearing the black felt hats with the rounded tops Cass had seen on the other men. But the Rebbe was wearing a fur *shtreimel,* more streamlined than the one he'd be wearing on Shabbes, but still an impressive piece of pelt.

The Rebbe stood up and came around in front of his desk and held out his hand to Jonas Elijah Klapper.

"Extreme Distinguished Professor Klapper of Frankfurter University," he said in clear English without an accent. "Welcome to New Walden."

"I am honored, Grand Rebbe, that you have permitted me this private audience."

"And you, Reb Chaim Yisroel Seltzer," the Rebbe greeted Cass. "It is wonderful to see you again." Cass was surprised to learn that the Rebbe remembered ever having seen him. Of course, the Rebbe had been at his bubbe's funeral, but he had been such a lofty figure, surrounded by his courtiers. Cass had assumed he hadn't noticed, and certainly not remembered, the one person who had cried. "Your bubbe, of sainted memory, could never stop singing your praises," the Rebbe said to him now, which made Cass almost tear up again. Being in New Walden brought her back so vividly. He could recall the smell of her house, a special Hasidic-certified scouring powder that used to make his mother gag. "May her praises continue to intercede on your behalf from On High. How is your mother, Devorah Gittel?"

Cass's mother had never clued him into the Rebbe's unusual mind, since she never had any praise to spare for the Valdeners. The Rebbe's remarkable recall for names was among the least of the wonders his Hasidim recounted. It was taken for granted that a Hasidic Rebbe would manifest extraordinary mental and spiritual attributes, since he was believed to inhabit a different spiritual plane, his soul garnering a greater share of the divine sparks that were, according to the Kabbalist cosmogony, scattered in the great metaphysical mishap that accompanied the creation of the world. The position was dynastic, passed down from father to eldest son—though, should the designated inheritor be deemed of unworthy spiritual or intellectual caliber, it could go to a younger son, or even another relative or a student.

Sometimes there could be feuds and factions, a War of the Rosens over succession. Such discord had never, thank God, rent the Valdeners. Though he had five older sisters, the current Valdener Rebbe was the eldest son, with three younger brothers. His intellectual sharpness and analytical skills had been apparent since childhood, though they manifested themselves with a zeal for matters more practical than mystical. The Valdener Rebbe would much prefer to discuss the requirements for New Walden's sewer system and water supply than the Kabbalist *Zohar, The Book of Splendor.* He had committed to memory a whole directory of doctors and their specialties, so that, if any of his Hasidim came to him with a particular ailment, he knew where to send him or her. The Rebbe's brilliance was often turned to the Talmudic complexities of attaining government subsidies—for housing, for health, for education—for the members of his community, the majority of whom lived below the poverty line, not surprisingly, since none were college-educated and they almost all had, thank God, large families.

"Please give your blessed mother my regards."

Cass was surprised that the Rebbe seemed to harbor no hard feelings toward his mother.

The Rebbe had retreated again behind his desk—for a small, round man he moved very quickly, giving the impression of forceful rolling—and now sat down. Cass and Klapper did the same.

"So your mother, Devorah Gittel, left the Hasidim. But you, Chaim Yisroel, have returned. You, too, are a Hasid."

Cass remembered how his bubbe used to call him a little Hasid. Had she told the Rebbe one of her *bubbe meisahs*, her grandmother tales? Cass felt compelled to clear up the confusion, as delicately as possible.

"I haven't been raised as a Hasid, Rebbe. I'm sorry. I don't think it's for me."

"Of course you're a Hasid! How can you deny that? Especially sitting right there beside your Rebbe!" he said, gesturing grandly toward Jonas Elijah Klapper.

A look of beatitude settled over Jonas Elijah Klapper's face. The Valdener Rebbe clearly recognized him as a fellow charismatic.

"We have many interests in common," Professor Klapper said now to the Rebbe. "I have a consuming passion for the esoteric texts of Jewish mysticism."

"You are an educator on the highest order. An Extreme Distinguished Professor at an accredited university. We Valdeners value education to the highest degree, too. Every Valdener Hasid is a scholar. Our boys are learning from the age of three on. In our *kollel*, which is our adult-learning institute, we have over fifty percent of our married men learning Talmud full-time, and for the first year after their marriage, every single man learns full-time, supported by the community until he has to go out and earn for his family. But even those who have jobs come in the evenings to study two or three hours. The ones with jobs support the ones who sit and learn full-time to the best of their abilities. All our men, young and old, are scholars, though some have special needs. You can imagine how hard it is on the community to support such demands of scholarship. In the outside world, only the chosen few, such as yourself, Rav Klapper, are permitted a life of study, but for the Valdeners every butcher, baker, and bus driver is also involved in a life of study."

"Indeed. The scholarship is, I presume, intensely esoteric. I am a student myself of Yehuda Ickel, the pre-eminent secular scholar of Jewish Kabbala. Ickel shrewdly brings the strategies of Heideggerian hermeneutics to the study of Jewish mystical texts. Heidegger lamented man's forgetfulness of Being, at the same time pointing out that it is Being that now hides itself from man. I quote now from memory: 'We come too late for the gods and too early for Being.'"

"But not, fortunately, too late or too early for help from the federal government," responded the Valdener Rebbe. "The United States government believes, together with you, Rav Klapper, and with your own Rav Heidegger, in the importance of education. And they have made available special grants both for advanced study and for those among us who have special needs if their divine spark is to reveal itself. You do believe, Rav Klapper, that all our holy children have divine sparks?"

"Ah, you refer, of course, to the 'breaking of the vessels,' the *shevirat hakelim*. I am familiar with the opinion of Chaim Vital, the foremost disciple of Isaac Luria, the holy Arizal, that the vessels are to be thought of as representing the womb of the Cosmic Feminine Presence, so that the shattering of the vessels signals not only the broken waters of birth but also the erotic displacements that the catastrophic aspect of creation unleashed."

"It is very true what you say, Rav Klapper. We have here right now in New Walden many families who are shattered because they have children who have been, from their birth, in need of whatever additional resources the government—

federal, state, and county—can provide so that their divine spark, too, can be rejoined to all of Klal Yisroel."

"Ah, the work of *tikkun olam*, the healing of the world! Yehuda Ickel, who is a close and valued friend, has . . ."

"Exactly as you say, Professor Klapper. And we have received letters of support in our efforts to get the needed funds from many prominent people such as yourself. Well, no, I shouldn't really compare. We don't yet have an Extreme Distinguished Professor, though Dr. Platinsky, a leading cardiologist at Mount Sinai School of Medicine, has been very helpful in backing our application for Pell funds."

It was a shame that Roz was missing this exchange between the Valdener Rebbe and Jonas Elijah Klapper, though things had livened up in the windowless waiting room where she'd been stored.

A little group of four had entered the room, arranged in height like a stepladder, all of them wearing identical long black winter coats. Very pretty girls, the oldest about nine or ten and the youngest about three or four.

No, Roz had been wrong. They had taken off their coats, the oldest one helping the youngest with the row of buttons, and when the coats came off Roz saw her mistake. The second-to-smallest was a boy.

The three girls were dressed in identical pleated brown plaid skirts that came down to their mid-calves, even the baby of three or four, and in starched white button-down blouses and brown wool cardigans, while the boy was dressed in black pants and a white button-down shirt, with a black velvet vest that was buttoned over the shirt. He was also wearing the knee-high leather boots that Cass had said the men wore only on the Sabbath, his pants tucked into the tops. The girls were wearing clunky lace-up brown shoes. The whole ensemble had the sort of eerie charm you see in photographs of Victorian children, dressed up in the somber clothing of adults. The girls had their hair severely held back in elastic bands, plastered down smooth and solid on their heads. They looked like nuns in training. They were blonde like the little boy, but because his hair was allowed to flow into the long swirling side locks, his looked shades lighter and silkier.

It wasn't just the hair that made him outshine his companions. He was an exceptionally beautiful child. His eyes were large and luminous, and there was something about the delicate folds around them that made him look both vulnerable and wise. He had the white skin of the very fair and a sculpted, round little chin. He might have been a cherub in the sort of paintings that would be deeply offensive, Roz suspected, to his community.

He turned his eyes and stared at her, and she stared back, and the effect he produced was even stronger. Was it the odd getup, the little velvet vest and the knickers and boots, that made him seem as if he had traveled far to get here, from some other time or even farther?

The oldest girl said something to him in a low chastising voice, unintelligible to Roz, presumably in Yiddish. She heard *"froy,"* and assumed he was being told not to stare at the lady. But then the sister, maybe regretting her tone of voice, kissed him on the top of his head, right on his black velvet yarmulke. He whispered something in her ear, and she shook her head.

"Are you all brother and sisters?" Roz asked.

The oldest girl took it on herself to nod yes.

"How nice that there are so many of you. It must be fun! I always wanted to have a sister or brother."

"You don't have?" It was the little boy who spoke.

"No, I don't. It was just me when I was growing up."

"Were you sad?" The child's voice was high and chimelike.

Again the older sister felt compelled to issue a gentle "shah."

"No, I don't think so. I had lots of friends. And my parents were my friends, too. They were my playmates!"

All four of the children stared at her with concentrated seriousness, even the youngest, as if they were trying to interpret her words. Perhaps their English wasn't very good.

Roz was not sentimental when it came to children. She found the standardized cuteness of kids about as inspiring as the standardized intelligence of grown-ups. She'd never been the kind of girl who spent much time with kids. She hadn't babysat, and she hadn't taken summer jobs as a camp counselor. Children had always left her cold until she studied the Onuma kids as part of her field research. She found most of them to be pains in the neck, though she'd grown fond of a few of them, particularly one, whom she had nicknamed Tsetse, and who was such a creative liar that even the elders admired him.

"Still, I think it must be lovely to be four like the four of you."

"We have more," said the little boy.

This time the older sister gave her brother a warning look that needed no interpretation.

Just then, a tall, thin woman came into the room. She was in a dun-colored dress and thick flesh-colored stockings, and the same clunky style of shoes as the girls. She was wearing a matching dun-colored wig. Her face lit up when she saw the children. Actually, it was the little boy she directed her glow to, and she cooed at him in Yiddish, apparently telling him to come to her.

He got up and walked over to her, and she took his hand

and brought it to her lips lovingly. Was this the mother? She didn't look like the children, certainly not like the enchanting little boy. And she didn't spare a glance for the girls.

She asked the little boy something, and he answered "Ya" and turned back to Roz.

"I have to go now. I'm going to see my *tata*," he said to her. She surmised that this meant "daddy."

"Is your *tata* the Rebbe?" she asked.

The children, even the little boy, looked down at the floor in response, and the dun-colored woman sharply asked Roz, whom she hadn't deigned to notice before, "Who you?"

"I'm here to see the Rebbe." Roz extravagantly rolled the *r* of "Rebbe," which was both fun and, she thought, helpful in convincing them of her respectful attitude. "I had an appointment to see him at four o'clock. I drove in from Boston with my two friends."

"Yes, they're *mit* da Rebbe now. If you want, come."

Holding the little boy's hand—the sisters were left behind, never glanced at—the woman led the way down a corridor into a little antechamber, where she knocked at a door. A bearded man poked his head out, took a look at the boy, and opened the door for him. Roz slipped in behind the child. The man quickly looked at her sideways and then closed the door behind her.

They were in a book-lined study, with a large desk behind which was sitting a pudgy man in a shiny black coat and a beard in the white, flowing model they stick on soldiers of the Salvation Army around Christmastime, and one superlative fur hat. There were two full-bearded subordinates standing guard behind him, and seated in front of the desk, cozy as could be, were Cass and Klapper. The seated man in the headdress could only be the tribal chief, and, judging by his cir-

cumference, the choicest matzo balls went to him. (The
Valdeners, from what Roz had seen of them, were a pale, mal-
nourished lot.) The Rebbe took no notice of Roz's entrance—
nobody did—but he smiled broadly when he saw the boy,
and he gestured for him to come. The boy went straight over
to the chief—perhaps *tata* meant "grandpa" rather than
"papa"—and was lifted up onto the ample royal lap.

"My son," he said to Cass and Klapper. "Your sisters
brought you, *tateleh*?"

"Ya, Tata."

"How many sisters do you have, *tateleh*?" Roz asked, even
though it had been impressed on her that the rules of female
modesty required her to render herself as close to nonexistent
as possible.

The boy stared at her, wide-eyed. It wasn't the endearment
that had startled him: it was her question.

"Don't you know, sweetie? Don't you know how to count?"

"He knows to count," the Rebbe said forcefully, "Believe
me, miss, that he knows how to do!"

Klapper turned back to where Roz was standing against the
wall, gave her a glance, and then turned back.

"There is an ancient prohibition against the counting of
people, which we learn from the account of the sin of King
David recorded in both Samuel and 1 Chronicles. King David
ordered his lieutenants to count the men of fighting age and
displeased God with his action, and God began to smite
Israel. David repented of his sin and asked for God's forgiveness and was given his choice of punishments, either three
years of famine, three months of being vanquished by enemies, or three days of 'the sword of the Lord,' which would
consist of a deadly plague that would sweep through the land.
David chose the latter, and a great many of Israel fell dead."

Klapper might have been answering Roz, but his response was directed to the Valdener Rebbe, and it had impressed him.

"That's some good head you've got on your shoulders, Rav Klapper! No wonder you're an Extreme Distinguished Professor! That's a first-class *Gemara kop,* a head for Talmudic study. Do you have scholars in your family perhaps, rabbinical scholars?"

"I've always assumed I must. It is more than possible to be of a plebeian family with no discernible learning and still have towering Talmudists and Kabbalists in one's lineage, whose erudition one carries in one's genetic memory."

Leave it to the Klap, Roz thought, to mangle the math and science in the most self-aggrandizing way possible. Everyone is guaranteed to find famous people in his family tree, since the number of ancestors explodes the farther back you go. Every Jew is going to find some legendary rabbi, every Wasp is going to find some aristocrat. Throw in intermarriage and the Jew will find an aristocrat and the Wasp a Talmudic sage. And could even the Klap believe that erudition was transmitted in one's genetic memory?

Suddenly the boy piped up from his father's lap.

"The number of my sisters is special."

"Of course it is," said Roz in that sudsy voice some women get when they talk to children, though it was a surprise to Cass—and to Roz—that she was one of those women. "Your sisters are special."

"Ask him what he means," said the Rebbe. "Tell our guests what you mean, *tateleh.*"

"If you put my sisters in a group, then there's no way to make equal groups of them."

All three visitors stared at the boy. The Rebbe was stroking his beard and smiling.

"Go on," he said to Cass and Klapper. "Ask him what he means."

"If I have a group of six things, could I make equal groups out of it?" Cass decided to ask, seeing that Jonas Elijah Klapper was sitting there impassively, and Roz was supposed to keep all manifestations of herself to a minimum.

"Yes, two ways. You could make two groups with three things, or you could make three groups with two things." He had a way of gesturing with his hands, very Hasidic.

"What about six groups with one thing?" Roz asked.

The child looked at her and laughed. He seemed to think she'd made an uproarious joke.

"You can always do that!"

"You're right," said Roz. She didn't know much developmental psychology, but having the concept of a prime number seemed pretty advanced for a child this age. It was touching to see the Grand Rabbi's face, irradiated with love. Mystic shmystic, this guy was a proud papa.

"Do you know what we call the kind of numbers that you can't make any equal groups out of?" she asked him. "We call them prime numbers."

"Prime numbers," the boy repeated, carefully. And then he smiled at Roz. The look of bliss was baffling, moving. Why did he look as if she'd just given him the present he'd secretly wished for as he blew out the candles on his last birthday cake, if Hasidic children engaged in such practices?

"Yes, prime numbers. And they're exactly as you said. You can't divide them up into groups that have equal numbers, except of course groups with one thing in them."

"Groups with one thing in them!" he repeated, smiling. "And as many groups as were in the first big group."

"That's right. You said it just right." She smiled back at the boy.

"Do you know what I call prime numbers?" he asked her, the only one of the males in the room who didn't seem to hold it against her that she was a woman who spoke. "I call them *maloychim*. Special *maloychim*."

"Angels," the Rebbe translated. "The heavenly hosts."

"And I call *you* an angel!" Roz said.

The child stared at her as if she'd just announced that she thought he could fly. That's probably what he did think that she'd announced. And then he laughed out loud in a high soprano. The kid's amusement amused her so much that she couldn't resist. Klapper bristled, but the Valdener Rebbe tolerated the tainted noise of a woman's laughter with surprising sangfroid. Unlike his Hasidim, he was often exposed to the outside world, meeting with politicians, agency heads, social workers, medical specialists, and building contractors. The Rebbe had to know how to talk to a variety of people whose assistance his community required. He had developed a level of worldliness to save his Hasidim from having to deal with the world.

"So, *tateleh,* can you tell our visitors any more of your special *maloychim*?" he asked his son, lightly glancing the back of his hand over the child's cheek.

"I'll start with one. And then there's two, and then three, and then five."

"That's good!" Roz said, enjoying both the look of pride on the Rebbe's face and the look of exasperation on Klapper's. She'd edged around the side of the room, still hugging the wall, just so that she could get an angle on Klapper's face and still keep the child and his dad in her sights.

"After five, there's seven, eleven, thirteen, seventeen, nineteen, twenty-three, twenty-nine, thirty-one, thirty-seven, forty-one, forty-three, forty-seven, fifty-three, fifty-nine, sixty-one, sixty-seven, seventy-one, seventy-three, seventy-nine. . . ."

"Exactly how long does this go on?" Klapper broke in testily.

Lord knew, he had the patience of a Job, but it was beginning to wear thin. He hadn't risked his life by driving down from Boston with that wild Rastafarian so that he could listen to an infant perform like a circus seal.

Meanwhile, the Valdener Rebbe was chiming in with "I told you the boy knew to count!" and Cass and Roz were exchanging looks of incredulity.

"Who taught him this?" Cass asked.

"Who taught him? The angels! *Min ha-shamoyim*—from the heavens. This is nothing. He likes to play with numbers. For him they're toys, and we let him play. He can learn a page of Torah or Talmud like *lamdin*—like scholars—three, four, five times his age. The way he learns now, at six years old, most men will never catch up."

Meanwhile, the child had settled on Klapper, staring at him wide-eyed. The visiting rav had asked an important question, and he was waiting to hear the answer. He thought that he knew the answer, a wonderful answer, but he would have liked to hear it spoken by this rav. He whispered his own rendition of the question softly, so softly that no one caught it.

"Have you ever had him tested?" Roz asked. "His IQ must be off the charts."

"We don't need to test. For the other special children, those who need the government's help, for them we have testers coming. We take care. But for a child like this? Why do we need to test? All our children are special, one way or the other."

"Tata?"

"Yes, *tateleh*."

"Tata, I know someone who isn't special."

"Is it possible?"

"Yes and no."

"Why yes and no?"

"If he's the only one who isn't special, so then he's special for not being special."

"So he's special. Everybody is special, one way or another, and this one, too."

"But no, Tata." The Rebbe's son squirmed off of his father's lap and turned around to face him, gesturing with his two hands in the motions of explanation. "He can't be special anymore if he's special for not being special. If he's not special, then he's special, and if he's special, then he's not special. *Du siest*, Tata?"

"You see," the Rebbe said, in either translation or demonstration, "this is the way the child is. There are children who are born as if knowing. He can go on like this all day long."

"No doubt," Klapper remarked dryly.

But Roz was relishing the spectacle and was determined to keep it going. The Rebbe's son was astounding, as everyone in the room was aware, with the exception of the child and Jonas Elijah Klapper.

"So the number of your sisters is a prime number. What if you add one to the number? Is it still a prime number?"

The boy walked around the desk and came over to where Roz was standing against the wall. He looked at her tenderly, a little sorrowfully, as if he worried that she might be one of those special people who needed his *tata*'s government funds.

"One, two, three. Three *maloychim,* holding hands. But after three, they can't hold hands. Because, if one number can't make two groups, then the number after it, that one can make two groups. Back and forth they go. Do you see?" he asked her gently, and he took her hand as if to help lead her.

"Now I do. You explained it very well to me."

He smiled at her. She felt strangely grateful to the tot for singling her out in this room of males who were all conspiring to pretend she wasn't there. Even Cass was keeping his eyes resolutely away from Roz.

"But the number of my sisters and me is still special. Sometimes you take a number a certain number of times. You repeat it the number of times of itself. So take two two times over and you get four. Or you take three three times and you get . . ."

"Nine!" Klapper shouted out the answer, actually raising his hand as if he were back in P.S. 2.

"Good!" the child commended the visitor, making Roz start to laugh, though she hastily tried to make it sound like a cough. "So those numbers, like four and nine and sixteen and twenty-five and thirty-six, they're also special."

"Are they angels, too?" Cass asked, smiling.

"Yes, also," he answered, so seriously that Cass felt a pang for the patronizing tone he'd taken. "There are different kinds of angels."

"Indeed," said Klapper. "The *malach,* translated as the 'messenger' or the 'angel,' is only one variety of numina. Psalms 82 and Job 1 refer to an entire *adat el,* or divine assembly. There are Irinim, who are Watchers or High Angels;

Sarim, or Princes; Seraphim, or Fiery Ones; Chayyot, or Holy Creatures; and Ofanim, or Wheels. The collective terms for the full array of heavenly beings, those who straddle the sphere between the human and the ultimate divine principle, include Tzeva, translated as 'Host'; B'nei Ha-Elohim, or B'nei Elim, or Sons of God; and Kedoshim, or Holy Ones. And of course there is some, albeit limited, migration between the sphere of Adam and the Kedoshim."

The person who seemed most intrigued by Klapper's words, in addition to Klapper himself, was the little boy. He was staring at his father's guest with a smile.

"What is numina?" he asked softly.

Klapper ignored him, staring around the room in an unfocused sort of way, his nose slightly wrinkling.

"Can you tell us about more?" Roz asked the child. "Some more special angels?"

"Yes. You take two two times, like before, and then another two times. That's eight. Eight is special. Or three three times, like before, and then another three times. That's twenty-seven. Twenty-seven is special. Or four four times and then another four times. That's sixty-four." His gestures, with his little palms turned upward, must have been in imitation of the rabbis he had watched, his father and teachers. "Those are special numbers, too. Also angels," he said turning to Cass, anticipating his question. "My sisters and me together have a number like that."

"Wow. You sure do have a lot of sisters, sweetie," Roz said.

The child looked stricken, as if he'd just been slapped across the face. His cheeks immediately blazed red, as if they bore the bruise. Cass and Roz understood right away what was going on. If the number of his sisters was prime, and he together with his sisters made the number a perfect cube, then the number of his sisters had to be seven. He had given out too many clues, and so, in essence, had announced the number straight out, which was forbidden.

"It's okay, *tateleh*," said the Rebbe gently. "You made a mistake, but it's okay. Only take a little more care. So, with the numbers, his *maloychim*, he sometimes forgets himself. Only then. Come here, *tateleh, kumma hier*." He indicated his lap.

Klapper could no longer control himself. As far as he was concerned the situation had long passed the point of the abidable.

"Why don't you and the child continue your conversation outside, young lady?"

The little boy was still holding her hand, having ignored his father's summons.

"I can, Tata?"

"Tell me, please, what is your name?" the Rebbe said to Roz.

"I'm Roz. Roslyn Margolis."

The Rebbe cocked his head a bit to the side and regarded her for a long moment.

"We will have other chances to speak together, Miss Margolis."

"I hope so."

"Yes, Azarya. You can go with Miss Margolis. This is a very nice lady, Miss Margolis. A pearl."

Cass was tempted to ask if he could go along with them. Half an hour ago, he would never have dreamed that anything could upstage the meeting between Jonas Elijah Klapper and the Valdener Rebbe.

"How old was he when he began to think about numbers?" he asked the Rebbe.

"Mr. Seltzer," said Klapper sternly, "perhaps you would like to go and join the young lady."

Cass looked over at the Valdener Rebbe, who smiled and said, "I am glad to see you again, Chaim Yisroel, after all these years. God willing, we'll meet again, next time before so many years have elapsed. Next time, too, I hope you can bring your brother, Yeshiya Yakov, and your mother, too, who will always be loved by the Valdener Hasidim. Please tell her how much I would like to see her, either when she comes with you or with Yeshiya Yakov or by herself. Tell her that her Rebbe will always be her Rebbe."

Jonas Elijah Klapper spent another three-quarters of an hour holed up alone with the Rebbe, and the conversation that ensued between them must have compensated for the exasperating distractions created earlier in the hour. Professor Klapper emerged extolling Reb Chaim's relation as an estimable descendant of the sanctified Ba'al Shem Tov.

"The Valdener Rebbe has the slyness of Socrates, and is to be compared perhaps more to the metaphysical fabulist Borges than to the heresiarchs of the Dead Sea Scrolls."

For their part, Cass and Roz had spent an enchanting time with the Rebbe's son. They'd gone back to the windowless room where Roz had first been shelved. Cass probably wasn't allowed to be there, but nobody came and bothered them.

Azarya, away from his watchful older sister, was now able to indulge in his curiosity about these visitors, especially the lady whom he thought as beautiful as Queen Esther.

His first question to them was where they came from, fascinated to hear that they came neither from New Walden nor from Brooklyn nor from Eretz Yisroel, the Land of Israel. He could recount for them, and did, the seven generations of Valdener Rebbes and their wives and children, going all the way back to Reb Azarya ben Yisroel, who had been a direct descendant of the Besht. He knew exactly where he was situated on the family tree. But he didn't know that the name of the country he lived in was the United States of America. Roz wanted to draw him a map of America. He'd never seen a map of anything, and once she explained the idea of a map to him, he grew so excited that he went running out of the room, his silky blond side curls flying, to go find something to draw with. He came back a few minutes later with a box of crayons and a few sheets of coarse white paper.

Roz got down on the floor, since there was no writing surface in the room, with the little boy stooping down near her so that he could watch closely, his hands clasped between his knees. She drew a reasonably well-proportioned and accurate map of the United States, using red and blue crayons. She also drew an American flag for Azarya and explained about its stars and stripes. She colored the Atlantic and Pacific oceans for him. He knew about the ocean because of the splitting of the Red Sea. He had no idea that he lived within fifty miles of an ocean. One of his older sisters had been to Brooklyn, but he had never left New Walden. He hadn't realized that when his father had gone to Eretz Yisroel he had had to cross the blue water that Roz drew for him.

Azarya knew how to read Hebrew and Yiddish and Aramaic, but he hadn't been taught the English alphabet yet. Nevertheless, Roz labeled all the states, saying the names aloud as she wrote, and labeled "New Walden" and "Cambridge."

"This is where you live, and this is where Cass and I live. Maybe someday you'll come and visit us. Would you like that?"

"With my sisters, too?"

"Sure, why not." As long as they were dreaming the impossible anyway, they might as well make it to the child's specifications.

"Are you married?"

Azarya had settled down cross-legged on the floor next to Roz. He was as comfortable with strangers as the Onuma brats, which was remarkable, given the insularity of the Valdeners. Being the Rebbe's son, and a prodigy to boot, he'd probably been bathed in affection and powdered in praise his whole life.

"To each other? No." She smiled down at him.

"To someone else you're married?"

"No. We're not married at all."

"Will you invite me to the *hasana*?"

"The wedding," Cass explained to her.

"Of course we'll invite you! Do you think we'd have our *hasana* without you?"

The child broke into his wonderful smile.

"Now I'll draw *you* a picture!" He took another of the sheets and lay down on his stomach on the floor beside Roz with his box of crayons and got to work.

"It's a surprise for you," he told them. "I'm going to make one for each of you. For your *hasana*. Don't look yet."

He didn't get the chance, though, since the rail-thin woman who had taken Azarya and Roz into the Rebbe's study soon came to fetch Azarya. She, too, had some words of gentle chastisement for him, apparently having to do with his being on the floor. She glared at Roz, who was sitting there beside him. Azarya got up quickly and then handed the sheet of paper to Roz, telling her sadly that he hadn't had time to finish.

"The last one isn't finished. When you look at my drawing, you'll see many different *maloychim*," he said to her, for the first time looking a little bit shy. "I'm sorry," he said to Cass, "that I didn't make a drawing for you. *Ble nadir,* I'll make one for you next time." As he was being led away, he looked back over his shoulder and smiled the smile of a cherub, lifting his little hand and opening and closing his fingers to wave in the manner of the very young. Bye-bye.

"That's not only the most extraordinary child I've ever met," Roz said to Cass and Klapper as they walked back to the car in the quickly falling dusk, "I think that might be the most extraordinary person I've ever met."

Klapper stopped walking and looked at Roz.

"I think he must be some sort of idiot savant. The Rebbe spoke feelingly of the problem with genetic disorders that they have. It's the price of their marriage purity."

"Idiot sa*vant*! Are you *kidding* me, Jonas?" Cass winced at the many liberties Roz was taking. At least she didn't call him "the Klap" to his face—not yet. "If that kid's not a genius, then I'll eat his father's fur hat. Turn on the light, Cass." They were in the Lincoln Continental now. "I want to see that drawing he made for me."

Azarya had folded the sheet once in half. When she unfolded it, she saw a bunch of numbers written down, arranged in clumps that were somewhat triangular in shape, and that he'd written with different-colored crayons.

"Let's see," said Cass, and Roz held Azarya's picture up so that both Cass and Klapper could inspect it.

"Perhaps it's gematria," Klapper said, showing a momentary interest.

"What's gematria?" asked Roz.

"I'll explain it to you as soon as Reb Chaim turns off the interior lights and turns on the heat. When I say my teeth are chattering I am not speaking figuratively. Gematria, from the same Greek roots that give us 'geometry,' is an ancient ana-gogic means of extracting the hidden meanings out of sacred texts, by assigning numerical values to letters and then com-puting the values of a word or phrase. The Greek isopsephy, the Muslim *khisab al jumal* are examples of similar tech-niques, but the most intricately and cannily developed is the gematria of the Kabbalists. Take my name, for instance, which is a rather fascinating one."

"'Klapper'?" Roz asked, and Cass felt a buzz of alarm. It would be catastrophic were the conversation to yield revela-tions of Klepfish.

"No, I refer to my given name, Jonas Elijah. In Hebrew, my name is Yonah Eliyahu, and if you take the gematria of my first name it adds up to thirty-five: *yod* is ten, *vav* is six, *nun* is fourteen, and *heh* is five. If you then add the first letter of my second name, *aleph,* you get thirty-six—or in Hebrew, *lamed vav,* which is a number with profound mystical significance. The Lamedvavniks are the thirty-six people of impregnable purity who live in every generation and for the sake of whom the world is not destroyed. Their identity is kept so secret that even they don't know who they are. The name Yonah means, literally, 'dove,' but also can mean, paradoxically, 'the Destroyer,' as it also means 'a Gift from God.' And in Hebrew the name of Yonah, *yod vav nun heh,* is almost identical to the one and only true name of God, *yod heh vav heh,* or Yahweh, the Divine Tetragram. The only letter that distinguishes between the two is the letter *nun,* which is a letter known as the 'winged messenger.'"

Boy, you never knew what Krap the Klap was going to throw at you. Roz almost had to admire him.

"Azarya's drawing had a bunch of zeros in it. Does the zero mean anything in gematria?" she asked him.

"Nothing at all. I'm afraid that the child's drawing has no Kabbalistic significance whatsoever. An indulged and, I've no doubt, much-tutored child has learned to write his numbers without having much grasp of what they mean and drew you a picture out of them."

"I bet there's more to it than that. That child is something wonderful."

"There was indeed something wonderful back there, young lady, and it is unfortunate for you that it passed you by. You are the sort who, should she witness the Messiah walking on water, would be impressed that his socks had not shrunk."

Cass marveled at how well Jonas Elijah Klapper kept his temper with Roz. He just hoped she wouldn't push it. His hope was in vain.

"I'm just wondering. Did you follow what he was talking about?"

Cass winced, waiting for the onslaught. But Jonas Elijah Klapper's response was astoundingly mild.

"Are you questioning whether I have the resources to keep pace with the Valdener Rebbe? Granted, he is a daringly speculative charismatic, but I hardly think we are mismatched."

"I meant did you follow Azarya."

"Azarya?"

"The Rebbe's little son."

"What I am failing to follow is you, young lady."

"I'm wondering whether you were impressed when he started talking about numbers."

"You think it had some Kabbalistic meaning?"

"I don't know about Kabbalistic. But the child had figured out—and, according to his father, all by himself—the concept of prime numbers. He'd figured out squares and cubes. He's six years old. That doesn't impress you?"

"No doubt he's an unusual child," Jonas Elijah Klapper conceded. His forbearance toward Roz verged on the miraculous. "He is, after all, of the royal line going back to the Ba'al Shem Tov himself. But, no, I'm not impressed by the slide-rule mentality. I remain unimpressed with the mathematical arts in general. What are the so-called exact sciences but the failure of metaphor and metonymy? I've always experienced mathematics as a personal affront. It is a form of torture for the imaginatively gifted, the very totalitarianism of thought, one line being made to march strictly in step behind the other, all leading inexorably to a single undeviating conclusion. A proof out of Euclid recalls to my mind nothing so much as the troops goose-stepping before the Supreme Dictator. I have always delighted in my mind's refusal to follow a single line of any mathematical explanation offered to me. Why should these exacting sciences exact anything from me? Or, as Dostoevsky's Underground Man shrewdly argues, 'Good God, what do I care about the laws of nature and arithmetic if, for one reason or another, I don't like these laws, including the "two times two is four"?' Dostoevsky spurned the hegemaniacal logic, and I can do no less."

They drove back to Boston in near silence, though Klapper had perked up a bit when they stopped at a McDonald's on the Massachusetts Turnpike, where he had expatiated on the parallels between the junk food on American highways and the junk ideas on American campuses, launching into the ludicrosity of English professors who study the evacuations from the posterior of popular culture—for example, a colleague he had had at Columbia who analyzed the lyrics of a musical ensemble called the Sex Pistols. Professor Klapper managed to expound even while he put away two Quarter Pounders with Cheese, a large order of fries, and a cup of cola the size of a cocktail shaker. "The fried potatoes are superlative," he said, his lips glistening.

They dropped Jonas Elijah Klapper off at his house in Cambridge, which was on an exclusive cul-de-sac pocketed behind the Episcopal Divinity School. The house was fronted by an iron gate and struck Cass as vaguely English. There was an old-fashioned lawn lamp shedding soft light on the ivy climbing the walls. He watched Jonas Elijah Klapper heavily mount the front stairs of his porch, unlock his front door, and disappear without a backward glance. He had sunk back into silence as soon as they had left McDonald's, and Cass wondered whether it was because of distaste for Roz, or because his visit with the Rebbe had yielded a feast of insights upon which he was meditatively chewing. Or perhaps he had been lulled into the tranquillity of an infant by the large car's effortless gliding through the darkness of night.

XIII

The Argument from Taking Differences

As tired as Roz had thought she was, she couldn't sleep. The first thing she had to think about, and dispose of, was just how infuriating that gasbag of a Klapper was. Did he actually say, without irony, "I've always experienced mathematics as a personal affront"? How could Cass not see him as one of the most prominent, if not the pre-eminent, propounders of poppycock of our day?

Cass was asleep beside her, his arms around her. He was the only man she'd ever known who liked to cuddle so much that he did it in his sleep. Sleep-cuddling was all that he had managed tonight. When she got out of the bathroom after brushing her teeth, he had already dropped off.

It was just as well. She'd felt put out with him. He'd given no indication that he opposed his demented adviser's ukase that Roz make herself as if she were not. Even the Valdener Rebbe had been less a misogynist than the Klap. In fact, she'd ended up liking him.

Poor boy. She predicted disenchantment of major proportions for Cass Seltzer. And if disenchantment never came, then its absence was an even more disturbing eventuality to contemplate.

But she didn't want to lie here and think maddening thoughts about the Klap. She disentwined herself from Cass's arms and crawled out of bed, going to the front closet to retrieve Azarya's drawing from her coat pocket. She crawled back into bed and switched on the little reading lamp. Cass stirred, looked over at her, smiled, and fell back asleep.

She studied Azarya's sheet, hoping it wasn't some sort of mystical gibberish that they'd given him in order to channel his interest in numbers into acceptable nonsense. Several minutes of study showed her it wasn't. She felt her scalp prickling, something that happened to her in moments of fear or excitement.

Azarya had color-coded his mathematics. In each pyramid, the line of zeros was in blue, the line after that, repeating a single number, was in green. The last line was in red, and the colors of the lines in between, if there were any, he'd left as they were, as if trying to show that they weren't as significant.

```
          0 0 0 0 0                    0  0  0  0
           1 1 1 1 1 1                  2  2  2  2  2
            1 2 3 4 5 6 7              3  5  7  9  11 13
                                        1  4  9  16 25 36 49


             0   0   0                        0   0
            6   6   6   6                   24   24   24
          12  18  24  30  36            60    84   108  132
         7   19  37  61   91  127        50   110  194  302  434
       1   8   27  64  125 216 343    15   65   175  369  671 1105
                                         1   16   81   256  625 1296 2401



                  0
               120 120
```

The first thing she noticed was that the last line of each of the triangles, the ones he'd written in red crayon, consisted of the first seven digits raised to a specific power. In the first triangle, he'd taken the numbers to the first power: 1^1, 2^1, 3^1. In the second triangle, his red line had the first seven numbers raised to the power of 2—1^2, 2^2, 3^2, 4^2, et cetera—which gave him 1, 4, 9, 16, 25, 36, and 49. Then he did the same thing for his third triangle, only now the bottom row had seven cubes: 1^3, 2^3, 4^3, and for the fourth triangle he'd raised the seven digits to the power of 4.

Roz got out of bed again and found her calculator. She used it to check the last numbers in his fourth last line. He'd gotten them right.

But, then, what about the lines above the red lines? It didn't take her long to see that the line immediately above the red line in each of the triangles was generated by taking the difference between the consecutive numbers in the line below. He did that, beginning at the bottom and proceeding up until he got to the green line, which had all the same numbers—odd that that kept happening—and which therefore gave him, when he took it to the next line above, his blue line of zeros. So his triangles were generated by taking differences. She went through with her calculator, checking his subtraction and her own surmise, and found both to be right.

But then came his fifth triangle, the one he hadn't finished. What was baffling was that he'd started not from the bottom but from the top. Why would he have done that?

The first line, the blue line of zeros, wasn't mysterious. Azarya had seen the pattern, the fact that taking the difference from consecutive numbers raised to the same power eventually gives you a line with all the same numbers, 1 when the power was 1, 2 when the power was 2, 6 when the power was 3, 24 when the power was 4. Azarya knew that the same thing was going to happen when he raised the first seven digits to the power of 5. He knew that, taking differences, he was once again going to get a line with all the same numbers, so that he'd end up with a line of zeros. So he'd written his blue line of zeros.

But what Roz couldn't see was how he knew that his green line would consist of 120s. How could he have known that before working his way up from the bottom, taking his differences?

What was the relation between 5 and 120, or, for that matter, between 4 and 24, and 3 and 6? What was special about 120? It was 10 times 12, which was $5 \times 2 \times 2 \times 3 \times 2$. Or, in other words, $5 \times 4 \times 3 \times 2$. Or in other words, $5 \times 4 \times 3 \times 2 \times 1$. It was 5 factorial, what mathematicians write as "5!" Roz's scalp was tingling like crazy. She only now noticed what was special about all the green lines.

24 equals 4!—$1 \times 2 \times 3 \times 4$. 6 equals 3!—$1 \times 2 \times 3$. 2 equals 2!—$1 \times 2$. And 1 is equal to 1!—$1 \times 1$. Azarya had drawn a picture for Roz showing the nth difference of x^n is $n!$

One heard stories of this sort of thing, mostly in mathematics and music, the most self-enclosed of spheres. At five, Wolfgang Amadeus Mozart was composing ingeniously, if not yet immortally. It wasn't known until long after Gauss's death that the greater part of nineteenth-century mathematics had been anticipated by him before 1800, which was the year when he'd turned twenty-three. Generations of mathematicians had had to plod along behind him until they finally caught up with what he'd known in his adolescence.

And here was Azarya Sheiner cavorting with *maloychim*. No wonder the whole village cooed and petted over this child, rigid-faced women almost bursting into reckless laughter at the mere sight of him. He wasn't just the Rebbe's son, the Valdener Rebbe–to–be, the heir apparent, the Dauphin of New Walden. He was that accident of genes that happens only once in a very long while.

And even then, when such accidents happen, there has to be a blessed confluence of factors. A Mozart born to a family of slaves in the antebellum South would have created excellent spirituals while he was picking cotton in the fields, but not sublime operas. A Gauss growing up before the Arabs had invented the zero wouldn't have had a chance to carry mathematics into realms of infinite abstraction.

But when the alignment was right, then marvels ensued. If Azarya was discovering that the nth difference of x^n is $n!$ at six years old, then what would he be doing at sixteen, at twenty-six? The Rebbe himself had put it well. "There are children who are born as if knowing."

She wondered how much the child understood of what he'd drawn here. Had he discovered his theorem by playing with the numbers and noticing a pattern emerging, which would be astounding enough, especially since it would have required his discovering on his own the idea of raising numbers to a power—which he'd already spoken to them about—as well as factorials? Or had the child, even more astoundingly, discovered these patterns by seeing why they *had* to form? Did he see the reason for these patterns? Roz sure didn't. To her it just seemed uncanny, though not nearly as uncanny as a six-year-old's discovering it.

She looked over at Cass. He had put in a lot of driving miles, and under pressure, too, with that tyrannical buffoon breathing down his neck all day, oblivious to everything except his own obsessions—certainly oblivious to how emotionally complicated this trip back to New Walden must have been for Cass.

She gently swept the silky hair off of his high forehead, and the gesture of tenderness made her feel tender. Now she knew where that auburn hair came from. Redheadedness ran rampant in New Walden.

She shouldn't wake him. She herself would have snarled like a trodden cat if she was woken in the middle of the night because somebody with something to tell her couldn't control himself until the morning. But she couldn't control herself.

"Wake up, you crazy Valdener Hasid," she whispered in his ear. "Let me tell you about your next Rebbe."

XIV

The Argument from Inconsolable Solitude

Something jolts Cass into wakefulness at 2 a.m., and he can't get himself back to sleep. He had conked out early, falling into a deep and dreamless sleep, but now he's fully awake, groping around for provocations for feeling guilty, because that's the normal behavior when you wake up in the middle of the night. You wake, you feel guilty, you search for reasons to justify your guilt. Anyway, that's normal behavior for Cass.

It could be Shimmy Baumzer. Shimmy had served the salmon over guilt. The president had exacted a promise from him to think about "what sort of goodies you might like to see in a retention package.

"For example, I notice that you don't own your own house but rent a place in Cambridge. I could call up the Comptroller's Office right now, my friend," and he gestured with his elegant hand toward the phone, "and have them cut you a check that would cover the down payment for a house in Weedham. Maybe even in Cambridge. Another idea for you to kick over is whether you'd like to have your own Center for the Psychology of Religion, with a discretionary fund at your disposal. I can be creative, Cass. Just promise me you'll give it some thought."

Could it be around Lucinda that his unease is congealing? Yes, definitely. He's been holding back on her, not sharing the news about his offer from Harvard, and that's a troubling thought in the middle of the night.

His conversation with her tonight had been brief. She had been anxious to go through her PowerPoint one more time before getting her seven and a half hours of sleep. Rishi Chandrakar, the unworthy keynote speaker, had been mentioned again.

This isn't easy for her. She's such a proud person, in the best sense of the word. She had lifted up her transformed face to Cass in the twilight as he held the door of Katzenbaum open for her, and she had laid bare her vulnerability. She had been so terribly betrayed, both by the despicable David Prentiss Cuthbert, chairman of Princeton's Psychology Department, and by the system, and she's still bruised and uncertain, though nobody but he knows. Mona, for example, for whom his affection has cooled, hasn't a clue. Mona is very hard on Lucinda. Lucinda is right that she provokes irrational responses from envious people. It's obviously ludicrous to complain of being both brilliant and beautiful, and of course Lucinda isn't complaining, even when she sounds as if she is, but, still, she's been hurt by the people she calls griefers. His darling girl! He wishes he could be more helpful, but she's so beyond him. What can he say that will give her what she needs? He keeps trying.

"The first time I gave a talk at one of Pappa's conferences, he told me that if it had been any better he would have had to shoot me," she had told him tonight on the phone, sounding both proud and sad at the same time.

"Well, then, please don't make it any better this time," he'd responded, which at least had made her laugh.

The textbooks for his self-tutorial in game theory are piled up on his night table, and he decides to use his sleeplessness to make some more progress toward understanding the Mandelbaum Equilibrium. The farther he gets in the textbooks, the more he's been enjoying his foray into her science, finding himself increasingly resorting to its form of reasoning in order to clarify things for himself. The first thing to figure out always is whether a situation is a zero-sum game or not. Sum games are the ones where what's up for grabs—say, some pot of money—stays constant, and zero-sum games are the kind in which one person's gain is another person's loss: the addition of all the players' winnings add up to zero. You win, I lose; I win, you lose.

All sorts of situations can be analyzed as games, whether zero-sum or not. Take love, for example. Let's say you've got two people in a romantic relationship and neither has said "I love you."

Let's call them X and Y.

No, let's call them Cass and Lucinda.

What are the risks and what are the possible benefits of one of them saying "I love you" first?

Cass grabs a pen from Lucinda's night table, and, using the inside of the cover of one of the texts as his sketch pad, he draws himself some boxes:

	Lucinda: "I love you"	Lucinda: Silence
Cass: "I love you"		
Cass: Silence		

If Cass were to say "I love you" and Lucinda responded "I love you," which is what the top box on the left represents, then there would be a huge payoff. For Cass there would be bliss, and, presumably, for Lucinda there would be bliss as well, so the result would be bliss times two.

	Lucinda: "I love you"	Lucinda: Silence
Cass: "I love you"	Bliss × 2	
Cass: Silence		

But what if Cass said "I love you" and Lucinda didn't reciprocate? That would probably result in some degree of discomfort for Lucinda, and a huge loss for Cass, especially if Lucinda was discomfited enough to decide to move out: they had both agreed that the arrangement was experimental.

	Lucinda: "I love you"	Lucinda: Silence
Cass: "I love you"	Bliss × 2	Lucinda: Discomfort Cass: Hell
Cass: Silence		

Cass supposes he has, for the sake of thoroughness, to fill in the box in which the situation is reversed, the lower box on the left, with Lucinda confessing her love and Cass keeping silent, even though he knows that this square exists only in the realm of the purely theoretical. Still, they call it game *theory*, don't they? Better call them X and Y.

	Y ~~Lucinda~~: "I love you"	Y ~~Lucinda~~: Silence
X ~~Cass~~: "I love you"	Bliss X 2	Y ~~Lucinda~~: Discomfort X ~~Cass~~: Hell
X ~~Cass~~: Silence	Y: Hell X: Discomfort	

The last box is the one in which neither of them said "I love you." That is the status quo.

	Y ~~Lucinda~~: "I love you"	Y ~~Lucinda~~: Silence
X ~~Cass~~: "I love you"	Bliss X 2	Y ~~Lucinda~~: Discomfort X ~~Cass~~: Hell
X ~~Cass~~: Silence	Y: Hell X: Discomfort	Status quo; neither great loss nor great gain for either

So now how is Cass supposed to figure out from these boxes the rational thing to do?

If he says, "I love you," then, considering the situation only from his own point of view, there is possible bliss but also possible hell, which, he supposes, cancel each other out. If he doesn't say "I love you," there is neither bliss nor hell to be gained. He will maintain the present situation, which is certainly a positive one for him—not as positive as bliss, of course, but definitely positive. It seems as if it is rational to keep silent—so rational, in fact, that he wonders why anyone would ever risk saying "I love you" first, which is a bit of a paradox.

Perhaps the lesson to be learned is that it isn't always sensible to be rational.

Or perhaps the Bliss × 2 that can possibly result if a lover speaks out his love is so hugely positive that it blows all the other boxes out of the water. Could that explain why anyone dares to say "I love you" first?

And here's another thought: If he shows Lucinda his little grid, it would be a way of indirectly saying "I love you" without taking the risk of saying the actual words. If Lucinda wants to accept his reasoning as a way of saying "I love you" and reciprocate, then they will keep the huge payoff of the first box on the left: Bliss × 2. But if she doesn't want to reciprocate, then he won't have blurted out an indiscretion that can't be taken back. They can keep up their present relationship, maintaining the imperfect-but-preferable-to-nothing status quo. So, by indirectly saying "I love you," Cass, or X, can possibly get the biggest payoff without risking the biggest payout.

Cass extends his grid to test out his calculations:

	Y ~~Lucinda~~: "I love you"	Y ~~Lucinda~~: Silence
X ~~Cass~~: "I love you"	Bliss × 2	Y ~~Lucinda~~: Discomfort X ~~Cass~~: Hell
X ~~Cass~~: Silence	Y: Hell X: Discomfort	Status quo; neither great loss nor great gain for either
X: shows grid	Bliss × 2	Status quo: neither great loss nor great gain for either

It is cogent. It is elegant. He has to admit he thinks it pretty damn near brilliant.

The Seltzer Equilibrium, he decides. Now he has an equilibrium to call his own.

XV

The Argument from Sacred Circles

There was no doubt among the seven students that something new and momentous was gathering itself around Jonas Elijah Klapper. His interests were precipitously veering away from literature and into theology, and a paradox shift of untold proportions was working its way out. The intensity of the cerebration going on before their eyes was both exalting and humbling. The ovoid seminar table was like the sacred circle that used to be drawn around the inspired poet-prophet to make a safe place for his wracking genius. His sentences emerged with the profundity, sententiousness, and obscurity of Gideon's favorite poets, so that Gideon might have said that Jonas Elijah Klapper had become a crucible for poetry, only he knew, as they all knew, that something even beyond poetry was being spilled. His invocations of the thing beyond genius amazed them all, including Jonas Elijah Klapper, who sometimes sat back blinking his eyes in wonder over words he had heard himself speak.

They were scheduled to meet from four until six-thirty on Wednesdays, but time ceased to behave conventionally once the seminar was under way. One week Jonas went on for four and a half hours without a break. Then there was the week in which he had abruptly gotten up and left after barely twenty minutes had elapsed.

Nothing surprised them anymore. They felt, at times, as if they themselves were careening toward the Sublime. The Subliminal and the Self had dropped out of the picture.

The syllabus had dropped out as well, and the seven of them never knew which books they ought to have read, only that the number was formidable, even for Gideon Raven, who was struggling with the rest of them to keep up with this thunderklap-in-the-making, as well as having his own undergraduate classes to prepare, not to speak (really, Cass wished that he didn't) of the continuing problems he had in his marriage.

At the top of the list of the books on Jonas Elijah Klapper's mind was the *Zohar*, also known as *The Book of Splendor*, as well as the *Yetzirah*, also known as *The Book of Formation*, both of them fundamental texts in Kabbala, or Cabala, or Qabalah, which last was now Jonas's preferred spelling, upon which, indeed, he would need henceforth to be insistent, because it was his informed suspicion that the alternative orthographic representations preserve far more sinister distortions. "Kabbala" was the spelling preferred by "Pharisaic normative Judaism," the mainstream Judaism of conventional rabbis, about which Jonas Elijah harbored harsh reservations; "Cabala" was the spelling adopted by the Christian Cabalists, who, beginning sometime around the twelfth century, spuriously argued that Romanism had assumed full ownership of Jewish esotericism.

"The Christian spelling can most likely be traced to the influential grimoire *Opus Mago-Cabalisticum*, which was authored by the Bavarian alchemist and theosophical thinker Georg von Welling, and appeared in 1735. Both variations are distortions of the Hebrew קַבָּלָה—nota bene, the single *beth*, the letter *qoph*, not *kaph*—which orthographic distortions are not unrelated to the distortions that had been imposed on the ancient proto-Hebraic Gnosis, the Tree of Life, in which all the great religions, from Zoroastrianism to Tantric Hinduism to the New Age of the redwood-hot-tub crowd, have their roots, just as the Tree of Life itself has its roots in the grounding of all existence, which is the pure negativity of absolute unity, referred to sometimes as *LO*, the Hebrew for 'no' or 'not,' as in the *Detzniyutha, The Book of That Which Is Concealed*, which begins, and I quote: 'The Book of That Which Is Concealed is the book of the balancing in weight. Until LO existed as weight, LO existed as seeing Face-to-Face. And the Earth was nullified. And the Crowns of the Primordial Kings were found as LO. Until the Head, desired by all desires, formed and communicated the Garments of Splendor. That weight arises from the place which is LO Him. Those who exist as LO are weighed in YH. In His body exists the weight. LO unites, and LO begins. In YH have they ascended, who LO are, and are, and will be.'"

They were all scrambling to get English-translation copies of *The Book of Splendor,* and *The Book of Formations,* and *The Book of That Which Is Concealed,* since Professor Klapper had never sent his reading list to the campus bookstore. It was Gideon who went and found *The Book of Splendor* in the stacks, the only one of the books yet translated, and put it on reserve in Lipschitz so that they would all have access to it.

Another event that seemed to herald great-things-in-the-making was Professor Klapper's exchanging his office for the adjacent one of Marjorie Cutter, his secretary. Marjorie was now occupying the large and sunny corner office, with its thick carpets and sectional sofa, and Professor Klapper was squeezed into quarters that duplicated more than ever the office he had left behind at Columbia. His students half expected to look out the window and see the traffic of Amsterdam Avenue creeping below.

Zackary Kreiser had suggested that Professor Klapper's retreat to a confined space might signify his symbolic return to the womb while he was in the process of gestating some immense new idea. But Miriam Chan had shot down Zack's suggestion, since it would entail that Jonas Elijah Klapper was the gestatee rather than the gestator.

Cass had defended Zack's intuition, remembering Klapper's words to the Valdener Rebbe that the Qabalist cosmic vessels, shattered in the birthing of the world, are to be thought of as representing the womb of the Cosmic Feminine Presence. Cass had left out the story of how he had happened to hear Professor Klapper speaking on the subject of gynecologico-cosmogony, but he convinced them that the Qabalist account of the *shevirah,* the violent bursting of the vessels that brought forth the flawed world, was not irrelevant to Jonas Elijah Klapper's seeking the narrowed space of Marge's former office.

The seven had done the moving and rearranging for the professor. They had just been able to squeeze Klapper's huge desk into his new office, but there wasn't space for much more, only his own green-cushioned chair and a flimsy metal folding chair that he kept folded up near his desk but could, if he wished, set up for a visitor, which he had done when Cass came by this afternoon to discuss the next phase of his independent study on faith. They were supposed to meet every Tuesday afternoon, but the last two Tuesdays, Cass had found the door closed and his knock had drawn no response. The first week, he went to the next office over to ask

Marge whether she knew when Professor Klapper would be back.

Marge had been in the navy after high school and seemed to Cass still to have a military no-nonsense-ship about her. She could hold her own with the professors, including Jonas Elijah Klapper, who didn't scare her, even when he got grouchy. "I think it's just his blood sugar that gets low, and I keep a bunch of those butterscotch candies that he loves on my desk and just hold them out to him when he gets cranky and he calms down," she'd tell the other secretaries. But she had a soft spot for some of the students, and Cass was her favorite, as good a kid as she had ever met outside the military.

"Isn't he there?"

He shook his head. She picked up the phone and dialed the professor, letting it ring for a while.

"He might have stepped out to the gents'," she'd said. "Why don't you wait here a bit."

But it was quite a bit more than a bit, since Cass had asked her if that adorable little blonde girl with the wide grin that showed the missing tooth was her daughter, and learned that it was Krista, her daughter Kimberly's daughter, and then he was shown more photos—it was like looking at a depressing time-lapse sequence go from bright-eyed, pigtailed Krista, to slack-jawed, slatternly Kimberly, to slit-eyed, triple-chinned Marjorie—and heard how Marge had had to take them in, Krista and Kimberly and Kimberly's good-for-nothing layabout husband (Cass didn't learn his name, though he did learn his brand of beer), and build on to the back of her house so that they wouldn't be out on the street, and now she didn't know when she would be able to retire, though it was all worth it for Krista, who was the sunshine of her life. After about forty-five minutes, Cass asked whether he should try Professor Klapper's door again, since he was expected there, and Marge let him go, but not before forcing him to take a handful of butterscotch candies.

Cass hadn't checked with Marge the next week, when Professor Klapper hadn't answered Cass's knock again, but the week after that, Cass had found the office door open, the professor sitting at his desk and reading. Professor Klapper had looked up startled at Cass's knock, peering at him intently over his bifocals before telling him where he might find the chair, which Cass, after a moment of hesitation, interpreted as an invitation to sit.

"That Moses Maimonides would be highly esteemed within normative Judaism was by no means a foregone conclusion," Professor Klapper had launched in, even before Cass had finished unfolding the metal chair. "Maimonides, after all, was the rabbi who performed the mixed marriage between the Aristotelian Unmoved Mover and Yahweh. Be that as it may, Maimonides has been pronounced kosher, gathered, as it were, into the folds of the four-fringed garment. Maimonides lived in trying times—indeed, when have great men not? He was a physician who ministered to no less a personage than the Sultan Saladin, and his prescription for the Jewish soul was a large pill of Thirteen Principles that he said all Jews must swallow if they are to merit entrance in the world to come. I myself have always queried whether belief could be prescribed—take thirteen and call me in the morning—but, then, I am by nature querulous.

"The twelfth principle concerns the Messiah, in whose coming we are adjured to believe: 'He who doubts or diminishes the greatness of the Messiah is a denier in all the Torah.'

And yet he forbids one to think on the time when he shall come: 'You should not calculate times for him to come, or look in the verses of the scriptures to see when he should come.' And where does that leave us?"

Cass was well aware by now that these questions were not intended to be answered, but the slim possibility that this one could be the exception, and the professor was awaiting a response, was always enough to set up a raucous commotion in his chest.

"We must believe that he will come but never believe that he *is* come. There is no Messiah but an uncome Messiah. Is it not extraordinary?"

Cass nodded.

"At the heart of the cold Aristotelian rabbi's exegesis, the bloodred blossom of antinomian chiasmus. And can you not help but compare it with the observation of the poet who might have been giving voice to his Jewish ancestry when he proclaimed that the only paradise is paradise lost?"

Cass was pretty sure that Professor Klapper was talking about Proust here; but was Marcel Proust Jewish?

"But my concern here is not with Proust per se, and it is only the striking parallelism that has brought me to Proust, raised a Roman Catholic, though born of a Jewess"—ah!— "and though Marcel was as devoted a son as any Jewish mother could have desired, who, in renouncing the hell's fire of sexual passion, implied that the only authentic love is for the woman who gave one the gift of one's life, the gift of one's genius"—Klapper paused here several long moments, his trembling eye focused on the silver-framed picture on his desk—"yet, though he was a model Jewish son, he was *not* a self-identifying Jew and was unfamiliar with any of the canonical Jewish texts, though of course one cannot be certain, the presence of knowledge being easier to ascertain than its absence. And yet who would deny that Proust's pronouncement is a temporal transposition of the Maimonidean position that the only Messiah is an uncome Messiah?"

Klapper settled an inquisitorial stare upon Cass, and this time he really seemed to be wanting an answer, and what could be offered in answer to his last question other than "Nobody?"

"Reb Chaim!" Professor Klapper cried out, and Cass's heart heaved so hard his shirt collar might have perceptibly moved.

"It all reminds me of a Hasidic tale, in the tradition of wisdom storytelling which you, Reb Chaim, with your exalted lineage, will be able to appreciate on multitudinous strata. An innkeeper and his wife are awakened in the middle of the night by the heartrending sobs of one of the guests. He goes to investigate, entering the room of sobbing and finding there a simple Jew, barefoot and dressed like a peasant, sitting on the cold wooden floor and weeping. There is nothing about him to betray the fact that he is a renowned Hasidic master, traveling incognito in order to see the state of the world. Each night at midnight, he climbs out of bed and mourns the destruction of the Holy Temple and the scattered nation of Israel. 'Why the tumult, my good man?' inquires the distressed innkeeper. 'What calamity has befallen you?' 'I cry over our Diaspora and the suffering it has wrought, and I beseech the Almighty to send the Messiah, who will restore the kingdom and return us to the Holy Land.'"

Klapper rocked his upper body back and forth as he spoke the master's words, impersonating the motions of Orthodox

Jews in prayer, and the thick layer of posh that usually over-
laid his pronunciation was temporarily removed, leaving bare
the cadence of the Tillie E. Orlofsky projects on East Broadway, itself an echo of the singsong cadence of Eastern Europe.

"The innkeeper is relieved. 'Is that it? You'd had me worried! I thought maybe my wife's beet borscht had, God forbid,
been off. Just try to keep your holy wailing down so that you
don't disturb the other guests.' The good man goes back to his
bedroom and explains the situation to his wife. Five minutes
later, he's back at the master's door. 'My wife sent me to ask
you whether, when the Messiah comes and restores us to the
kingdom of Israel, we will be allowed to take our chickens
with us.' The master is taken aback by the question. 'Chickens? As far as I'm aware, it doesn't say anything about chickens. You might have to leave your chickens here when the
Messiah comes.' 'I'll tell my wife.' Five minutes later, there's
another knock on the door. 'My wife requests that you please
not pray anymore for the Messiah to come. We are doing fine
here and would prefer to stay with our chickens.' The master
is confounded by this reaction. 'What do you mean, you are
doing fine? Don't you know how precarious our exile is? At
any moment the Cossacks could arrive and take your chickens, your wife, all your money, and even your life! Are we not
better off in our Promised Land?' The Rebbe's words make
sense to the innkeeper, but he still has to inform his wife. Five
minutes later, another knock. 'My wife requests that you pray
for the Messiah to come and take the Cossacks to the Land of
Israel—so we can stay here with our chickens.'"

Klapper's face was completely deadpan as he finished the
tale, and Cass, who was certain the story was supposed to be
as funny as he found it, was uncertain whether Jonas Elijah

Klapper agreed. The uncertainty choked the laughter somewhere around his epiglottis, but not before a smile briefly
fanned out.

"You smile, Reb Chaim. And, indeed, there is a comical
element, brought to bear by the risibility of the word 'chickens.' Retell the tale with the substitution of 'cattle' for 'chickens' and the humor will substantially diminish. The wife's
poultry-centric worldview signifies the untenability of the
Maimonidean position. The presence of 'chickens' is a
shrewd evocation of the absurd, similar in ploy to the koans of
Zen Buddhism, which, I presume, make you smile as well."

Cass nodded.

"The absurd is here employed as a means to incite the Messianic exigency, kept alive in Judaism only by the subversive
counter-modality of Hasidism, against the establishment
effort to contain the destabilizing energies of Messianism. I
here but follow the explication of the pre-eminent secular
authority on Qabalah, Yehuda Ickel, who maintains that
the Qabalist embrace of the insurrectionist ideal of the non-
tarrying Messiah was the deepest point of conflict with the
mainstream rabbis, who would have us believe wholeheartedly
in a Messiah so long as he is not here! The true Hasid believes
that if his own Rebbe is not the Messiah—or Moshiach, as he
is called in Hebrew, and which literally means 'the anointed
one'—then maybe his brother-in-law's Rebbe is Moshiach."

Again, there was that inquisitorial stare, demanding at the
very least a question.

"So Hasidim all believe their own Rebbe is the Messiah?"

"The point I am making, Reb Chaim, is that for the Hasid
the Messiah will not present a rupturing of history, with the
ordinary giving way before the extraordinary. For the Hasid,
the ordinary is already brimming with the extraordinary, or, to

put it in plainer terms, the extraordinary is immanent within the ordinary as the ordinary is immanent within the extraordinary, and the role of the Messiah, who is a man both more ordinary and more extraordinary than all others, is to reveal the divine depths of the extraordinary-cum-ordinary. As shall become, I trust, manifest to you on our next voyage to New Walden—which, I am sure you concur, ought to occur on the holy Sabbath day, so that we can experience the Valdener Hasidim in their full glory, from sundown to sundown. I leave the practical arrangements to you. I request only that this time the Rastafarian not accompany us."

XVI

The Argument from the Longing on the Gate

```
to: GR613@gmail.com
from: Seltzer@psych.Frankfurter.edu
date: Feb. 28 2008 5:15 a.m.
subject:

Are you awake?


to: Seltzer@psych.Frankfurter.edu
from: GR613@gmail.com
date: Feb. 28 2008 5:16 a.m.
subject: re:

Yes.


to: GR613@gmail.com
from: Seltzer@psych.Frankfurter.edu
date: Feb. 28 2008 5:18 a.m.
subject: re: re:

Are you worried about the child?
```

```
to: Seltzer@psych.Frankfurter.edu
from: GR613@gmail.com
date: Feb. 28 2008 5:21 a.m.
subject: re: re: re:
```

It's hard not to worry.


```
to: GR613@gmail.com
from: Seltzer@psych.Frankfurter.edu
date: Feb. 28 2008 5:25 a.m.
subject: re: re: re: re:
```

I dream of having such worries.


```
to: Seltzer@psych.Frankfurter.edu
from: GR613@gmail.com
date: Feb. 28 2008 5:28 a.m.
subject: re: re: re: re: re:
```

You're right to dream of such worries. And
to worry about such dreams.

XVII

The Argument from Strange Laughter

Since Roz was in the Amazon for several weeks with Absalom Garibaldi, Professor Klapper's request that she not come along with them on this second trip to New Walden was easily met.

Professor Klapper had instructed Cass to pick him up at his house at noon, sharp. Cass had been so nervous about getting lost or hitting traffic or encountering any contingency that might make him late that he had gotten to the house on Berkeley Place at eleven-twenty and parked the car in front, happy to lean back and wait out the forty minutes in the rented Lincoln Continental. Cass had made certain to reserve the same car, since Professor Klapper had remarked on its roominess and solid feel, once Roz had been safely restrained in the back. The sidewalk leading to the front porch was poetic with daffodils. Could Jonas Elijah Klapper himself have had them planted, in homage, perhaps, to Wordsworth's jocund company? But then one of Klapper's students would have been made to ply the spade. They were always called upon to take over the tasks the professor knew better than to request of the naval verteran, Marjorie Cutter. The daffodils must have come with the house.

He hadn't been there for more than five minutes before the front door opened and a towering figure stepped forth, and all the world went reeling, the thirty-odd areas of the primate brain devoted to interpreting visual input—especially the circuits that neuroscientists call the "What" system —struggling to apprehend what it was that Cass was seeing, and while they were struggling, Cass heard background laughter that was infuriatingly familiar, though he couldn't quite identify it— no, wait a minute, that was Roz's laughter that his overworking brain was imagining as the reaction to what it still couldn't assemble into an image that could cohere with the web of his beliefs, starting with his belief that he wasn't given to visual hallucinations in the brightness of nearly noon on a perfect spring day, the crowd of daffodils nodding on a street in Cambridge, Massachusetts, that looked so unmistakably like a street in Cambridge, Massachusetts, except for the phantasm manifesting itself in gleaming black leather boots into which the bottoms of its pants were tucked, which was enfolded into a capacious iridescent black satin caftan, which was ornamented with a jet-black velvet strip of paisleys and curlicues, tied with a wide and long satin sash encircling it right under its belly, and a snow-white dress shirt, buttoned to the top, emerging above the collar of the caftan to choke the monumental neck that supported a head swathed in a halo of the dimensions of those golden auras that encircle Jesus and the saints in Quattrocento paintings, only this nimbus was made of dead animals and was lodged more firmly and lower down on the pate of the author of twenty-eight books and the object of literary reverence the world over with the exception of Great Britain.

Jonas Elijah Klapper was locking his front door, and the crashing surf of Roz's laughter was swelling, so that Cass thought he should look away as Professor Klapper got himself down the stairs awkwardly—the boots hadn't been broken in—but found that he could not, for all its risks, avert his gaze. He half expected the hat to disintegrate as Klapper approached, for the mad mirage to yield to what was actually there.

Klapper placed the small suitcase he was carrying down on the sidewalk and stood beside the passenger door, his hands dangling helplessly at his sides, and the homunculus in Cass's head broke off her laughter briefly enough to demand, "Why the hell doesn't he open the door?"—which was enough of a cue to make Cass jump to action, leaping out of the car to scurry around and open the door for Jonas Elijah Klapper and place the bag on the backseat, taking care to keep his eyes away from the professor's face, lest he see that the solemn expression he expected was there. But he did take a quick, furtive glance from close range, just to dispel any lingering doubts that his brain had been playing tricks on him, as when he was a child, lying on his bunk bed under Jesse, and the bathrobe hanging on the door had become an intruder approaching the bed, and Cass had known to pretend to be asleep but was terrified that his little brother would wake up and start screaming and get them both killed.

There was no delusion now. The *shtreimel* was the shape of a layer cake, large enough to feed a Hasidic family. Klapper had it pushed down on his high forehead so that it rested above his turbulent eyebrows and ascended to at least six inches above his head, making a man of five foot nine tower over a man of six foot two.

Cass got back in the car and buckled himself in. Klapper was having trouble with his seat belt, but Cass didn't trust himself yet to lean over and help, so he sat quietly, staring down at his hands, and waited. Finally, he heard the click of success and turned on the ignition, carefully pulling away from the curb, trying to concentrate on his breathing like a woman in labor—no, like a Zen practitioner. He'd had a girl-friend in college, Felicia Lebowitz, who had been a yoga prac-titioner, and she used to say, when she was teaching him how to meditate, "If a thought comes to you, observe it and let it go," or "Instead of thinking the thought, just let it be thought," which he thought sounded pretty close to what was usually going on in his head, and it certainly had never led to any nirvana, and in all likelihood it wasn't going to help him now.

He maneuvered through the traffic of Harvard Square, and there was silence in the car, but it was a thin silence, which couldn't be trusted, and Cass realized that the thoughts in his head, the ones he was letting be thought without thinking them, came from a song he'd learned in first grade that was sung to a waltz with a Viennese lilt, the kind they play on the organ at ice-skating rinks—he and Jesse often went on Satur-day mornings, and Jesse had been on a local hockey team until there had been an incident and he was asked to leave—and whose words were:

Ice-skating is nice skating
But here's some advice about ice-skating
Never skate where the ice is thin
Or else it might break and you'll fall right in
And come up with icicles under your chin
If you skate where the ice is thin!

They were across the Larz Anderson Bridge now, heading for the Massachusetts Turnpike, and Cass was finding that his meditative techniques had not improved since the days of Felicia, and Roz's laughter was still dangerously coiling in the dark water beneath the thin ice, and he decided to visualize the cover that *Time* magazine had had a few months before, emblazoned with the word "FAMINE" and asking the question "Why are Ethiopians starving again?" with the picture of a mother staring down with eloquent sorrow at the dying child on her lap, his head bulbous compared with the shrunken body, the match-thin arms prematurely wrinkled, and his eyes filled with the precocious knowledge of his own doom. It was surely immoral to use an image of others' tragedy to counteract the painful urge to laugh, but he was a poor meditator and a desperate man.

Somewhere around the Natick/Framingham exit, Jonas Elijah Klapper broke the silence.

"You are probably wondering how I procured these garments."

Cass nodded, not glancing over, knowing that Klapper would understand and heartily approve his taking his driving so seriously.

"I had Ms. Cutter arrange for a car service to pick me up and drive me to Williamsburg, Brooklyn, to a store that specializes in Hasidic vestments. I was able to purchase the *kaputa*"—Klapper indicated his caftan with a flourish of his hands—"and the *shtreimel*"—he gestured upward to his fur piece—"at one place. I had to go to another establishment for the boots."

Cass nodded his head again, his eyes fixed on the road. He had questions, but he wasn't sure he could trust himself to ask them. For example, was it Marjorie Cutter who had located a store selling fur hats shaped like giant hockey pucks? Did they have his size of *kaputa* in stock, or did they need to special-order? Had the money for the car service to and from Williamsburg come out of the discretionary funds that Frankfurter had conferred on Jonas Elijah Klapper? And what species of dead animal was it that was perched on Professor Klapper's head?

The professor removed the *shtreimel*, laying it carefully on his lap.

"It is toasty warm. I could have used such a defense against the elements back in frore February."

Cass had a bad moment as the image came unbidden to him of Jonas Elijah Klapper clambering over the snowdrifts of Plotnik Quad dressed like a Valdener.

"Please be so good as to pull over at the earliest convenience."

The Charlton Full Service Rest Stop was coming up, and Cass pulled off the turnpike and into the parking lot and turned off the ignition.

"In the zippered pocket at the side of my satchel you will find a large blue plastic bag. Please take it out and place this within it, and then carefully deposit it on the backseat. I know I needn't tell you, Reb Chaim, that this *shtreimel*, which is Russian sable and made out of thirteen tails, represents an expenditure in the thousands."

There was an answer to two of Cass's questions, and to one that he hadn't thought to ask.

"As long as we have stopped," said Professor Klapper, when Cass got back behind the steering wheel, "I would like to use the facilities. I don't know why they have chosen to make it such a trek to get from the parking lot to the rest stop. Please drive up to the building and wait for me in front."

A young woman who was heading inside held the door open for the sad-eyed fat man in the splendid black robe and boots. Even though he waddled, you could see he had a great deal of dignity, and she thought he must be a religious dignitary, maybe a Greek Orthodox priest or a Wiccan. He passed through without acknowledgment.

As soon as Jonas Elijah Klapper disappeared into the building, Cass let the laughter that had been pushing up through his trachea come gushing out, gaining a new understanding of the cliché "to laugh so hard it hurts."

When Roz's laughter had finally expended itself, he found that he urgently needed to use the facilities himself, but he was nervous about leaving the car. It would be a disaster if Professor Klapper came out and the Lincoln Continental was nowhere in sight. Could Cass leave it illegally parked here and just dash in? But he'd have to leave it unlocked so that Klapper could climb in and wait, and he'd just been informed that the thirteen tails of Russian sable curled up in the blue plastic bag on the backseat represented an expenditure in the thousands. He compromised and left the locked car parked right in front, so Professor Klapper would see it when he got out.

By the time the professor exited, carrying a cone with a double twist of vanilla and chocolate ice cream—there was a Baskin-Robbins in the plaza—Cass was sitting in the car, fully composed. He popped out and held the cone for Professor Klapper while he settled himself into the car, struggled with the buckle, and then reached out his hand for the ice cream. He tiled several paper napkins across the expanse of his lap and tucked one into the collar of his *kaputa* and proceeded to lick.

They spoke little on the way. Cass had gone from resisting the awful attack of laughter—a sort of Zen laughter demanding to be laughed even if Cass didn't want to laugh it—to being overcome by a despondency that was like feeling sick before any of the symptoms had appeared.

He thought a lot about Gideon. He thought about that first night at The View from Nowhere, when Gideon had told him to go back to pre-med. How would Gideon react if he were to see Jonas Elijah Klapper now? Would it matter as little to him as the remarks of a random philosophy student in The View from Nowhere? "*Wovon man nicht* knows the first fucking thing, *darüber muss man schweigen?*" That was pretty powerful stuff, and it hadn't shaken Gideon in the least. Gideon was brilliant, and he had seen fit to study with Jonas Elijah Klapper for the past twelve and a half years, and he was as convinced as the rest of them that Klapper was on the verge of a breakthrough of epochal proportions. Who was Cass to challenge that view? Was he so influenced by the sight of Klapper looking ridiculous—but why more ridiculous than the Valdeners themselves? why more ridiculous than the Rebbe?—that he was ready to throw up his hands and agree with Roz?

That had been Roz's laughter, not his own. He loved Roz, but that didn't mean he had to adopt her cynical view of Professor Jonas Elijah Klapper. Gideon and the rest of the seminar would only have been awed by Jonas's capacity for throwing himself so completely into another Weltanschauung, appropriating it so that he could understand it as those within could not hope to, reading it as he read the great poets, so that they yielded their innards to him far more torrentially than the poets themselves could have experienced, so that he might crisscross all the vast reaches of human conception and see its arteries coursing with the ichor of psychopoiesis.

And if he'd charged the car service and the leather boots

and *kaputa* and Russian sable *shtreimel* to his discretionary funds, so what? This was research as legitimate as any, a measure of the creative limits to which a master like Jonas Elijah Klapper would travel, as daring an experimenter as any particle physicist with an accelerator—no, more daring, because it was his own soul that he offered up in the spirit of empiricism.

Jonas Elijah Klapper was like William James, who had experimented with nitrous oxide in order to determine whether it could induce something like mystical experiences. It could, he found. He wrote about it in *The Varieties of Religious Experience*. Cass pictured William James, sitting in his worsted-wool vest behind a closed door in his office in Emerson Hall and stoned out of his gourd, a high-pitched giggle emerging from the spread of his long Victorian beard, as he tried to write down the metaphysics floodlighting his mind: "What's a mistake but a kind of take? What's nausea but a kind of -ausea? Sober, drunk, -unk, astonishment . . . Agreement—disagreement!! Emotion—motion!!! . . . Reconciliation of opposites; sober, drunk, all the same! Good and evil reconciled in a laugh! It escapes, it escapes! But— What escapes, WHAT escapes?"

You'd be laughing at William James, too, he chided himself, but William James would never have laughed at Jonas Elijah Klapper. The thought helped to sober Cass more effectively than picturing starving Ethiopian children, but it was a good thing that Professor Klapper, absorbed by the passing scenery, was disinclined to speak. The professor loved being driven in large fancy automobiles. Zackary Kreiser, who chauffeured him back and forth between Cambridge and Weedham, owned a cramped jalopy that rattled him to the limits of endurance. Might he prevail upon the university to procure a car of this model to be used soley to convey him between his place of work and domicile?

The professor was overtaken by a brief spasm of loquacity when he saw the forest-green sign announcing that they were on the Merritt Parkway, a scenic highway, he explained, landscaped with native plantings and shrubs, and the result of a Depression-era public-works project.

"To keep with the aesthetics, there were to be no intersections of local roads, in consequence of which sixty-eight bridges—no two of them alike, and with expert masonwork and ornamentation, some representative of the Art Deco movement, which was then in its heyday—were constructed to channel the local traffic aerially. I happen to remember the surname of the architect who designed all sixty-eight bridges, because it was so droll. The name was Dunkelberger.

"Imagine Dunkelberger as a man of letters, a man of the abstract instead of the concrete," said Professor Klapper. "No one would have read him! But 'designed by Dunkelberger' has never stopped a motorist from traversing a bridge."

And, succumbing to his wicked sense of humor, Jonas Elijah Klapper went into the contortions that were his laughter, and Cass, still harboring strange laughter within him, was happy to join in.

XVIII

The Argument from the Arrow of Time

Cass comes up the back stairs of his apartment, which lead directly into the kitchen. He pauses at the stove to put some water up for tea and then goes into the living room.

Last night had been his second night of sleeplessness this week, and the deprivation is taking its toll. He had stayed alert during his early-morning taping of an interview for National Public Radio's *The Cutting Edge*. The interviewer had introduced him in his famous plummy tones as "Cass Seltzer, the eminent philosopher and one of our deepest divers into the choppy waters churning between religion and science." Cass has learned to take it all in stride, even the mislabeling of him as a philosopher, which used to embarrass him, making him feel as if he had illegitimately been awarded a few extra IQ points. He had rushed from the radio studio to Frankfurter's campus, to teach his afternoon advanced seminar, "Psychology of Religion." The topic today had been the Concept of the Quest in religious contexts.

But at four in the afternoon, he had slumped. He had begged off keeping his date with Mona for a drink, pleading exhaustion, which was true but also convenient.

On and off, all day long, he's been thinking of Lucinda, wondering how her talk would go, is going, had gone. She had set the bar high. Anything less than spectacular success will be counted as failure, and Lucinda isn't made for failure, in much the same way as he hadn't been made for success, despite the strange happenings of the last year, which he has spent walking around in someone else's coat.

He hasn't turned on any of the lights, but a soft glow from the streetlamp drapes itself across various sections of the furniture and rug, a black-and-gold-and-orange adaptation of a Klimt painting that had been left behind, along with everything else, by Pascale when she took off with her plundering neurologist.

When he found this place, he couldn't wait to show it to Pascale. It occupies the two top floors of a spacious Victorian house on gracious Upland Road. It has three bedrooms, high ceilings, and ample light; the rent was surprisingly reasonable, too. But Pascale had at first balked.

"It is for us too much space."

She had scowled, her thin, dark brows drawing themselves into one elegant line of rejection. Too much space seemed an odd drawback. Perhaps what was in her mind was that her emphatic "No!" had not entirely vanquished the delusions of breeding to which Cass had several times confessed. What did her husband have in mind with all those bedrooms? But the dormered room that would be her study, with windows looking out at the park across the way, had made her relent. Sheltered in the closest corner of the park were a few playthings for children—a seesaw, a jungle gym. Perhaps she pictured herself hanging upside down there, for the vertigo and the images. Or perhaps she detected the spirits of the muses thick in the air around her. She had stood there a long time and had finally turned to Cass, her trademark red lips smiling, and said "Yes."

There's a little side yard with a blue spruce that reaches down to the ground in an invitingly cozy way. He often pictures it inhabited by little people playing hide-and-seek. "Please close the gate, remember our children." The inscription provokes a feeling akin to nostalgia, only directed at the future.

The kettle is whistling, and he gets up and makes himself some strong tea and takes it back to the couch and picks up the phone and dials Lucinda's cell and hears her voice on the recorded message and leaves one for her:

"It's me. I've been thinking about you all day, wondering how your talk went. Call me when you can. I love you."

Before he's even replaced the receiver, he's gagging on regret. What had he done? What had possessed him? He's circling the living room in a blurry haze, and he's bashing his forehead with his open palm to the down-down-down beat of his idiocy.

It was hearing her voice on the recorded message—her formal voice that held a tinge from the year she'd spent at Oxford. "Lucinda Mandelbaum here. Leave your coordinates, and I shall return your call." Those tones in his ear had sent that bolt of longing through him. It had bypassed his own will and ended up in his larynx, and, without any intent to do so, he was blathering out those three explosive words. *Cass here*—that elusive metaphysical substance he had been trying to chase down ever since he was a kid—was collateral damage.

So much for his late-night cuddles with textbooks on game theory. So much for his grids. So much for his dreams of the Seltzer Equilibrium.

He considers calling her back, leaving a message to cancel out the other. He could pretend to be drunk, so that she'd conclude that he had been drunk when he called the first time and couldn't be held responsible. Better yet, since he's not much of an actor, he can get himself drunk.

Stop thinking like one of your undergraduates, he tells himself out loud. (He's talking to himself out loud.)

He has a vivid sense that if only he concentrates forcefully enough he can rewind the tape of his disaster. What happened isn't irreversible, it can't be, Lucinda hasn't even heard it yet, and also it's three hours earlier in Santa Barbara, which he knows is irrelevant, but, still, there must be some way to undo that swerve of recklessness that had momentarily knocked him off course, flip that arrow of time back, but, no (he is still circling the room), no force of exertion is going to return him to that moment before this disaster happened so that he can make it not happen, the irrevocable past, so close and yet so closed, it's fleeing his grasp, hurtling, hurtling, and then the phone rings.

"Hello."

"Hi, Cass. It's me."

"Lucinda!"

"You sound surprised." She sounds amused.

"No, I'm not surprised. In fact, I just called you." She must not have listened to the message, and what reason will she have to listen to it now, after all, when she's already speaking to him, making that past message obsolete, she'll just delete it, and it will be as if it had never been, and all shall be well, and all shall be well, and all manner of things shall be well.

"Yes, I know. I got your message. So, anyway, my talk went very well. The Q & A was certainly the liveliest of the conference so far."

So she'd heard his message. She must have heard him say, "I love you."

"So you're happy with the way it all went?"

They were having a conversation as if nothing had changed. Maybe she hadn't heard the message through to the end? Or maybe she just hadn't noticed?

"Yes, I suppose. I can't really judge yet. Rishi is speaking later tonight."

Can it be that he's landed in neither bliss nor hell? Can it be that his midnight grids are all wrong?

"Yes, I know."

She's acting as if he had never uttered the words, and his autonomic nervous system is returning to baseline, and he decides to continue the conversation as if nothing has changed, because quite possibly nothing has.

"Well, that's the thing, you see. I'll only know how well I did when I know whether I did better than Rishi."

Or maybe she's signaling something more?

"I'm not sure that makes sense, Lucinda. Intellectual achievement isn't a zero-sum game."

"Listen, Cass, you may be the expert on my soul, but I'm the expert on zero-sum games."

Her voice is smiling.

"And this is a zero-sum game?"

"It is, Cass. Most of what matters in life is a zero-sum game."

He laughs at her joke, and they hang up soon after, Lucinda

rushing off to dinner, which will be followed by Rishi's backward-causative talk.

It's only later, after they hung up, that it occurs to him to wonder whether her zero-sum comment had been a joke. She hadn't laughed, and Lucinda always laughs at her own jokes.

XIX

The Argument from the Overheard Whispers of Angels

They had bad Friday-afternoon traffic almost the entire way, and though Klapper was serenely oblivious, Cass was acutely aware of the sinking of the sun as they approached the witching hour of 6:44, when, as Cass had been informed by Cousin Henoch, the Sabbath would begin and travel was prohibited. They had made far too many stops, sometimes for scenic purposes but more often to sample the "facilities and comestibles." The Merritt Parkway's rest stops were deemed by the professor to be vastly superior to those of the Massachusetts Turnpike.

Henoch had arranged that Professor Klapper, as an honored guest, would be staying with the Rebbe, and finally they arrived at the redbrick house across the street from what Roz had dubbed the Costco House of Worship.

The door was opened by the Rebbe's little son, Azarya, the child who Roz was convinced was meant to be the future Gauss, "if we can get him away from all that kosher baloney.

"They'll have the kid calculating how many Hasidim can dance on the top of a *shtreimel*. They'll have him counting the hairs in his father's beard and multiplying it by the hairs in his side curls to figure out the date of the Messiah's arrival. It's a goddamn tragedy. I'd kidnap the kid if I thought I could get away with it, and if I knew what the hell to do with a kid."

"Why would you kidnap a child from a loving family?"

"Because that loving family are a bunch of zealots."

"Zealots aren't allowed to have children? That sounds pretty zealous."

"I guess I wouldn't outlaw zealots' having children, if only on practical grounds, but, frankly, I think that what they do to kids is immoral. It's immoral to indoctrinate children so that they never develop the tools to think for themselves. It's our birthright to think about things for ourselves."

Cass laughed.

"What?"

"You sound like my mother."

"Well, your mother is right. She knew what she was doing when she got the hell out. I'd have thought twice about sleeping with you if you had those side curls. What do they call them again?"

"*Payess*. I think my mother's rebellion had more to do with her hating her own mother so much."

"On the contrary, I think that her hating her mother gave her the emotional distance to be objective and to judge the beliefs she was raised on with an open mind and conclude that they're full of shit."

"You've got to meet her. You and my mother are going to love each other."

"I'd love to meet your mother. I'd love to team up with her about Azarya. Did you tell her about him? She might be our only chance to save him from the forces of benightedness."

"I don't know why you're being so hard on this struggling

sect that only wants to be left alone. There surely have been lots of gifted children born to families who weren't in a position to appreciate their talents."

"And that's a tragedy! Wouldn't it be tragic if Gauss's father had had his way and his genius son had never been educated?"

"Would it? I don't know. Not if it didn't make anyone unhappy. Not if Gauss himself didn't realize what he could have been."

"Oh yeah, Gauss a happy bricklayer, or whatever his dumbass father had wanted for him."

"It's a different situation." There were times when Cass regretted sharing what he had learned from *Men in Mathematics* with Roz. "Gauss would have known what he was missing. He'd had enough schooling for that. Azarya belongs to a community that's completely insular."

"So what you're saying is that the best thing we can do for that child is to ensure that his ignorance is never threatened! Do you hear what you're saying?"

"Azarya belongs to a group that reveres knowledge. Okay, so maybe he won't be a professor of mathematics, but he'll be a rabbinical scholar. He'll be the Rebbe someday!"

"So you'd be okay with Gauss's going into a monastery and counting the angels on the head of a pin."

"Gregor Mendel did okay for himself in a monastery."

"Because they left him alone with his pea plants! The whole *problem* is that Azarya belongs to a sect that thinks it reveres education, but their idea of education has nothing to do with real knowledge! The kid doesn't even know how to read English."

"He's only six, for crying out loud."

"But you know that they're never going to teach him. They

wouldn't know how to begin to teach him what he needs to learn. You heard his dad. 'For him they're toys, and we let him play.' I swear I'd kidnap him if I could."

"Roz, cut it out. It's upsetting."

"Why?"

"Your values are skewed. You'd take him away from a family that loves him and that he loves. The child would be miserable. Do you think genius is the only thing that matters?"

"Oh, for chrissakes, Cass. I'm not saying I'd really kidnap him. I'm making a point. But just as an aside, I don't think he'd be miserable if I did kidnap him. Instead of giving him candy and ice cream, like other kidnappers, I'd ply him with theorems and proofs. I'd hire MIT professors who'd make him so delirious on equations that he'd forget all about New Walden."

"Enough."

"No, not enough, because I haven't yet responded to your gross hypocrisy. You're criticizing me for placing too much emphasis on genius, when that's what you Klapperites are totally obsessed with!"

"That's entirely different."

"Oh yeah? You want to explain how? Other than the major difference that Azarya Sheiner really is a prodigy."

"Before you get in touch with my mother to hold the ladder while you abscond with Azarya in a pillowcase, you might just try speaking to his family. Tell them what you think. Tell them about Gauss. Maybe they'll see to it that he develops his talents."

"Oh, of course. Right after my appointment with the pope, when I explain to him why celibacy is such a disaster. And in case you didn't notice, I'm a woman, and in that community women don't exactly have clout. Tell them about Gauss!

They'll say, sure, wasting your life on mathematics is okay for some German goy, but not for the future Valdener Rebbe. Why don't you try to speak to the family? Or, better yet, get the Klap to do it."

"Doubtful."

"Yeah, you're right there. That child is an affront to his monumental ego."

Azarya was standing there, shyly smiling up at Jonas Elijah Klapper, who craned his neck around, looking to see who was there to welcome him.

"I remember your question," Azarya said to him now.

"What?" Jonas stared down past the obstruction of his own *kaputa*-upholstered stomach at the child looking up at him.

"I remember your question."

"To which question are you referring, little boy?"

"How many there are. The prime angels. How long does this go on? I remember your question."

Jonas Elijah Klapper stared down at the child a little longer, as if trying to figure out what language he was speaking. He turned to Cass.

"I wonder why nobody is here to greet me. I need to take care of a few things in the short time left until *licht benching*."

Klapper had used the Yiddish expression for the lighting of the Shabbes candles, the same expression as Cass's bubbe had used.

"Come, please, Rav Klapper," Azarya said, beckoning with his tiny finger for the professor to follow.

Klapper shrugged and marched up the stairs after the child. Cass followed along, toting the small suitcase and the blue plastic bag with the thirteen-tailed *shtreimel*.

Azarya led them down the narrow hallway to a bedroom, and Jonas Elijah Klapper entered and indicated for Cass to put his things on the bed and dismissed him. Azarya walked Cass back downstairs to the tiled vestibule. He reached up to open the heavy front door for Cass; he was taking his role as host seriously. Cass smiled down at him, and the child smiled back, raising his little round chin.

"Do you remember me?" he asked in a soft voice.

"Of course I remember you! You're Azarya!"

The child's smile spread, so that not only were his wide-spaced blue eyes lit, but his pale skin, translucent in the way of fair-haired children, glowed.

"I remember also you, Mr. Seltzer. And Miss Margolis. Is she coming also for Shabbes?"

"No, I'm afraid she isn't."

"She's in Cambridge, Massachusetts?"

"No, she's far away. In another country."

"Not in the United States of America?"

"Not in the United States of America."

"In Eretz Yisroel?"

"No, not Eretz Yisroel either, but another country."

"Which?"

"Venezuela."

"Venezuela." He repeated it carefully, and then he smiled, a bit impishly. "Will you draw me a map?"

"I don't think there's time now. It's almost Shabbes. Maybe after Shabbes."

The child nodded, understanding that time was short, and stood out of the way as Cass moved toward the open door.

"I can read English now."

Cass was already halfway down the sidewalk that led to the street. He turned back. The door was half open, and Azarya was inside, peeking around the side, his head at an angle, so that his side curl fell over the shoulder of his fancy white dress shirt, similar to the one Jonas Elijah Klapper was wearing under his *kaputa*.

"That's wonderful!" So much for Roz's hysteria. She was letting her pique over the Hasidic attitude toward women color her whole view. "Who taught you?"

"From the map. I learned from the map."

Roz had told Cass how she'd felt her scalp prickling as she figured out the meaning of Azarya's crayoned drawing. Cass had resisted her effusiveness. He understood that the child was uncommonly intelligent, but he knew better than to leap to the sort of wild romanticizing that his girlfriend was indulging in. Mathematical talent often shows itself early. Probably a good fraction of top-notch math professors at places like Harvard and Princeton and MIT and Caltech had seemed, when they were small children, like geniuses to their classmates and teachers, not to speak of their families. Not all of them—in fact *none* of them—had grown up to be a Gauss. The overwhelming odds were that Azarya fell into this category. He'd take the SATs when he was in sixth grade, which is how the Center for Talented Youth at Johns Hopkins tests for entrance into its summer program, and he'd score high enough to take the special classes designed for kids like him. Or, in any case, that's the kind of thing that would happen if he weren't a Valdener. Azarya might be at the extreme tail of the bell curve, but there were enough like him to make a program like CTY worthwhile.

Roz, pressing her case, had given Cass a short story by Aldous Huxley called "The Young Archimedes." An Englishman, who has rented a villa in the Italian countryside, discovers that a sweet-natured peasant boy, Guido, is an untutored mathematical genius. The Englishman, kind and cultured, alone understands the prodigious nature of Guido, but has to go away. The venal woman who owns the land the peasants work has seen the Englishman's interest in the boy and takes him away from his family, thinking she can make a performing musician out of him—Guido is musical as well—and become rich off his talents. The boy, missing his Euclid and his family, ends up leaping to his death. The conclusion has the Englishman walking back from the cemetery in Florence, where the child has been buried, the grief-stricken father beside him. They pause on a hill to look down at the inspired city laid out in the valley below. "I thought of all the Men who had lived here and left the visible traces of their spirit and conceived extraordinary things. I thought of the dead child."

The story was beautiful, but he still wasn't going to accept that Roz had proved anything by presenting him with Aldous Huxley's fiction.

"I never would have pegged you for the Jewish-mother type."

"Me, a Jewish mother?" She cocked her head in a considering sort of way, as if she were trying on an outlandish outfit and finding it didn't look bad. "How do you mean?"

"You're letting your imagination run away with you."

"Was Huxley letting his imagination run away with him when he imagined that child jumping out of a window when he wasn't allowed to study his Euclid?"

"Yes, that's exactly what he was doing. Letting the imagination run away is what fiction writers do. A piece of fiction doesn't make predictions the way a scientific theory does. You can't cite a fictional Guido to convince me of the danger to the non-fictional Azarya!"

"Spoken like a true pre-med!"

Pre-med or not, he felt something like Roz's prickling rising up over his surface as he took in what the Rebbe's son was

telling him. Goosebumps are a legacy from our furry ancestors, who could contract the muscles around each hair follicle
to fluff themselves up when they were frightened, making
themselves look more formidable. Were our quadrumanous
grandparents also capable of awe? Did their fur rise as the
wind of the uncanny blew cold over them?

The child put up his left hand and waved in the same infantile way he had that first time that Cass and Roz had met him,
opening and closing his fingers. Bye-bye.

Henoch lived in a black-and-white two-family house; it
reminded Cass of a Linzer torte. Cass had first rung the bell of
the wrong side. Henoch's in-laws lived there, Yocheved's parents, who were Israelis. Yocheved, who was already the
mother of quite a few children—Cass knew better than to ask
how many—was the oldest child of her parents, and there
were, between the two families, a massive number of interlaced children, who seemed to mingle so inextricably he wondered if the parents always remembered who belonged to
whom. Certainly Cass never got it straight. Several of Henoch
and Yocheved's children were older than the aunts and uncles
they played with.

"It's late," Henoch greeted him. He had looked harried and
impatient the first time Cass had met him, at the meeting
between Professor Klapper and the Rebbe, so it wasn't surprising to find him looking harried and impatient now. He
was a tall man, with a bony and intelligent face, his narrowed
eyes looking like they were scanning the world for the details
he had to record and rectify. "I'm already on my way to shul.
Licht benching is in less than fifteen minutes, and there is a
tish tonight at the shul. You and your professor will see something special. Berel"—and here Henoch indicated one of the
gaggle of children gathered in the vestibule, ready to walk

with their father, or their brother-in-law, to the synagogue; blonds and redheads preponderated, the little girls in plain dresses, their hair tied primly back with bands, and the boys in suits—*"bleibt du. Ven dein cuzin wert zein zugegrayt nem im zu dem shul."*

Berel stepped obediently from the crowd and nodded to Cass to follow him. Cass was going to sleep in a bedroom that was off the living room and was already jammed with two bunk beds and four small dressers. There was a cot set up in a corner for Cass, with sheets and towels neatly folded on top. Cass washed up hurriedly and changed into the dark-blue suit he was carrying in a plastic bag from the cleaners. His mother had bought it for him for a cousin's wedding on his father's side. She skipped all family gatherings on her own side.

He hurried downstairs to Berel, patiently waiting at his post, and they walked quickly to the shul. As they got in sight of the vast white ornamented warehouse of a synagogue, Cass saw the last of the stragglers, hurrying in that distinctive walk he'd noticed: leaning precipitously forward from the waist, the straight back almost parallel to the sidewalk, taking furiously fast strides. "Scurrying" was the verb that suggested itself, but it carried the taint of the Nazi propaganda that had been shown in his pre–Bar Mitzvah classes in Persnippity, the disturbing film that showed swarms of rats pouring out of a sewer segueing into Jews who looked like the Valdeners scurrying down mazelike European streets.

The sun had just disappeared, spraying the sky with a rosy gold that spread itself thickly onto the white turrets and tablet-shaped windows of the synagogue, so that the awkward architecture seemed, in the few moments of its illumination, almost as beautiful as the Valdeners themselves probably thought it was.

"Tonight *ist der tish*," Berel spoke for the first time to Cass. He was around twelve or thirteen, a somewhat pudgy red-head, with freckles and a sweet and docile manner. Cass couldn't tell what Berel thought of him, a cousin who looked so different from the other cousins, who might not even know what a *tish* is. Was he intrigued, bemused, pitying, indifferent?

"Yes," said Cass to him now, and added, "I've always wanted to be at a *tish*," to let Berel know that he knew what it was.

Tish is the Yiddish word for "table." In Hasidism, *tish* refers to the Rebbe's table, and, metonymically, to the public event of sharing a meal with the Rebbe, or in any case watching him and his family and closest associates consume a meal and then receiving the *shirayim*, or remains. The *shirayim* consists of small portions of food—of fruit or kugel, or a glass of wine—that are distributed from the hand of the Rebbe. It's a peculiarly Hasidic custom. There's nothing like it in main-stream Judaism, and it underscores one of the stickier arguing points that separate the two: the locating of the Rebbe on a different scale of being, as possessing both a soul and a body closer to the divine than that of other mortals. In mainstream Judaism, the position of intermediary between man and God is left conspicuously vacant. In Hasidism, it's occupied, and the major qualification is heredity.

"I've never actually seen a *tish*," his mom had told him. "It's so important, the most intimate connection between the Rebbe and his Hasidim, that of course the Valdeners reserve it only for the men and boys. My bratty little cousins were taken, but I never even could get anybody to tell me what went on there. Except that my father once told me that, back in Hungary, the Hasidim would actually grab for the food on the Rebbe's plate when he was done, scrambling belly-first over the *tish* top in a free-for-all for farfel."

"Tish-tish."

"My impression is that things are a bit more civilized now, with food given out instead of grabbed from the plate. But first it's all passed through the hands of the Rebbe to get some of his holiness in it. It's all part of the primitive folk biology mixed in with the dubious theology." Deb Seltzer, the former Devorah Sheiner of New Walden, delighted in describing the Valdeners in antiseptic, clinical terms. "The food that goes into a holy man must itself be holy, seeing how it's going to become the Rebbe's own flesh. It's got sparks of the divine essence, which got misplaced in the great commotion that accompanied the creation of the world, little bits of God that got trapped inside matter the Rebbe tries to return to the heavens by ingesting—I kid you not. So the Rebbe shares his food, spreading the holiness around."

"So luckshen are holy?"

"Well, not as holy as potato kugel. I bet there are tracts written on potato kugel."

As soon as they entered the doors of the synagogue, Cass heard male voices massed together in the sumptuous folds of song. The strains of melody didn't prepare Cass for the sensory assault as they now entered the vast room where the Hasidim were gathered for prayer. For the second time that day, the neuronal circuits of his "What" system were overloaded, transposing sights, sounds, smells, so that the melody struck his nostrils with spices he couldn't identify, and he heard beneath it the contained roar of the vast boiling sea of black, which gradually individuated into discrete men, hundreds rising steeply to the rafters in tiered waves from the small cleared center, dazzlingly white, a rectangle of gentle foam floating in the blackened sea. It was the homogeneity of the Valdeners' appearance and the synchronization of their motion that liquefied them, the individuating features smoothed away by the identical beards and the *payess* and *kaputas* and *shtreimlach,* undulating waves made up of Valdeners swaying in unison in great sweeping arcs in time to the powerful surge of their song, though now Cass could see that the four banks of tiers splayed outward and upward from a pure white platform, and that lining its perimeter were evenly spaced artifacts, ceremonial perhaps, and wavering ripples of glossy air drifted over and blurred the white rectangle, the mirage of scorching summer days, so that Cass had to peer a little longer before he could make out that the ceremonial objects were just regular plates and glasses and silverware, and now he saw it wasn't a platform but a table, and the foam was a linen tablecloth, and those were men seated round the table, each aligned with a plate of food.

The *tish!* Of course! This was the famous *tish!* Cass had a better view of it now, pulled onto a tier by a stranger's hand— though for all he knew the man could be a cousin, since those *payess* had red highlights. His arm was linked into that of the next Valdener, who was linked with the next, and he felt himself assimilated into the row and so into the room and so into the mystique of fellowship, and slipped, too, into the powerful hold of the male voices fused into a strength that was somehow also delicate, carrying the haunting melody, the *niggun,* that was like large hands gently carrying a fragile being, and the melody was haunting Cass not only because of the depth of its beauty but also because of its eerie familiarity, Cass knew it immediately, intimately, like a newborn knowing the voice of his mother, and he softly began to sing with the others.

From his tier he could look down on the *tish*, where now he could discern the Rebbe—a lone spot of color in the vastness of black. The Rebbe was resplendent in his unique *kaputa*—a *tish bekeshe*—blue velvet shot through with gleaming gold, and his *shtreimel* may not have exceeded all others—the one on the head of the Hasid next to him rivaled it in luxuriance— but the gold from the *kaputa* emanated outward with a quickening glow, so that everything about the Rebbe seemed more vibrant. The Rebbe's chair, too, was magnificently regal, a throne of elaborately carved wood the soft brown of a pecan and upholstered in red velvet.

The black-clad men around the *tish* held hands and swayed, the Rebbe bisecting the ring so that both sides swayed inward toward him. The Hasid sitting to the right of the Rebbe, the one with the rivaling *shtreimel*, was as eerily familiar to Cass as the haunting song that he was singing. Like the *niggun*, Cass knew that Hasid with an immediacy and intimacy that defied explanation.

No, it didn't defy explanation. There in the seat of honor beside the Rebbe was Jonas Elijah Klapper.

The singing changed to a different melody, slower and sadder, and the Rebbe's eyes were closed. He gestured expansively, shrugging his shoulders, his palms facing upward and then downward, then pointing an index finger out toward the Hasidim, and then upward into the heavens, as the tune slid out of its mournful key and ascended into a soaring, ecstatic scale, bursting the constraints of mere sound, and the rows and rows of Valdeners were jumping, like one large organism they rose upward and returned to earth in perfect unity, it was a rapturous intermingling of melody and movement, the heat in the room, the density of all the people, only driving the exultation further in its ascent, and Jonas Elijah Klapper, too, had his eyes closed, there beside the Rebbe swaying, and his own shoulders also doing a dance of little shrugs and rolls, and his lips moving as if he knew the words, as maybe he did, the capacious repository that was his mind would continually astonish, two visionaries, side by side, emanations of the extraordinary, so that even when the singing subsided, and the room stopped bubbling with ecstatic men, and they quieted on a single sustained note and took their seats in unison, as if by unvoiced command, the silenced melody still hung in the air as the Rebbe began to speak.

He was speaking in Yiddish, loud enough so that each syllable could be heard by the Valdeners up in the rafters, in the very last tiers, and Cass was pressed not only by the men on either side of him but from behind as well, the Hasid behind him placing his hand on Cass's shoulder, leaning forward, so that Cass, too, leaned forward, placing his hand on the Hasid in front of him, the entire room of Valdeners were fused into one and pressing down toward the *tish,* where the Rebbe spoke his words that were somehow so penetrating in their pronunciation that Cass, who knew only a few words of Yinglish, felt that he could somehow understand what the Rebbe was saying, and the longer the Rebbe talked, sometimes slapping his hand on the *tish* for emphasis, the more it seemed to Cass that he was getting it, until he was seamlessly understanding everything, but only, he realized a few seconds later, because the Rebbe had switched to English.

He was speaking of the week's Torah portion, which spoke of the strange fire, the alien and foreign fire—*aysh zarah*—that Nadab and Avihu, the two sons of Aharon the High Priest, brought into the Holy Tabernacle, the Mishkan, that the Hebrews carried with them as they wandered the desert, and on which the presence of *der Aybishde,* the Eternal, rested in a cloud of glory. Aharon was the first of the descending line of High Priests, and he was the brother of Moses the Law-giver, Moshe Rabenu, Moses our Rabbi, our Teacher. Nadab and Avihu were High Priests as well, since the priesthood is hereditary, passed down from father to son until this very day, and Nadab and Avihu went with their father into the Mishkan. The Torah tells us, "Each took his fire pan, put fire in it, and in it laid the incense. And they offered before Him a strange fire, *aysh zarah*." And fire came down from above, and, in a flash, consumed them, before their father's eyes.

"The Torah tells, 'And Aharon was speechless.' His silence was not only of words but of all reaction. Not a single tear crossed his cheek. Not a groan or a wail escaped his lips. Was he speechless from horror? From grief? Maybe from self-protection, afraid to cross a line when, at that moment, the Judgment from On High had descended? Or was Aharon's the silence of an understanding that has answered its own ques-tion? Had the High Priest, wearing his vestments of purity, wrapped himself in the purity of his understanding? And what could a grieving father of two princes like Nadab and Avihu understand that would silence him? They stood beside him in their holy service, and—in an instant—snatched! What could have kept him from crying out after them?

"Hear, then, what the holy Arizal said of the sons of Aharon! In the last *dr'ash* that the Arizal gave before his death in the sacred city of S'fat, the Arizal spoke of Nadab and Avihu. The Arizal compared them to the fawns of the gazelle. Just as the gazelle, as it is written in the Zohar, requires the serpent's bite in order to give birth, so Nadab and Avihu were *korbanim*, sacrifices, to hasten the coming of Moshiach.

"The gazelle is the Shechinah, the indwelling Presence; the snake is the snake; the child being born is, if the moment is right, the Moshiach of the line of David, but otherwise just another Moshiach of the line of Joseph, doomed himself and not yet capable of returning Israel from its exile.

"The strange fire, *aysh zarah,* was not *avodah zarah,* not idol worship! Not at all! Do not make the mistake of thinking that, *chas ve-shalom,* heaven forbid, Aharon's sons, Moshe Rabenu's own nephews, succumbed to idolatry!

"The strange fire was the redemptive fire that leaps out to purify the world, consuming the innocent only to return them back again into the holy service, as it will always be, the *gilgul* turning round and round until the redemption of our days, may it be in our lifetime, Amen."

A thunderous "Amen" answered the Rebbe's own.

The Rebbe switched back to Yiddish now, and Cass found that his knowledge of Yiddish was really as limited as he'd remembered. He didn't understand another word. Still, he enjoyed listening to the Rebbe's words, watching the expressions on his face and the dance of his hands.

When the Rebbe stopped speaking, a little commotion started up beside him—not on Professor Klapper's side but on the other side. Cass hadn't noticed the tiny figure of a child sitting there, who now was being lifted up onto the *tish,* placed beside gigantic bowls of apples and oranges.

Unlike all the other unmarried males, he was wearing a fur hat, smaller than those of the grown men but still enormous on his tiny head, and he was wearing a shiny little *kaputa* of pale blue.

It was a strange sight, the child standing on the table. In his little *shtreimel,* he resembled an oversize mushroom displayed beside the fruit. The disturbing thought of child sacrifice came to Cass's mind. He knew that the idea had been, from the earliest days, anathema to the Hebrews. The prophets had ranted about the child sacrifices of the neighboring tribes. They had denounced as abominations the pagan practice of burning children at altars to the cruel gods of Baal and Baal-zebub. But there was also that horrific story of the binding of Isaac to set off a chain of unwanted associations, of the father, Abraham, rising early in the morning to heed Yahweh's terrible command to offer his son as a burnt offering on a mountaintop. Like Aharon the High Priest, Abraham, too, hadn't cried out in protest or grief, but wordlessly prepared for the sacrifice.

"I give my *dr'ash* in the honor of the visitor, Rav Klapper," the child announced in his chimelike voice, and the black sea of men drew in toward the tiny figure standing poised on the foam. Cass could feel the irresistible undertow straining toward him, the prodigious child and future Rebbe, whose lineage of chosenness traced back all the way to the holy Ba'al Shem Tov.

"The beauty of the *maloychim* comes down on us. The *maloychim* are above. But also they are here, everywhere, in everything." He patted the air down in front of him, and then he turned his hands over and gestured with them in the classic Hasidic gesture of explanation. "As they are, it must be.

"The *maloychim* are in everything. They are even in some of the *maloychim*!" And now he smiled, and all the Valdeners smiled. "They are there, side by side, and above and below and in the center.

"Here at the *tish,* we are sitting, and the *maloych* 36, *lamed vav,* also sits, and in *lamed vav* is sitting 2, *beys,* 2 times, and that 2 times 2 is sitting 3 times, *gimel,* and that 2 times 2 times 3 is sitting 3 times. There in the *maloych, lamed vav,* the maloychim *beys* and *gimel* are sitting at a *tish.* Their *tish* sits here with us at our *tish*!

"But there are differences between the *maloychim*. *Beys* and *gimel* are not like *lamed vav*. *Beys* and *gimel* are more simple and more beautiful. You look and look, and each is one *maloych*. In them there are no other *maloychim* sitting above and below and to the side. These are the prime *maloychim*. They are in all the other *maloychim*, and they are in them exactly so. As they are, it must be."

And again he paused to let the Valdeners admire the sight before him.

"Rav Klapper asks: How many prime *maloychim* are there? How long does this go on?" He cast his smile on the honored guest who stared back at him. "*Ayn sof!* Without end! Just as, with all the *maloychim*, there are always more, so it is also with the prime *maloychim*. Not one of them is the biggest. How long do they go on? Forever! *L'olam va-ed!* The prime angels are singing their own *niggun*, and they are singing that they are always more!"

He looked around at the room full of his father's followers, whose faces told him that they were as joyous to hear this *niggun* as he was to sing it for them.

"Here is how they are singing. This is their *niggun*. Find the biggest prime *maloych*. Call it Acharon, for the last, and stand him at the end of a line, with all the prime *maloychim* that came before him. Here is 2 and 3 and 5 and 7 and 11 and 13 and 17 and 19 and 23 and 29 and 31 and 37 and 41 and 43 and on and on, all of the prime *maloychim* up until Acharon, the last. Do to them like this. Take 2 three times and then take that number five times, and then take that number seven times, and then take that number eleven times, and if the Cambridger Rebbe asks me how long this goes on, he knows what I will say: take it each time by another, the next in line, all the way up to the last and biggest of the prime *maloychim*,

Acharon. And then . . ." He threw his arms out and up into the air, a little Valdener in ecstasy. "Add one more to Acharon! That is a new *maloych*. His name is Acharay Acharon, the One Who Comes After the Last. And Acharay Acharon can't be! You see! If there is Acharon, there is Acharay Acharon, and it can't be, so there is no last, *l'olam va-ed!*"

He stood stock-still, an extraordinary expression on his face, entranced with what he was seeing. The look was replicated around the *tish,* up and down the bleachers, all motions stilled, snuffing the last blink and breath.

His father broke the silence with a question:

"Do you know the *niggun* of the prime *maloychim*? Can you sing it?"

"That was the *niggun,* Tata. I tried to sing it."

"A beautiful *niggun*. But now sing us one of yours, *tateleh*."

The child began to sing. The dense room pressed itself forward, trying to get as close as possible, even if they didn't outwardly move, the lines of invisible force drawing them down to the foamy rectangle on which the Rebbe's small son floated. His singing was beautiful, as could have been guessed from his speaking voice, and his pitch was perfect. He raised his little hands and gestured like his father, turning his palms up and then over. The Valdeners let him sing the pretty melody through once, and then, when he began it again, they joined in.

Ever since the Ba'al Shem Tov, the Master of the Good Name, rebelled against the intellectualized strain of Judaism prevailing in his day, the Hasidim have cultivated a worship of the divine that is experiential, sensual, ecstatic. This is why they dance. This is why they sing. But the Valdeners of New Walden possessed a path to ecstasy that was theirs alone, and it was obvious on every face up and down the tiers. The

Rebbe's son was their ecstasy. They understood little of his words, but the melody they could understand, and they knew that they were in the presence of the divine. Their arms were linked again as they swayed, and many had tears overrunning their eyes, trickling down faces as enraptured as Azarya's own face had been, a few moments ago, while he was contemplating the beautiful proof that there is no largest prime number.

He hadn't bothered to go through the last steps of the proof. He had taken them far enough and pointed and expected that they all would see the wondrous thing that he was seeing.

Assume that there is a largest prime number. Give it a name, as Azarya had. Call it P. And now take all the prime numbers that precede P and multiply them together, just as Azarya had said: 2 times 3 times 5 times 7 . . . times P. Take that product and add 1 to it. Call that new number Q. Is Q a prime or not? Since P has been assumed to be the largest prime number and Q comes after P, Q can't be a prime. But then Q must be divisible by a prime number, because all non-prime numbers, or composites, are divisible by a prime. As Azarya had seen, composite numbers are all the products of primes. So there must be, at least, one prime number that is a perfect divisor of Q. None of the prime numbers less than Q can be a divisor of Q, because 1 had been added to the product of all of them in order to construct Q. So there has to be a prime number larger than P to be Q's divisor, which contradicts the statement that P is the largest prime number. And so there cannot be a largest prime number.

Cass recognized the proof from *Men of Mathematics*. It was Euclid who first discovered it, though his proof had been slightly different, more geometrical than Azarya's. And the Alexandrian giant had not been six years old.

The angels pour their beauty down on us, Azarya had said. They are above, yes, but also here, in everything. 36 descends from on high to sit at the Rebbe's *tish*. It carries the beauty of its own composition, and of its invisible bonds with the immaculate others of its realm, transporting this beauty down to us to grace our humble table. As it is, so it must be, and that is the nature of the beauty. In every row, in every tier, in the whole assembled crush of Valdeners, carried on cantillated waves of explosive love, blasted with their gratitude for having been born Valdeners, there are numbers, and this very room, filled with so much shifting strangeness, which before had been an undifferentiated black and bubbling sea, and then had resolved into individual men, now yields its surface again so that Cass can glimpse the silent presence of Azarya's angels conspiring with one another to bring about what is, because as it is, then so it must be, and this is the nature of the beauty.

The room is reeling for Cass with Azarya's angels, beating their furious wings of diaphanous flames, this is what it must be like for the child, what he must see out of those luminous blue eyes, only Cass knows that for Azarya there is infinitely more to be seen, even now, at six years old, and this is all the divine that we need, this is the strange fire that is worth almost anything, the angels within angels in their infinite and necessary configurations, a fleeting glimpse, let it last a little longer, let me savor this tiny bit tossed from the *shirayim*, the remains, of the infinite that is *ayn sof*, without end, emanations of the extraordinary that burst on us in rapture, and look how that small boy is laughing and clapping his hands, riding up on top of his adoring father's shoulders, and Cass thinks that he can hear a child's laughter rippling like water over the din.

The melody continued. The Valdeners were deep into their ecstasy. They loved their Rebbe's son, the Dauphin of New Walden, heir to the most royal of all lineages, necessary to the continuity that made their lives worth living, this small, laughing boy who was bouncing on his dancing father's back, with the Valdeners kissing their prayer shawls and reaching them out to touch him as they do when the Torah scroll is paraded among them. The wonderful child was to them a proof more conclusive than Euclid's of all that they believed. They couldn't know who it was they were loving. But Cass knew, and his face was as wet with tears as any in the room, his trance as deep and ecstatic as that of any Hasid leaping into dance.

XX

The Argument from Tidings of Destruction

Cass's cup of tea has grown cold while he was speaking with Lucinda, and he is going back to the kitchen to put the kettle back on when the phone rings again.

It's Roz.

"So how did it go down with Shimmy?"

"Not so great. He's pretty upset."

"Over your leaving?"

"That, but also that whole fraternity-fracas thing you helped to stir up on Tuesday."

"You're kidding me, right?"

"There are posters, protesters, banners hung from the dorms, petitions. Shimmy called it a tinder keg, a powder box."

"The slim edge of the wedgie!"

"Don't laugh, Roz." She's laughing. "He made me feel so sorry for him that I promised him I'd think about what kind of retention package would tempt me to stay."

"Oh, Cass. He's playing you for a shlemiel, using that *Saturday Night Live* sketch of a protest to guilt you into staying. What an ox-shit artist."

"Well, maybe. But Shimmy really did seem shaken."

"I can imagine. It's Gamma Gamma Gamma, or he can just forget about his yes indeedee." As an alum, Roz has kept abreast. She even knows the name of the expert doctor that Deedee and her sorority sister Bunny share.

"His weak spot is that woman."

"Isn't it always?"

"I could feel his pain. He kept talking about being squeezed."

"That Southern belle of his can probably squeeze them like they were limes for mint juleps."

"Ouch."

"Oh, Cass! I'm sorry, but this is one beautiful hoot!" She breaks off a spell to demonstrate just how beautiful a hoot she thinks it is. She's a bit breathless when she returns. "I guess I might have contributed some to this kankedort."

"Don't start getting a swelled head."

"Did any of the kids use my motto?"

"At least a dozen. I have to say, though, that the banner I liked the best was one that had 'Toga Party!' written out in Greek letters. *Tau, omicron, gamma, alpha, pi, alpha, rho, tau, iota!*"

"Wait a minute, wait a minute, give me a moment to think." He gives her a moment to think. "Okay, here's what we do to end Shimmy's Hanukkah Wars. Tell him to Hebraicize the Greeks! So, instead of some fraternity named Alpha Delta Kappa, make it Aleph Daleth Qooph!"

He can't help joining in her laughter. "Deedee's Gamma Gamma Gamma could be Gimel Gimel Gimel."

"Instead of sororities and fraternities, they can call them sisterhoods and brotherhoods—like in a synagogue! It's so ridiculous, it just might work!"

"As Shimmy likes to say, 'Stranger things have gone down the tubes.'"

"But whether it works or not, you're out of there! Stop letting the Shimmys of the world work you over. Get it through your head, you're a star. Speaking of which, I can't wait for your big God debate tomorrow."

"What big God debate?"

"The debate with Felix Fidley! I was over at Harvard today, and there are posters plastered all over the place! 'Resolved: God Exists.' You can't have forgotten!"

"But I did! Fuck! I totally forgot. Fuck!"

"It's upsetting when you curse, Cass. You're the only person I know who only curses in extremis."

"Fuck, Roz. Fuck."

"Really upsetting."

It's all coming back to him. Felix Fidley, a Nobel-laureate economist who has been taking his stand on a wide range of issues by publishing in the neoconservative magazine *Provocation,* has been challenging the so-called new atheists to debate him on the existence of God. He'd written to Cass with a mixture of arrogance and flattery:

I'm having too easy a time with these debates. The reason is that some of the "new atheists" know something about one thing but very little about other things. Twickenham, for instance, admits he knows nothing about science. Fitzroy seems to know little about anything else. You, on the other hand, with your extensive knowledge of religion, psychology, philosophy, science, and history, would present a more than worthy adversary. A Fidley-Seltzer debate would be a real highlight, entertaining but intellectually provocative.

"What do you think of Felix Fidley?" he had asked Lucinda. They were in bed, Lucinda tucked neatly into the pockets of the comforter, reading.

"Felix Fidley?" Lucinda looked up from *A Proper English Murder.* She's addicted to mysteries. "He's got a Nobel."

"Yes, but what do you think of him?"

"He's one of the most brilliant economists of the last twenty years. In fact, I co-authored a paper with him, 'Mandelbaum Equilibria in Hostile Takeovers.' Why?"

"He wants to debate me."

"Really?" Lucinda marked her page with her bookmark and set *A Proper English Murder* down on her night table. "About what?"

"The existence of God."

"I should have guessed!" She laughed. "Are you telling me Felix Fidley believes?"

"Belligerently."

"How odd. He's such a rationalist—University of Chicago and all. Are you sure?"

It was touching how sincerely Lucinda believed in reason. It was difficult for her to get her mind around the fact that believers weren't all high-school dropouts who used their fingers and toes to add and subtract.

"For lots of people it's become a matter of political coalitions more than anything having to do with theology. The enemy of my enemy is my friend. If liberals are going in one direction in the religion-versus-reason debates, defending the theory of evolution and secular humanism, neocons feel they have to head off in the opposite direction. Or they think that it's okay for people like them, who are thoroughly civilized, to question God's existence, but that it would be moral anarchy

if the teeming masses started to doubt God. I suspect that
that's what Fidley believes."

Provocation is a good example of what Cass was describing.
It was founded by left-wing intellectuals in the 1940s, but its
editors had been profoundly insulted by the new leftism of
the sixties and reacted by lurching to the right. By now *Provocation*'s policy of opposing anything advocated by the liberals—
a word it had helped besmirch—has carried it into open
warfare against the entire project of the Enlightenment. Darwin has come in for multiple attacks, and religious scientists
have shown off their creativity. There was an article by an
Orthodox Jewish linguist who used Noam Chomsky's theory
of a universal grammar to vindicate the Bible's story of the
Tower of Babel. There was an article authored by a fundamentalist geologist on the movement of the tectonic plates of the
earth as consistent with a worldwide flood on the order of
Noah's. There was an article by a Catholic anthropologist
arguing against the liberal denial of distinct races and backing it up with Genesis 10, where the begettings of Noah's
three sons are explained. *Provocation*'s review of *The Varieties
of Religious Illusion* had been so negative as to border on the
actionable.

"Are you going to debate him?" Lucinda had asked him,
turning over on her side so that she was facing Cass, her head
propped up on her palm.

"Do you think I should?"

"What day did you say this thing is?" he's asking Roz now
on the phone.

"February 29. I think that's tomorrow."

"It *is* tomorrow! I'm fucked. And that's when Lucinda is
getting back from Santa Barbara. What was I *thinking*?"

"Well, if anyone is worth debating on this issue, then Felix Fidley is," Lucinda had said. "It would certainly be a major win for you, and I don't see how you could fail to win." She'd smiled, and her delicate nostrils flared ever so slightly. "I'd like to see that."

She'd reached out her hand and laid it on Cass's stomach and then had slid it slowly up his chest. She reached up for Cass's glasses and gently removed them, leaning over him to place them on his night table, her brandy-glass-shaped breasts just grazing his uplifted face.

That minute adjustment had come over her face, unstiffening her upper lip and unloosing the full extravagance of her beauty, flooding all of Cass's modules, seizing him up with the one and wordless premise that composes the Argument from Lucinda.

"I'm fucked for real," he says now to Roz.

XXI

The Argument from the Remains

Jonas Elijah Klapper had intimate knowledge of all the prominent thinkers across the ages. There was not a novelist, poet, essayist, critic, historian, metaphysician, ethicist, theologian, or belletrist worth the reading (an emphatically necessary qualification) of whom he had not taken the reckoning. He had expended himself in exhaustively computing the ranking of anyone meriting mention in the great chain of genius. His project had been demanding. It had demanded neither more nor less than omniscience. The (all but) universal ovation was not disproportionate to the accomplishment. He had organized the vast reaches of human thought in a way that could be compared, mutatis mutandis, to the commendable efforts of Miss Ching in helping him to settle into his Frankfurter suite of offices, her admirable zeal in conceiving categories for the color-coded files, craftily alphabetized.

So, when Jonas Elijah Klapper stated that the Grand Rabbi of the Valdener Hasidim was a religious genius on the order of Meister Eckhart, Emanuel Swedenborg, and Nathan Benjamin ben Elisha ha-Levi Ghazzati (also known as "Nathan of Gaza" or "Nathan the Prophet"), it was quite a statement. Professor Klapper confided in Cass that the Valdener Grand

Rabbi was among the most extraordinary men of his lifetime—and he had met all the extraordinary men of his lifetime, including the pre-eminent secular scholar of Qabalah, one of the few non-Americans granted membership in the American Academy of Arts and Sciences (Jonas had been initiated as a mere pup of thirty-eight), the Jerusalemite Yehuda Ickel.

Cass had liked the Valdener Rebbe quite a lot, almost in spite of himself, and certainly in spite of his mother. In fact, one of the Rebbe's most endearing traits, at least to Cass, was the warmth he still harbored toward the former Devorah Sheiner. The Rebbe seemed to regard her with none of the severity with which she regarded him, though perhaps this was just part of his Socratic slyness. Still, listening to Professor Klapper's assessment, he had to conclude that it was probably his own ignorance of Yiddish that had blocked him from seeing the full extent of the Rebbe's extraordinariness, though he couldn't dismiss the possibility that the blame lay in his intrinsic soul-shortage.

According to Professor Klapper, the Valdener Grand Rabbi was like the Palomar Observatory, which he had been compelled to visit with his fulsome hosts at the University of California at San Diego when he had been out there to deliver, soon after the publication of "my little book *The Perversity of Persuasion*," the prestigious John Shade Lecture in Literature and Truth. They had organized quite the tour for him, in consequence of which he had immediately resolved never to accept another invitation from anywhere in the entire state of California, a ban he had, over the years, gradually widened until it included everything west of the Hudson. Jonas Elijah Klapper was ready to confess his vagueness on such details, since Sigmund Freud was as far as he would venture in the direction of the hard sciences, but he had carried away the impression that the contraption took the compass of the infinite cosmos. If that was so, then it was still as nothing compared with the observatory that was the Valdener Grand Rabbi.

"For it is the measure of the infinite soul that is taken by your inestimable relation, Reb Chaim."

Everything the Valdener Rebbe said and did was both liminal and luminant. That is what Jonas Elijah Klapper might choose to call the graduate seminar next year:

"The Liminal, the Luminant, and the—"

The professor was brought up short by a rare aposiopesis. He looked over to his erstwhile student to see whether he might offer some help. The word that seditiously leaped into Cass's mind was so inappropriate that Cass suspected Roz's insidious sense of humor was infecting him again—long-distance, since she still hadn't returned from the Amazon.

"Well, never mind that for now. We shall think of the apposite trinomial in time," the professor was continuing.

The Valdener Sage had the capacity to speak the liminal words that transported the Self through the narrow threshold within the Self to enter into the hushed precinct where the Sublime sat on its throne of glory, an ecstatic knowledge that transformed the Self even as it revealed the Self, for it awoke within the Self the knowledge of what is immortal in the Self, not in the sense of duration, definable by time, but, rather, the Self that dwells, like the Place—or Ha-Makom, one of the monikers for YHVH—outside of time, the Self that cannot die because it was never born, begotten by no seed of man.

Professor Klapper had found everything relating to the Grand Rabbi fraught with hidden meanings, the humblest word or action setting off tremblings in the highest spheres, in what the Qabalists refer to as the Keter, the Crown of Being, the last gate behind which the Ayn Sof, That Without End, has withdrawn itself, coiled within the End of Thought.

"It is as the Valdener Rebbe himself masterfully put it: the Acharay Acharon, the One Who Comes After the Last."

"That was Azarya."

Cass couldn't help himself. He had spoken before he had thought. "Azarya? Who is Azarya?"

"The Rebbe's son. He was the one who spoke about the Acharay Acharon."

Klapper widened his eye into his practiced glare but then, deciding upon leniency, waved Cass's irrelevance away with a magisterial flourish of his hand.

"I am quite certain you are mistaken. The little boy sang a *niggun,* which I believe he had composed. Perhaps that is the source of your errancy. The child decidedly did not delve into the mysteries of the Ayn Sof. The suggestion is a preposterition."

"Preposterition," meaning "preposterous proposition," was a neologism of his own coinage, and, employing it, he felt irked all over again by this presumptuous young person who was crowding his office and squandering his time. But then he recalled the young man's lineage, the majestic luster that clung to his bloodline, manifesting itself in the very tint of his hair, and decided to forgive.

"The Valdener Rebbe has supplied some information that may yet prove to be surpassingly significant. It is as I suspected. To non-initiates it appears as if the denizens of New Walden have closed themselves off to the increments in human knowledge that have, it is commonly believed, proceeded *pari passu* with the so-called advancements in the sciences, which too often amount, I am forced to inform you, to

no more than the merest scientism. Unlike the colossal confusions of pedantry in which I have been forced to collude—
by which I mean a pedagogical cartel that could not begin to
understand the meaning of the term 'higher education,'
which misprision it manifests in its increasing insistence that
every Tom, Dick, and Harry should misspend his youth, not
to speak of his parents' lucre, by parking his dullard head at
an undergraduate institution for four years—the Valdeners
recognize that not every Tevye, Dudel, and Hershel are meant
to be introduced to subjects beyond their comprehension.
The Rebbe, as an exalted master, does the learning for them
and then transmits to each according to his capacity to
receive. And of course his mastery extends to full command
of the non-verbal lineaments of communication. There was
no doubt in my mind that transmission at the profoundest
level was taking place during the ritual of the *shirayim*. Each
person who partook of the Rebbe's food received a commu-
niqué that was fashioned for his individual quiddity, the
measure of which the Rebbe takes in ways that can only be
divine."

Cass was surprised to hear Professor Klapper's impression
of the *shirayim*. For his part, Cass had found the proceedings
anything but edifying. It had not been quite as civilized as
Cass's mother had been led to believe. There had been a grab
for the actual remains on the Rebbe's plate, and it had
seemed to Cass, though he could not be sure, that Frankfurter's Extreme Distinguished Professor had gotten the better part of what was there. The Rebbe had then begun to pitch
the apples and oranges from the great cut-glass chalices on
the table, and as the fruit flew, so rose the Valdeners. They
looked like the fans in Fenway Park when a long foul ball was
hit into the grandstand. Hasidim had flung themselves onto

the gigantic table, squirming forward on their bellies to get a piece of fruit that hadn't made it into the tiers. There had also been pieces of potato kugel that the Rebbe had distributed with his bare hands. The pandemonium of the event—there was shouting and tussling, not to speak of food being flung— had ripped Cass entirely out of the rapture that had seized him while Azarya spoke. He had found nothing to inspire him in the *shirayim.*

But Jonas Elijah Klapper had. He did not reveal, not even to Reb Chaim, the full extent of what had been received in the Rebbe's remains. He had been awakened to a knowledge that he had always held within him, nestled inside like something rare and precious, now delivered into the conscious Self that had been prepared for its reception.

It had concerned food, since that, after all, at its simplest level, is what the ritual of *shirayim* concerns. Here, too, the soul of Jonas was in a state of heightened preparation. It had been given to him to experience the profounder intimations of food since his earliest childhood. At three years of age, he had devised his two-fork method, one in each hand, so that he would not have to wait between mouthfuls. Sometimes his mother made a dish—her Friday-night chicken fricassee with dumplings, her brisket braised with potatoes, her calf liver fried with onions—that moved him to a hedonic delirium far beyond the carnal.

The most exquisite of these experiences had been afforded by her chicken soup—always suffused with emanations of the divine, but most especially when it came blessed with what she called *fleishig eier,* or "meat eggs." This was a delicacy as indescribable as it was rare, dependent as it was upon circumstances beyond anyone's control.

His mother purchased her slaughtered chickens from the

poultry market on Essex Street. She would then have to open and eviscerate them, soak and salt them, in accordance with the laws of *kashrut* (taboos he had discarded, with the exception of that relating to the flesh of the pig). The *fleishig eier* were the unlaid eggs, clustered in varying stages of immaturity and circumference, that his mother would sometimes find nestled within an old laying hen. They were called *fleishig eier* because the rabbis had ruled that they belong to the meat category (a logical decision, since they were still a part of the chicken) and thus were immiscible with dairy. His sainted mother would put the *fleishig eier* in her chicken soup, and they would be served to Jonas alone, placed reverentially before him by one of his sisters. They were orbs of pale yellow, all yolk, their texture denser and firmer than that of matured yolks, and with a concentrated flavor that held suggestions of an otherworldly sweetness.

The rituals prevailing over the Rebbe's *tish* harked back to the rites of the High Priest Aharon making his offerings on the altar, which had been described in such an abundance of detail in the Torah portion fated to be read the very Shabbes of Jonas's visit to New Walden, when the Valdener Rebbe had explained the secret meaning of the *aysh zarah,* the strange fire, that the sons of the High Priest had introduced, immolating themselves to the cosmic agenda. None of the allusions had been lost on Jonas. He had, at long last, received (the very meaning of the term "Qabalah") a complete and clarified understanding of (among other receptions) a truth he had always instinctively known—to wit, that the appetitive soul is emphatically not the unrefinable sensibility that the pagan thinkers, through either ignorance or cunning deception, had described. Intelligence operating through longing—*orektikos nous*—or longing operating through thought—*orexis dianoetike*—has always been essential to the spiritual and intellectual exertions that alone can redeem.

Jonas was brought back, with a start, to the student sitting inches away from him in his office. He had a task for him. He wished the student to explore the full implications of the traditional Jewish menu. Each of the traditional dishes had symbolic significance: gefilte fish, the balls of ground pike or carp simmered in broth; blintzes, stuffed pancakes; kishke, a sausage made by stuffing a cow's intestines with a filling of carrots, onions, and matzo meal; farfel, a kind of pasta; tzimmes, a sweet stew made with carrots, sweet potatoes, and prunes; cholent, the Sabbath stew of beans and potato, a bit of beef if one was well-to-do, put into a low oven before sundown on Friday and served hot on Saturday for lunch; luckshen, or noodles; and, of course, kugel, the sacred pudding.

"All of the dishes have Qabalist significance, which must be why, as I have finally come to understand, a Jewish high cuisine never developed. If nothing can, hermeneutically speaking, exceed the potato kugel, then there can be little point in culinary refinement. The refinements are of an entirely different order."

Professor Klapper reached into the chaos reigning on the surface of his desk and pulled out a book. He opened it to a page that had been marked, pulled his bifocals down from the top of his head, bringing tufts of hair down along with them, and read from the Yiddish, looking up at Cass, when he had finished, in a quizzical fashion.

"Is this not extraordinary?"

"I'm sorry. I didn't understand it."

"What?"

"I don't understand Yiddish."

"Indeed." The professor examined him closely over the top

of his glasses, his chin ruffling out against his shirt front. "Is that not unusual for someone of your background?"

"We're fallen-away Valdeners, my mother and I. My father doesn't come from that background at all."

"In any case, with your privileged pedigree, it should not be difficult for you to assimilate the *mama lashon,* the mother tongue, with winged speed. In the interim, I shall translate. 'The *tzaddikim,* or righteous ones, proclaimed that there are profound matters enfolded in the kugel. For this reason they insisted that every Jew must eat the Shabbes kugel. Rabbi Menachem Mendel of Rimanov recalled that once, when he went out for a walk with the holy rabbi of Ropshitz, all that they talked about for three hours were the secrets that lie hidden inside the Shabbes kugel.'"

He gave Reb Chaim a meaningful gaze and then pulled another book out of the pile on his desk, found the place he had marked, and read:

"'Reb Itzikel of Pshevorsk taught that there is a special chamber in paradise in which the particular reward for eating kugel on the Shabbes is granted. Even he who has eaten kugel out of low physical desire will receive his reward.'"

Jonas closed the book, at the same time closing his eyes and sighing, sinking into reflection. Suddenly he roused himself with a start, eyelids snapping open like a window shade out of control.

"All of these primary sources, I am certain you will be delighted to learn, Reb Chaim, have been recommended to me by your sanctified relation, the Sage of the Palisades. There is a treasure trove more. Here is one by Rabbi Aaron Roth, of Jerusalem, which leaves no doubt concerning the covenantal significance of the kugel. 'Kugel is the one special food that all Jews eat, one food in the service of the one God, so that anyone who does not eat kugel on the Shabbes in this country should be investigated for heresy.'"

He placed the book down on his pile, as always making certain to keep the space around the framed picture of Hannah Klepfish cleared.

"You can see the direction in which I am going here." Again he stared at Cass over his bifocals, the high dome of his forehead corrugated with the inquisitorial ascent of his brows.

"To tell you the truth, Professor Klapper, I'm not exactly sure."

"I am, I believe, your dissertation adviser?"

There was no need to answer.

"I venture to assert that I have located in this matter a topic that will not only satisfy the requirement of Faith—you have, I may remind you, to attain competence, under my supervision and to my satisfaction, in the areas of Faith, Literature, and Values—but might very well provide you with a topic for your dissertation for the degree of *Philosophiae Doctor*. You shall embark by first confronting the intriguing mystery of the kugel, both noodle and potato, although the sages favor potato. The potato stands for Yesod, which can be translated as Foundation, and is one of the ten Sephirot, the emanations of the revealed God radiated throughout the created physical world. Beyond the ten Sephirot is where the Ayn Sof lurks. Yesod is the channel through which the emanation Tiferet— another of the ten Sephirot and to be translated as Beauty, Glory—strives to unite with the Shechinah, which is God's indwelling Immanence and which shares the cosmic exile that must be redeemed through the processes of ongoing history."

He took a pause, perusing the face before him to see

whether he could safely assume his meaning had been received. Satisfied, he continued.

"Nothing, Reb Chaim, is as it seems. The homeliest object or act can be of cosmic proportions. That which is common, undignified, vulgar—*proste* in Yiddish, which I submit to you is related to the ancient Greek *prostychos*—a potato or the *fleishig eier* floating among the shining globules in a mother's chicken soup—is, when contemplated by the singular Self, numinous. *Mysterium tremendum et fascinans.* The Qabalist masters were able to divine that the potato symbolized Yesod, but how they did so I am not yet sure."

There followed another protracted stare that lasted long enough for Cass to wonder whether the session had been concluded. It had not.

"I have made progress regarding other mysteries of the kugel. *Kugel* means, in both German and Yiddish, a circle, and the fact that the dish is called by this name, even when it is made in a square or rectangular pan, as my own mother most often prepared it, indicates we are dealing with the sacred nature of the circle. A kugel is always made with generous amounts of oil, which recalls the ritual of unction. 'Messiah,' or 'Moshiach,' literally means the Anointed One. In the Shabbes kugel one consumes and makes flesh the essence of the Qabalist message, that the created world is striving to repair the brokenness of the scattered shards, to unite the ten emanations, the Foundation acting to conjoin Beauty and Glory with the indwelling Immanence, so that the Anointed One will complete the sacred circle and repair the world.

"And yet one question of the kugel still remains: why the potato rather than the luckshen? I am vehemently disinclined to believe that, in identifying the potato with Yesod, the masters were resorting to its being a root vegetable. The potato's significance is surely derived anagogically, and yet I have exhausted every numerical combination and rewording of which I could think, and have also dipped into the alternative methods of assigning numerical values to the letters, to no avail. There is a manuscript in the Bodleian Library at Oxford that lists more than seventy different systems of gematria, and it might become necessary—indeed, I cannot see how it could fail to become necessary—for your research to take you there. According to one alternative system, for example, the value 1 is assigned to the first letter of the alphabet, *aleph,* but instead of counting the second one, *beys,* as 2, *beys* is given 1 plus 2—in other words, 3—and *gimel* is given 1 plus 2 plus 3, and so on, which is enough to drive one mad. To add to the complexity, the Qabalists often mixed and matched the systems, so that a word that is gematricized under one method can be held as equal to a word gematricized under another. A method of this sort must lie behind the potato's enshrinement. I bestow upon you, Reb Chaim, a quest."

Without having to unseat himself, Jonas retrieved six books from around his office, all of them in Yiddish, and handed them to Cass, pointedly indicating the door—he pointed—and sending the scholar on his way.

XXII

The Argument from Fraught Distance

to: GR613@gmail.com
from: Seltzer@psych.Frankfurter.edu
date: Feb. 28 2008 10:08 p.m.
subject: a friend in need

I seem to have committed myself to debating
Felix Fidley, the Nobel laureate. Resolved:
God exists. Guess which side I'm on. Not
only did I commit, but I then promptly
forgot all about it. Can you call me? Can I
call you? I know it's a little early in the
night for you, but I'd much appreciate if we
could talk tactics. Roz has been trying to
tell me that there's nothing Fidley can put
over on me, that I should just use my
Appendix as my cheat sheet, but I'm not so
sure. Fidley could use my Appendix as *his*
cheat sheet. I've made it easy for him. He
knows all my moves.

One more thing I forgot to mention. The
debate is tomorrow, so I need, if it's at
all possible, to speak to you tonight. It's
at Harvard, being sponsored by the Agnostic
Chaplaincy, and I'm not making this up just

to get you to call me. According to Roz, the
whole campus is plastered with posters about
this thing. I know how busy you are, but the
fate of all freethinkers hangs in the
balance.

XXIII

The Argument from the Disenchantment of the World

Roz had been delayed in returning from the Amazon, and when she came back she had been transformed. There were no more dreadlocks. She was deeply tanned and on first glance looked hale and hearty. But a second glance revealed that all was not right. She looked pale beneath the tan. There was something drawn and almost haggard in her noble face.

"Did you lose weight?" Cass asked when she answered the door of her apartment. She had just gotten back that day. She had been incommunicado while she was with the Onuma, and the only word that Cass had gotten from her was a quick phone call from the airport in Miami saying she was on her way home.

"Lose weight? I don't know."

It didn't take her long—in fact, only till the next sentence— to tell Cass of her real losses. Tragedy had swept through the immune-depressed Onuma, a mortal outbreak of measles. The children had been particularly hard hit, including—and here her eyes overwhelmed with tears—Tsetse. Roz was in mourning.

She sat cross-legged across from cross-legged Cass in her apartment, which she always joked had been bugged by her landlords, the Wilde man and his wife, to keep tabs on their oestrous offspring, and she pulled out the few pictures she had taken on her previous trips of Tsetse, smiling with a mischief so delighted with itself you could all but hear the guffaws.

"And look at this one. This is him offering me a taste from the jar of peanut butter he had stolen out of my hut."

Tsetse, with a solemn look, was holding out a piece of leaf dabbed with brown, to a Roz doubled-up with laughter.

"That's why I stayed on longer. Absalom was trying desperately to get vaccine sent in, by way of the missionaries, and then he and I went from village to village vaccinating. But it was too late for many of them, most of all the children." She broke down and sobbed.

"Okay," she finally said. "That's it for me, at least for now. I've got lots more stories, but I don't have the heart for them now. Tell me what's been going on with you. Anything new?"

"I've been back to New Walden. Klapper wanted to go back for a Shabbes."

"What? Without me? How could you?"

"I didn't exactly have a choice in the matter."

"That I can believe. So how was it? Did you see Azarya again? Did you get to speak to him?"

"Just a little bit, when I dropped Klapper off at the Rebbe's house. Azarya let us in. He asked for you."

"You're kidding?" She still looked like hell, her face disarranged from her jags of crying, but she was smiling.

"I think he has a little crush on you."

"Oh!" And her eyes, not entirely dried out yet, began to well anew.

"Listen, Roz, here's something to cheer you. He knows how to read English."

"They taught him?"

"He taught himself. From your map of the U.S. You said all the words as you wrote them down, and he memorized them and used the map to teach himself how to read."

"How do you know?"

"He told me."

"Did you test him? Did you see whether he really knows how to read?"

"Roz, I believe him."

"What is it? What's that look on your face?"

He told her about how the Valdeners had assembled in celebration as the sun sank, and about how the child, in his little *shtreimel* and pale-blue *kaputa,* was lifted up onto the enormous table—"it was bigger than your apartment and mine put together"—and how he had spoken about his angels.

"He calls the prime numbers 'prime angels' now. Prime *maloychim*. Roz, he knows that every composite number can be factored into primes."

"How do you know he knows that?"

"Because, Roz, because . . ." Cass had to take a breath to control his voice and face before going on. "Azarya proved that there's no largest prime number. He proved that there are an infinite number of primes. He used the factorization theorem to prove it. I'm pretty sure I was the only one there who had any idea of what he was talking about. His father didn't get it. Azarya was so happy, thinking that he was showing all the Valdeners the wonderful thing that he had found and sharing it with them, but he was all alone. It was the most exhilarating and the loneliest thing I'd ever seen in my life."

They were both churned up by emotional turmoil. Cass had never been able to resist Roz's laugh. He wouldn't have known, until tonight, that her tears had the same effect.

"You can laugh at me all you want," she said in between their tears, "but I'm terrified for that kid. The fragility of children is the most terrifying part of this whole terrifying world."

"Terrifying world? Come on, Roz! What happened to my fearless warrior woman, Suwäayaiwä? The wild Rastafarian who could set the Extreme Distinguished Professor of Faith, Literature, and Values jiggling with terror?"

"How is the Klap?" Roz asked when she could find her voice again. "He enjoy himself in New Walden?"

He hadn't planned on telling her anything at all about the irregularities of his professor's behavior during the Shabbes at New Walden. But the poor girl so clearly needed a laugh that he poured it out to her, starting with his pulling up in the Lincoln Continental in front of the faux-English manor on Berkeley Place and beholding the emergence of Jonas Elijah Klapper in full Hasidic drag.

"No! You're making it up!"

"I'm not capable."

"Oh God! Did you get a picture?"

"I only wish! If I'd only known, I'd have brought a camera."

"And send it to the Frankfurter Board of Trustees. Show them where their money is going!"

"The *shtreimel* was sable, Roz. Russian sable, with thirteen tails!" It was a long time before either of them could say anything again.

Roz had to have noticed that Cass's attitude toward Jonas Elijah Klapper was not as reverential as it once had been. But Cass held off speaking of his more particular and personal misgivings. The topic was depressing. For the second time since coming to study at Frankfurter, he had to consider what to do with his life if he was no longer going to be Jonas Elijah

Klapper's student. He wasn't ready to air his doubts with Roz. He knew that to bring them up with her was—"ipso facto," as the Klap would say—to have made the decision to leave Klapper. And at this point, he realized, the hardest aspect of that decision was his abandonment of the group. Gideon had urged him, that first day, to quit while he was ahead, but that was so long ago, before Cass had become woven into the texture of their shared devotion.

He had shoved the books that Klapper had assigned him under his bed. He didn't want to see them, and he most certainly didn't want Roz to see them.

But, with her unerring instincts for fieldwork, she located them by herself. It was late morning, the light in Cass's basement apartment the dirty gray of twilight that it achieved at its brightest. Roz called Cass's digs "Suicide Manor" and claimed to be able to make out the chalk outlines of the body of the last tenant.

Cass was in the bathroom, and Roz was searching for a black thong that she had flung off an hour before.

"What are these?" she asked Cass as he emerged in his shorts. He only shook his head.

"Is this Hebrew?" she demanded.

"Yiddish."

"You know Yiddish?"

"No more than you."

"I know *mishegoss*."

"Me, too."

"Craziness, right? That's what *mishegoss* means? What's it about?"

"I think he might be going off the deep end."

"Might? Going?"

She was stark naked, having still not located the thong. She must have gone pretty skimpy in Venezuela, judging by her tan line.

"At least you've only wasted a year. Look at poor Gideon. He's wasted almost thirteen. He lost his poetry. He's probably going to lose his wife."

"Lizzie?"

"She's had it. All that elaborate exegesis about every cocka-mamie thing the Klap says or does. Lizzie's poured her heart out to me."

"Fuck." Cass sat down on the bed, dazed.

"Wow. I've never heard you curse. It's disturbing."

"Fuck. Fuck."

"Really, really disturbing."

"I can't believe Lizzie would leave him. He's going to be devastated. Lizzie is the center of his world."

"No, she isn't. That's the problem. Klapper is." She paused, but Cass made no response. "Seven good minds gone bad, wasting themselves on trying to figure out the Kabbalist meaning for why Nut Boy switched offices with his secretary. How long do you think a woman can listen to that?"

"Six minds. Six minds going bad. There's no way I'm writ-ing a dissertation on the hermeneutics of potato kugel."

Lunatic. That had been the word that had occurred to him in Klapper's office. The Liminal, the Luminant, and the Lunatic. Cass had hastily disowned it.

But now the thought wasn't just being thought.

Cass was thinking it.

XXIV

The Argument from the Ethics of the Fathers

The phone rings, and Cass is relieved. It must be a response to his desperate summons. But when he answers, he's momentarily confused. It's Lucinda. He calculates quickly. It's 9 p.m. in Santa Barbara. Rishi must have given the keynote, and Cass hears the triumph restored to Lucinda's voice. She had fanged the sucker. She had fanged him but good.

"And you're not going to believe this, but *you* actually helped me out here!"

"Me?"

"Believe it or not! Or maybe your ne'er-do-well brother."

"Jesse?"

"None other. You remember how I'd mentioned the Saint Petersburg Paradox to you, tried to explain that that's what did Jesse in?"

His younger brother's high-risk finance strategies had been responsible for Jesse's briefly seeing the inside of a minimum-security federal prison for white-collar offenders.

"Yes."

"Well, that had made me think through the S P P in a different way, and that's exactly what I needed to squash that cockroach Rishi. I won't go into the technical details, since you wouldn't be able to follow. I'm not even sure how many at the conference followed. But Rishi did, and that was enough. He crumpled."

"So it really was the anticlimax rather than the keynote."

"It kind of was. Pappa told me if it had been any better he would have had to kill me!"

"And Pappa's latent aggression makes you feel good?"

"Of course!"

"Okay," he said, and then laughed, Lucinda joining in.

"You know, it was incredibly nice of you to devote all that time to the Saint Petersburg Paradox just to help me understand Jesse's situation."

"Don't thank me. I was glad to do it. Fascinating stuff. And then there it was, come to my rescue. What goes around, comes around."

Cass cringed at that saying, even coming from Lucinda.

"Rational self-interest is always what morality boils down to," she continued in a reflective tone of voice.

"Do you think so?"

"Of course. I've always figured you must, too."

"Why's that?"

"Well, isn't that basically the core of Jewish ethics?"

"I never thought of it that way."

"The way I heard it, Judaism is the religion of rational actors. My father explained it to me. His grandfather was religious, so he knew all about it. The great rabbis had a saying: 'If I am not for myself, then who will be for me?'"

"And?"

"And what?"

"That's only part of it."

"It is?"

"The rest of the quote is: 'And if I'm *only* for myself, then what am I?'"

"Are you sure? That's not the way I heard it."

"I'm sure."

"Well, that's a disappointment."

"You don't mean that."

There's a pause.

"Lucinda?"

"I'm kidding, I'm kidding! Give me a little credit for complexity, will you! It was a joke!"

But she hadn't laughed. Again, Lucinda hadn't laughed.

XXV

The Argument from Cosmic Tremblings

It was the most painful and most exalted of his memories.

He had gone with his mother, the abandoned wife, to seek assistance from the rabbinical court on East Broadway. She had begged the attending rabbi to force her husband to grant her a *get*, a Jewish divorce. By Jewish Law, it is the husband's power alone to grant a *get*, and a woman in Hannah Klepfish's position inhabits a despised no-woman's-land, not married but not not-married, wandering in desolation between two worlds. The rabbi had sat there in judgment of her, with his barbed beard of dirty red, like the rusted pads of steel wool that she used for scrubbing her pots. But the Pharisee would not be moved. The Law would apply. Until this day, Jonas could not recall his mother's sobs without feeling that his body might split apart from the agony.

And it came to pass in that house of judgment, amidst the humiliation heaped upon them, that the decree had come down. As they were being shown out—Jonas, six years old, supporting his prostrated mother—an ancient rabbi, hardly taller than little Jonas, had placed his opened palms atop the child's head, and had shouted out, in the voice of the prophet,

"*Hoy, hat der kleiner ein moah godol uneshomo niflo'o!*"—"Oh, the little one has such a great brain and a wondrous soul."

In an instant, the woman and her son had gone from being cast down to lifted aloft. Hannah Klepfish was the mother of a child of whom prophecies were foretold.

The prophecy had unfolded on a day of jubilation when the letter of acceptance from Columbia University arrived at the Tillie E. Orlofsky projects on East Broadway. His blessed mother had danced—yes, whirled around like a Jewish maenad—on the faded but spotless kitchen linoleum. In her faded blue flannel bathrobe and her terry-cloth slippers, the cream she skimmed off from the top of the bottled milk smeared onto her face as a moisturizer, she had kicked up her legs in some jig she must have learned as a young girl back in Kishinev, Bessarabia. A simple woman who had never mastered the English language, who had had to ask Jonas to write his own "Please excuse my son's absence" notes to his elementary-school teachers, Hannah Klepfish held the acceptance letter in her right hand and offered a corner to Jonas, so that they had danced together like a bride and groom in a Jewish wedding, only not with a white handkerchief dangling between them but with the paper embossed with the blue shield and the Latin words *In lumine Tuo videbimus lumen*—"In Thy light shall we see light."

She had lived to see her Jonas's light spread throughout the world. He had become a professor at the great institution. Framed book jackets in every language papered the walls of her little apartment from floor to ceiling. He had never tainted her joy by disclosing the treachery of Great Britain.

Also never mentioned were the mortifications closer to home that Jonas underwent. As the decades passed, Columbia University had shown itself increasingly unworthy, finally assuming the proportions of perfidy in its failure to recognize the singularity of his achievements.

He had detested his colleagues. Oh, he had suffered, *suffered*, most especially when one of his mortal enemies, a most fearsome creature by the name of Harriet Horn (specialties: post-colonialism, gender and cultural studies), assumed the chair and proceeded to advocate positions for which no possible rationale could exist other than delivering hot irons to the exposed soul of Jonas Elijah Klapper. After every contentious department meeting, as he hurried away before anyone could detain him in chitchat, he would chant to himself a scrumptiously suitable verse adapted from the prophet Jeremiah:

> *Oh, my suffering, my suffering!*
> *How I writhe!*
> *Oh, the walls of my heart!*
> *My heart moans within me,*
> *I cannot be silent;*
> *For I hear the blare of horns,*
> *Alarms of war.*
> *Disaster overtakes disaster,*
> *For all the land has been ravaged. . . .*
> *In a moment, my tents have been ravaged.*
> *How long must I see [no] standards*
> *And hear the blare of horns?*

He had naughtily inserted the word "no" before "standards," and taken what comfort he might, an epicerastic to temper the acrimony of the humors (cf. *epikerastikos*, Galen).

He understood the nature of his trials: Where he trod, cosmic tremblings reverberated. Wherever he stood in the disputed terrain—whether it concerned syllabus reforms or the hiring of the latest imposter arrayed in foppish theory—that place became an arena for the hot conflict between heaven and hell engineered with a view toward universal issues. He had put his sufferings in their context, and he had endured.

But at Frankfurter University he required no such quaffs from balance-restoring epicerastics. Aside from a generous salary, sabbaticals, and territory—an entire floor of office space—they offered him the best of all possible relations with his colleagues—which is to say, none at all. None! Κανένας από αυτούς! No Harriet Horns to barge in red in the face, brandishing a copy of *The Collected Works of Transvestite Balladeers* and bellowing about dead white males. Jonas could—he would!—pack his syllabi with nothing but dead white males! He need never attend another departmental faculty meeting again, not unless he called one—and then, being the sole faculty member, he could boycott! Frankfurter's terms made him want to break out into a dance, into a wild Slavic *kazachoc*. Inside, he was dancing, squatting down and kicking out a right leg, a left, a right!

To top it off, Frankfurter University had offered a taxonomic penthouse they would construct for his sole habitation. "Distinguished Professor," the highest honor that was accorded a faculty member, was deemed incommensurate with Jonas Elijah Klapper's stature. The title that was to be Jonas's, and Jonas's alone, in perpetuity, was Extreme Distinguished Professor of Faith, Literature, and Values. If only that paragon of selfless maternality, who had been pitifully chained to the classification of an *agunah*, a deserted wife, had lived to see the change in academic nomenclature necessitated by her Jonas. And the signs and wonders had come pouring.

And now another.

The week after Roz's emotional return from the Amazon, Cass went for his Tuesday meeting and found Marjorie Cutter sitting in the small office where Cass had expected to find the professor. Her face, normally stolid, was churned up with the agitated eagerness of a bystander at a fatal accident, and she placed her index finger vertically against her mouth, forming the crucifix of silence, and motioned for Cass to stay put. The door of the next office was closed, but Cass, following Marge's urgent facial signals, listened, and an irate voice could be heard leaking through the wall.

Cass couldn't share in Marge's fevered excitement about a confrontation of soap-opera proportions happening in real life and within hearing. On the contrary, he felt his innards clenching. For a few minutes, while the voices remained muffled, it was conceivable that there was nobody but Jonas Elijah Klapper in the next office, either talking on the phone or having a psychotic breakdown, but the raised voices soon partitioned into two.

And suddenly there he was. He stood at the threshold, staring unseeingly, or so it seemed to Cass, his features distorted in that silent-film shriek of horror that recalled to Cass a moment he would just as soon have forgotten, when Klapper's wrath over "Dover Beach" had nearly annihilated Cass. Professor Klapper pushed past Cass, who tried to retract himself, and elbowed Marge to reach for his briefcase on the floor near the desk. He said not a word and turned away to flee, but not before Cass had caught sight of the wild gleam of triumph snaking its way across his face.

While Cass and Marge remained frozen like hands on a clock in a blackout, another apparition materialized at the threshold.

The dean of the faculty, often accused of being a bloodless prig, was giving the lie to the accusation. Browning Crisp's face was an apoplectic shade of red. He, too, stared unseeingly, or so it seemed to Cass, for several long moments.

"That is the most impossible man on the face of the earth!" he finally announced, which was as out of character as the pounding blood in his face, since Browning was the soul of decorum, and it was hardly decorous for someone at a certain rank, in this case a dean, to address those at a lower rank, in this case a secretary and a graduate student, regarding a personage above them, in this case a professor, not to speak of an Extreme Distinguished Professor.

"Professor Klapper?" ventured Marge in a small voice, hoping to push the dean to a few more indiscretions.

"Indeed!"

"You look like you've been given a terrible time," Marge urged gently.

"Well," Crisp said, collecting himself, "I daresay I'll recover."

The dean had gone to the Extreme Distinguished Professor to discuss his giving up some of his building space—he was using most of it for storage anyway—because it would be needed for the new brain and cognitive sciences center. Klapper had stared him down with the most intimidating of his glowers.

"I shall not relinquish a cubit!"

With his entreaty to Klapper's sense of collegiality rebuffed, the dean reminded Jonas that the space belonged to the university. Brain science and cognitive science were dynamic and expanding fields. To stay in the first rank, Frankfurter had to allow them to grow. Harriet and Manny Katzenbaum had generously donated the funds for renovation if the university could come up with the available space. It was Browning's responsibility as dean to allocate space according to the greater good of the university. Jonas's underused offices were the logical option for the time being.

Perhaps it was the word "logical" that had touched off the ensuing tirade. Klapper had insulted Browning Crisp up and down the canon, accusing him of being an academic apparatchik of the noetic *nomenklatura,* a moral Quisling who was reneging on the covenant of trust and who would be reduced, if he were remembered at all, to an ignominious footnote in the history of Jonas Elijah Klapper.

At this point, Browning Crisp lost his own temper and wielded his decanal power. There was no more negotiation: some of Jonas's space would be taken away. Klapper told him that in that case he would resign. It may have been said in the heat of the moment, but Browning Crisp was going to hold him to it.

Jonas had shown, under the circumstances, the restraint of a saint. The insult was historic. They were proposing not only to reduce his square footage but to bestow the stolen property on his sworn enemies. These were the illiterate mob intending to trample out intellectual and spiritual life as Jonas Elijah Klapper had known and shaped it, the light-spun span of all the faith, literature, and values of the ages. This brain and cognitive sciences center represented the worst of scientism, for it had set its sights on the study of Man. "Go, wond'rous creature! mount where Science guides, / Go, measure earth, weigh air, and state the tides; / Instruct the planets in what orbs to run, / Correct old time, and regulate the Sun"—but keep your filthy fingers off the study of Man! This was but a small share of his thoughts on the matter that he had seen fit to impart to the odious dean of faculty.

The ex–Extreme Distinguished Professor hadn't gotten in touch with any of his graduate students, nor had anyone from the administration. At the designated time, the seven of them were assembled round the seminar table, awaiting the Sublime, the Subliminal, and the Self.

Vague rumors had reached them, but they were uncertain of everything. It fell to Cass to tell them quietly of the scene that he had witnessed, and they received the news in wounded silence. The few desultory speculations concerned where he might go next, and they along with him.

"He could go anywhere."

"Not Great Britain."

"Well, of course, not there."

"He could always go back to Columbia. I'm sure Columbia would be thrilled to have him back."

"It would be good to go back to New York."

"Who knows where it will be? We could end up almost anywhere in the world."

"It's kind of exciting. Disorienting but exciting."

"You have to expect the unexpected with Jonas."

They sat there for the full two and a half hours of the seminar, long after they had given up on Professor Klapper's appearing, feeling that it would be disloyal to leave before the allotted time was over. When Cass left them, they were heading as one toward the View from Nowhere.

XXVI

The Argument from Chosen Individuals

Cass had decided against informing Klapper of his change of plans. He would go and speak to the dean of graduate students. His hope was that some other Frankfurter department would accept him. He had some ideas about what he wanted to study. But Cass received word from Klapper himself, a scrawled note left in his box summoning him.

Cass wasn't sure in which of the two offices he'd find him. The door to the smaller of them was ajar, and Klapper was sitting at his desk, calmly writing. He didn't turn at the sound of Cass's footstep, so Cass knocked on the open door, and the professor turned around in slow motion.

"Ah, Reb Chaim. Take a seat."

Jonas Elijah Klapper was smiling, and Cass recalled that inexplicable gleam of triumph that had vied with righteous fury for control of the professor's face, as if the screaming match with Browning Crisp was the realization of all that he could hope for.

"So, Reb Chaim, here we are!"

Cass nodded. Professor Klapper's face looked almost glazed with well-being.

"But not for long," Klapper continued in response to Cass's

nod. "I shall soon be departing Frankfurter University. Indeed, I am going to a distant land. I shall be telling you where before too long. There are things I cannot yet say. I am enjoined to preserve the silence of the Dura Valley, or, to paraphrase the Valdener Rebbe, the silence of the Hudson Valley."

The creases in his pate that had been pressed into place by ceaseless cerebration were smoothed, the blued shadows that mottled his jowls and the half-circles beneath his eyes were lightened, his coloring, usually cement-gray, was roseate, and even the down slope of his eye seemed raised several degrees. Perhaps this was the face of beatitude.

"The Valdener Rebbe, may his name be blessed, spoke to me in the allegorical mode, this being the only means by which certain things may be imparted, a threefold interpretation being customary. And so it was that the Rebbe spoke of the special-needs children in the community. These children are beloved of God and yet separated from Him through no fault of their own. They lack the means to find their way through the sacred paths of learning. I alone, the Rebbe said, of all the men whom he had ever met, had the connections to help these children.

"'The special-needs children of the community' refers to the nation of Israel in exile, and the connections of which he spoke became clearer to me as he went on.

"He spoke of a child, one child. 'On such a child I never dreamt to rest my eyes.'"

Klapper was a good mimic. Cass could hear the Rebbe's voice lurking beind Klapper's.

"He called the child 'my son,' and as he spoke his eyes glistened with the purity of his tears. 'Abraham despaired of a son, and then Isaac was born. Hannah, too, despaired of a son. She went with her husband to the temple at Shiloh and prayed with such ardor that Eli the priest thought she must be drunk or out of her mind and wanted to throw her out.'"

And though Cass knew that Klapper's eyes would move inexorably in the direction of the photograph, when they did he had to resist the urge to flee.

"'I, too, knew such despair.'" He was still speaking in the Rebbe's voice. "'And as it is written of the Arizal, the lion of S'fat, so it was with the child. The child grew and was weaned and was brought to school and learned more and faster than any child his own age, following in the footsteps of Isaac on the way to Moriah.'"

Cass's desire to flee had grown so urgent that he could feel it as a physical sensation spreading through his limbs.

Klapper had now sunk into profound reflection, and Cass cautiously began to rise from the green metal chair.

"Stay!" Klapper bellowed.

Cass sat down swiftly.

"I have alluded to the fact that I shall shortly be leaving these shores. It will not surprise you to learn that I shall be going to the holy city of S'fat, where my footsteps have always been pointed. In a manner of speaking, I am going into exile, at least for some years. I can take only one student with me. I have chosen you."

"*Me?*"

"You seem surprised. I wonder why. Perhaps it is the humility of the true disciple."

"But what about the others? What about Gideon Raven? He's been studying with you for almost thirteen years. He understands your ideas better than anyone."

"Gideon is a more-than-adequate student of my past. But you, Reb Chaim, shall be the student of my future. You have already had a taste of the bitterness of exile. I had a divination concerning you, even before I knew who you were, and I tested you. You are aware of what I allude to?"

"'Dover Beach'?"

Klapper's smile was benedictory, and he nodded once.

"I have too soft a heart and could not extend your trial too long. You see how nothing is as it seems? In a moment of abject humiliation, the loftiest of futures can be received. As Hannah and her son were lifted aloft, so, too, the tested student."

Even Roz was stunned when Cass related this conversation with Klapper.

"S'fat? Where the hell is S'fat?"

He had gone to her place on Francis Avenue, hoping to find her there. She answered the door in a purple towel, her hair dripping wet. She had gone for a late run and had just gotten out of the shower.

"It's in Israel. It's where the Jewish mystics congregate. One of the hot spots."

He wished that she didn't go running at night. She was fearless, and he loved that about her, but he also worried.

"The Hot S'fat!" she said, laughing.

It would be wonderful to take care of her. She was a woman, even if she was Suwäayaiwä, and he wanted to take care of her.

"It's not really funny."

She was beautiful and brilliant, strong and immensely kind.

"It's not?"

And she loved with such force. She had loved Tsetse, and she loved Azarya, and she loved him, too. She loved Cass Seltzer.

"He wants to take me along with him. Only me. None of the others. Not even Gideon. He's abandoning them all."

As wild and unpredictable as she was, she was always on his side. That was and would always be predictable. And he was on hers. Even without always getting what her side was, he knew with certainty that he'd be on it, and she'd be on his.

"What a shit. Still, you have to admit it's all for the best."

What a thing it is in this world to have somebody always on your side.

"I hope Gideon sees it that way. I worry that he's about to become the most disappointed man in the world."

"I don't know. He's got a lot of contenders."

Cass was staring at Roz.

"What is it, Cass? Do I still have shampoo in my hair?"

He stooped down swiftly to one knee.

"I love you, Suwäayaiwä!"

"Well, I love you, too!"

She followed suit and got down on one knee in her purple towel.

"No, no. You have to stand, and I have to kneel!"

"Okay." She got back up. "What are we playing?"

"We're not. I'm proposing."

"What are you proposing?"

"Marry me! Marry me and become Suwäayaiwä Seltzer."

"Good one!" She laughed. "No, wait a minute! You mean it! Darling boy, get up. You're upsetting me down there."

He got up. She put her hand on his cheek.

"I can't marry you, Cass."

"Never? I know I'm young, but I'm getting older quick."

"Cass, I can't think about marriage, and you're only thinking about it because you're having a breakdown and haven't realized it yet."

"I don't think I'm having a breakdown. I think I'm realizing that you're the most perfect woman in the world."

"Well, of course I am." She gently stroked his hair. The tender gesture made her feel even more impossibly tender. "I'll always be there for you, but I need a life of maximal options."

"Don't you think you could live with maximal options married to me?"

"I have all kinds of things I need to do with my life. You do, too, only you don't know what they are yet. Don't look so woebegone! You're going to have a lot more loves in your life."

"That's supposed to cheer me up?"

"You know what you're doing, don't you?"

"I'm asking you to marry me."

"You're trying to replace your infatuation with Jonas Elijah Klapper with an infatuation with me. You're trying to do it so quickly that the loss won't register on your mind. It's a rebound reflex."

"That's not what love is."

"Okay, I'm game. What's love?"

"Love is this. It's real. It's not infatuation or bewitchment or enchantment. It's the splendor that's still there after the disenchantment of the world."

If they got married, they would be able to tell their children that he had proposed to their mother while she was wearing a purple towel. It was the purple towel that gave him hope as he waited for her to break her long silence.

XXVII

The Argument from the Bones of the Dead

Cass was grateful—and surprised—when Pascale remembered to scrawl him a note and leave it where he would be certain to see it, telling him that his mother had called.

"Deb. Call. Urgent."

She had put it on a front burner of the kitchen stove. Of course he would be certain to notice it when he came home from work to start dinner, as he did every night except when they ate out. The symbolism was perfect, worthy of Pascale, whose every gesture was touched by her poetry. Was she aware of the English idiom "putting something on the back burner"? Was there a similar expression in French? Cass's colloquial French wasn't good enough for him to know. It would be like her, though, the poetic economy and compression that wrapped the message in metaphor.

Still, his stomach lurched at the three words. His mother's tone must have been truly urgent to break through the heavy fog of Pascale's poetic distractions. He was almost sure the urgency had something to do with Jesse. There was no reason to think that Jesse had collided with disaster, unless one considered as a reason Jesse's whole history, the reckless belief in his ability to push past the limits of the strictly moral, not to speak of the legal, and assume that he'd get away with it.

Things had been going well for Cass's little brother for the last two years. He was working on Wall Street, for a firm called New Empire Reinvestment Opportunities, and he had soared to the top. He was living largely and glamorously. His girlfriends were supermodels, his apartment in SoHo so fabulous that Woody Allen had used it to film one of his movies, paying him twenty thousand dollars a day, which was chump change, Jesse said, but he'd agreed to it because it was so cool.

All of this made his mother nervous. Cass could tell because when she spoke about Jesse she only quoted him and never added her own commentary—as if she was willing herself to believe no more and no less than what he was telling her. It didn't reassure her that the acronym for Jesse's firm was NERO.

But the phone call had nothing to do with Jesse. It was Azarya Sheiner that his mother was worrying about.

"Things have reached a crisis state. He wants to leave. He doesn't feel he can do anything else. He needs to go to a university. He needs to meet mathematicians."

"He must be going through hell."

"If it was hard for me, I can only begin to imagine what it's like for him."

"What do you think we can do for him?"

"That's why I'm calling you. You know he's been corresponding with that professor at MIT."

"Gabriel Sinai."

"Right. Gabriel Sinai. Seems like a lovely man."

"He does."

In the past few years, his mother had had more contact

with the town where she'd grown up, America's only shtetl, but only because of Azarya. It was because of Azarya that she'd overcome her aversion and reconnected with her extended family and with the Rebbe. Cass had enlisted her help ten years ago, in her capacity as a school psychologist, when he and Roz had realized the nature of the Rebbe's son.

Three years ago, Azarya had turned thirteen, the age that marks the end of childhood for an observant Jewish male.

Cass hadn't been able to go to Azarya's Bar Mitzvah, since he couldn't very well take Pascale to New Walden—it would have been overwhelming for her—and he hadn't wanted to leave her at home. In fact, he hadn't seen Azarya in years. It was his mother who kept him up to date. The festivities for Azarya's Bar Mitzvah had lasted an entire week, with all of New Walden, as well as many Hasidim from other sects, participating. Azarya's birthday was in May, and the streets of New Walden had overflowed with celebration, the Valdeners dancing beneath the lilacs.

His mother had gone to the opening event. She'd planned to go to more, arranging to stay over with her cousin Shaindy for the Shabbes that would crown the tumult, but realized that she couldn't take any more of it, not even for Azarya's sake. And she couldn't get close to him anyway, claustrated as she was in the curtained-off women's section. The event she had attended had begun with the Rebbe and Azarya handing out awards to Valdener students who had excelled in special examinations that had been given in honor of the Bar Mitzvah. Each of the children came up to the dais, where the Rebbe and his son stood, and picked up a plastic cup of grape juice, whose contents had been mingled with a cup from which the Rebbe himself had sipped, toasted *l'chaim*—to life—and then received a holy book, the difficulty of which varied with the student's age.

After that the Rebbe had made a long speech recounting the saga of the Valdener Hasidim, the story of one sect but also of one family, going back from the Bar Mitzvah boy to his father, the present Valdener Rebbe, to Azarya's grandfather, who had brought a portion of his followers over to America in time to escape Hitler, though many had perished, and past that time to the other rebbes, fathers and sons with the occasional son-in law, ending finally back at the root of it all, the Ba'al Shem Tov himself. The story of the Rebbe's family was the story of the Valdeners, which was the story of Hasidism, which was the story of the Jews. Azarya's becoming a Bar Mitzvah was a triumph in a long, unlikely tale of survival.

The Rebbe had spoken of the vision of the prophet Ezekiel—Yechezkel in Hebrew. "The King of Babylonia, Nebuchadnezzar, threw Chananya, Mishael, and Azarya into the fiery furnace, and at the same time the Holy One, blessed be He, said to Yechezkel, 'Go and restore the dead in the valley of Dura.' And those bones came and slapped Nebuchadnezzar in the face!

"There is no resurrection of the dead greater than this! Our valley of Dura is the Hudson Valley. Here stands Azarya, a Bar Mitzvah! Azarya the Rav lives! Azarya *ha-Rav chai*! Azarya the holy one lives! Azarya *ha-kodesh chai*! The gematria adds up to 719. And the gematria of the sentence describing how Yechezkel breathed life into the dry bones is also 719! *Va-tevo ba hem ha-ruach vi-yichiyu*. And the breath came into them, and they lived!"

Cass and his mother's Bar Mitzvah present to Azarya had been a subscription to *Annals of Mathematics*. Cass had consulted a mathematician at Frankfurter, Barry Fine, as to which mathematics journal to order. Barry had shown an interest in the story of the Hasidic boy with the unusual mathematical gifts, and he'd told Cass that if Azarya wanted he could write to him. Azarya did, and Barry and he were still corresponding. But at a certain point, Barry had suggested that Azarya needed a better mathematician than himself and had gotten in touch with Gabriel Sinai. Not only was Gabriel a legend, but he had also been a child prodigy, back in Augusta, Georgia. And he was also an Orthodox Jew, although with nothing like the insularity of the Valdeners. He'd become observant when he was an undergraduate at Harvard and, feeling lost on campus, had started eating his meals at the Harvard Hillel, liking the crowd he'd found there. Their lives were more ordered and restrained than the bacchanalia in his dorm, and he had felt comfortable. He liked that the religion was more about deed than creed. If you stopped eating Kraft cheese because you worried that the rennet from the stomach of an animal was the ingredient used to solidify the milk, you were a good Jew, whether you believed in God or not. Judaism was behaviorist. Carry out the behavior and the beliefs would take care of themselves. Or not. This seemed a sensible religion to Gabriel, a religion that freed you from having to waste brain-power on the mundane choices of your physical existence but didn't bother you too much about your beliefs. And he continued to take his meals at the Harvard Hillel, which was as convenient as it was congenial, since at forty-one he still wasn't married.

He had also found a certain solace in the idea of a day of rest. He liked to think that the 14.3 percent of the week in which he was conserving his mathematical activity might extend his productivity a few more years. Like many in his profession, Gabriel was sensitive about the premature senescence that hangs above the heads of mathematicians like the sword of Damocles. The Fields Medal, the highest accolade in mathematics, is restricted to mathematicians forty or younger, and many will tell you that's because if a mathematician hasn't produced remarkable work by then, then he is never going to do it. The medal isn't given for a single result but for a body of work, which makes the age restriction all the more telling.

Gabriel had won his Fields Medal at the age of thirty-one, and among the theorems that had gotten him the math world's equivalent of a Nobel was a result concerning prime numbers, which had fascinated him since his days as a prodigy. For centuries, mathematicians have tried to find patterns in the way the prime numbers are distributed among the whole numbers. Is there, in that infinite sequence of primes, a stretch that is as long as you like and in which the difference between each prime number and its successor in the stretch is always the same number n? Mathematicians had long suspected there was, and Gabriel had proved a theorem that showed that their intuition was correct.

"Sinai wants Azarya to come to MIT to meet with him," Cass's mother continued. "He's prepared to sponsor him, or whatever the term is, to get him into MIT, even though he doesn't have any of the conventional qualifications."

"I wouldn't say that," said Cass. "He got a perfect 1600 on his SATs."

Cass's mother had used her connections as a school psychologist to arrange for Azarya to take the standardized exams.

"True. Even though your old girlfriend Roz was worried when she met him that he'd never learn to read."

"So what does Azarya think about Sinai's plan?"

"He's excited. He wants to come up as soon as possible."

"He's told his father?"

"You know Azarya."

"So how'd the Rebbe take it?"

"That I don't know. I didn't ask."

There was a heavy silence on both ends.

"He'll stay with us, of course."

"Of course. But maybe you should check with Pascale."

"I know it will be okay with her. She loves mathematicians. She grew up with them. And you know how kind she is."

"I think you should check with her anyway."

Cass found Pascale perfectly amenable when he told her. He explained that Azarya Sheiner was a sixteen-year-old prodigy, and that he would be spending a few days at MIT. "It will be better if he stays with us rather than at a hotel."

"Why?"

"He's a stranger in the world."

"All mathematicians are strangers in the world."

"He's especially a stranger, even for a mathematician. He comes from an insular background, very religious."

"Jewish?"

"Yes. In fact, he's a distant cousin on my mother's side."

"I've never met a religious Jew. It will be interesting for me."

"You'll like him. He's amazing."

"Perhaps yes, perhaps no. It is annoying for one person to command another to like someone."

"It was more of a prediction."

"That is even more annoying."

There was a flurry of telephone conversations between

Cass and his mother. Azarya would take a New Walden Kosher bus to the Port Authority Terminal in New York, then a Greyhound to South Station in Boston. From there, the Red Line on the T would take him to Porter Square, and he could walk from there to Cass's house. Cass would get back from Frankfurter as soon as possible, but Pascale would be there to let him in.

Unfortunately, Cass wasn't able to leave his office as early as he'd planned, and on the drive home he worried about how Pascale and Azarya had interacted. They were both strangers in the world, which meant that they might hit it off fantastically, though also might not.

Cass drove back from Frankfurter fast, even through the speed traps that separated Weedham from Cambridge. It was true that Pascale was an extraordinarily kind person—he'd seen her hand over a sandwich she'd just bought at Au Bon Pain to a homeless man haranguing the passersby of Harvard Square—but the thick smoke of distractions in which she lived often obscured her vision of anything outside it, and sometimes her obliviousness could result in unintended rudeness. And she was right that a person couldn't predict whom she'd like and whom she wouldn't.

Pascale had taken an instant dislike to Roz when she had visited, to the extent that she had not sat down with them at the table when they ate, instead taking a tray with bread and cheese and fruit up to her study. Cass knew that Roz could come on strong and was an acquired taste, but he hadn't understood what Roz had done that was so objectionable. Something must have passed between them that he hadn't seen, and he suspected it must have been Roz's fault. Were he to list Pascale's attributes, he would put kindness first, even before her poetic passion and brilliance, her fierce and fragile beauty, that ethereality that was such a part of her essence that its scent emanated from her hair.

When Cass pulled up, he was surprised to see Azarya sitting on the steps with a suitcase next to him. It had to be Azarya, even though Cass would not have recognized him, because what other Hasid would be sitting on his front steps? Azarya stood as Cass got out of the car, and smiled, coming down the stairs to meet him at the front gate.

Azarya probably wouldn't grow to be a tall man, though who knew? At sixteen, he could still shoot up. Cass had been one of the smaller kids in his class until around Azarya's age, though he'd had unusually big hands and feet, and his mother had predicted he would grow into them. Azarya was reaching out to shake his hand, and Cass's big mitt enfolded it completely.

"Azarya! At long last! But what are you doing out here? It's cold!"

It was mid-March and still wintry, especially at this hour, the sun having disappeared over the horizon.

"I was waiting for you."

"But why out here?"

Azarya smiled with a shrug.

Cass suddenly recalled the complicated Jewish laws about a man being alone with a woman who was not his wife. How stupid of him to have forgotten! Of course, he wasn't sure what he could have done about it anyway. He couldn't very well have ordered Pascale not to be in her own house when Azarya arrived, while leaving the key with a neighbor.

"Come on in. Let's warm you up."

But when Cass got inside the house, it was dark and empty.

"Where's Pascale?" he asked Azarya.

Again Azarya smiled and shrugged.

"You were sitting out there because there was nobody home?"

"I didn't sit here the whole time. I walked around. I saw Harvard. I walked to MIT. It was good."

"What did you do with your suitcase?"

"I carried it."

Cass smiled, a bit confused. Should he start worrying about Pascale? They had only the one car, so she couldn't have gotten into an accident, but she could have been hit crossing a street, or been a hostage in a bank robbery, tied up in the vault, her small hands helplessly trussed. Before he could get going, he heard the key in the door, and Pascale was running up the front stairs as swift and light as a child, wiggling out of her black sheepskin coat, and hanging it in the hall closet.

She came into the living room and stopped short, looking from her husband to the strange young man standing next to him. She had seen pictures of people who looked like this, but she was shocked to see one in her own house.

"Pascale," Cass said. "This is Azarya. Azarya, Pascale."

Fortunately, Pascale was not in the habit of extending her hand at introductions. Cass didn't know how Azarya would have handled that. He was, of course, not allowed to touch a woman.

Pascale stared. She was dressed in her usual narrow black slacks that hugged her round little derrière, and had on a fuzzy sweater, vividly rose. Her white skin had a faint wash of color from the cold outside, and there was the slash of red over her mouth.

"Here, Azarya. Let me take your coat," Cass said to break the silence.

"No, it's okay. I'll keep it on."

"But you're staying here. Make yourself at home!"

Azarya smiled.

"It's so kind of you both. I hope I'm not putting you out."

"Are you kidding? This is great! Pascale, if it's okay with you, I'll just show Azarya his room and let him get settled. Then I'll start dinner. Azarya, don't worry about food. I went to Brookline yesterday and bought everything from a takeout place that's strictly kosher. I have paper plates, plastic utensils, everything. I got the strictest instructions from my mother, and I followed them to the letter. She even called Cousin Shaindy to make sure that the takeout place met the Valdener standards, but I bought a lot of fresh fruits and vegetables in case you don't feel completely comfortable, not knowing the place for yourself."

"Ah, so that is what that food is!" Pascale murmured.

Azarya smiled at her voice. She did have a charming voice, thickly accented, smoky soft.

"Yes. And I threw out all the food that wasn't kosher, so you don't have to worry about contamination."

Azarya laughed, turning red as he did so.

"You didn't have to go to all that trouble. It's enough that you let me sleep here."

"Would our food really contaminate his?" Pascale asked. "This I do not understand. How would the contaminants be transmitted? Like spores in the air?"

"No, I was exaggerating. I just didn't want anything to get mixed up."

"It is strange," Pascale softly observed.

Azarya laughed again, and again you could see the flush creeping along his translucent cheeks. He didn't look as if he had started shaving. No, of course he hadn't, or he would have a beard.

His hair had darkened since he was a little boy, at least judging by his *payess*. They were no longer the color of flax, but of baked whole wheat.

"You sure you don't want to give me your coat?"

"It's okay."

It occurred to Cass that Azarya just wanted to warm up first. He'd probably been freezing, sitting on the porch waiting for them.

"Come, you'll be staying here on this floor."

Cass led him into the bedroom that was off the living room.

"It's private here. There's your bathroom. Pascale and I are upstairs."

"It's good. Much more space than I have in my own home, with all the sisters."

"How many is it now? Oh, I'm sorry! I'd forgotten."

"No, no, it's okay. I have eleven sisters. But the five oldest are already married and have children of their own—so far all of them girls, eight of them!"

"So you're still the only boy. What are the odds of that?"

"One in 524,288."

Cass smiled.

"And you still have a prime number of sisters. And your nieces are a perfect cube."

"You remember that. Amazing."

"It's more amazing that you remember. You were only a small boy."

"But for me, it was a big event. To meet you and Professor Klapper and Miss Margolis. To learn that there were names for things like prime numbers. To learn that I lived in a place called the United States of America."

"I remember. She drew you a map. Did you really teach yourself to read from that map?"

"It wasn't so hard. She'd said all the names as she wrote them down, and I remembered them. And I already knew how to read Hebrew and Yiddish and Aramaic, so I had the idea that letters could represent sounds."

Cass smiled at him. Now that he was looking more closely at Azarya's face, he could see that the child he remembered was preserved there. The expression was eerily similar, and the wide-spaced eyes, a deep blue almost verging on violet. His features were still delicate, though his face had become thinner, the petal-shape curve of his cheek elongated and flattened. He still looked young enough so that the term that came to mind was "beautiful" rather than "handsome."

"Come, let's give you something to eat."

Azarya took off his coat and hung it in the closet.

"Warmed up now?" Cass asked, and of course Azarya only laughed in response, since to do anything else would be to admit he'd been cold in the first place, which would be to imply that his host and hostess had been remiss in leaving him to fend for himself for four and a half hours. Cass was beginning to catch on.

Azarya took off his felt hat. Under it he had a black velvet skullcap, which he kept on.

They went to the kitchen, and Cass took out the food he'd gotten from Tirza's Batampte Kitchen—Tirza's Tasty Kitchen—and started warming the carrot tzimmes and the mushrooms with barley in the microwave, leaving the food in the sealed containers so that, as Pascale had put it, none of the spores could infect it. There was also a large pickled fish that Cass set out on the table in the aluminum pan it had come in.

"Sorry for the inelegance." He laughed.

"It's very kind of you to go to all this trouble. I'll set the table," Azarya said.

"It's only these paper plates and plastic knives and forks."

"Really, I didn't expect this, or I wouldn't have bothered you at all."

"Nonsense. This is such a pleasure for me! Looking at you, I realize how quickly the years have gone. Here, just put them at these three places." Cass indicated where they'd be sitting at the huge table, with its six oversize chairs. "When do you see Gabriel Sinai?"

"Tomorrow morning at nine."

"I can drive you over."

"Oh no, no need. I know the way. I went by Professor Sinai's office this afternoon, just so I'd know how to get there. It will take me a half hour at the most, now that I know where it is."

Cass smiled. He was elated. Azarya had had this effect on him when he was a child, and now Cass hadn't spent more than ten minutes with him and he was already giddy. Why not? The boy was there intact, you could see the child still lurking in his expression. Only by now, at sixteen, his mind must have traveled infinities. Barry Fine certainly thought so, and, according to Barry, Gabriel Sinai, himself one of the best mathematical minds alive, was willing to go all-out to get the boy to MIT. And if that happened, then of course Azarya should live with Cass and Pascale. He was too young to be in a dormitory, and that world would be too disruptive anyway. How could Azarya go from New Walden to coed dorms and friends with benefits? No, it made sense for Azarya to live here with Cass and Pascale, who were his own family and would ease his transition. Cass was already heady on the fantasy.

Cass ran upstairs to Pascale's study to bring her down for dinner. She was standing at the window that looked out on the park across the street, and turned around at his footstep.

"Is the Jewish food ready?" she asked.

He laughed. "It's just regular food, really. You won't be able to taste the difference."

"It is very strange to me."

"It's pretty strange to me, too."

"Not in the same way. That much is obvious."

"How do you mean?"

"The obvious meaning. You are Jewish."

"But not a practicing Jew. Not a believing Jew."

"Still, it is very different for me. It makes me see you differently, too."

"Me?"

"I had never thought about it, that you are Jewish. It made no difference. It was not part of my conception." She pronounced this as a French word.

"Does it make a difference now?"

"It is just that I am seeing it now. I had not even seen it before, and now I wonder how it is I could not. It is like when I noticed that the Klimt rug in the living room has circles that are ovaries. I had never seen them until I saw them. Now to look at the rug is to see the ovaries."

Cass felt the elation draining out of him, though it was understandable that Pascale would, at first, think of Azarya as alien, an intergalactic voyager. The whole point of the distinctive hair and clothes was, of course, to keep the Hasidim separate from the outside world. These things were as effective as Cass's tossing all the unkosher items out of the refrigerator, meant to ensure that no mix-ups occurred. It would be hard for Azarya at MIT if even Pascale was having difficulties seeing past the *payess*.

They sat down at the table.

"But why do you have the paper and the plastic? Can our plates also infect his food? You did not throw out all our dinnerware, I hope!"

Cass shook his head, the blush on Azarya's face painful to see. Then, to divert the conversation as quickly as possible, he said to Azarya, "Pascale's father is a mathematician. He's at the Institut des Hautes Etudes Scientifiques."

"Oh, in Bures-sur-Yvette!"

"Ah, you know!" Pascale's tone was instantaneously warmer.

Azarya smiled.

"Is it okay if I ask who your father is?"

"He is Claude Puissant."

"The Puissant Manifold?"

"Ah! You know this, too!" This time she raised her glass of Carmel kosher wine at him in a toast. Her eyebrows had interlaced over her nose as she'd studied the label, finally shrugging and taking a cautious sip, grimacing slightly before taking another one.

"I assumed the manifold was named 'Puissant' because it's such a powerful tool." He smiled self-effacingly. "I have a lot to learn."

"I am also interested in mathematics. Most especially probability theory, which I reject without qualification."

Azarya's smile wavered a little uncertainly.

"I will explain. An event that happens happens. Its non-occurrence, therefore, cannot happen. When something happens, its not happening cannot happen. If it is happening, then it is happening one hundred percent, and it is zero percent that it is not happening. Therefore"—she puffed into the second syllable in her distinctive way—"there is only the absolutely impossible, with the probability of zero, and there is the thing that happens with absolute necessity, so that its probability is complete and infinite. *C'est tout.*"

The blood rushed to Azarya's cheeks, and he got a look of panic in his eyes.

"Would you like some wine?" Cass asked him, and Azarya, who had declined any wine before, dumbly nodded yes, and then, not bothering to examine the label as Pascale had done—he must simply have trusted Cass to have obtained kosher wine—took a long sip.

Pascale excused herself early from dinner, carrying another glass of the Carmel with her upstairs. Cass poured the rest of the bottle into Azarya's glass.

"Pascale is a poet," Cass said.

"A poet," Azarya said. "I never met a poet before." He smiled. "She's how I would have pictured a poet. She's very . . . poetic."

"Maybe sometimes a little . . . imprecise."

"Poetic license." Azarya laughed.

Cass wondered whether Azarya realized that Pascale wasn't Jewish. It was hard to gauge how worldly Azarya was, but for him even to know a phrase like "poetic license" showed that he was reading. He was obviously less of a stickler for the Law than the other Valdeners—at the very least, he didn't count counting people as a transgression. The question that was quivering on Cass's lips was what the Valdener Rebbe thought of his son's venture into the outside world. Was this sojourn to Cambridge an act of rebellion? As if reading the unspoken question, Azarya brought up his father.

"My father sends you his greetings. He says that it's more than long enough between your last visit and your next."

"How is he?"

"How is he? I am wondering that myself. The whole time on the bus, walking around Cambridge, even sitting here at dinner with you and Pascale, I am asking myself how he is."

There was quiet in the room. Cass sighed, and Azarya answered him with another sigh, staring down at the tzimmes on his plate.

"I'm thinking about my mother," Cass said. "I'd never really asked her too much about her leaving New Walden. She just told me recently that it had been hard for her."

"Your mother is my angel. Remember when Miss Margolis—"

"I think you should call her Roz. If I know her, and I do, she'd be offended to hear you calling her 'Miss Margolis.'"

Azarya smiled.

"Yes, I like that. Roz had said I was her angel. I thought that was the best joke I had heard in my life. But now that's how I think of your mother. She's my angel."

Cass smiled.

"She's a wonderful mother to me and Jesse."

"And a second wonderful mother to me. In many ways, I'm closer to her than to my own mother. Your mother sends me books, journals, tapes of Bach, Mozart."

"You like music?"

"Very much."

"Do you play an instrument?"

"Not to speak of. I listen."

Azarya cast his deep-blue eyes in the direction of the baby grand.

"Do you play?"

"Like you, I listen. Pascale plays, though not often enough. But if you like, we could listen to the stereo now. Come take a look at my CDs while I clean up."

"I'll help you first."

"There's really nothing to do here. There's something to be said for eating on disposable plates."

They tossed the remains, and then Cass showed Azarya his CD collection, which he examined at length. He chose Glenn Gould playing Bach's *Goldberg* Variations, and the two of them settled down on the couch and melted into the music. And when the last measure was played, Azarya asked if they could listen to it again.

XXVIII
The Argument from the Mandelbaum Equilibrium

This time, when the phone rings at 2 a.m., Cass is certain that his desperate plea for help preparing for the Fidley debate has been answered at last, but once again he's wrong. For the third time in the last seven hours, it's Lucinda.

"Lucinda!"

"Are you up? Did I wake you?"

"No, you didn't wake me. I don't seem to be sleeping much since you went away."

"Well, I'll be home tomorrow."

"And don't forget I'm picking you up at Logan."

"I really could take a cab. Pappa's picking up all expenses."

"No, I want to come get you."

"But that's double the driving time. You'll have to drive to Logan and then drive back." She doesn't have much confidence in Cass's mathematical abilities, and he laughs.

"Don't worry about it. And if I'm a few minutes late, don't assume I'm not coming. I have that debate with Fidley tomorrow—well, actually today. It should end in plenty of time for me to get to Logan, but give me a few minutes, just in case."

"Debate with Fidley?"

"Felix Fidley."

"Oh, right. I remember. Tell me again what you're debating him on?"

"God. The existence of God."

"Right. I still can't believe that Felix Fidley wants to argue for religion. It's just a way for him to show off his brilliance, to take a far-out position and then overwhelm everybody with the way he can make it sound persuasive."

"I hope he doesn't overwhelm me."

"I hope not, too."

"Hey, can I get a little more encouragement going here?"

"You know this stuff inside and out. There's nothing Fidley can pull on you. I have absolute confidence."

"My girl," he says gratefully.

"I'm sorry that I've been calling you so much today," Lucinda says, changing the subject. "I'm being something of a nuisance."

"You never have to apologize for calling me. Call me three times, thirty times, three hundred times a day."

"I'm still worried that maybe you didn't get my joke about being for yourself as the core of Jewish ethics. That you still think I was actually being serious."

"Lucinda." He's moved that she cares so much what he thinks about her. "Don't you think I know your sense of humor by now?" He's not only moved; he is, he now has to admit, relieved that he can eliminate any nagging, disloyal doubt.

"Oh, good. Well, I better let you get some sleep if you're going to fang Felix Fidley tomorrow."

"Good night, Lucinda. Sleep well."

"Good night, Cass. You sleep well, too. I love you."

XXIX

The Argument from Rigid Designators

Cass came down the next morning at seven, still wet from his shower, anxious that Azarya be on time for his appointment with Gabriel Sinai. He wanted the boy to have a good breakfast, too. The door to the spare bedroom was open. Cass walked over to it and saw that the bed was neatly made. In the bathroom, the bath towel was still damp from the boy's shower. But he was gone, no signs of his having had a glass of juice or milk. Cass imagined that either Azarya wanted to get out before Pascale and Cass woke up so that he wouldn't get in their way, or that he was too excited to stay put.

Cass was disappointed. He had woken eager to come down and talk to Azarya. He'd given him a key to the house so he wouldn't have to worry about the boy's having to wander around until somebody got home.

Azarya called Cass at his office during the day to say that Professor Sinai wanted to take him to the Harvard Hillel that night for dinner, and would that be okay? Cass assured him it would be, but again was disappointed—stupidly, of course, since Azarya had come here to spend time not with Cass and Pascale but with Professor Sinai.

Azarya had asked Cass whether there was a time by which

he ought to be home, and Cass had said no, he should feel free to come and go as he wanted. That's why he had given him the key.

"But you have to be careful. Not all parts of Cambridge are safe. It's not like New Walden."

Azarya assured him, telling him that Professor Sinai was going to drive him home.

Azarya came back a little before midnight. Cass didn't have to ask him how his day had gone. His flushed face said it all. He began by apologizing for the late hour.

"We lost track of the time."

"Are you tired now, Azarya? Do you want to go to bed, or do you want to stay up and talk a little?"

"If you're not too tired, it would be wonderful to talk. I'm too excited to sleep."

"It was that good?"

They sat at the table, and Cass went to the refrigerator to get some water, juice, and fruit and laid it out, his instincts telling him that this was the thing to do.

"Better. How good I can't describe. When I tried to put into words something, Professor Sinai knew already what it was before I'd said two syllables, and he had the perfect formulation ready for it. He speaks in music. Mathematical music. He wasn't teaching today, and he thought I should see what the classes at MIT are like. I sat in on a class on topology, which was wonderful, and then another class on modern philosophy that was also wonderful."

"Did you and Professor Sinai talk about your future?"

"He wants me to come to MIT next year. We didn't talk that much about it. We were too busy speaking math."

"You're not too young?"

"He did mention the William James Sidis rule. Do you

know who is this William James Sidis? Professor Sinai was vague on the details."

"He's the cautionary tale of how not to raise your prodigy. He was the son of two doctors, and according to legend taught himself eight languages by the age of eight and lectured on four-dimensional bodies when he was eleven. He graduated from Harvard at sixteen, burned out early, spent his adult life doing menial jobs and collecting subway transfers, and would run screaming if anyone mentioned mathematics to him."

"That would explain it. He said there's an unofficial rule at MIT, that they call the William James Sidis rule, not to accept kids who are too young, that just because a student is ready to do advanced math doesn't mean he's mature enough to live away from home and go to college."

"That makes sense."

"But I'll be seventeen next year, an old man compared to William James Sidis. Professor Sinai doesn't think there will be a problem, even though my education has been what he's kind enough to call 'unconventional.'"

"What do you call it?"

Cass knew he was pushing, asking such a direct question, but it seemed to him that Azarya wanted to talk about this subject. He was right.

"I call it nonexistent."

"Do you really think so? You've been studying your whole life."

"What I've been studying isn't going to help me with anything I'm interested in knowing."

"What are you interested in, besides math?"

"I hardly even know enough to know what I'm interested to know. I've only tried to teach myself mathematics. I haven't had time for much else, with all the studies heaped on me. I know nothing about your field, psychology. I'm interested in your specialty."

"The psychology of religion?"

"Yes. It interests me very much. So tell me, since this is your area, why do people the world over and in all times have such strong inclinations to believe what they have no evidence for, and to believe it so strongly that they shape their entire lives around it?"

Cass was floored.

"You think religious beliefs have no evidence?"

Azarya laughed. "Wait a minute. I've heard about you psychologists always answering a question with another question."

"That's a different kind of psychologist. A psychotherapist."

"Like your mother. She's more that kind of psychologist. You're more a scientist, doing research on how people think. I know a little about your work. I've asked your mother. She sent me one of your journal articles, 'Self-Definition and Religious Identification.' I liked it a lot. I liked the concept of a rigid designator. It made a lot of things clear for me."

"I borrowed it from the philosophers."

A rigid designator is a term that designates the same object in all possible worlds which makes it different from a mere description. So, for example, "Pascale Puissant's husband" is a description that refers to Cass Seltzer, but it didn't have to. It's not a rigid designator. There are logically possible worlds in which Cass was currently a bachelor or was currently married to somebody else. But "Cass Seltzer" is a rigid designator, as are all proper names. Rigid designators pick out an individual—that very thing and nothing else. One can even say, "Suppose that Cass Seltzer wasn't named 'Cass Seltzer,'" and that proposition has meaning because the first use of "Cass Seltzer" is a rigid designator. Terms that aren't rigid designators are called "non-rigid designators" or, more whimsically, "flaccid designators."

"That's another subject I know nothing about. Philosophy. I loved sitting in on that class. It was all arguments and proofs, almost like math. I'm going to have a lot of catching up to do when I get to MIT."

"So you've decided, then. You're coming here."

"I should have said '*if* I get to MIT.' At one point today it seemed perfectly clear. Professor Sinai had explained something to me that I had been confused about, and the thought came to me, how can you not take the opportunity to study with a *gaon* like this?" Azarya had used one of the Hebrew terms for "genius"—there are several—to describe Gabriel Sinai. Looking at him, Cass had the vivid memory of that little boy standing on the *tish,* trying to point his Hasidim's eyes at the proof that he was seeing, that same smile on his face.

"It was the first time you spoke to somebody who could understand you."

"Not the first time, no. The first time was Roz and you. But it's been a while." He said this softly and with a self-deprecating smile.

"If it makes your decision any easier, you ought to know that I would love for you to live with us if you come to MIT. It will be less strange than if you stay in a dorm."

"You open your home to me as if I were your son. How can I express how that makes me feel?" He managed to do it, with his eyes and the heat that rose in his cheeks. "Perhaps it will be. But, you know, I don't think I would feel strange at MIT. I maybe think I would feel less strange at MIT than I feel in New Walden."

Cass looked at Azarya's face, which was struck open with his confession.

"For how long has it been like this for you?"

"My Bar Mitzvah. That's when I remember feeling afraid for my future. That's when I saw clearly what I mean for the Valdeners."

"You became a man, according to the tradition."

"Yes, that's one tradition I had no trouble with."

"You still keep all the laws?"

"Yes, why not? I'd have to make a big effort not to, living in New Walden. It's not the laws that bother me. They're second nature." He thought for a moment. "One has to live some way, so why not that way? Professor Sinai is observant, but it doesn't stop his mind. He's not a Valdener. He's not the son of the Valdener Rebbe, with a whole community of people who mention him in their every prayer. It's foolishness, their prayers, I know that. Still, how can I not feel the burden of so many prayers? Every time I hear how they call me, *Azarya ha-kodesh,* Azarya the holy one, it sounds like shovels of dirt on a coffin."

Cass looked at him, taken aback by the note of melodrama. In addition to everything else that Azarya was, he was also an adolescent. Cass found this touching, just as he'd been touched by the small Azarya waving bye-bye.

"The problem is that 'Valdener MIT math student' is not a rigid designator. There are many possible worlds in which it doesn't pick me out."

"Is 'son of the Valdener Rebbe' a rigid designator?"

"Yes. It is. I had to be my father's son, or I wouldn't be me. I am Azarya ben Rav Bezalel. It's a rigid designator. Just as my father is rigidly Rav Bezalel ben Rav Yisroel. It was Rav Yisroel, my grandfather, who came to America in 1939, saving the few Valdeners he could. He built New Walden for them so that they could insulate themselves against the corruptions of America. He tried as best he could to duplicate Valden as it had been before it was destroyed. When you live in New Walden, then the old Valden is always in your mind. You go to the shul in New Walden and you are thinking of the old shul. That's where the Germans packed all the remaining Valdeners, left behind when Rav Yisroel came to America, before they set it on fire. And my grandfather was rigidly Rav Yisroel ben Rav Eliezer. Rav Eliezer, my great-grandfather, was rigidly Rav Eliezer ben Rav Bezalel. He had an older brother, Rav Azarya ben Rav Bezalel, who died the same year as his own father, and so Rav Eliezer ben Rav Bezalel became the Rebbe. Rav Eliezer ben Rav Bezalel is known as *'der shvagte Rebbe,'* the silent Rebbe. He had a saying: *'Man shvagt un man shvagt. Dernoch riet men abisl un man shvagt vater.'* 'We stay silent and we stay silent, and then we rest a little and we stay silent.' He's always been one of my favorite ancestors because of that. I think maybe he was a mathematician himself, to have had such a fine idea of paradox. Rav Bezalel, my great-great-grandfather, was rigidly Rav Bezalel ben Rav Itzikil. Rav Itzikil ben Rav Yosef, my great-great-great-grandfather, was the Borshtchaver Rebbe's son, but he married the Valdener Rebbe's daughter, Sura Sima, so Rav Itzikil ben Rav Yosef was the son-in-law of Rav Azarya ben Rav Yisroel, who was my great-great-great-great-grandfather. And Rav Azarya ben Rav Yisroel was a direct descendant of ha-Rav Yisroel ben Eliezer, as he was rigidly designated, but whose many non-rigid designations include *der heyliger Ba'al Shem Tov,* the holy Master of the Good Name."

They stared at each other over the dining-room table. Cass wished he were that other sort of psychologist, the kind that knows the right thing to say to a young person caught as Azarya was caught.

"But a name's being a rigid designator doesn't make the decision for you, does it?"

"No." He paused for a while, staring into space. Again, Cass remembered his own exalted vision that night at the Rebbe's *tish,* when he thought he'd caught a glimpse of what the world must look like to Azarya. "But if not rigid designation, then what does make the decision?"

"You. Only you."

"It's never only you. Not when your 'bens' iterate back to the Ba'al Shem Tov."

"But you also have a link to others. To Professor Sinai. And to his teacher and the teacher of the teacher, maybe going back to Gauss or Dedekind, or Euler or Archimedes. That's also a long chain of links going back in time. And it has more to do with you, with who you really are, than your connection with the Ba'al Shem Tov, rigid designator or no."

Azarya shrugged in a Hasidic way, his palms turned upward. "Maybe you're right. Anyway, if nothing else, I have this week."

"I think you're being, if anything, too philosophical here. Rav Hillel said, 'If I'm not for myself, then who will be for me?'"

"'And if I'm only for myself, then what am I?'"

"'And if not now, when?'"

"I know the formula, but I can't see my way clear to the solution. I try out every permutation, and nothing comes out right. How can that be? How can there be no solution? The only thing I seem to be able to prove is that there is no solution. No matter how many different ways I attack it, that's as far as I get. If I leave New Walden, I break the heart of every Valdener Hasid, a community that remade itself through the efforts of my grandfather, who did what he could to save a few, and it wasn't enough, which is what he was crying out the hour that he died. He was calling out by name Valdeners that he had left behind. I break the heart of my father, whom I love more than anything in the world. So that has impossible consequences and can be ruled out. So I stay. But if I stay, then I have no more days like I did today. I live among people who love me more than they love themselves, who think I'm their messenger to *der Abishda,* who will grab someday for the *shirayim* on my plate, and I'll never be able to share a single thought with them. I'll live the life of my father, and of his father before him, and of all the fathers who lived only to repeat the lives of their fathers. Where's the sense in that? How can one choose such a meaningless life? So I leave. And so it goes. Going to a university is necessary but impossible. Staying in New Walden is impossible but necessary."

"Azarya, do you know what you are? Has anyone ever told you? Do you understand why a man like Gabriel Sinai is so eager to bring you to work with him?"

"You don't need to tell me that I'm special. All my life, that's all that I've heard. All my life, the community has *kvelled* at my every word."

"But not for the right reasons, Azarya. Not because of who you are but because of your bloodline."

"Not because of who I am." He smiled ruefully. "I guess that's the question. Who am I?" He shrugged. "When my designator is rigidly picking me out in other possible worlds, what's it coming up with? What's the part that can go and what's the part that can't?"

It was extraordinary how young Azarya could still look, when the clarity in his eyes was overtaken by a helpless wonder and his mouth quaked.

"You're the boy who proved at six years old that there's no largest prime number. I can't imagine what you've proved since then. I can't imagine what you could go on and prove. You talk about your responsibilities to the Valdeners. Don't you have a responsibility to human understanding?"

"Believe me, human understanding will continue without Azarya Sheiner. The Valdeners are a different story."

"But should they continue? It's a harsh question, I know, harshly put."

"Yes. Harsh."

"But, Azarya, you don't seem to shy away from questions. So answer this one for me: Why should the Valdeners continue with their superstitions and their insularity and their stubborn refusal to learn anything from outside? Why is that something to perpetuate?"

"I was hoping that maybe you could help me answer that. Because that is your specialty, psychology of religion, no?"

"No. This question is meant for you alone, Azarya."

"As I've always feared," he said softly.

"Let's think about it together, then. Let's say you leave and the community suffers for a while, then disintegrates and disperses to other Hasidic groups; maybe even—because of the trauma of your leaving—the members become assimilated into the modern world. Tell me what's lost? A few fewer false beliefs knocking about in the world? The Valdeners end up being like my mother and me? Is that so bad?"

Azarya stared down at the table a while before he spoke.

"It's tragic, a diminishment, when a people goes out of existence, a way of life, a culture, a language." He spoke slowly, either from emotion or because he was thinking out his line of reasoning as he went. "But that's not even the heart of it. No. The heart of it is the story of *this* people, *my* people, *my* Valdeners. You are who you are." Cass saw with horror that Azarya's eyes were welling. "Had my grandfather Rav Yisroel ben Rav Eliezer not fought with all his life to bring over as many Valdeners as he could in 1939, then there would be none living now, and even so he wept on his deathbed for the lives he hadn't saved. That bloodline that every Valdener child can recite as easily as Shema Yisroel"—"Hear O Israel," the iconic Jewish prayer—"would have ended in that burning shul if not for him. So how can I, Azarya ben Rav Bezalel ben Rav Yisroel ben Rav Eliezer, decide to be the executioner now? How can it be by my hand?"

He's sixteen, Cass was thinking. Look at the quantities of agonized thought he's poured into his paradox, and look at the living agony twisting itself out on his face right now, welling over in his eyes and making his upper lip tremble.

It was enough for one night, more than enough, and Cass said so. As they were getting up from the table, he couldn't help putting his hand gently on Azarya's shoulder, remembering, as he did so, how the Valdeners had kissed their prayer shawls and touched the child with them as if he were a living Torah as he was bounced around on his dancing father's back.

"Azarya, I'm sorry. I shouldn't have pushed you so hard."

"It's for me wonderful to be able to share this with somebody. It's a gift that you are taking my decision so seriously. Often I think maybe I'm taking it too seriously myself, that the world will go on whatever Azarya Sheiner decides to do. Still, a person takes his life seriously. A person has to live his life. Who else's life is he supposed to live? Maybe together we'll figure out how something that's necessary but impossible can happen. We'll collaborate on a solution."

"It would be an honor to be your collaborator. And we'll bring Professor Sinai on board, too, as a collaborator. Why don't you bring him here tomorrow for dinner? I've still got piles of food from Tirza's Batampte Kitchen. I'd like to meet the man whom Azarya Sheiner calls a *gaon*."

Pascale was up in her study and Cass was in the kitchen, warming up the barbecued chicken and the potato kugel, when an excited Azarya arrived home with a burly man in heavy black-framed eyeglasses, his wavy black hair awkwardly mounding on random places of his head. He had the shy, uncomfortable grin that had probably not been revised since he was a child. He wore a green flannel shirt and an air of unkemptness, but it was hard for Cass to take him in because of a transformed Azarya beside him, holding three bunches of green-tissue-wrapped tulips in one hand and a bottle of wine in the other.

Before Cass had gotten a word out, Pascale came sashaying into the room, balanced on a spiky pair of red shoes that matched her lipstick. Her long black hair, the color of the rest of her outfit, was piled high on her head. She stopped cold at the sight of them.

"But is it you?" she asked Azarya with the directness of a small child, and he laughed.

"But where are your"—she curled her index fingers beside her ears—"your *baguettes à cheveux*?"

Azarya, who didn't know French but couldn't help getting Pascale's drift, pointed to the Red Sox baseball cap he was wearing. He lifted it off his head with a flourish, and two dark-blond *payess* came flopping down.

Pascale shrieked with laughter, which cracked them all up, Gabriel Sinai joining in with a high whinnying noise.

"*Non, non,* you must put them back *tout de suite!* It is so much better like that. *Oui, comme ça! Plus beau!* You are a beautiful boy! It is amazing how the beauty comes out. Better, why don't you just snip, snip?"

She ran with her frantic movements, the high heels clacking on the wooden floor, to the kitchen drawer, and pulled out the poultry shears—Cass was surprised she knew where to find them—and advanced toward Azarya, in a pretend menacing way, moving her black-sheathed legs like a stalking panther. She jiggled the poultry shears beneath Azarya's right ear. Cass uneasily wondered what Pascale was capable of in such an antic mood.

"I'm not quite ready for that." Azarya was laughing back at her, not looking worried himself—but, then, he didn't know Pascale. "One thing at a time."

"One thing at a time," she echoed back. "But of course! We will snip first the one and then the other!"

They were all laughing, Pascale most of all, suddenly thrust into one of her high-spirited moods. In one of those quick reversals that Cass had seen in her before—in fact, to which he owed his marriage—she now liked Azarya with all the savagery of her certainty. Pascale was kind, as Cass had always known, but with the kindness of a child. She'd been repelled by the sense of his strangeness, perhaps believing that his appearance entailed a rejection of the world outside his own, a smug assertion of superiority. But as soon as she had been able to recognize a fellow human being and see that he was a citizen of a wider sphere—or in any case longed to be—her natural kindness had blossomed.

Azarya handed Pascale the tulips, and with a happy little exclamation she tore off the paper from the bunch of purples and pinks and yellows.

"Very beautiful," she said, gathering them to her narrow chest. "The colors of spring."

"That's what I thought, too. Also the colors of the poet." He then presented her with the bottle of wine.

"I hope it's good. You can imagine how little I know about French wines. The man in the wine store said this was a good one."

"Bordeaux! Oh, it is very good! You are being civilized *rapidement*. Only now let me cut off the unlovely baguettes!"

Cass had never seen Pascale this animated. It occurred to him that having mathematicians around was probably familiar and therefore wonderful for her, reminding her of her girlhood in the idyllic Bures-sur-Yvette, which she'd spent benignly ignored by her distracted father and hanging upside down on the jungle gym with other mathematical offspring, who were "not so annoying as other children." Gabriel was fluent in French and clearly enjoyed speaking it, so he directed most of his comments to Pascale and in her native tongue, which put her in a jollier mood still. Gabriel knew Claude Puissant very well and thought that he might even remember Pascale as a young child, sometimes playing piano at gatherings.

"I did not play so well!" she said.

"That's true," he agreed, and she shrugged and poured some more of the Bordeaux for herself and Cass. Gabriel and Azarya were sticking to the Carmel.

But the real treat was to come after dinner, when Gabriel

loped over to Pascale's baby-grand piano. There was sheet music on top and Gabriel looked it over for a while, and then sat down and, without any sheet music, forcefully played the famous third movement of Mozart's *Turkish* Sonata. He immediately launched into something else, sounding vaguely familiar, though it was Azarya who got it first, laughing gleefully, and explained to Cass and Pascale that Professor Sinai was playing the same movement from the *Turkish* Sonata, only "upside down"—that is, inverted.

Azarya was elated with Gabriel's inversion of the Mozart and asked him if he could try something that he, Azarya, thought was possible, though he didn't have the technical proficiency to do it.

"The idea is to combine the harmonies from the Prelude in C Major, the first in Volume I of Bach's *Well-Tempered Clavier*, with the arpeggios of the first étude from Chopin's Opus 10, also in C major. I can hear it in my head, but I can't play the piano well enough to do it."

"I've never studied the Chopin," Gabriel said, but despite that disclaimer he instantly launched into the challenge, and played the entire Chopin étude from start to finish, with all the Bach harmonies substituted for the original ones, and then, without pausing, he did the reverse, combining the harmonies of the Chopin étude with the more reserved but beautiful figurations of the Bach prelude.

Azarya, who could follow much more closely than Cass or Pascale, was beside himself.

"This has been an impossible dream! It's as beautiful as I had imagined—more beautiful!"

Gabriel laughed in his high whinny. He was now completely comfortable, his rubbery mouth stretching into easy smiles, showing his full set of chaotic teeth.

"It's a terrific idea. I'm going to add it to my repertoire. Any other combinations you've been impossibly dreaming?"

"I've got something I can sing for you. Here's the idea. You take the thirty-two variations of Bach's *Goldberg* Variations, each with thirty-two measures. You take one measure of each of the variations, always in diagonal fashion—in general, the *n*th measure of the *n*th variation."

"Nice," Gabriel said. "Let's hear."

The chimelike voice of the child that Cass still remembered was now a tenor, each note struck pure. Gabriel's face was creased with concentration, and when Azarya had finished, he declared it a marvel.

"You're basing it on Cantor's diagonal proof, of course," he said, and Azarya smiled, and Gabriel said, "That's it. You're coming to MIT." Cass had known that Gabriel Sinai would be the ideal collaborator.

Gabriel launched into playing "Sheiner's Diagonal Variation on Bach's *Goldberg* Variations" for himself, more rapidly than Azarya had sung it, and was, by Cass's count, on the eighteenth measure of the eighteenth variation when Cass heard the phone ringing—nobody else noticed it—and quietly went off to answer it.

It was his mother. It was difficult to hear her over the laughing and music. He kept his eyes on the action at the piano, Azarya sitting there now and jamming with his *gaon*. Gabriel was playing the right hand of something that Cass didn't recognize, and Azarya was playing the left. He seemed to know more about the piano than he had let on.

"Mom, can you speak up a little? I can barely hear you. Azarya's here playing a piano duet with Gabriel Sinai. I wish you could see this."

Pascale stood behind Azarya, proposing alterations. She

had both her hands resting on his shoulders as she leaned over and watched the keyboard, and either he didn't notice or she was his relative so it didn't count as a strange female or he just didn't care.

His mother said something that he didn't catch. She barely sounded like herself.

It wasn't like Pascale to make casual physical contact. It wasn't only the faithful who couldn't help themselves from leaning inward toward Azarya, that crush in the Costco House of Worship, with the tiers of yearning Valdeners straining downward to the child standing on the *tish* between the gigantic bowls of oranges and apples that the Rebbe would soon be tossing to the scrambling Hasidim.

"Mom, what's the matter with you?"

She was softly crying. He listened to the strange sound of it. Not even his bubbe's madness-sharpened needling could ever make her break down and cry.

"Mom?"

His heart was pounding now, terrified. Was it Jesse? Was it his father?

"Cass, the Rebbe had a heart attack. He died two hours ago."

XXX

The Argument from the
Long Silence of the Night

```
to: GR613@gmail.com
from: Seltzer@psych.Frankfurter.edu
date: Feb. 29 2008 5:00 a.m.
subject:

Just on the chance that my last message
didn't get through to you I'm resending it.
Don't worry about waking me. Just call.
```

XXXI

The Argument from the New York Times

He must have fallen asleep at some point after dawn, since he's being rudely awakened now into the full brightness of morning. It's the telephone. He reads the caller ID and sees that it's Roz and unplugs the receiver and turns over, Lucinda's pillow muffling his head. The scent of her shampoo has faded over the course of the week.

Now his cell phone is tolling somewhere in the bedroom. With a sigh he gets up and traces the source to his jeans pocket. It's Roz again. He's up for the day now, but he doesn't have the strength yet for Roz. He pulls on the jeans and a sweater and goes downstairs to put up the coffee. He's feeling shaky from lack of sleep and has a moment of vertigo as he goes downstairs to pick up his *Times*. He tosses it on the kitchen counter as he pours himself a cup of the dark-roast brew, whose fragrance peps him up before he's swallowed a mouthful.

His cell phone is vibrating again in his jeans pocket. Roz again, being relentless. He sips his coffee as he skims the headlines and then flips to the Op-Ed page.

His first thought is that he really has fallen back asleep, but now the cell phone is ringing again, and it's Roz, of course, she must be going out of her mind with her need to reach him, and it only makes sense that she would be going out of her mind—at least, that is, if Cass is not at this moment fast asleep and dreaming bizarrely of the *New York Times.*

The New York Times

Friday, February 29, 2008

Cosmic Tremblings

By Jonas Elijah Klapper
Safed, Israel

I have watched for some years now, in silence but with mounting dismay, as a small sect has presumed to preach from on high. The sect speaks in the name of the false and hollow god, Scientism, claiming all the dominions under heaven for its faceless revelation. They accuse other faiths of intolerance, yet are contemptuous of all who dare believe that there is more than is dreamt of in parsimonious philosophies. They themselves have been indulgently tolerated, even celebrated, their books bought up at rates to enrich their coffers, their ubiquity a grotesque parody of the presence divine. A rough beast indeed is slouching toward Bethlehem.

For most of my sojourn on Earth my task has been to educate and elucidate. I have seen firsthand how our universities have been corrupted by the triumph of the number crunchers, permitted to crunch the very soul into ashes and dust. The sacred knowledge, preserved in imagery and metaphor, in incantatory language overheard from the higher spheres, has been forgotten, and forgotten, too, the few who remember.

My years as an educator yielded painful and intimate acquaintance with the band of the proud unknowers. Alas, it is to my own pedagogical failure that I painfully confess. Had I succeeded better, then at least one of the men of falsehood would not be laying evil hands on the evisceration of the world soul. Even here in my place of sacred exile I cannot escape his apostasy, the expression of defiance displayed behind plate glass. Betrayal is, of course, one of the stations on the road to redemption.

I have kept my silence, but I can no longer, for there are matters beyond me contending. The masters tell us that there are moments of cosmic trembling, when the future lies in the balance. It is always upon one man that the issue is poised.

The threats to such a one are commensurate with the enormity of what he is asked to do and to be. Every culture and every age has looked to its future and made out his dim form. "I behold him but not near," says the Hebrew Bible (Numbers 24: 17). He has been called by many names: Ras Tafari, Mahdi, Shiloh, Yinnon, Menachem, Haninah, the Saoshyant, the Hermetic Corpus, the Christ, the Redeemer, the Saviour, the Moshiach, the Messiah, the Anointed, the Son. The names persist even into our day of failing memory.

There have been far more true Messiahs denied than false messiahs proclaimed. He has been born many times. If the moment is right, then he is of the line of David; otherwise he is but another of the line of Joseph, doomed himself to die, incapable of achieving the foretold redemption.

The belief that he tarries is erroneous and is partly to be blamed on the equally fallacious belief that he is required to perform miracles. I do but quote here from Maimonides: "Do not imagine that the anointed King must perform miracles and signs and create new things in the world or resurrect the dead. The matter is not so."

How then shall he be known? For every age a different attribute is apt. In our day of prodigious forgetting what is more meet than prodigious memory? It is from the faithful rendering of all the world's words that the Word shall go forth, for in the beginning was the Word.

And how shall the Word go forth? Jesus chose the Mount to deliver his sermon, but Jesus was born, depending on various reckonings, between 8 B.C. and 6 A.D. To Jesus there was but one medium and that was the human voice. Today would it not be felicitous for the Good News to go forth from the newspaper of record?

Here then might it be said:

I am the way, the truth and the life. No one comes to the Father except through Me.

XXXII

The Argument from the Precipice

Cass feels a forceful hand on his shoulder clamping him from behind. He turns back and discovers it's Sy Auerbach, adorned in his fedora and impatience.

"Seltzer! What are you doing at the end of a line for your own debate? Haven't I taught you anything?"

"Sy! What are you doing here?"

"I'm here for your smackdown. I'm going to record it and put the transcript and video up on my blog."

Cass doesn't voice the first question that comes to mind: What if Fidley flattens him? Will his agent put that up on www.precipice.org?

"How did you even know about this?" is what he asks. He's pretty sure there hasn't been any publicity outside of Harvard.

"Roz Margolis told me. She got in touch with me about representing her and mentioned it. She said it was going to be big, but I had no idea."

"Neither did I."

"Obviously, or you would have gotten here sooner. Coming through," he bellows to the people up front. "Cass Seltzer coming through."

The crowd parts, and a student usher gushes, "Professor

Seltzer, we're so excited, please follow us," and he enters the beautiful nave of the church, where the whitewashed pews are quickly filling and heads swivel in his direction as he walks down the long center aisle with Sy Auerbach at his side, a red runner under their feet and a simple Protestant cross before their eyes. The immense windows have the shape of the sublime domes that had been carved into the ice on Cass's night on Weeks Bridge, and the walls are inscribed with the Harvard dead who had been lost in the wars of the twentieth century.

"You see that demented Op-Ed in today's *New York Times?*" his agent is asking him. "Perfect timing. Coincidence?"

"You mean could he have known about this debate? Unlikely. It was my book that had gotten to him."

"My congratulations." Auerbach gives his mirthless laugh.

A thin young man with a ponytail and a ring piercing his eyebrow yells "Cass-man!" as they walk past, and Cass gives a lopsided smile and a halfhearted wave.

"I heard a rumor you were once his student," Auerbach is saying.

"True."

Auerbach chuckles softly.

"Remind me to tell you a story about Klapper someday."

Cass will never remind him. He'll remember not to remind him.

They pass the chancel and enter the chaplain's office, tonight being used as the greenroom.

Five people are gathered there, and Cass's eye is drawn first to a tallish man who has the kind of conical build that gives the impression of taking up more volume than it actually does, with broad shoulders and an expansive chest. His hair is silvered and elegantly sheared, falling silky to the finely stitched collar, but his eyes are hard, glinting pebbles and his mouth is a firm line, no give at all in the upper lip. There's a suggestion of brute force as he stands there with a stillness that suggests reserves of strength that he is straining to hold in check. With an impassiveness that manages to be aggressive, he's listening to a man who is addressing him with a desperate affability. The setup has the look of a psychological experiment, a verbal analogue to the dollar auction that Lucinda had used to fang Harold Lipkin. The speaker has already doled out so much in trying to win this man's approval, and if he stops before getting anything at all, any flicker of humanity from those unblinking eyes, then he'll have nothing to show for his efforts, and there's no natural way to stop at this point, and Cass bets that the man behind the pebbles probably knows about the dollar auction, but then he commits an error, he glances over at Cass and Sy, which gives the desperate talker an excuse to stop talking as he rushes over to greet them. He's Lenny Shore, the spiritual leader of the Agnostic Chaplaincy of Harvard, the sponsor of tonight's event, and he's a slight man who looks as if he would bend easily, surprisingly young, with long lank brown hair and a fidgety mouth that isn't quite able to hold down an expression. He's wearing a corduroy jacket and black jeans over cowboy boots, and he's telling Cass—whose attire is the arithmetic mean between Fidley and Lenny, a dark wool jacket bought in France, a green silk tie—how much he admired *The Varieties of Religious Illusion,* and what a great day this is for the Agnostic Chaplaincy of Harvard, and how we are going to be at capacity crowd tonight, which means somewhere in the vicinity of eleven hundred, and how he feels that tonight the Agnostics of Harvard have really arrived, and is there anything that Cass needs or that Lenny or anybody else can do for him, and the crowd is just overwhelming, and Cass is smiling and nodding and trying to give the chaplain whatever he's needing so that he'll calm down and meanwhile also stealing sideway glances at the still and powerful man in the corner, who is standing next to an equally handsome and silver-haired woman—clearly his property and almost certainly responsible for the civilizing touches of his elegant haircut and clothes—and who has settled the tempered blade of his gaze onto Cass Seltzer.

Lenny Shore brings Cass and Auerbach over to make the introductions, and it is just as Cass has feared. The man sucking the energy out of the room is Felix Fidley, looking as if his manicured hands might be forming fists beneath his monogrammed shirt cuffs, a sense of menacing potency radiating out from the kind of man to have that kind of wife with that kind of cold beauty that ages so well, not so unlike Lucinda's, whom Cass desperately wishes he had beside him to give him some ballast, but instead he has Sy Auerbach, who brings ballast enough for any man, though Cass has never felt it as particularly steadying, not when it's this close, though he certainly appreciates it when it's representing his interests, it's made him rich, it's made him famous, it's brought him here, to this unlikely moment, about to face off with this man who is several times over more than his match.

Fidley extends his hand and shakes Cass's, and the grip all but crushes three metacarpal bones, and nothing is said, Cass feels that Fidley is daring him to open his mouth and offer up some drivel that he can then subject to his impassive stare that will put any inanity that's there—and there's always inanity there—up on vivid display. But when it comes to saying nothing, Cass has never had a problem, and sly Sy, too, is keeping his own counsel, and only pastoral Lenny feels compelled to soften the brutal wordlessness with patter.

Now there's an usher at the door, and Lenny rushes over, and gives a signal, and they file out of the chaplain's office back into the nave, Fidley and his wife following after Lenny. Fidley, when he sees the packed church, turns his head to give Cass a measured smile, mutually shared congratulations for having drawn such a crowd, it's a moment approaching almost warmth, or at least that flickering recognition of shared humanity that Lenny Shore had been desperately seeking.

There's a respectful hush as they take their seats up on the dais, their nameplates set out on the table together with glasses and pitchers of water, Cass on the left, Fidley on the right, Lenny Shore in the middle. There's a lectern on either side of the table, where each will stand when his turn comes.

Cass looks out at the filled pews, and he's searching for the fan with the ponytail, whom he finds after a few moments, talking animatedly to a girl who looks familiar, though he can't place her, and then he lets his eyes travel along the other rows, and he's startled to see Mona sitting front and center. She must have gotten here early to have nabbed that seat. She gives him two thumbs-up, and her gesture is immediately duplicated by a tall young woman sitting next to her who resembles Roz, and Cass looks again, and it *is* Roz. They both blow him kisses, and he leans forward in his chair and squints to make sure that his eyes aren't deceiving him, and Mona and Roz are laughing together, and how like them to have found each other.

Lenny Shore has risen and is at the lectern near Cass, welcoming the crowd for "this historic debate," and Cass is still struggling to get his neurons to line up in a way commensurate to the task at hand, but he's having trouble even paying attention to what Lenny is saying, as he launches into the history of the Agnostic Chaplaincy of Harvard, which was formed in the 1960s and whose intellectual roots go back to some of the most eminent minds of Harvard, like Ralph Waldo Emerson, who urged us to "take the bandages of doctrine off of our eyes and live with the privilege of the immeasurable mind," and William James, who observed that "rationality does not lie on one side or the other. It is a contest between our fears and our hopes, and both the scientist and the religious believer take a gamble," and who authored a book he had presciently entitled *The Varieties of Religious Experience,* as if he could foresee that a century later another psychologist of religion would write a book he'd call *The Varieties of Religious Illusion* (big laugh), and Lenny is finally getting a reaction, and his bendable body is weaving with the excitement, and Cass remembers where he's seen that girl before, she's the one who had asked him whether he signs body parts.

"The Agnostic Chaplaincy is here to serve the spiritual needs of the questioners and doubters, those who enjoy the journey more than the arrival. Our only doctrine is the open mind, and our ethics stresses tolerance for all points of view, which we practice by trying to see things all possible ways.

"There's an old Jewish joke about a quarreling couple that comes to the rabbi to get counseling. The rabbi listens to the wife's complaints about how all the problems are caused by her no-good husband, and the rabbi says, 'You know, you're right.' Then he listens to the husband's complaints about how all the problems are caused by his shrewish wife, and he says, 'You know, you're right.' The whole time, the rabbi's wife has been listening in, and as soon as the couple leaves, she asks him, 'What did you think you were doing in there? How can they both be right?' The rabbi says, 'You know, you're right.'"

There's a healthy laugh, and the chaplain is laughing along, and before it completely dies off, Lenny leans in too close to the mike, and his eagerness makes him lose control of his voice, so that it comes out as a squawk, "That rabbi is my role model!" and Cass finds he's stopped worrying about himself long enough to worry about the chaplain.

"Of course, everything may change for us tonight. The resolution of tonight's debate is: 'God exists.' We have on each side a masterful persuader, able to make the best case that can be made for his position, so perhaps the question of God's existence can finally be answered, tonight and at Harvard."

Lenny pauses, and the audience, wildly revved up, bursts into applause, pierced by two-fingered whistles. Cass is reassured about the chaplain, he's doing fine, he's just overexcited, and Cass can get back to worrying about himself.

"Felix Fidley is the Manfred Mannessen University Professor of Economics at the University of Chicago. He did his undergraduate work at Princeton and received his doctorate from Harvard. He received the Nobel Prize in Economics for his pioneering work combining military and economic strategies of rational decision making. His book *Welfare Warfare Wherefore* was cited by both the *Wall Street Journal* and the *Washington Times* as the best book of the year, and Nathan Paskudnyak of *Provocation* wrote that if he believed in evolution he would say that Felix Fidley is the most highly evolved thinker alive today. Professor Fidley will be affirming the resolution 'God exists.'"

There is a round of applause.

"Cass Seltzer is a professor of psychology at Frankfurter

University with a specialty in the psychology of religion. He did his undergraduate work at Columbia University and received his doctorate from Frankfurter University where he has been a professor ever since. He is the author of *The Varieties of Religious Illusion,* which spent forty-three weeks on the *New York Times* best-seller list, and has been translated into twenty-eight languages. The *New York Times* praised Cass Seltzer as being a different species of atheist, giving every indication that he intimately knows the world of the believer from the inside, calling him the William James for our day, and *Time* magazine christened him 'the atheist with a soul.'"

Sy Auerbach is flanked by his Boston and Cambridge clients: Roz's hero Luke Nanovitch on one side, and the cognitive scientist Arthur Silver on the other. The philosopher Nicholas Duffy, the physicist Eliza Wandel, and Cass's old colleague Marty Huffer are also there with him. Auerbach must have put out the word, demanding their attendance. He's been speaking into Silver's ear throughout Lenny's introduction, but the rest of the audience is applauding with gusto, and there are more ear-stabbing whistles, and Cass sees that his friend with the ponytail is pumping his fist. Cass knows that he should feel buoyed by the wave of good will, and he would be if only he felt he were going to perform in such a way as to earn it retroactively, but he doesn't, so instead he feels pummeled by the wave, sickened by the thought of how much disappointment he may yet inflict on the ponytailed student and his tender-armed lass and all the others who are recklessly giving him the benefit of their doubts. He glances sideways at Fidley, who has a slit of a smile slicing into his left cheek, the one closer to Cass.

"Professor Seltzer will be negating the resolution 'God exists.'"

Another burst of applause. Cass smiles wanly, catching Roz's eye, and she is staring at him steadily, as if she has caught the worrying current of his mood, and she smiles slowly and nods her head with a confidence that seems considered, as if she's taking to heart his implied admonition in the car and is not only resolved to think before she speaks but to think before she nods.

"Professor Fidley will be opening. He has fifteen minutes to make his statement, which will be followed by Professor Seltzer's fifteen minutes. Then Professor Fidley and Professor Seltzer will face off and ask each other questions directly. They'll have the chance to ask three questions each and shouldn't spend more than five minutes answering each question. I will be keeping time. And now may this historic moment commence, with the spirits of Ralph Waldo Emerson and William James smiling down on us . . . or not!"

Lenny has scored again, and he savors the audience's laughter and then undulates back down into his seat, and Fidley rises and moves to his lectern. Everything he does has a tone of authority.

"I want first of all to thank the Agnostic Chaplaincy of Harvard for organizing this debate, and thus, as the chaplain put it, giving Professor Seltzer and me a chance to decide this issue once and for all." He pauses for a brief soft chuckle. "I am particularly delighted to have the chance to debate, of all the atheists who are suddenly taking their responsibilities to enlightenment seriously enough to write best sellers, the one atheist who comes equipped with a working soul."

Cass is trying to pay attention to Felix Fidley's words, trying to keep his mind focused, but the strangeness of his being *Cass here* is threatening to carry him away.

"I can't help but believe that this will make my task easier.

If Cass Seltzer has a soul, then he already knows that God exists, even if he doesn't yet know that he knows. And that is what I'm going to convince him of tonight, and you will be here to witness it.

"In my spare time I'm a military-history buff," Fidley is saying, which is the kind of thing that he would be and Cass wouldn't be, and wouldn't it be nice if Cass could just sit back and admire the man's towering presence and assurance. "And so you will forgive me if I take my analogies from that sphere. My strategy tonight can be compared to Khalid ibn al-Walid maneuvers at the Battle of Yarmouk, a great and decisive battle that took place in August in the year 636, between the Islamic Caliphate and the Christian Byzantine Empire."

Cass Seltzer is thinking about how many times during the past year he has had the strange impression that he has been wearing somebody else's coat.

"Many military historians believe this to be among the most decisive battles of all times, since it was the first of the Islamic victories outside of Arabia, and was followed by a wave of triumph that carried the Muslim conquest to the very shores of Europe. Khalid ibn al-Walid was one of history's great military strategists, and the strategy he used at Yarmouk is a classic three-pronged attack," Fidley is saying when it occurs to Cass that Felix Fidley is the man whose coat Cass has mistakenly been wearing.

"That three-pronged attack is precisely the one that I'll employ tonight."

And tonight's the night when the legitimate wearer is going to demand his coat back.

XXXIII

The Argument from the Violable Self

He was still holding the *New York Times* Op-Ed page in his trembling hand.

"My God," he had answered the phone.

"You've seen it then, the Klop-Ed."

It had been a slip of the tongue that she hadn't even realized she had made until he laughed, grimly.

"Are you okay?" was what she mainly had wanted to know.

"I'm shaken. I'm really shaken."

"I can only imagine. Even I'm shaken."

"I wouldn't have predicted how important he still is to me, how much it all still hurts."

"You're obviously still important to him, too."

"That hurts, too."

"Why?"

"I don't know exactly. It's horrible to think of him thinking of me as his nemesis."

"Not to belabor the obvious, but he's stark-raving mad. How can anything he thinks about you bother you?"

"You'd think not, wouldn't you, but there it is. I wish I didn't have any part in his current story. I don't want to be in his story."

"That's the thing about people. They're free to use you in their stories as they see fit, and there's not a damn thing you can do about it."

"Most of the time we don't even know how we're being used."

"Better that way."

"But that he'd cast me as his Judas!"

"His is the kind of story that needs a Judas. You've done him a favor."

"My book's provoking him into writing that piece isn't doing him any favors."

"Why not? Is it going to ruin his academic reputation?"

"I'm afraid they'll come after him with a straitjacket."

"He's in Hot S'fat, according to the byline. Probably half the town thinks they're messiahs and the other half are the messiahs' believers."

"This piece will put all of his work into doubt."

"If you ask me, that's where it always should have been."

"No. The early work was a revelation. He was a revelation."

"I'd be careful with that kind of language, Cass, after that Klop-Ed."

"You've got a point."

"It's interesting how that religiously charged language comes back to you when you talk about him."

"You've got a point."

"Even after all these years of studying the ways that religious emotions are fungible."

"You've got a point."

"You really are in shock, my poor darling. That's three times in a row that you said I have a point. Do you want me to come over?"

"Thanks, no. Somehow or other I need to get my mind back on the debate tonight."

"You've got fodder in the Klop-Ed. Use it to argue that religion is nuts."

"Only that's not what I believe."

"Maybe you should."

"Now's not the time for me to rethink my stand. Now's the time for me to try and remember what my stand is."

"You sure you don't want me to come over?"

"Thanks, Roz. I need peace and quiet."

The phone had rung all day. He had let the machine pick up. He'd get back to them tomorrow. The only phone call he had taken had come from London.

"Baby Budd, Jimmy Legs is *down* on you."

"Gideon? Is that you? Gideon!"

"How you holding up there, Baby Budd?"

"I read that piece and it's as if the past twenty years had never been."

"It had the same effect on me. I heard that voice again. That's all I can hear. All those years getting his voice out of my head, and then six hundred and forty-eight words get published in the *New York Times* and he's taken over my thought processes. I heard myself telling my wife, Fiona, to take our offspring for a perambulation so that I might be allowed the society of my own inviolable self. There I was, channeling him once again."

"You counted the number of words?"

"Six hundred and forty-eight is the product of thirty-six and eighteen," Gideon said quietly.

There was a long trans-Atlantic pause, while Cass tried to think of what to say, and, before he'd decided, there came the laughter. Cass was delighted to learn that Gideon still had his infantile giggle.

And all day long, no e-mail from GR613. It was so utterly unlike him. In the middle of all his other concerns today, Cass couldn't stop worrying about Azarya.

XXXIV

The Argument from the
View from Nowhere

Lenny Shore has proved not to be a strict enforcer of the time. Felix Fidley had used close to fifteen minutes to lay out his first prong, and Cass is still groping for the general shape of the argument.

The first prong had seemed a version of what Cass had called The Argument from the Unreasonableness of Reason (#33):

"Atheists talk a great deal about reason," Fidley had said, coating the last word with sarcasm. "They claim to be ruled by reason and reason alone. Their allegiance to reason is so strong that they profess themselves to be outraged by anything less than reason—by, in other words, faith. If anything is sacred to a man like Cass Seltzer, it's reason.

"Bertrand Russell, a famous English atheist, who wrote an essay entitled *Why I Am Not a Christian* and who was barred from teaching in this country in the 1940s because of his views concerning marriage and sexuality, said that the difference between faith and reason is like the difference between theft and honest toil. So here was a man who was proud of scandalizing the trustees of the City College of New York with his views about free love, but he was shocked—*shocked*—by believers caught *in flagrante fideo*."

He had gotten the laughs that he was going for, though Mona and Roz, front and center, stiffened with lack of amusement, Roz's upper lip listing one way under the weight of her scorn and Mona's listing the other way.

"But the thing about reason is that, if you're truly consistent, which is the first rule of reason, then you will be able to prove that reason has its own strict limitations. The claim that everything must be legitimated through reason is self-refuting. How, after all, can you legitimate that claim? Through reason? That would be viciously circular. In other words, we have to accept reason on faith. We have to accept logic on faith. A man like Bertrand Russell, and presumably a man like Cass Seltzer, is faithful to logic. Can he justify his logic? Is there some logical principle he can use that will prove the legitimacy of logic? And even if he proves it, why would he accept his own proof, if he's really being logical, since accepting it would already be taking for granted that he accepts logic, the very acceptance he's trying to justify? Logic has to be accepted without any proof at all. Logic has to be accepted on faith. Every time an atheist uses a logical principle, or draws a conclusion from premises, or believes a conclusion because he's got a sound argument, he's relying on faith."

Cass had a printed-out copy of his own Appendix folded up in his breast pocket, just in case, and he had taken it out to quickly review #33, discovering as he did so that he was having trouble moving his handshake-crushed right hand.

"So faith is unavoidable. If Bertrand Russell was right that faith is akin to theft, then he was thieving throughout his life. When he and Alfred North Whitehead were working on their

Principia Mathematica, trying to deduce all of mathematics from logic, they were robbing left and right.

"I'm relying on faith in reason right now in making my argument that reason always involves faith. But of course that doesn't bother me, since I already recognize the legitimacy of faith. You won't find me cringing from embracing faith. But a man like Cass Seltzer supposedly keeps himself pure of all contact with faith."

Fidley's tone wasn't pretty. If there was a stylistic war going on within the man, represented by the monogrammed cuffs on the one hand and the bone-crushing grip on the other, it was sounding as if the bone-crusher was prevailing.

"Now let's take this a bit further, shall we? Let's talk about that other great higher power called upon by the Bertrand Russells and Cass Seltzers. Let's talk about science.

"The linear progress of science, we're told, has carried us further and further away from religion. The whole great enterprise of modern science began in the sixteenth century with the Copernican revolution, which turned the old Aristotelian-Ptolemaic system on its head and showed us that we are not the center of the universe."

Again, Cass thought he knew where Fidley was heading, though he seemed to be jumping around before finishing any arguments. Cass shuffled his papers so that the arguments from the Big Bang (#4) and from the Fine-Tuning of Physical Constants (#5) were in front of him.

"Now, I'm not going to argue tonight—at least, not right now—that any of the recent and most sophisticated of scientific discoveries, coming from the best physicists and cosmologists of our day, are showing that the deeper we go into the mysteries of the physical universe the closer to religion we get. The line away from religion reversed itself in the twentieth century, right around the time that the biggest break-throughs in physics and cosmology were happening. Mark Twain said that when he was fourteen his father was so stupid he could hardly stand to have him around, but that when he got to be twenty-one he was astonished at how much the old man had managed to learn in seven years. That's how it's turning out to be with religion and science, and maybe we can talk about that later.

"But right now I'm going to continue to show that those who protest the most against the reliance on faith are, even in their protests, manifesting their supreme faith.

"It was the philosopher David Hume who demonstrated just what a faith-based enterprise science really is. Science is in the business of discovering the laws of nature. It bases its conclusions about the laws of nature on empirical evidence. Sometimes we discover that what we thought was an inviolable law of nature actually isn't, and so we discard it and try to find one to replace it. But when we find out that some particular law of nature isn't quite right, we don't give up on the lawfulness of nature. We never give up on that. We just give up on our old formulation of the laws of nature, and start searching for a new formulation that can accommodate the new evidence. And so we can ask—this is what David Hume in effect did ask—what *would* make us give up on the lawfulness of nature? Is there *any* kind of empirical evidence that would make us give up on that belief—not just give up on our belief that *this* or *that* is a law of nature, but on the whole belief that nature is lawful? Of course not. Anytime we get some counterevidence against a law, we go off searching for the right law. We never consider that maybe that counterevidence should be used against the whole idea that nature is lawful. Never! The idea just wouldn't arise, because the whole enterprise of science is ruled by the search for laws. The unlawfulness of nature is unthinkable, not because there's no evidence for it, but because nothing would ever be deemed evidence for it. And we can't even offer any evidence for the lawfulness of nature—this is the tricky part of Hume's argument—because even the notion of evidence already presumes nature's lawfulness. If we were really going to ask for evidence for nature's lawfulness, we wouldn't be able to offer up any evidence without already presuming nature's lawfulness. That's what Hume showed."

Fidley had paused and given a grand survey of the packed chapel. He had the audience's full attention, and he knew it. Roz was not looking happy, and Mona was downright grim.

"Reason—logic and science—themselves demonstrate that faith is unavoidable. So it can't be true, as this flock of ardent unbelievers has been trying to convince us, that there's faith and religion on one side, and reason and science on the other, and that they are irreconcilable antagonists. Just as faith without reason is blind, reason without faith is crippled."

So is Fidley claiming that Hume showed that faith in the lawfulness of nature is necessary for science to proceed, and that faith in religion is also necessary (for what?), and that science can't say anything against it? That seems blatantly fallacious, and hardly the tactic that, in Lucinda's words, "such a rationalist—University of Chicago and all" would take. But is that where he's headed?

"And there you have it, my first prong of attack. Faith is unavoidable.

"Prong two," Fidley says now, and calmly takes a sip from his glass of water. "Given that we sometimes have to rely on faith, when should we do it? What should we have faith in?

Well, reason and science certainly. But what else? We need standards. To say that faith is necessary doesn't throw open the floodgates to all beliefs willy-nilly. We can't just start believing in superstitions, populating our world with leprechauns and Easter bunnies.

"You see, there's serious faith, which is necessary, and then there's frivolous faith. Faith in the laws of logic and the laws of nature is necessary if the world is going to present itself to us coherently. If I doubt logic itself, I don't know how to proceed. There *is* no way to proceed. My knowing that all men are mortal and that Socrates is a man will give me no reason to think that Socrates is mortal. Same thing if I were to start doubting the lawfulness of nature. If I doubt that nature is lawful, then I will never use the past as a guide to the future. Just because light has always traveled at 186,272 miles per second up until today, that would give me no reason to believe that it will do so tomorrow.

"The moral: there are faiths that are unavoidable if coherent lives are to be lived. That's presumably why Cass Seltzer has faith in logic and in science. Cass Seltzer is a man of faith because he can't live his life coherently otherwise.

"These kinds of faiths can be compared to financial investments. When you make an investment, you can't know whether it's going to pay you back. You can only make the investment and see what happens. Has your money worked for you or not? The same principle applies here. Does investing in a faith in logic and science work for us or not? Obviously it does. Without it, we're flat broke. So this is a faith we should keep in our portfolio.

"Are there other faiths that are like this, that are comparable to the faith in science and reason? Well, what about the faith that your own individual life has a purpose? What about the faith that human life in general has meaning, that it matters to the universe that we are here and that we survive and flourish? What about the faith in the dignity of human life, your own and others'? How is it possible to live coherently, leading lives that are worthy of us, without faith in a transcendent purpose and meaning and dignity? These, too, are faiths that pay a good rate of return. To accept them is to see the value of one's life increase exponentially.

"Skepticism in regard to reason and science renders our lives incoherent to the point of unlivable. So, too, does skepticism about the purpose and meaning of our lives, skepticism about whether we have any right to pursue our lives with the seriousness they demand of us. A David Hume could demonstrate the non-demonstrability of reason, but that didn't keep him from reasoning. A Bertrand Russell or a Cass Seltzer can argue for the purposelessness of our individual lives, yet that doesn't keep them from living purposefully, from living as if it all matters. Cass Seltzer pursues his life; in fact, from the looks of it, he pursues it pretty well. Even if he argues that he thinks his life is devoid of purpose, of worthiness, the very vigor with which he is pursuing it gives the lie to his claim. It's just like the person who argues that we shouldn't have faith in reason—he gives the lie to his argument by expecting that his argument will be taken seriously, since if his argument really worked we couldn't take it seriously. Some faiths are unavoidable because without them our very lives become incoherent. Faith that we have a reason to live is a faith like that.

"That is my second prong." Eighteen minutes have elapsed, and he has yet to affirm the resolution that God exists.

"But I haven't said anything yet about God." Aha! "I've

waited for my third prong of attack to introduce Him. I should have convinced you by now that certain faiths are necessary for coherence, and I should have convinced you that among such faiths is that in our own purposefulness, our sense that our lives matter. You know, even someone who ends his life is taking that life seriously, so seriously that he can't stand to live it. We just can't inhabit our lives without taking them seriously."

Cass could be projecting—he's been known to project before—but he seems to sense a slightly more sympathetic note creeping into Fidley's delivery as he swerves toward the existential.

"But how can an individual life acquire this seriousness? What can confer it? It requires something outside an individual's life to make it matter, and that something must *itself* have agency and purpose. It must have intentionality, which means it must have a mind. And that is exactly what God is. The mind of God is the purposeful agency that confers purposefulness on each of us, even on Cass Seltzer."

No, Cass had definitely been projecting.

"The faith in a God who loves each one of us, who cares about whether we each reach our full potential as human beings, is the very faith required for us to reach our full potential as human beings. The faith in a God who has made us in His image is the faith that confers worth on each of us. How else can mere human lives acquire transcendent meaning if not through a transcendent agency?

"How am I doing for time?" he finally thinks to ask Lenny, who answers jauntily that he'd used up his time several minutes ago, and earns himself a huge laugh. Lenny is now having the time of his life.

"Okay, then, I'll make just one more point," Fidley says,

because obviously Lenny is not going to stop him. "And that's that, if you have any doubt that rejection of faith in God impoverishes life and robs men and women of that sense of meaningfulness that makes their lives coherent, then all you have to do is look around at the hollow hedonism, neurotic narcissism, and dissolute degeneracy of a secular age that can't even be alerted to the seriousness of life by a wake-up call like 9/11. It's not just the immorality of our godless age that makes a person want to weep, but also the sad sight of human life untouched by transcendence."

Cass can see Fidley's trapezius muscles contracting, and his right hand slashes the air one time each on the downward beat of "hedonism," "narcissism," and "degeneracy."

Fidley walks back to his seat, and Cass remains sitting a bit too long, so that Lenny actually turns to him with a wide smile and a flourish of his hand to indicate the podium, which of course gets another laugh; at this point, Lenny can do no wrong. Cass stands and walks over to his lectern and looks out at the overflow audience, and the awareness of the absurdity of his standing here, before all these people, in order to negate the resolution "God exists," threatens to transport him clean out of who he is supposed to be and what he is supposed to be doing.

Here I am.

No, if any moment is the wrong moment for him to yield to his version of transcendence, this has to be it. He takes a good long look at the kid with the ponytail, he takes a good long look at Roz, and he brings himself back to the question at hand, which is: is he going to go after Fidley's argument?

He doesn't feel he has a grip on it yet. Fidley has appealed to elements of The Argument from Personal Purpose (#19), and The Argument from the Unreasonableness of Reason

(#33), and he's even introduced a snatch of The Argument from Pragmatism (#32) in speaking of beliefs that pay good rates of return; but he's jumbled them up in such a way that the whole is giving the appearance of being greater than the sum of its parts, and Cass can't see his way through the jumble yet. And then he'd thrown in Hume, too, for good measure. What would Azarya say about Fidley's deployment of Hume? Hume is one of Azarya's heroes. He'd all but memorized Hume's essay "On Miracles" when he was an adolescent. Azarya would never stand for Humean skepticism's being misused as a defense of theism.

Back when Cass had been a pre-med and taking exams, sometimes he would look at the questions for the first time and think in a panic that nothing was familiar, that because of some terrible misunderstanding he had studied the wrong text, and that there wasn't a single question on the page that connected with anything that he knew. But then, like a cloud of silt settling out of turbid water and revealing the riverbed below, his mind cleared and the panic subsided, and each question of the exam emerged as an exemplar of a familiar principle. He's hoping that will happen very soon.

On the spot, as Cass is making his preliminary remarks thanking Chaplain Shore and the Agnostic Chaplaincy of Harvard for sponsoring the debate, and thanking Professor Fidley for "initiating the discussion by firing such an intellectually serious salvo," he's decided to postpone discussing Fidley's argument, and instead start out by making his own case independently. Why let Fidley define the terms of his opening argument anyway?

"Professor Fidley, in apologizing for the necessity of faith, concedes too soon in admitting that belief in God must rest on faith. If God makes any difference to the world—and what would be the point of believing in any God that didn't make a difference to the world?—then we should be able to see indications of his existence when we observe the world we find ourselves in. And the fact is that this world does not present itself as being one in which there exists a powerful creator who cares about us. On the face of it, it seems a very different kind of world, which is what has inspired the theological line of argument that's called theodicy: the attempt to reconcile the existence of God with the facts about our world that seem to suggest his absence.

"We can observe one feature of our world that is particularly relevant: suffering. Children die of disease; individuals are crippled by accidents and wracked with pain; whole peoples get exterminated. Just on the face of it, the obscene amounts of suffering we observe are not compatible with a God who's both good and in control. Mind you, that's just on the face of it. Believers look for ways of accommodating God's existence with the searing facts of suffering, but they have to work hard at it, and the hard theodical work they need to do is what I mean by the world's offering empirical evidence against God's existence.

"So what are the ways that believers have offered to reconcile so much suffering with the existence of God? First there are the preconditions for free will. If we are truly to be moral agents rather than robots, then we must have the freedom to choose between good and evil. And, given that freedom, the possibility of evil must be there; and, given that possibility, sometimes it will be realized, and when it is realized, suffering will ensue.

"But the requirements of free will can only account for a small part of the suffering we see. It will, perhaps, allow the believer to write off, as cosmically accounted for, the child who was overheard to whisper to his mother as they were both being marched to their deaths at the extermination camp at Belzec, 'But I tried to be so good, Mama!' Yes, people are given free will, and Belzec was a consequence, and so the theist can write off that child's pathetic cry as accounted for.

"But there is also abundant suffering that comes about not because of the exercise of others' free will but because of natural disasters and accidents and the ravages of disease. And believers have to come up with some other way of dealing with these cases, since their occurrence has nothing to do with the exercise of free will. At this point you hear about the potential for achieving a greatness of the soul in overcoming tragedy. You hear that there are virtues—such as forbearance, and courage, and transcendence in the face of suffering, and compassion and love for those who suffer—which can only be exercised because suffering gives us the opportunity. The moral purpose of life, under this view, has to do with soul-making, and the full extent of what our souls can become can only unfold under the adverse conditions that God generously provides us.

"These are ingenious attempts to reconcile the facts of our world to the existence of a God who cares, and the very ingenuity they require shows how difficult the reconciliation is.

"And of course even here the explanation can't cover all the cases, since so many of those who suffer are never given the opportunity to achieve soul-making at all—like people whose lives are snuffed out in an instant, together with all those who might have developed virtues in the grieving for them, or children who have no way to make sense of their suffering. Once again, their suffering, according to this rationalization, can perhaps serve the moral needs of others, and so can find justification.

"I don't know about any of you, but I find this rationalization, as ingenious as it is, morally offensive. The suffering sacrifice of some so that *others* are afforded the opportunity to achieve moral transcendence doesn't strike me as descriptive of a moral universe. At the very least, shouldn't all God's creatures be given an opportunity for transcendence? The believer who's satisfied with this ingenious answer isn't paying close enough attention to the facts of suffering. His moral calculus of costs and benefits doesn't add up.

"And it's at this point that the believer, if he feels this objection at all, will take refuge in the inscrutable will of God. Or perhaps he'll argue that the very resistance of these facts of suffering to any explanation that we can come up with points to the existence of God, since there must be a way in which this suffering is redeemed, and since it's not in this world, then it has to be in the next. But, of course, to believe that there must be some way in which this suffering is ultimately redeemed is already to assume a level of transcendent explanation, which is the same thing as assuming God, which makes an argument of this kind circular.

"So at some point the believer, no matter how ingenious his attempts to reconcile the existence of God to the nature of the world, will have to fall back, when it comes to some of the most heartrending of cases, on the inscrutable ways of God. But to speak of the inscrutable ways of God is to acknowledge that the moral complexion of our world doesn't favor the existence of a benevolent deity, which is the very point that I'm making.

"How am I doing for time?"

"You have a minute left," Lenny says, without looking at his watch. Cass has the feeling Lenny is keeping time or not, as the spirit moves him.

"Okay, then, I'll wrap it up. It's often said that, just as the-ism can't be proved, so, too, atheism can't be proved. Just because no argument manages to establish God's existence doesn't show he doesn't exist. Both beliefs depend on faith alone. But to this I respond that there is so much about our world—in particular, its moral complexion—that makes it appear to be unruled by a beneficent being, there is so much that we either have to callously ignore or else lay at the feet of God's inscrutability, that in the absence of any argument for God's existence so compelling as to overcome these facts of suffering—and I haven't heard one tonight—the reasonable conclusion is that God does not exist."

Cass stops speaking, and there's some rustling and whis-pering and thumping out in the pews as people rearrange their bodies and prepare for the next round.

Fidley goes to his lectern, while Cass remains standing at his, and Cass finds he no longer feels intimidated. He thinks he's acquitted himself well so far, and he wistfully wishes that Lucinda were here to see it. But there are Roz and Mona, both looking optimistic—in fact, Roz looks radiant—and now that he's no longer nervous, he feels grateful to Sy Auerbach for traveling all the way from New York, and to the Agnostic Chaplaincy and to Harvard University, to whom he feels dou-bly grateful, and he realizes that he's once again on the verge of ascending on the flapping wings of his grateful soul, and so he takes a good hard look at his adversary to bring him back down to this moment and to what still lies ahead. Fidley has struck a formidable pose, his shoulders looking wider than ever, and he's been hastily scribbling while Cass has been doing nothing but counting his blessings like a fool. He con-centrates now and thinks he knows what Azarya would say about Fidley's enlisting of Humean skepticism, and thinking that he knows how Azarya would respond calms him down again.

Lenny Shore comes over to Cass's lectern and speaks into his mike.

"Before we go on to the next phase of this debate, I just want to say to Professor Fidley: You know, you're right! And I would like to say to Professor Seltzer: You know, you're right!"

The audience laughs, and Lenny laughs with them, right into the mike.

"So—now on to the questions. Professor Fidley, you have the first question." Lenny returns to his seat.

"Thank you very much. I'm more grateful than ever to have the opportunity to question Cass Seltzer after having listened to him. Only now do I fully understand why he is referred to as 'the atheist with a soul.'"

Felix takes a little longer this time to smile and then waits for a few snickers to join him. Is Lenny keeping time? Roz has murder in her eyes.

"That was an impressively soulful homily on the virtues of atheism. Cass Seltzer makes it sound as if anyone who cares sufficiently for his fellow man is duty-bound to be an atheist. A believer such as Mother Teresa, who devoted her life to serving the most suffering of God's creatures, apparently isn't paying enough attention to the facts of suffering, at least not as much as academicians like Bertrand Russell and Cass Seltzer are paying attention, ministering to God's unfortunates by being professors and writing best-selling books."

This is the second time that Fidley has gotten in a dig about best sellers. Perhaps the sales for *Welfare Warfare Wherefore* had been disappointing.

"The Reverend Dr. Martin Luther King, who forfeited his life in the struggle to alleviate the misery of his people, apparently didn't pay close enough attention to how people suffer, or he would never have been a man of God. Despite lives of self-sacrifice—to which, I think even Cass Seltzer will agree, the religious are far more prone then the irreligious—such people as these are cold of heart compared with the atheists, who care too much for their fellow man to be able to believe in God.

"My first question to Professor Seltzer is whether he really does mean to suggest that Mother Teresa was a callous woman."

Fidley spaces out those last six words so that they make their full impact, and there's a faint rushing noise that Cass is pretty sure is coming from the audience and not from inside his own head, as if of the collective intake of breath.

"I'm sorry if I gave the impression that I think believers are callous and uncaring. That certainly isn't something that I believe."

Cass swallows. This head-on attack is unnerving. He's unnerved. He takes a sip of water.

"You and I are here today, Professor Fidley, to debate the resolution 'God exists.' We're evaluating arguments for and against that resolution. As those of you who have read my book know, that's not how I think religious beliefs are generally formed. When it comes to religion, arguments usually come after belief, not before. Far more potent than arguments are certain emotional attitudes that permeate one's whole sense of being in the world, emotional attitudes that orient a person in the world rather than say something true or false. Theistic propositions like 'God exists,' or 'God is good,' or 'God loves me,' are metaphorical expressions for these permeating attitudes and emotions—metaphors that can seriously confuse us. For me to debate the truth or falsity of the proposition 'God exists' with you tonight therefore has nothing much to do with the psychology of religion as I understand it, with what it feels like to hold a spiritual attitude toward the world and to live accordingly. So, when I criticize theodical arguments as being cavalier toward suffering, I'm not criticizing religious *people* as being cavalier toward suffering, since the whole point of my book is that the psychology of religious conviction has little to do with arguments.

"But here tonight we *are* debating arguments, arguments for a proposition, not an emotion, and I maintain that the argument *against* the existence of God, based on the great amount of suffering that the believer must lay at the inscrutability of God, is stronger than any arguments *for* the existence. And any theist who thinks he's helped clear up the mystery by appealing to such things as the potential for achieving greatness of soul that suffering presents to some sufferers, but by no means all sufferers, is, yes, cavalier toward suffering, at least while he is consciously making that argument. In some sense, perhaps, the very fact that compassionate people, people who devote themselves to alleviating suffering, can get themselves to believe that the degree of suffering we witness can be explained, is itself a measure of how powerful the psychological mechanisms are."

Cass had felt discomfited by Fidley's question, not only the hostile way in which it had been asked, but by the substance of it as well. He doesn't want to be forced into criticizing religious people. He suspects that Fidley has figured this out about him and is going to exploit it.

Now it's his turn to ask a question, and he looks at Fidley as he speaks, but Fidley doesn't look at him.

"Professor Fidley, you've argued that the belief in God is as necessary to our living coherently as is our belief in logic and our belief in the lawfulness of nature. As you pointed out so eloquently, there can be no thought at all without believing in the fundamentals of thinking, in the rules of logic and the rules of scientific induction. Likewise, you want to argue, our living coherently requires our sense that we matter, and that this mattering in turn requires a Transcendental Underwriter, something beyond ourselves that ensures that we do actually matter. How is it possible to live coherently, you ask, leading lives that are worthy of us, without faith in a transcendent purpose? But there's something about this line of reasoning that strikes me as viciously circular. If we already *know* that we're worthy of having a transcendent purpose coming to us, why would we need the transcendent purpose? The transcendent purpose would be redundant. And if we don't know that we're worthy unless we acquire that transcendent purpose, then who says we have a transcendent purpose coming to us in the first place? This demand for a transcendent purpose seems either unneeded or unearned, or am I wrong?"

All the talk about Hume, Cass had seen, had been just so much silt-stirring. Fidley's three-pronged argument is an elaborate variation of The Argument from Personal Purpose. Fidley's argument is only as sound as Cass's #19.

Fidley smiles again, that same thin gash cutting into his left cheek, and he keeps his face turned toward the audience.

"It's hard for me to accept anything Cass Seltzer has to say about my argument, since his entire discussion has begged the question in a way I think must be obvious to everyone here, including Cass Seltzer himself. He's coming at my argument from a moral high ground that he can't legitimately claim. There is simply no way for an atheist such as himself to be able to claim any sort of objective morality.

"Cass Seltzer spoke of the tragedy of a child being exterminated by the absolute evil that was Nazism. But how, coming from his worldview, can he possibly maintain that there's anything like absolute evil? It's on the basis of the evil in this world that he argues that our world yields empirical evidence against God's existence. But the absolute distinction between good and evil can be maintained only on the basis of God. According to the Nazi system, it was perfectly okay to send that child to his death. And without God, who's to say the Nazis were wrong?

"Now, Cass Seltzer, of course, is not a Nazi. He has another system from which he judges the Nazis' actions wrong, the suffering inflicted on that child evil. But if it's just some people's systems going up against other people's systems, with no higher authority to adjudicate between them, then it all dissolves into moral chaos and ethical relativism, and Cass Seltzer isn't entitled to talk about the moral complexion of the world at all.

"*I* can talk about it, but only because I know that there's a God who establishes the objective difference between right actions and wrong actions, between immoral systems like Nazism and moral systems like Judeo-Christian ethics. But how can Cass Seltzer claim such objective moral distinctions?"

Fidley stops speaking, and he still isn't looking at Cass, and Cass isn't quite sure if this is the second question that Fidley is lobbing at him or just a rhetorical flourish.

"Is that your second question to me?"

"Yes, it is." Still the man won't look at Cass, and it's beginning to irk him.

"I'd be glad to answer that question, Professor Fidley, but first I do want to point out that you didn't answer my question, and that disappoints me. Instead, you've switched the topic and are arguing that my own argument makes no sense because it's a moral argument and without God there can be no moral truths. I'm more than happy to address that point.

"Morality is often claimed by the theists to come much easier to them than to the atheists. It's a natural thing to think. The claims of morality seem so mysterious—involving, as they do, not just claims about what *is* the case but about what *ought* to be the case—that it's natural to feel that you have to ground them in a mysterious foundation. Morality is mysterious, God is mysterious, let's reduce one mystery to the other and assume that the mystery of God takes care of the mystery of morality. Morality has to be more than just one people's system of values clashing with another people's system of values, Professor Fidley says, and I agree. But then he also says that the only way that it can be more is if there is a higher authority adjudicating between them.

"But grounding morality in God doesn't work at all. After all, you have to ask the question whether *God* has any reason for his moral adjudication. Does God have some reason for endorsing a system that enshrines a moral principle like 'Do unto others as you would have them do unto you,' while he rejects the principles of Nazism that sent that child and so many like him to their deaths? Professor Fidley asked me how we humans can adjudicate between moral systems if we don't have recourse to God's adjudication. Now I'm asking the same question about how God adjudicates. Either God has a reason for his moral decisions or he doesn't.

"Let's say he does. Well, then, there are reasons independent of his will, and whatever those reasons are provides the justification for what makes those moral decisions the right ones. God's reasons for wanting us to do unto others as we would have them do unto us are the very reasons that we *should* do unto others as we would have them do unto us. The reasons are what make such actions moral, and God himself is redundant.

"The alternative is that God has no reason at all because there are no moral reasons independent of God. But if he really has no moral reason pushing him one way or the other—because otherwise *that* would be the moral reason and we could leave God out of it—God could just as well have reversed himself. He might want each of us to do unto others the very thing we lie in bed worrying that someone might, God forbid, do unto us. He might order a loving father to take his son and prepare him for sacrifice, binding the terrified boy as one binds an animal to be slaughtered, and, because there is no morality independent of God, the father will obey without demurral. Ah, you say, but the Lord stayed the father's hand, as we knew that he would, since he would never demand something as morally heinous as child sacrifice. But that's to bring in a morality independent of God. If there really isn't any morality independent of God, then we would all be in the position of Abraham, prepared to commit the filicide he came close to committing in Genesis 22. We would all be prepared to commit the genocide that God commands in Numbers 31, when he is outraged that not every last woman and male child of the Midianites had been killed. Without any moral reasons independent of God, God's adjudication becomes the whim of an entirely arbitrary authority, and it doesn't clear up the mystery of morality in the least. Without an independent concept of morality, how can we even say that God is good and that therefore his adjudication is relevant to our moral decisions?

"This argument goes back to Plato, and it shows that appeals to God don't help with the problem of grounding morality. Either God has his reasons and *those* are the reasons and reference to God is unnecessary, or God has no reasons and then morality consists of the arbitrary diktats of a God who we can't even say is good.

"How, then, *do* we ground morality? Professor Fidley has done part of the work for us by identifying the fundamental adherence that each of us has to our own lives' mattering. He's right in claiming that we can't live coherent lives without feeling that we matter, but that is quite a different thing from our *actually* mattering in some cosmic sense. We can't get that automatically, just from our wanting to matter or feeling that we do matter. The upward move that Professor Fidley tried to make in the third prong of his argument doesn't work.

"But I do think we can move horizontally outward, and that's the direction to go to legitimate morality. I can't look at other creatures who are committed to their existence and flourishing in the same way as I'm committed to my existence and flourishing without feeling a certain degree of identification, empathy, sympathy, compassion. The intuition that we ought to do unto others as we would have them do unto us flows naturally from this outward move. I don't see any way to get it by some upward move. I presume, however, that you do, Professor Fidley. And I'd like for you to explain how, especially how you get around Plato's argument, which is my question to you."

"Indeed I do, Cass Seltzer. Not only do I think that what you call the 'upward move' can ground morality, I don't believe that anything else can, certainly not your floundering gesture in what you call the outward direction."

Well, this is at least some improvement, as far as Cass is concerned. Fidley may be snarling, but at least he's addressing him directly, and he's actually turned toward him, the two hard pebbles locking onto Cass's gaze.

"As far as I can make out, this sideways movement that's supposed to give you the Golden Rule just comes down to this: seeing the meaninglessness of your life moves you to compassion for the meaninglessness of other lives."

He says this with a smile—his most convincing one yet—and he ends it with a brief bark of a laugh. It's a good line, and Cass laughs, too.

"And from this you want to derive morality, Cass Seltzer? That is, to say the least, a pretty tepid system of morality you're offering us, which, even if you could get it to make internal sense, doesn't have much force. I don't see it getting anyone to overcome their immoral impulses.

"As far as that argument from Plato that you are so impressed with is concerned, I can't say that I find it convincing. There's nothing arbitrary about God's moral grounding. It's rooted in God's very character. The being of goodness lies in God. Our life has moral value, sufficient so that Cass Seltzer can pity the suffering of humans, only because we are made in the image of God. There is nothing in the nature of a human being that, in and of itself, entails worthiness. Our worthiness, if it exists at all, has to be derived from something outside us.

"And from what is it derived? From that of which we cannot think without seeing Its worthiness. Seltzer's question—how do we know that God Himself is good?—is as misguided a question as asking what time it is right now on the sun. If you understand that what we mean by the time of day is the relation between the sun and the earth, then you're not going to ask what time it is on the sun. And if you understand that the being of God contains the grounds of goodness in Its very essence, then you're not going to ask whether God is good or not.

"Cass Seltzer is patently confusing *how* we know with *what* we know. People can recognize moral values independently of God, and they can use that recognition to understand that God is good. But their recognizing moral values independently of God doesn't mean that moral values *themselves* exist independently of God. There's knowledge that's independent, and then there's existence that's independent, and these are two different things.

"My belief is that God, who is the foundation of moral values, implants intuitions of these values in each of us. This is what the Bible happens to say, and as Cass Seltzer of all people should know, this is what many psychologists are now reporting, that, beneath the surface differences in our moral points of view, there are deep universals. So it can seem to people like Cass Seltzer that, just because his knowledge of these values can be attained independently of his knowledge of God, the values themselves are independent of God. In fact, there can be no morality independent of God, but that doesn't mean that morality is arbitrary. Morality could not be different, because God is God; He has to be the way He is, and could not be some other way if He is God at all."

Cass has been brought to the point of wondering how sincere Felix Fidley really is. Does he believe what he's saying, or is he trying, as Lucinda predicted, to overwhelm him? His argument has all the structure and verbiage and feel of a philosophical argument, with its familiar distinction between how something is and how we know that something is, but it doesn't really apply to the issue they're debating. The philosophical distinctions glance off the surface without digging in. Even Fidley hadn't sounded completely convinced as he delivered his last few lines, as if he had to get them out but didn't like the taste of them in his mouth. Perhaps Cass will find a way to frame his last question that will expose Fidley's unease with his own sophistry.

But at this point Chaplain Lenny steps in and says that this has been so fascinating, and the time has flown by so quickly, that there's only time for one more question, which he guesses will go to Professor Fidley. Fidley again takes several moments to scan the audience.

"It seems apparent to me, and I certainly hope to many of you who are here tonight, that the Judeo-Christian system of morality, founded on the appeal to an authority beyond us, is the only thing that can confer the sort of worth on each individual that wrings tears from an atheist like Cass Seltzer. Nothing else can do it. No 'is' statement can entail an 'ought' statement. No statement about what people are like, what matters to them, entails that we *ought* to do unto others as we would wish them to do unto us. If we just stay on the horizontal level of 'is' statements, then we can't possibly get out any 'oughts.' This is why we have to move to a whole other level, which is the level of God, the level on which the distinction between 'is' and 'ought' disappears, a point which neither Plato nor Cass Seltzer appreciates. Plato's excuse is that he lived before the great monotheistic discovery had spread to Greece. What's Cass Seltzer's excuse?

"But even if I were to grant Cass Seltzer his tepid sideways moral system, what motivation can he drum up to get anybody to do the moral thing? What motivational force can he put behind it? That's yet another crucial problem with a secular system of morality. It has no muscle. It's a legal system with no means of enforcement, no police to arrest people who break the law—in other words, anarchy. In the end, given a secular morality—if such a thing is even coherent—what you get is a system that is utterly toothless, so the result is the same as if there were no moral system at all: anarchy, anomie, a society consisting of people doggedly acting only in their own self-interest, in fact little more than brutes.

"But a moral system based on the will of God has enforcement built into it. What motivation do people have for doing the morally right thing? If they don't, they will be displeasing God, and there will be, as we say, hell to pay.

"Cass Seltzer is an atheist with a soul, who feels sympathy for all sentient beings and thinks that others ought to, too. Lovely sentiments. But what if they don't feel as he feels, and what if they don't want to? What means does he have of compelling them to do the right thing?

"For him there's no immortality. Death is the end, and everyone ends up exactly the same. It doesn't make any difference whether you live as a Hitler or a Mother Teresa. There's no relationship between the moral quality of your life and your ultimate fate. Death is final, over and out, and, given its finality, what reason could there be for consistently living the moral life rather than living only for one's self?

"My last question to you, Professor Seltzer, is, what motivation for adopting the moral point of view can you possibly offer without a belief in God and immortality?"

Fidley's tone of belligerent confidence has returned with this last speechifying question. The line about a morality with muscle is, clearly, something he really believes. Roz is sitting on the edge of her seat—literally, as she would say—and her hands are clasped in front of her almost in supplication, and he can't help smiling at the sight of her. She's a good friend, but she's also distracting him.

"Professor Fidley worries that, without a belief in God, people will act only for reasons of self-interest instead of behaving morally. But then what does he offer as the only persuasion to adopt the moral point of view? Concern for one's self, in this life and the next. Without this, he says, there's no reason to act morally. In the end, it's Professor Fidley who reduces morality to self-interest.

"And it's no wonder that in the end he has to fall back on self-interest as the ultimate motivation for morality. He can't see what can be morally compelling about morality, in and of itself. If he did see that, he wouldn't think that he needs God to magically inject the morality into morality. And since, according to him, there's nothing compelling about morality in itself, he also thinks morality requires some lash to punish us in an afterlife if we don't comply. So, in the end, all that he can appeal to are motivations of self-interest. In the end, all that he can offer people as a reason to act morally is for them to act in their self-interest, currying favor with an authority that can dole out rewards and mete out punishments.

"But if the moral point of view is something that we humans can, with a great deal of effort, reason our way into, then morality itself provides the motivation to be moral. The reason to do the moral thing is that it's the moral thing to do; to do anything else is to make a shambles of our thinking, of our values, of our mattering. Our seeing *for ourselves* why it's the moral thing to do is what compels us.

"When we're trying to teach a child why it's wrong to pick on another child, do we say, 'It's wrong because if I catch you doing it again you'll be spanked,' or do we, rather, say, 'How would *you* feel if someone did that to *you*?' And when we're wrestling with our own conscience, trying to resist a temptation we know is wrong, do we think to ourselves, 'If I do it, then I'll be flambéed in hell's fires,' or do we think, 'Would I want everyone in the world to behave this way? Wouldn't I feel moral outrage if I learned of someone else doing this?'

"There is a point of view that's available to all of us. The philosopher Thomas Nagel called it the 'View from Nowhere.' It's the source of so much of our philosophical reasoning, including our moral reasoning. When you view the fact that you happen to be the particular person that you are from the vantage point of the View from Nowhere, that fact shrivels into insignificance. Of course, we don't live our life from the perspective of the View from Nowhere. We live inside our lives, where it's impossible not to feel one's self to matter. But, still, that View from Nowhere is always available to us, reminding us that there's nothing inherently special or uniquely deserving about any of us, that it's just an accident that one happens to be who one happens to be. And the con- sequence of these reflections is this: if we can't live coherently without believing ourselves to matter, then we can't live coherently without extending that same mattering to every- one else.

"The work of ethics is the work of getting one's self to this vantage point and keeping it relevant to how one sees the world and acts. There are truths to discover in that process, and they're the truths that make us change our behavior. To assert that there has been no cumulative progress in discover- ing moral truths is as grossly false as to say there's been no cumulative progress made in science. We've discovered that slavery is wrong, we've discovered that burning heretics in autos-da-fé is wrong, we've discovered that depriving people of rights on the basis of race or religion is wrong, we've dis- covered that the legal ownership of women is wrong.

"Religious impulses and emotions are varied. There are expansive, life-affirming emotions that can find a natural expression in the context of religion, which is why I can never offer a wholesale condemnation of religion, even though Professor Fidley seems to think I do. But when religion encourages what I can only describe as a moral childishness that blocks the development of true moral thinking, then I do condemn it. When religion tells us that there is nothing more we can say about morality than that we can't see the reasons for it, but do it if you know what's good for you, then I do condemn it. We can do better than that. We can become moral grown-ups. And if there were a God, surely he would approve."

Cass stops speaking, not because he has found the perfect parting shot, but because he is spent. His opening statement had been shorter than Fidley's by half, so he had felt it only fair to help himself to as much time as he wanted at the end, when the words just kept coming. There's a silence for several long moments, an uncanny silence considering how many people are crowding Memorial Church, and Cass wonders whether he went on too long and too emotionally, and whether he has embarrassed himself and everyone here. Then the hall erupts. Lenny stands at the lectern beside Cass, waiting for the applause to die down so he can say the few words that he's been saving for the end, including the best of the agnostic jokes. But he doesn't get the chance, because when the applause dies down the crowd surges forward, and Cass is surrounded.

XXXV

The Argument from Solemn Emotions

It's only when Cass is settling himself into his car that he realizes that he's euphoric. He hasn't had the time to observe the state of his mind, or maybe the euphoria has descended on him right at this moment. I'm drunk, he thinks, pushing the Start button of his Prius and silently steering onto Massachusetts Avenue.

William James, cataloguing the varieties of rapture that can seize hold of a person, hadn't scorned to include intoxication: "Sobriety diminishes, discriminates, and says no; drunkenness expands, unites, and says yes. It is in fact the great exciter of the *Yes* function in man. It brings its votary from the chill periphery of things to the radiant core. It makes him for the moment one with truth."

Yes, Cass thinks, making a left onto Bow Street, driving past the Harvard river dorms. He feels as if he hardly has a need to breathe, as if he's holding his breath as the *Yes* function is pumping, and that for as long as he can sustain this breathless *Yes* he is in perfect harmony with the world, no matter the wildness and pang of life. All the irreconcilabilities are melded sweetly together, the pulling-apartness that shreds the human heart is stilled in the yesness that's resounding, and all manner of things shall be well.

My soul is blotto, he says, and laughs out loud, and William James himself would approve. Straight ahead of him, Weeks Bridge is spectrally glowing, the wide white steps leading into a self-enclosed space of solemn emotions, and he gazes lovingly at it as he makes a right onto Memorial Drive.

The traffic light on the corner of Memorial Drive and JFK, which is always red, is green for him, and as he turns left and glides over the river, he glances left to get another glimpse of the mystical radiance of Weeks Bridge, and it induces a surge of love that would be more appropriate if directed toward a person than a brickwork structure. He turns left onto Storrow Drive and gets another loving look at the bridge and at the redbrick and pristine jewel-colored domes and spires of the Harvard skyline, the architecture that had impressed him twenty years ago with the insistence of its purity and American authenticity, and his love for it, too, is inappropriately tender.

As he makes the right that will take him to the turnpike, he realizes that the reason these loves feel as if they're directed toward a person is that they are. All are expressions of his love for Lucinda. It's Lucinda who has reset the vector of his life, giving a vigorous spin to the wheel of his fortune. No wonder his soul is intoxicated—shit-faced, as Mona might put it and he loves Mona again, now, too, mindful Mona, front and center—and he laughs as he exits for Logan Airport, and then parks the car in the short-term lot.

He's twenty minutes late and his *Yes* function is still pumping at capacity, and the sound of it is laughter. He laughs when he checks the American Airlines monitor and learns that her plane is only now landing, and he laughs when he remembers that she had had to check her luggage, since she had taken her running and swimming clothes and the creams she has for every body part; and again he laughs when he sees that Carousel D is labeled "AA 211, Dallas," which is the flight she was on, and then the carousel starts to spin and he recognizes the first suitcase to emerge and rushes to retrieve it, but another hand deftly lifts it before he makes contact, and it's hers.

"Lucinda!"

She looks up at him, startled.

"Cass?"

"Lucinda!"

"Wow, you did come."

"Of course! I said I would."

She smiles, and again there's that slight tremor in her vermilion bow that softens the hardness that sometimes settles over it.

"I'm glad you're here," she says simply, and she kisses him sweetly, and it doesn't surprise him, and he relieves her of the green leather bag with the monogram "LM," and they walk together toward the terminal exit.

"I'm tired," she says.

"Of course you are. If you want to wait here, I'll get the car and bring it round."

"No, I want to walk. It's the staying still that's wearying."

They settle into the car, and she leans back and closes her eyes, and the solemn joy he feels is the solemn joy that William James describes.

"Anything happen while I was gone?" she asks.

A solemn joy, James had written, preserves a sort of bitter in its sweetness. A solemn sorrow is one to which we intimately consent.

"Well, I'm coming straight from the debate at Harvard."

"Debate?"

"With Fidley."

"Ah yes, Felix. You know that he and I published a paper together?"

"'Mandelbaum Equilibria in Hostile Takeovers.'"

"Right! You fang him good?"

"I don't know whether it would be what you would call good fanging. I think it was a good debate."

"Well, who won?"

"I kind of think I did."

"Kind of?"

"Afterward, Luke Nanovitch said, 'Score one for our side.'"

"Luke Nanovitch was there?"

"Yes. A lot of Auerbach's cartel were there. He must have ordered them to attend. Arthur Silver and Nicholas Duffy and Eliza Wandel and Marty Huffer."

"Sounds like quite the event. Those are brand names."

"There was only one brand name I wanted there. Lucinda Mandelbaum."

She opens her eyes and looks sideways at Cass and smiles and then closes her eyes again and leans back.

"The debate is going up on my agent's Web site, if you want to watch it. There were over a thousand people there. If I had had any idea, I would have been too terrified to show up."

"My talk for Pappa is posted on the Internet, too, if you want to watch it."

"Of course I want to watch it! The question is, will I understand it?"

"Maybe not all the technical points, but the general ideas, sure."

"Is it related to the Mandelbaum Equilibrium?"

"Only tangentially. It's related to regret."

"Regret, as in wishing you could change the past?"

"Exactly. Regret is a form of counterfactual thinking, and it can be modeled in game theory. People measure how well their strategy was not only by what they win, but by what they *could* have won. I developed some mathematics that puts regret into the equations."

"The mathematics of regret. It sounds hopeful."

"Yes," she says and smiles again, "it's very hopeful," and the silence in the car is charged with their intimacy and the sweet naturalness they've easily found their way back into.

"Something else happened while you were away."

She opens her eyes and looks at him.

"What?"

"I want to show you when we get home. I've been looking forward all week to showing you."

She smiles and leans back again.

"Oh, then, it's something good."

"Yes, very good."

"I'd thought for a moment it was something bad."

"Bad? Why?"

"Your voice sounded ominous."

"Ominous?"

"Well, solemn. I thought maybe some long-lost love of yours had shown up on our doorstep."

"Well, that, too," he says, and they both laugh.

They've exited onto Storrow Drive now, and there's Weeks Bridge rising up before them, and Cass says, "The first night you were gone, I couldn't sleep, and I finally just went for a walk at four a.m., and I found myself on Weeks Bridge," and he points right and her eyes follow where he's pointing. "The river was frozen except where it flowed through the three arches. It looked as if a cathedral had been carved into the ice."

"Has it melted now?"

"Yes."

"Too bad. It sounds sublime."

"That's exactly the right word. That's the word I had thought at the time. Sublime."

She smiles again, and they cross back over Larz Andersen Bridge and through Harvard Square, and Cass is contemplating how irresistible that drunken sense is that makes you feel that you and the world are in silent cahoots.

"Was Fidley fierce?"

"Pretty fierce."

"Yes, I imagine he'd be a tough antagonist."

"Before I even walked into the place, he was intimidating the poor Agnostic Chaplain of Harvard."

She opens her eyes.

"Did you say the Agnostic Chaplain of Harvard?"

"I did. It was the Agnostic Chaplaincy that sponsored the debate."

"How droll!"

"Yes," he says, laughing, "it *is* droll!"

"I guess I'll never understand the religious mind."

"What about the agnostic mind?"

"No, not that one either."

They drive down Massachusetts Avenue and turn onto Upland Road, and he pulls into the driveway, and the light from the streetlamp falls lavishly on them both.

"You look so tired I feel I should carry you in."

She smiles. "I feel so tired I might let you."

He gets her suitcase out of the backseat and shoulders her computer bag and her purse, and they go through their gate and up the porch stairs, and he unlocks the door, and they climb the narrow stairs to their first floor side by side.

"Why don't you sit down, and I'll make you some tea?"

"I ought to unpack first. I always unpack first thing when I get home."

"I'll help you unpack later. You just sit and have some tea. Are you hungry?"

"I ate dinner during the stopover in Dallas. What about you? Have you eaten?"

"I guess I haven't. I didn't have time after the debate."

"Hungry?"

"Not at all. We can both have some tea and some McVities Original Digestive Biscuits. Heath and Heather Night Time or Rather Jolly Earl Grey?"

"I'll have the Rather Jolly Passionfruit." She smiles and angles her head coyly.

"My girl," he says, his voice a little hoarse with emotion.

He puts the kettle on, and then gets her suitcase and trots it up to their bedroom. He knows how disciplined she is, so that the sight of it sitting there, unattended to, will spoil her fun. He comes back down, and she's settled onto the couch, her shoes thrown off, and her long legs curled beneath her.

"I feel quite decadent not unpacking straightaway, but I guess I can be a bad girl sometimes."

"Of course you can. Life's a thrill!"

She's wearing one of her short skirts, this one tight and black with pinstripes, and a pearl-gray sweater, and her languor is luscious, and he wonders whether he should put off telling her his news, but he can't wait any longer.

He has the Harvard letter out on their dining-room table, and he walks over and picks it up and hands it to her without a word.

She places it on her lap and tilts slightly downward to read it, the fluffy halo of her pale hair falling away to reveal the lotus stem of the back of her neck, and Cass, standing there above her, gazes lovingly down on it. He would bend and softly kiss it, but she hates to be disturbed while she reads, even if it's just the ingredient list on a food product, and he restrains himself from placing his lips on the tender exposure of her sweet neck. She straightens her back and stands and hands the letter back to Cass.

"How nice for you," she says. Her voice sounds as if it has turned blue with cold, and the coldness has hardened her thin upper lip, and the sight of it, the transformation it casts over her face, brings an ungainly unreality into the room.

She turns away, and as soon as she does, and he doesn't see her face, he's sure that he hasn't seen what he thought he had seen. She's heading toward the stairs to their second floor, and there's a howling sound, a long thin note as if of pain, and he realizes it's the teakettle boiling.

"Wait a sec," he says, and runs to the kitchen to take the kettle off and runs back to the living room, and she isn't there. He starts heading up the stairs, but she hears his footsteps and calls down, "I'll be down jolly soon," so he turns around and heads back into the kitchen, and mechanically starts to make their tea.

He figures that her obsessional discipline has overpowered her, her sense of order asserting its tyranny. She's unpacking, and then she'll be down.

He arranges the biscuits on a plate and sets them out on the table with folded napkins, and he has strawberries, too, which he washes and hulls, and he scoops some of Lucinda's Double Devon Cream into a bowl, and she still hasn't come down from the bedroom.

She's put out, he understands that. Her voice gets British when she's annoyed, and that "jolly soon" was, to use her word, ominous. He had made a terrible mistake in not telling her immediately about Harvard's offer. His wiser self has known it all week long and made him feel guilty. She read the date on the letter, and she can see that it was posted a week ago, and it's jarring to learn that your lover is capable of such expert dissembling. If he can hide this particular thing so well, who knows what else he can hide? Of course she's upset, she has every right to be. But he'll make it clear to her that he's not the kind to keep secrets from her, and that he never will again, never. And he shouldn't have told anyone else either, certainly not Roz, and he'll confess to Lucinda that he did, and he'll hope that she will forgive him.

He wonders whether he ought to go up to her now. He knows that she's hurt, and the longer she dwells on it without their talking, the more firmly the hurt will take hold. He knows this as a psychologist, and he knows this as a man. He moves toward the stairs and begins to climb them, heavily, so as to give her fair warning, and again she calls that she'll be down soon and just to wait.

The tea has gone cold, and he empties out the two cups in the sink. Lucinda likes her tea just short of scalding, and he puts the kettle up again, and steps out from the kitchen, and Lucinda is standing there in the living room. She's holding the green leather suitcase in one hand, her briefcase and purse in another.

"I thought you were unpacking," he says stupidly.

She takes a big breath and puts her things down and then

says, "We have to talk," and in those four words he knows it all.

"This isn't going to work," she says.

"Because of the way that I told you about the Harvard offer."

"That's part of it. The insensitivity with which you just flung the offer in my face, not even waiting for me to unpack, with that terrible gloating on your face—well, it's hard to take. I hadn't realized how competitive you are."

Her intonation is so British that it's hard to believe she grew up near Philadelphia.

"Surely you can't believe that. I'm not capable of feeling competitive with you."

"Well, if it wasn't competitiveness, it was still insensitivity of monstrous proportions. Did you never stop to consider how it might make me feel, given my professional situation at the moment?"

Her face has assumed a look of frigid hauteur that he's never seen before, no matter how much contempt she's displayed toward members of their department.

"I had thought of the offer from Harvard as being something good for both of us."

"Well, that is, to put it generously, bizarre beyond belief. How could *your* professional success possibly be interpreted as benefiting *me*? Ah, wait. I think I see. I hadn't pegged you as yet another *man* who just doesn't get it, but I am incurably naïve that way. You can't possibly appreciate what it is like for me, how hard I have had to struggle to be taken seriously. It's never enough, no matter how much I do. And now you think I shall be content to bask in your reflected glory."

"That's preposterous, your basking in my reflected glory. I

would never dream of thinking that my work could even be compared to yours."

"And it can't. I don't mean to be hurtful, I'm not that kind of person, but you and I both know that this boon you're enjoying has nothing to do with science. I know that the psychology of religion is topical, but it's soft, and it's shoddy, and if the world hadn't suddenly gone mad on religion, no one would be lauding you like this. It's deplorable that academia should prostitute itself, but there it is. Not even Harvard is above it. In fact, Harvard least of all, with that ludicrous delusion of self-importance that makes every Harvard professor feel he's a public intellectual, qualified to comment on issues far beyond his expertise. You'll do very well there."

Lucinda, holding herself ramrod-straight, walks over to the bay window overlooking the street and peers out, and then comes back to Cass.

"I'm just watching for the cab. I'm spending the night at the Charles Hotel. I'll get in touch with you about collecting my things."

"You don't think there's anything for us to talk over? Your mind is completely made up?"

"This was only an experiment, as you know. I'd been explicit, from the very start. You can't deny that."

"Of course not."

"Look, Cass, I wish you well. No matter what I might think about the injustices of academia, I have been trained to accept facts as facts. It was only rational of you to take advantage of the current interest in religion and to work the contemporary traumas to your self-interest. You've done well for yourself, and I'm happy for you. But I don't respect what you do, and the fact that you have now acquired more prestige than I have, when my work is so much more important, is not something I can tolerate. I can't degrade myself by being regarded as your female companion, the pretty young woman at the inferior institution who will be patronized by the Harvard elite. To be with you is to have everything that is wrong with academia constantly rubbed in my face."

She walks again to the bay window.

"Ah, the taxi's here."

Cass goes to pick up her suitcase.

"I'll take it myself."

"But you're so tired. At least let me help you down."

"I'm not tired anymore. Goodbye, Cass. I'll call you about my things."

She goes down the steps, and as he hears the front door close, he darkens the living room so that he can see her more clearly outside in the night.

The driver emerges from the cab, taking her suitcase and her computer bag, and Cass can see her halo of pale hair catching the gleam of the streetlight as she turns back and carefully fastens the latch: "Please close the gate, remember our children." The taxi drives off, and Cass hears a keening wail, the counterpart of the laughter that had risen like vapor off of his joy, only this, he thinks, is the sound of solemn sorrow, until he realizes it's the kettle boiling.

XXXVI

The Argument from the Silent Rebbe's Dance

Cass drives into New Walden in the late afternoon of a wind-lashed day. The clouds are streaming across the sky, shadow and shimmer rippling over surfaces. It makes the ground look as if it's in motion, as if it's a carpet unfurling underfoot.

There's still more than an hour until the sun goes down, but the Valdeners are already out en masse, dressed in their Shabbes finery, the sartorial and tonsorial splendor of the men in full display. The winds coming off the Hudson are playfully pulling on *payess* and *kaputas,* and married women are laughing almost audibly as they hold on to their wigs and hats, their high spirits verging on disregard for the rules of female modesty.

The Costco House of Worship, gargantuan as it is, has been outgrown, and there's an additional warehouse of a synagogue constructed right behind it and the happy Hasidim are streaming in that direction. The streets are too clogged with walkers for Cass to drive on farther. He leaves his car not far from the parking lot where the mismatched buses are jammed, and continues on foot.

Everyone Cass passes gives him a smile and a hearty *mazel tov,* and he answers in-kind. *Mazel tov* literally means "good luck" but is the phrase pronounced on someone to whom something fortunate has happened. You say *mazel tov* to a Bar Mitzvah boy and his family, to someone who gets engaged or gets married or has a baby. *Mazel tov* is the all-purpose response to all the good things, big and small.

There are lots of out-of-towners visiting this Shabbes. Cass can tell by the garb of the men. It's only the Valdeners who wear the knee-high black boots with their britches. Other sects wear long black stockings, with their black knickerbockers tucked in, and still others do the same only with white stockings, and still others let the bottoms of their pants extend over their socks. The Valdeners' tradition of boots had derived from a compromise reached before a wedding, when the family of one side of the couple wore white stockings and the other side wore black.

The styles of *kaputas* and *shtreimlach* differ, too. Cass is hardly an expert at the semiotics of the sects, but he's pretty sure there are a lot of Satmars, Belzers, and Bobovers. Even the Gerers are represented. There used to be a rift between the Valdeners and the Gerers, but this has been mended in recent years through the masterful diplomacy of the Valdener Rebbe.

The women and girls are less distinguishable. Cass thinks perhaps the other sects dress with a little more panache than the Valdeners, but this, too, takes a practiced eye, and when Cass is in New Walden he follows the mores and averts his eyes from females.

Cass is on his way to his brother's house. It was when Jesse was, as they say, away, that he had found religion, or religion had found him. He had been visited by the Hasidim—not Valdeners but Lubavitchers, who have an outreach program for Jewish prisoners—and eventually he made his way back to New Walden, where he goes by his Hebrew name, Yeshiya.

Cass has to walk past the old Valdener synagogue to reach Jesse's house, and the spectacle of masses of Hasidim converging as one has the convulsive effect on Cass it always does.

The likeness in attire is partially responsible. Cass may be able to pick out the subtle differences in hosiery between a Valdener and a Satmar, but the overall effect is of an undifferentiated mass of humankind, a category mistake that writhes with a life of its own, and Cass is never indifferent to it, no matter how well he understands the psychology behind his reactions.

The Friday-evening sun is descending behind those flitting clouds, and Cass is in a hurry to get to his brother's house, but he pauses a moment in front of the Rebbe's house to take in the scene, vibrating with kinetic men and boys rushing everywhere.

A little boy, blond and beautiful, about the age that Azarya had been when Cass had first met him, skips past him and lisps out a *mazel tov* in a shy soprano. The child's face is flushed, his cheeks pomegranates of excitement. If Cass were to stop him and ask him what he was feeling, what would he say?

I'm happy, of course, he would say. I'm happy.

And if the little boy were to ask what he, Cass Seltzer, the atheist with a soul, is feeling, standing stock still in the middle of the commotion, what would *he* say?

He'd say what he's been saying all along. That his Appendix was only an appendix, and that it has little to do with the text; and that the text is written not out there but in here, in the emotions that are so fundamental that we spread them onto a world of our imagining, or onto a world of our making, so that we end up beholding a world that is lavished with our own disgust at the uncleanliness that pollutes us, and with our yearning for a mythical purity that remains untouched, and with our vertiginous bafflement at the self that is inviolably me and here and now, and with our desperate and incomplete sense of the inviolable selves of the others that we need so crucially, and with our fear of all that's unknown out there and that can hurt us, and with our suspicion that almost everything out there will turn out to be unknown and able to hurt us.

The little boy has disappeared into the throng entering the synagogue. In Cass's reverie, he's still there, speaking in the voice of Azarya, peeking his head around a half-open door and shyly announcing that he can read English now, and in that voice he now asks him: and then what happens?

This is what happens, Cass answers him. All of this. The rituals of purification; and the laws of separation, with *menner* on one *seit* and *froyen* on the other. The communities that define themselves in distinction from others, and the hatred in those others who can burn them alive. The young people clashing over sensuality and piety, and the dreams of our bodies or our souls outwitting death. The longings for redemption and for redeemers, and our imbuing others with the perfection that escapes us. The elected circle of disciples, and the ordeals that try their faith, and the sinner born again as a Hasid, a pious man. The signs and the portents of the coming of the Messiah, and the descent into madness of the false messiahs. The forces of our soul that press us outward and dissolve the boundaries of the self and burst us open onto the

world, so that all of existence feels the way New Walden feels
to a Valdener, an intimate world that will embrace us in coherence and connection and purpose and love, and whose caring
is no more open to doubt than is the Valdener Rebbe's love for
his own Valdeners.

The crowd in front of the synagogue is thinning, and the
young men in the Rebbe's front yard are no longer singing,
and Cass hurries on. In three minutes, he can see the ram-
shackle two-family house where Jesse is living.

Cass is pretty sure his brother can afford better. He probably likes the shabbiness, because it exaggerates the disconti-
nuity between his former life and this one. The front yard is
littered with pastel plastic toys. The family that Jesse shares
the two-family house with have the typical Hasidic brood.
Cass wonders whether Jesse is going to find a Valdener girl
and start having children himself. Their parents' Volvo is
parked in the unpaved driveway.

"You made it!" Cass's mother greets him, as he stoops and
she stands on her tiptoes to kiss his cheek.

"Of course I made it. Did you have any doubt?"

"How long did the drive take?" his father asks, the same
question with which he's been greeting him ever since Cass
got his license.

Ben Seltzer used to be almost as tall as Cass himself,
though he's lost an inch or two. Cass's mom is a bit less than
average height, trim and athletic. She's been a tennis player
since her twenties, and she still looks like one in her late sixties. Her hair is gray now, and she wears it short and sensible,
as she always has, except when Cass was very young, when
her hair had flowed over her shoulders and down her back
like a river of red. Jesse's side locks and beard have emerged

in the same vivid shade. Cass wonders whether he'll ever stop having the urge to yank one of his brother's *payess* to test whether they're real. He has an image of Jesse detaching them every once in a while, taking time off from Valdenerism to connect with some model he'd dated in the past.

Their mother had been philosophical about Jesse's becoming a *ba'al t'shuva,* a penitent who returns to the fold.

"If it will help quiet his troubled spirit, then how can I object? I've never understood him, and I don't think you do either. Maybe, when it comes to your brother, Hillary was right. It takes a village."

"Over four hours," Cass answers his father. "I hit rush-hour traffic coming over the Tappan Zee Bridge. And the winds are fierce. You could feel them slamming into the car."

"I know. We almost went airborne coming in from New Jersey."

"Where's Jesse?"

"He's already left," his father says. "It's going to be a mob scene, according to him."

"It already is."

"Let's get going, then. We were just waiting for you."

Ten minutes ago, Cass couldn't get his car through, and now there are only a few stragglers on the streets. Cass's mother obediently crosses to the *froyen seit,* without making a sarcastic comment.

"Look at that," Cass's father says. "She must be growing out of her rebelliousness."

As they near the synagogue, Cass notices a thin young man in a long black wool coat and an elegant *shtreimel* on the women's side, and then he looks again and it's a tall young woman, and then he looks again and it's Roz in her mink hat.

"Roz!" he calls out.

His mother hears him and goes up to her and says, "You're not really Roz Margolis, are you?"

"I am!"

"My goodness. I'm Deb, Cass's mother. I've been wanting to meet you for twenty years."

"Me, too! That's how long I've been waiting to meet you!" And she throws her arms around Deb, and the two women hug.

"Roz!" Cass calls over to her again.

"It looks like Cass wants to talk to you." Deb is laughing. "I'll save you a seat in the women's section. We'll finally get acquainted. *Mazel tov!*"

"*Mazel tov!*" Roz answers, and Cass tells his father to go on to the synagogue without him, and Cass and Roz leave their respective sides and meet in the middle of the road.

"*Mazel tov,*" Roz says.

"*Mazel tov,*" he answers her.

"Look where we are."

"Look where we are," he answers her.

"Have you seen him yet?"

"No, I just drove in. He got in touch with you?"

"He sent me an e-mail. Believe it or not, he was worried about you. He wanted to make sure you acquitted yourself well with Fidley."

"I got an e-mail from GR613 apologizing that he hadn't been available." Cass laughs. "Only Azarya would send an apology under the circumstances!"

"Only Azarya," she agrees.

"How did it go for you in New York?"

"It went great. I've got myself a book deal. *Immortality Now!* All I have to do is write it."

"So Auerbach has taken you under his wing."

"I should say so! He gave me the coat off his back." She gestures downward. "The one I brought with me was a bit too flamboyant for New Walden."

"Ah, that explains it," Cass says, smiling.

"Explains what?"

"I thought you were a young man flouting the rules of *menner seit* and *froyen seit,* especially with that *shtreimel.*"

"I'll accept the 'young' part." She laughs. "Have you noticed?"

"I've noticed."

"We're almost there. You're not going to stop us."

"When have I ever wanted to stop you, even if I could?"

"But will you come with me?"

"It's too early for me to say."

"We're almost there," she repeats.

He looks at her closely.

"Promise you'll keep a few laugh lines."

"But will you come with me?" she asks him a second time.

"Too soon to say," he repeats.

"I might get lonely living so long without you."

"You seem to have managed quite well for the past twenty years."

"That's what I've been trying to tell you. I've been trying to tell you that it's our living that teaches us how to live. There's a lot to learn. That's why we need all the time we can get."

"All shall be well, and all shall be well, and all manner of things shall be well."

"What's that from?"

"The Catholic mystic Julian of Norwich."

"A world-famous atheist quoting a Catholic mystic in the middle of a Hasidic shtetl in twenty-first-century America. By the way, I thought you were magnificent in the debate."

"I'm glad to hear you say that."

"Come on. You know it. I think you may even have convinced the Agnostic Chaplain."

"I thought that maybe you weren't so pleased with my performance."

"How's that?"

"You didn't say anything to me afterward. You were hanging back like a stranger."

Roz doesn't say anything for a few moments, and then she changes the subject.

"Why isn't Lucinda here?"

"I was waiting for you to ask me that. Lucinda left me."

"She *left* you? Since last *week,* she left you?"

"She left me the night she came home. I picked her up from the airport, brought her home, and she left me."

Surprising them both, Cass laughs.

"You've got to be leaving something out of the story."

"I picked her up from the airport, brought her home, showed her the offer from Harvard, and she left me."

Cass is still smiling, and Roz studies his face for several moments before speaking.

"How are you?" is what she finally says.

"Surprisingly well, to tell you the truth."

"Are you putting on a brave face for me?"

"I'm not. I was devastated for seventy-two hours, and then I wasn't. Do you want to hear my latest insights on the varieties of religious illusion?"

"I always want to hear your insights."

"Romantic infatuation can be a form of religious delusion, too."

"Sweetie," she says softly, "anyone who's watched you with your women has known that for years."

"Ah."

"You still believe in love, though, don't you?"

"As if it were a matter of belief," he moans, and she moans softly in response, and takes his hand, and then, remembering where they are, lets it drop.

There's another long silence as they walk past the synagogue and then circle back.

They've stopped walking, poised midway between the *menner* entrance and the *froyen* entrance to the Valdener synagogue, and the shadows and the shimmers of the day are rippling over their closely watched faces, and both of them say nothing.

"I made a rational-actor matrix, figuring out whether it's ever rational to say 'I love you' first," Cass says after a while.

"What's the conclusion?"

"It turns out not to be rational."

"That's depressing."

"Only for rational actors."

"I still say your mate-selection module got knocked out of whack twenty years ago."

"And I say you're right. I'm thinking of following my brother's lead and yielding responsibility for my life to the Grand Rabbi. Maybe we Valdeners don't have the instincts anymore for choosing our own mates. Maybe I should let the Valdener Rebbe pick one out for me."

"But he did. We promised to invite him to the *hasana*."

He laughs and places his large hand on her *shtreimel* and mashes it down.

"Hey," she says, "have a little respect! That's mink on my head."

"I'd rather you were in a purple towel."

"That can be arranged."

They enter their gender-appropriate doors, and as soon as Cass is inside he hears the explosive euphoria of the thousands of rejoicers, singing and stamping, and he's slammed hard by the sight of that vast room's life, it sends him reeling and jostles his senses out of alignment, so that he can discern the spicy fragrance of the melody and the shifting colors of the emotions, and what does it feel like for Roz up there looking down, what is she making of the soulful wildness of the Valdeners?

He'll never find a seat and has no intention of trying, but if he stands here in the aisle he will have a sight line to the clearing in the middle of the room, and he might catch a glimpse of the grand event.

A flushed man comes hurrying down the aisle and says to him, "Excuse me? You're maybe Cass Seltzer?"

"Yes, I'm Cass Seltzer."

"I've been looking! You don't remember?"

"I'm sorry." The man is neither young nor old, and he has a sweet yeasty blandness that makes Cass think of his bubbe's round babka.

"I'm Berel! I'm Cousin Berel!"

"Berel! Cousin Berel! How are you? How have you been?"

"I'm well, *baruch Ha-Shem!*" Bless His Name. *"Mazel tov, mazel tov!"*

"Mazel tov!"

"Come, come. I have a seat in the front saved for you. The special friend."

Berel leads Cass down the narrow aisle between the crushed tiers to the front row of seats, probably occupied by dignitaries, though Cass doesn't know one from another, but the beards and *shtreimlach* are impressive, and everybody is on his feet, singing and exulting.

As Cass makes his way to his space, everyone he passes interrupts his singing to shout *"Mazel tov!"* into his face, and to wrap an arm around him or thump him on the back.

Somewhere up there in the women's gallery, hidden from sight, is Roz in her *shtreimel,* savoring the absurdities to their succulent cores, the wildness and pang that will always confound us; even if she gets her way and we live for centuries, still we'll be confounded, as nobody in all the world knows better than the young man who is now standing quietly in the center of the room and smiling, dressed in a white satin *kaputa* streaked with gold, so that the singing rises to a crashing crescendo and the floor is heaving with the weight of frenzied exaltation, and they come and place the swathed infant in his outstretched arms.

Somewhere in the women's gallery is Tirza, the daughter of the Grand Rebbe of the Borshtchavers, a girl from Israel who was brought here to marry the Rebbe, a mating between two royal lines that's brought joy to Hasidim around the world. This baby is their firstborn, destined to be the future Valdener Rebbe, delivered a week ago during a long and difficult labor, while Cass had been desperately trying to reach Azarya.

It's one of the traditions of the Valdeners, distinguishing them from other sects: the dance of the Rebbe with his firstborn son on the first Shabbes of his life.

It had begun with the current Rebbe's great-grandfather Rav Eliezer ben Rav Bezalel, the one known as 'der shvagte Rebbe,' the silent Rebbe. Perhaps Rav Eliezer had wanted to dance so that he wouldn't be forced to speak. He was the one who composed this melody, sung only on the occasion of welcoming the future Rebbe into their midst.

It's surprising how well everybody seems to know the *niggun,* since it hasn't been sung in twenty-six years. It seems to Cass that even he knows it as it's being softly hummed, a sumptuous melody that's an abrupt change in tone after the stampeding boisterousness.

The melody is frothy white and streaked with gold and sung exactly as it had been sung when the current Rebbe was placed in his own father's arms, and when his father had been placed in his father's arms, and when his father had been placed in his father's arms, in the little town in Hungary that the Valdeners refuse to forfeit to the flames and to forgetfulness.

The Rebbe raises the child up to the heavens as his father had done before him, so that the Valdeners' collective heart can soar as they behold their future, and the Valdeners lift as one with his upward motion until they seem to hover several inches from the floor.

What does he think at this moment, what does he feel? Cass is certain he knows the Rebbe better than anyone else, and Cass has no idea. At the heart of Azarya Sheiner is the solitude that he had prophesied for himself when he was sixteen. The decision was made for him in the agony of a terrible moment, when he was far too young to have to decide. But he's decided since then, and if he struggles still, then he struggles alone and he never lets on.

To the Hasidim, their Rebbe is not a human like others, and Cass knows it is true of this Rebbe. Cass is awed by the grace with which the Rebbe accepts the responsibilities that come from his being loved by his Hasidim as much as they love existence itself, so that they batter him with the needs of their love every day of his life, from early morning until late at night. Only in the small, lonely hours does the Grand Rebbe let himself return to being Azarya, wandering among the abstractions, pursuing reason wherever it takes him, especially in the questions that his way of life might seem to answer but doesn't at all. As Cass had once been astonished by a little boy's genius, so he's been astonished by the way in which that genius has been laid aside. It grieves him, and it moves him, and for Cass Seltzer, Azarya Sheiner will always stand at the place where our universe touches the extraordinary.

Still, if to be human is to inhabit our contradictions, then who is more human than this young man? If to be human is to be unable to find a way of reconciling the necessary and the impossible, then who is more human than Rav Azarya Sheiner?

And if the prodigious genius of Azarya Sheiner has never found the solution, then perhaps that is proof that no solution exists, that the most gifted among us is feeble in mind against the brutality of incomprehensibility that assaults us from all sides. And so we try, as best we can, to do justice to the tremendousness of our improbable existence. And so we live, as best we can, for ourselves, or who will live for us? And we live, as best we can, for others, otherwise what are we? And the Valdener Rebbe holds his son and dances.

APPENDIX:
36 ARGUMENTS FOR THE EXISTENCE OF GOD

1. The Cosmological Argument
2. The Ontological Argument
3. The Argument from Design
   A. The Classical Teleological Argument
   B. The Argument from Irreducible Complexity
   C. The Argument from the Paucity of Benign Mutations
   D. The Argument from the Original Replicator
4. The Argument from the Big Bang
5. The Argument from the Fine-Tuning of Physical Constants
6. The Argument from the Beauty of Physical Laws
7. The Argument from Cosmic Coincidences
8. The Argument from Personal Coincidences
9. The Argument from Answered Prayers
10. The Argument from a Wonderful Life
11. The Argument from Miracles
12. The Argument from the Hard Problem of Consciousness
13. The Argument from the Improbable Self
14. The Argument from Survival After Death
15. The Argument from the Inconceivability of Personal Annihilation
16. The Argument from Moral Truth
17. The Argument from Altruism
18. The Argument from Free Will

1. The Cosmological Argument

1. Everything that exists must have a cause.
2. The universe must have a cause (from 1).
3. Nothing can be the cause of itself.
4. The universe cannot be the cause of itself (from 3).
5. Something outside the universe must have caused the universe (from 2 and 4).
6. God is the only thing that is outside of the universe.
7. God caused the universe (from 5 and 6).
8. God exists.

FLAW 1 CAN BE CRUDELY PUT: Who caused God? The Cosmological Argument is a prime example of the Fallacy of Passing the Buck: invoking God to solve some problem, but then leaving unanswered that very same problem about God himself. The proponent of The Cosmological Argument must admit a contradiction to either his first premise—and say that, though God exists, he doesn't have a cause—or else a contradiction to his third premise—and say that God is self-caused. Either way, the theist is saying that his premises have at least one exception, but is not explaining why *God* must be the unique exception, otherwise than asserting his unique mystery (the Fallacy of Using One Mystery to Explain Another). Once you admit of exceptions, you can ask why the universe itself, which is also unique, can't be the exception. The universe itself can either exist without a cause, or else can be self-caused. Since the buck has to stop somewhere, why not with the universe?

FLAW 2: The notion of "cause" is by no means clear, but our best definition is a relation that holds between events that are connected by physical laws. Knocking the vase off the table caused it to crash to the floor; smoking three packs a day caused his lung cancer. To apply this concept to the universe itself is to misuse the concept of cause, extending it into a realm in which we have no idea how to use it. This line of reasoning, based on the unjustified demands we make on the concept of cause, was developed by David Hume.

COMMENT: The Cosmological Argument, like The Argument from the Big Bang and The Argument from the Intelligibility of the Universe, is an expression of our cosmic befuddlement at the question, why is there something rather than nothing? The late philosopher Sidney Morgenbesser had a classic response to this question: "And if there were nothing? You'd still be complaining!"

2. The Ontological Argument

1. Nothing greater than God can be conceived (this is stipulated as part of the definition of "God").
2. It is greater to exist than not to exist.
3. If we conceive of God as not existing, then we can conceive of something greater than God (from 2).
4. To conceive of God as not existing is not to conceive of God (from 1 and 3).
5. It is inconceivable that God not exist (from 4).
6. God exists.

This argument, first articulated by Saint Anselm (1033–1109), the Archbishop of Canterbury, is unlike any other, proceeding purely on the conceptual level. Everyone agrees that the mere existence of a concept does not entail that there are examples of that concept; after all, we can know what a unicorn is and at the same time say, "Unicorns don't exist." The claim of The Ontological Argument is that the concept of God is the one exception to this generalization. The very concept of God, when defined correctly, entails that there is something that satisfies that concept. Although most people suspect that there is something wrong with this argument, it's not so easy to figure out what it is.

FLAW: It was Immanuel Kant who pinpointed the fallacy in The Ontological Argument—it is to treat "existence" as a property, like "being fat" or "having ten fingers." The Ontological Argument relies on a bit of wordplay, assuming that "existence" is just another property, but logically it is completely different. If you really could treat "existence" as just part of the definition of the concept of God, then you could just as easily build it into the definition of any other concept. We could, with the wave of our verbal magic wand, define a *trunicorn* as "a horse that (a) has a single horn on its head, and

(b) exists." So, if you think about a trunicorn, you're thinking about something that must, by definition, exist; therefore, trunicorns exist. This is clearly absurd: we could use this line of reasoning to prove that any figment of our imagination exists.

COMMENT: Once again, Sidney Morgenbesser offered a pertinent remark, in the form of The Ontological Argument for God's Non-Existence: Existence is such a lousy thing, how could God go and do it?

3. The Argument from Design

A. *The Classical Teleological Argument*
1. Whenever there are things that cohere only because of a purpose or function (for example, all the complicated parts of a watch that allow it to keep time), we know that they had a designer who designed them with the function in mind; they are too improbable to have arisen by random physical processes. (A hurricane blowing through a hardware store could not assemble a watch.)
2. Organs of living things, such as the eye and the heart, cohere only because they have a function (for example, the eye has a cornea, lens, retina, iris, eyelids, and so on, which are found in the same organ only because together they make it possible for the animal to see).
3. These organs must have a designer who designed them with their function in mind: just as a watch implies a watch-maker, an eye implies an eye-maker (from 1 and 2).
4. These things have not had a human designer.
5. Therefore, these things must have had a non-human designer (from 3 and 4).
6. God is the non-human designer (from 5).
7. God exists.

FLAW: Darwin showed how the process of replication could give rise to the *illusion* of design without the foresight of an actual designer. Replicators make copies of themselves, which make copies of themselves, and so on, giving rise to an exponential number of descendants. In any finite environment, the replicators must compete for the energy and materials necessary for replication. Since no copying process is perfect, errors will eventually crop up, and any error that causes a replicator to reproduce more efficiently than its competitors will result in the predominance of that line of replicators in the population. After many generations, the dominant replicators will *appear* to have been designed for effective replication, whereas all they have done is accumulate the copying errors, which in the past *did* lead to effective replication. The fallacy in the argument, then, is Premise 1 (and, as a consequence, Premise 3, which depends on it): parts of a complex object serving a complex function do not, in fact, require a designer.

In the twenty-first century, creationists have tried to revive the Teleological Argument in three forms:

B. *The Argument from Irreducible Complexity*

1. Evolution has no foresight, and every incremental step must be an improvement over the preceding one, allowing the organism to survive and reproduce better than its competitors.
2. In many complex organs, the removal or modification of any part would destroy the functional whole. Examples are the lens and retina of the eye, the molecular components of blood clotting, and the molecular motor powering the cell's flagellum. Call these organs "irreducibly complex."
3. These organs could not have been useful to the organisms that possessed them in any simpler forms (from 2).
4. The theory of natural selection cannot explain these irreducibly complex systems (from 1 and 3).

5. Natural selection is the only way out of the conclusions of The Classical Teleological Argument.
6. God exists (from 4 and 5 and The Classical Teleological Argument).

This argument has been around since the time of Charles Darwin, and his replies to it still hold.

FLAW 1: For many organs, Premise 2 is false. An eye without a lens can still see, just not as well as an eye with a lens.

FLAW 2: For many other organs, removal of a part, or other alterations, may render it useless for its current function, but the organ could have been useful to the organism for some other function. Insect wings, before they were large enough to be effective for flight, were used as heat-exchange panels. This is also true for most of the molecular mechanisms, such as the flagellum motor, invoked in The New Argument from Irreducible Complexity.

FLAW 3 (the Fallacy of Arguing from Ignorance): There may be biological systems for which we don't yet know how they may have been useful in simpler versions. But there are obviously many things we don't yet understand in molecular biology, and, given the huge success that biologists have achieved in explaining so many examples of incremental evolution in other biological systems, it is more reasonable to infer that these gaps will eventually be filled by the day-to-day progress of biology than to invoke a supernatural designer just to explain these temporary puzzles.

COMMENT: This last flaw can be seen as one particular instance of the more general, fallacious Argument from Ignorance:

1. There are things that we cannot explain yet.
2. Those things must be attributed to God.

FLAW: Premise 1 is obviously true. If there weren't things that we could not explain yet, then science would be complete, laboratories and observatories would unplug their computers and convert to condominiums, and all departments of science would be converted to departments of the history of science. Science is only in business because there are things we have not explained yet. So we cannot infer from the existence of genuine, ongoing science that there must be a God. In other words, Premise 2 does not follow from Premise 1.

C. *The Argument from the Paucity of Benign Mutations*

1. Evolution is powered by random mutations and natural selection.
2. Organisms are complex, improbable systems, and by the laws of probability any change is astronomically more likely to be for the worse than for the better.
3. The majority of mutations would be deadly for the organism (from 2).
4. The amount of time it would take for all the benign mutations needed for the assembly of an organ to appear by chance is preposterously long (from 3).
5. In order for evolution to work, something outside of evolution had to bias the process of mutation, increasing the number of benign ones (from 4).
6. Something outside of the mechanism of biological change—the Prime Mutator—must bias the process of mutations for evolution to work (from 5).
7. The only entity that is both powerful enough and purposeful enough to be the Prime Mutator is God.
8. God exists.

FLAW: Evolution does not require infinitesimally improbable mutations, such as a fully formed eye appearing out of the blue in a single generation, because (a) mutations can have small effects (tissue that is slightly more transparent, or cells that are slightly more sensitive to light), and mutations contributing to these effects can accumulate over time; (b) for any sexually reproducing organism, the necessary mutations do not have to have occurred one after another in a single line of descendants, but could have appeared independently in thousands of separate organisms, each mutating at random, and the necessary combinations could come together as the organisms have mated and exchanged genes; (c) life on Earth has had a vast amount of time to accumulate the necessary mutations (almost four billion years).

D. The Argument from the Original Replicator

1. Evolution is the process by which an organism evolves from simpler ancestors.
2. Evolution by itself cannot explain how the original ancestor—the first living thing—came into existence (from 1).
3. The theory of natural selection can deal with this problem only by saying that the first living thing evolved out of non-living matter (from 2).
4. That original non-living matter (call it the Original Replicator) must be capable of (a) self-replication, (b) generating a functioning mechanism out of surrounding matter to protect itself against falling apart, and (c) surviving slight mutations to itself that will then result in slightly different replicators.
5. The Original Replicator is complex (from 4).
6. The Original Replicator is too complex to have arisen from purely physical processes (from 5 and The Classical Teleological Argument). For example, DNA, which currently carries the replicated design of organisms, cannot be the Original Replicator, because DNA molecules require a complex sys-

tem of proteins to remain stable and to replicate, and could not have arisen from natural processes before complex life existed.

7. Natural selection cannot explain the complexity of the Original Replicator (from 3 and 6).

8. The Original Replicator must have been created rather than have evolved (from 7 and The Classical Teleological Argument).

9. Anything that was created requires a Creator.

10. God exists.

FLAW 1: Premise 6 states that a replicator, because of its complexity, cannot have arisen from natural processes, i.e., by way of natural selection. But the mathematician John von Neumann proved in the 1950s that it is theoretically possible for a simple physical system to make exact copies of itself from surrounding materials. Since then, biologists and chemists have identified a number of naturally occurring molecules and crystals that can replicate in ways that could lead to natural selection (in particular, that allow random variations to be preserved in the copies). Once a molecule replicates, the process of natural selection can kick in, and the replicator can accumulate matter and become more complex, eventually leading to precursors of the replication system used by living organisms today.

FLAW 2: Even without von Neumann's work (which not everyone accepts as conclusive), to conclude the existence of God from our not yet knowing how to explain the Original Replicator is to rely on The Argument from Ignorance.

4. The Argument from the Big Bang

1. The Big Bang, according to the best scientific opinion of our day, was the beginning of the physical universe, including not only matter and energy, but space and time and the laws of physics.
2. The universe came to be ex nihilo (from 1).
3. Something outside the universe, including outside its physical laws, must have brought the universe into existence (from 2).
4. Only God could exist outside the universe.
5. God must have caused the universe to exist (from 3 and 4).
6. God exists.

The Big Bang is based on the observed expansion of the universe, with galaxies rushing away from one another. The implication is that, if we run the film of the universe backward from the present, the universe must continuously contract, all the way back to a single point. The theory of the Big Bang is that the universe exploded into existence about fourteen billion years ago.

FLAW 1: Cosmologists themselves do not all agree that the Big Bang is a "singularity"—the sudden appearance of space, time, and physical laws from inexplicable nothingness. The Big Bang may represent the lawful emergence of a new universe from a previously existing one. In that case, it would be superfluous to invoke God to explain the emergence of something from nothing.

FLAW 2: The Argument from the Big Bang has all the flaws of The Cosmological Argument—it passes the buck from the mystery of the origin of the universe to the mystery of the origin of God, and it extends the notion of "cause" outside the domain of events covered by natural laws (also known as "the universe"), where it no longer makes sense.

5. The Argument from the Fine-Tuning of Physical Constants

1. There are a vast number of physically possible universes.
2. A universe that would be hospitable to the appearance of life must conform to some very strict conditions. Everything from the mass ratios of atomic particles and the number of dimensions of space to the cosmological parameters that rule the expansion of the universe must be just right for stable galaxies, solar systems, planets, and complex life to evolve.
3. The percentage of possible universes that would support life is infinitesimally small (from 2).
4. Our universe is one of those infinitesimally improbable universes.
5. Our universe has been fine-tuned to support life (from 3 and 4).
6. There is a Fine-Tuner (from 5).
7. Only God could have the power and the purpose to be the Fine-Tuner.
8. God exists.

Philosophers and physicists often speak of "the Anthropic Principle," which comes in several versions, labeled "weak," "strong," and "very strong." They all argue that any explanation of the universe must account for the fact that we humans (or any complex organism that could observe its condition) exist in it. The Argument from the Fine-Tuning of Physical Constants corresponds to the Very Strong Anthropic Principle. Its upshot is that the upshot of the universe is . . . us. The universe must have been designed with us in mind.

FLAW 1: The first premise may be false. Many physicists and cosmologists, following Einstein, hope for a unified "theory of everything," which would deduce from as-yet unknown physical laws that the physical constants of our universe had to be what they are. In that case, ours would be the only possible universe. (See also The Argument from the Intelligibility of the Universe, #35, below.)

FLAW 2: Even were we to accept the first premise, the transition from 4 to 5 is invalid. Perhaps we are living in a "multiverse" (a term coined by William James), a vast plurality (perhaps infinite) of parallel universes with different physical constants, all of them composing one reality. We find ourselves, unsurprisingly (since we are here doing the observing), in one of the rare universes that does support the appearance of stable matter and complex life, but nothing had to have been fine-tuned. Or perhaps we are living in an "oscillatory universe," a succession of universes with differing physical constants, each one collapsing into a point and then exploding with a new big bang into a new universe with different physical constants, one succeeding another over an infinite time span. Again, we find ourselves, not surprisingly, in one of those time slices in which the universe does have physical constants that support stable matter and complex life. These hypotheses, which are receiving much attention from contemporary cosmologists, are sufficient to invalidate the leap from 4 to 5.

6. The Argument from the Beauty of Physical Laws

1. Scientists use aesthetic principles (simplicity, symmetry, elegance) to discover the laws of nature.
2. Scientists could only use aesthetic principles successfully if the laws of nature were intrinsically and objectively beautiful.

3. The laws of nature are intrinsically and objectively beautiful (from 1 and 2).

4. Only a mindful being with an appreciation of beauty could have designed the laws of nature.

5. God is the only being with the power and purpose to design beautiful laws of nature.

6. God exists.

FLAW 1: Do we decide an explanation is good because it's beautiful, or do we find an explanation beautiful because it provides a good explanation? When we say that the laws of nature are beautiful, what we are really saying is that the laws of nature are the laws of nature, and thus unify into elegant explanation a vast host of seemingly unrelated and random phenomena. We would find the laws of nature of any lawful universe beautiful. So what this argument boils down to is the observation that we live in a lawful universe. And of course any universe that could support the likes of us would *have* to be lawful. So this argument is another version of the Anthropic Principle—we live in the kind of universe that is the only kind of universe in which observers like us could live—and thus is subject to the flaws of Argument #5.

FLAW 2: If the laws of the universe are intrinsically beautiful, then positing a God who loves beauty, and who is mysteriously capable of creating an elegant universe (and presumably a messy one as well, though his aesthetic tastes led him not to), makes the universe complex and incomprehensible all over again. This negates the intuition behind Premise 3, that the universe is *intrinsically* elegant and intelligible. (See The Argument from the Intelligibility of the Universe, #35, below.)

7. The Argument from Cosmic Coincidences

1. The universe contains many uncanny coincidences, such as that the diameter of the moon as seen from the earth is the same as the diameter of the sun as seen from the earth, which is why we can have spectacular eclipses when the corona of the sun is revealed.
2. Coincidences are, by definition, overwhelmingly improbable.
3. The overwhelmingly improbable defies all statistical explanation.
4. These coincidences are such as to enhance our awed appreciation for the beauty of the natural world.
5. These coincidences must have been designed in order to enhance our awed appreciation of the beauty of the natural world (from 3 and 4).
6. Only a being with the power to effect such uncanny coincidences and the purpose of enhancing our awed appreciation of the beauty of the natural world could have arranged these uncanny cosmic coincidences.
7. Only God could be the being with such power and such purpose.
8. God exists.

FLAW 1: Premise 3 does not follow from Premise 2. The occurrence of the highly improbable can be statistically explained in two ways. One is when we have a very large sample: a one-in-a-million event is not improbable at all if there are a million opportunities for it to occur. The other is that there are a huge number of occurrences that could be counted as coincidences, if we don't specify them beforehand but just notice them after the fact. (There could have been a constellation that forms a square around the moon; there could have been a comet that appeared on January 1, 2000;

there could have been a constellation in the shape of a Star of David, etc., etc., etc.) When you consider how many coincidences are possible, the fact that we observe any one coincidence (which we notice after the fact) is not improbable but likely. And let's not forget the statistically improbable coincidences that cause havoc and suffering, rather than awe and wonder, in humans: the perfect storm, the perfect tsunami, the perfect plague, et cetera.

FLAW 2: The derivation of Premise 5 from 3 and 4 is invalid: an example of the Projection Fallacy, in which we project the workings of our mind onto the world, and assume that our own subjective reaction is the result of some cosmic plan to cause that reaction. The human brain sees patterns in all kinds of random configurations: cloud formations, constellations, tea leaves, inkblots. That is why we are so good at finding supposed coincidences. It is getting things backward to say that, in every case in which we see a pattern, someone deliberately put that pattern in the universe for us to see.

ASIDE: Prominent among the uncanny coincidences that figure into this argument are those having to do with numbers. Numbers are mysterious to us because they are not material objects like rocks and tables, but at the same time they seem to be real entities, ones that we can't conjure up with any properties we fancy but that have their own necessary properties and relations, and hence must somehow exist outside us (see The Argument from Human Knowledge of Infinity, #29, and The Argument from Mathematical Reality, #30, below). We are therefore likely to attribute magical powers to them. And, given the infinity of numbers and the countless possible ways to apply them to the world, "uncanny coincidences" are bound to occur (see Flaw 1). In Hebrew, the letters are also numbers, which has given rise to the mystical art of gematria, often used to elucidate, speculate, and prophesy about the unknowable.

8. The Argument from Personal Coincidences

1. People experience uncanny coincidences in their lives (for example, an old friend calling out of the blue just when you're thinking of him, or a dream about some event that turns out to have just happened, or missing a flight that then crashes).

2. Uncanny coincidences cannot be explained by the laws of probability (which is why we call them uncanny).

3. These uncanny coincidences, inexplicable by the laws of probability, reveal a significance to our lives.

4. Only a being who deems our lives significant and who has the power to effect these coincidences could arrange for them to happen.

5. Only God both deems our lives significant and has the power to effect these coincidences.

6. God exists.

FLAW 1: The second premise suffers from the major flaw of The Argument from Cosmic Coincidences: a large number of experiences, together with the large number of patterns that we would call "coincidences" after the fact, make uncanny coincidences probable, not improbable.

FLAW 2: Psychologists have shown that people are subject to an illusion called Confirmation Bias. When they have a hypothesis (such as that daydreams predict the future), they vividly notice all the instances that confirm it (the times when they think of a friend and he calls), and forget all the instances that don't (the times when they think of a friend and he doesn't call). Likewise, who among us remembers all the times when we miss a plane and it *doesn't* crash? The vast number of non-events we live through don't make an impression on us; the few coincidences do.

FLAW 3: There is an additional strong psychological bias at work here. Every one of us treats his or her own life with utmost seriousness. For all of us, there can be nothing more significant than the lives we are living. As David Hume pointed out, the self has an inclination to "spread itself on the world," projecting onto objective reality the psychological assumptions and attitudes that are too constant to be noticed, that play in the background like a noise you don't realize you are hearing until it stops. This form of the Projection Fallacy is especially powerful when it comes to the emotionally fraught questions about our own significance.

9. The Argument from Answered Prayers

1. Sometimes people pray to God for good fortune, and, against enormous odds, their calls are answered. (For example, a parent prays for the life of her dying child, and the child recovers.)
2. The odds that the beneficial event will happen are enormously slim (from 1).
3. The odds that the prayer would have been followed by recovery out of sheer chance are extremely small (from 2).
4. The prayer could only have been followed by the recovery if God listened to it and made it come true.
5. God exists.

This argument is similar to The Argument from Miracles, #11, below, except that, instead of the official miracles claimed by established religion, it refers to intimate and personal miracles.

FLAW 1: Premise 3 is indeed true. However, to use it to infer that a miracle has taken place (and an answered prayer is certainly a miracle) is to subvert it. There is nothing that is *less* probable than a miracle, since it constitutes a violation of a law of nature (see The Argument from Miracles, #11, below). Therefore, it is more reasonable to conclude that the conjunction of the prayer and the recovery is a coincidence than that it is a miracle.

FLAW 2: The coincidence of a person's praying for the unlikely to happen and its then happening is, of course, improbable. But the flaws in The Argument from Cosmic Coincidences, #7, and The Argument from Personal Coincidences, #8, apply here: Given a large enough sample of prayers (the number of times people call out to God to help them and those they love is tragically large), the improbable is bound to happen occasionally. And, given the existence of Confirmation Bias, we will notice these coincidences, yet fail to notice and count up the vastly larger number of unanswered prayers.

FLAW 3: There is an inconsistency in the moral reasoning behind this argument. It asks us to believe in a compassionate God who would be moved to pity by the desperate pleas of some among us—but not by the equally desperate pleas of others among us. Together with The Argument from a Wonderful Life, #10, The Argument from Perfect Justice, #24, and The Argument from Suffering, #25, it appears to be supported by a few cherry-picked examples, but in fact is refuted by the much larger number of counterexamples it ignores: the prayers that go unanswered, the people who do not live wonderful lives. When the life is our own, or that of someone we love, we are especially liable to the Projection Fallacy, and spread our personal sense of significance onto the world at large.

FLAW 4: Reliable cases of answered prayers always involve medical conditions that we know can spontaneously resolve themselves through the healing powers and immune system of the body, such as recovery from cancer, or a coma, or lameness. Prayers that a person can grow back a limb, or that a child can be resurrected from the dead, always go unanswered. This affirms that supposedly answered prayers are actually just the rarer cases of natural recovery.

10. The Argument from a Wonderful Life

1. Sometimes people who are lost in life find their way.
2. These people could not have known the right way on their own.
3. These people were shown the right way by something or someone other than themselves (from 2).
4. There was no person showing them the way.
5. God alone is a being who is not a person and who cares about each of us enough to show us the way.
6. Only God could have helped these lost souls (from 4 and 5).
7. God exists.

FLAW 1: Premise 2 ignores the psychological complexity of people. People have inner resources on which they draw, often without knowing *how* they are doing it or even *that* they are doing it. Psychologists have shown that events in our conscious lives—from linguistic intuitions of which sentences sound grammatical, to moral intuitions of what would be the right thing to do in a moral dilemma—are the end products of complicated mental manipulations of which we are unaware. So, too, decisions and resolutions can bubble into awareness without our being conscious of the processes that led to them. These epiphanies seem to *announce themselves* to us, as if they came from an external guide: another example of the Projection Fallacy.

FLAW 2: The same as Flaw 3 in The Argument from Answered Prayers, #9, above.

11. The Argument from Miracles

1. Miracles are events that violate the laws of nature.
2. Miracles can be explained only by a force that has the power of suspending the laws of nature for the purpose of making its presence known or changing the course of human history (from 1).
3. Only God has the power and the purpose to carry out miracles (from 2).
4. We have a multitude of written and oral reports of miracles. (Indeed, every major religion is founded on a list of miracles.)
5. Human testimony would be useless if it were not, in the majority of cases, veridical.
6. The best explanation for why there are so many reports testifying to the same thing is that the reports are true (from 5).
7. The best explanation for the multitudinous reports of miracles is that miracles have indeed occurred (from 6).
8. God exists (from 3 and 7).

FLAW 1: It is certainly true, as Premise 4 asserts, that we have a multitude of reports of miracles, with each religion insisting on those that establish it alone as the true religion. But the reports are not testifying to the *same* events; each miracle list justifies one religion at the expense of the others. See Flaw 2 in The Argument from Holy Books, #23, below.

FLAW 2: The fatal flaw in The Argument from Miracles was masterfully exposed by David Hume in *An Inquiry Concerning Human Understanding,* chapter 10, "On Miracles." Human testimony may often be accurate, but it is very far from infallible. People are sometimes mistaken; people are sometimes dishonest; people are sometimes gullible—indeed, more than sometimes. Since, in order to believe that a miracle has occurred, we must believe a law of nature has been violated (something for which we otherwise have the maximum of empirical evidence), and we can only believe it on the basis of the truthfulness of human testimony (which we already know is often inaccurate), then even if we knew nothing else about the event, and had no particular reason to distrust the witness, we would have to conclude that it is more likely that the miracle has not occurred, and that there is an error in the testimony, than that the miracle has occurred. (Hume strengthens his argument, already strong, by observing that religion creates situations in which there *are* particular reasons to distrust the reports of witnesses. "But if the spirit of religion join itself to the love of wonder, there is an end of common sense.")

COMMENT: The Argument from Miracles covers more specific arguments, such as The Argument from Prophets, The Argument from Messiahs, and The Argument from Individuals with Miraculous Powers.

12. The Argument from the Hard Problem of Consciousness

1. The Hard Problem of Consciousness consists in our difficulty in explaining why it subjectively *feels* like something to be a functioning brain. (This is to be distinguished from the so-called Easy Problem of Consciousness, which is to explain why some brain processes are unconscious and others are conscious.)

2. Consciousness (in the Hard-Problem sense) is not a complex phenomenon built out of simpler ones; it can consist of irreducible "raw feels" like seeing red or tasting salt.

3. Science explains complex phenomena by reducing them to simpler ones, and reducing them to still simpler ones, until the simplest ones are explained by the basic laws of physics.

4. The basic laws of physics describe the properties of the elementary constituents of matter and energy, like quarks and quanta, which are not conscious.

5. Science cannot derive consciousness by reducing it to basic physical laws about the elementary constituents of matter and energy (from 2, 3, and 4).

6. Science will never solve the Hard Problem of Consciousness (from 3 and 5).

7. The explanation for consciousness must lie beyond physical laws (from 6).

8. Consciousness, lying outside physical laws, must itself be immaterial (from 7).

9. God is immaterial.

10. Consciousness and God both consist of the same immaterial kind of being (from 8 and 9).

11. God has not only the means to impart consciousness to us, but also the motive—namely, to allow us to enjoy a good life, and to make it possible for our choices to cause or prevent suffering in others, thereby allowing for morality and meaning.

12. Consciousness can only be explained by positing that God inserted a spark of the divine into us (from 7, 10, and 11).

13. God exists.

FLAW 1: Premise 3 is dubious. Science often shows that properties can be *emergent*: they arise from complex interactions of simpler elements, even if they cannot be found in any of the elements themselves. (Water is wet, but that does not mean that every H_2O molecule it is made of is also wet.) Granted, we do not have a theory of neuroscience that explains how consciousness emerges from patterns of neural activity, but to draw theological conclusions from the currently incomplete state of scientific knowledge is to commit the Fallacy of Arguing from Ignorance.

FLAW 2: Alternatively, the theory of panpsychism posits that consciousness in a low-grade form, what is often called "proto-consciousness," is inherent in matter. Our physical theories, with their mathematical methodology, have not yet been able to capture this aspect of matter, but that may just be a limitation on our mathematical physical theories. Some physicists have hypothesized that contemporary malaise about the foundations of quantum mechanics arises because physics is here confronting the intrinsic consciousness of matter, which has not yet been adequately formalized within physical theories.

FLAW 3: It has become clear that every measurable manifestation of consciousness, like our ability to describe what we feel, or let our feelings guide our behavior (the "Easy Problem" of consciousness), has been, or will be, explained in terms of neural activity (that is, every thought, feeling, and intention has a neural correlate). Only the existence of consciousness itself (the "Hard Problem") remains mysterious. But perhaps the hardness of the Hard Problem says more about what *we* find hard—the limitations of the brain of *Homo sapiens* when it tries to think scientifically—than about the hardness of the problem itself. Just as our brains do not allow us to visualize four-dimensional objects, perhaps our brains do not allow us to understand how subjective experience arises from complex neural activity.

FLAW 4: Premise 12 is entirely unclear. How does invoking the spark of the divine explain the existence of consciousness? It is the Fallacy of Using One Mystery to Explain Another.

COMMENT: Premise 11 is also dubious, because our capacity to suffer is far in excess of what it would take to make moral choices possible. This will be discussed in connection with The Argument from Suffering, #25, below.

13. The Argument from the Improbable Self

1. I exist in all my particularity and contingency: not as a generic example of personhood, not as any old member of *Homo sapiens,* but as that unique conscious entity that I know as *me.*
2. I can step outside myself and view my own contingent particularity with astonishment.
3. This astonishment reveals that there must be something that accounts for why, of all the particular things that I could have been, I am *just this*—namely, me (from 1 and 2).
4. Nothing within the world can account for why I am *just this,* since the laws of the world are generic: they can explain why certain *kinds* of things come to be, even (let's assume) why human beings with conscious brains come to be. But nothing in the world can explain why one of those human beings should be *me.*
5. Only something outside the world, who cares about me, can therefore account for why I am *just this* (from 4).
6. God is the only thing outside the world who cares about each and every one of us.
7. God exists.

FLAW: Premise 5 is a blatant example of the Fallacy of Using One Mystery to Explain Another. Granted that the problem boggles the mind, but waving one's hands in the direction of God is no solution. It gives us no sense of *how* God can account for why I am *this* thing and not another.

COMMENT: In one way, this argument is reminiscent of the Anthropic Principle. There are a vast number of people who could have been born. One's own parents alone could have given birth to a vast number of alternatives to oneself. Granted, one gropes for a reason for why it was, against these terrific odds, that oneself came to be born. But there may be no reason; it just happened. By the time you ask this question, you already are existing in a world in which you were born. Another analogy: The odds that the phone company would have given you your exact number (if you could have wished for exactly that number beforehand) are minuscule. But it had to give you *some* number, so asking after the fact why it should be *that* number is silly. Likewise, the child your parents conceived had to be *someone*. Now that you're born, it's no mystery why it should be you; you're the one asking the question.

14. The Argument from Survival After Death

1. There is empirical evidence that people survive after death: patients who flat-line during medical emergencies report an experience of floating over their bodies and seeing glimpses of a passage to another world, and can accurately report what happened around their bodies while they were dead to the world.
2. A person's consciousness can survive after the death of his or her body (from 1).
3. Survival after death entails the existence of an immaterial soul.
4. The immaterial soul exists (from 2 and 3).
5. If an immaterial soul exists, then God must exist (from Premise 12 in The Argument from the Hard Problem of Consciousness, #12).
6. God exists.

FLAW: Premise 5 is vulnerable to the same criticisms that were leveled against Premise 12 in The Argument from the Hard Problem of Consciousness. Existence after death no more implies God's existence than our existence before death does.

COMMENT: Many, of course, would dispute Premise 1. The experiences of people near death, such as auras and out-of-body experiences, could be hallucinations resulting from oxygen deprivation in the brain. In addition, miraculous resurrections after total brain death, and accurate reports of conversations and events that took place while the brain was not functioning, have never been scientifically documented, and are informal, secondhand examples of testimony of miracles. They are thus vulnerable to the same flaws pointed out in The Argument from Miracles, #11. But the argument is fatally flawed even if Premise 1 is granted.

15. The Argument from the Inconceivability of Personal Annihilation

1. I cannot conceive of my own annihilation: as soon as I start to think about what it would be like not to exist, I am thinking, which implies that I would exist (as in Descartes's *Cogito ergo sum*), which implies that I would not be thinking about what it is like not to exist.
2. My annihilation is inconceivable (from 1).
3. What cannot be conceived, cannot be.
4. I cannot be annihilated (from 2 and 3).
5. I survive after my death (from 4).

The argument now proceeds as in The Argument from Survival After Death, only substituting "I" for "people," until we get to:

6. God exists.

FLAW 1: Premise 2 confuses *psychological* inconceivability with *logical* inconceivability. The sense in which I can't conceive of my own annihilation is like the sense in which I can't conceive that those whom I love may betray me—a failure of the imagination, not an

impossible state of affairs. Thus Premise 2 ought to read "My annihilation is inconceivable *to me*," which is a fact about what my
brain can conceive, not a fact about what exists.

FLAW 2: Same as Flaw 3 from The Argument from the Survival
After Death.

COMMENT: Though logically unsound, this is among the most
powerful *psychological* impulses to believe in a soul, and an afterlife, and God. It genuinely is difficult—not to speak of dishearten-
ing—to conceive of oneself not existing!

16. The Argument from Moral Truth

1. There exist objective moral truths. (Slavery and torture and
   genocide are not just distasteful to us, but are actually
   wrong.)
2. These objective moral truths are not grounded in the way the
   world *is* but, rather, in the way the world *ought to be*. (Consider: should white supremacists succeed, taking over the
   world and eliminating all who don't meet their criteria for
   being existence-worthy, their ideology still would be morally
   wrong. It would be true, in this hideous counterfactual, that
   the world ought not to be the way that they have made it.)
3. The world itself—the way it is, the laws of science that explain why it is that way—cannot account for the way the
   world ought to be.
4. The only way to account for morality is that God established
   morality (from 2 and 3).
5. God exists.

FLAW 1: The major flaw of this argument is revealed in a powerful
argument that Plato made famous in the *Euthyphro*. Reference to

God does not help in the least to ground the objective truth of morality. The question is, why did God choose the moral rules he did? Did he have a reason justifying his choice that, say, giving alms to the poor is good, whereas genocide is wrong? Either he had a good reason or he didn't. If he did, then *his* reasons, whatever they are, can provide the grounding for moral truths for *us,* and God himself is redundant. And if he didn't have a good reason, then his choices are arbitrary—he could just as easily have gone the other way, making charity bad and genocide good—and we would have no reason to take his choices seriously. According to the *Euthyphro* argument, then, The Argument from Moral Truth is another example of the Fallacy of Passing the Buck. The hard work of moral philosophy consists in grounding morality in some version of the Golden Rule: that I cannot be committed to my own interests' mattering in a way that yours do not just because I am me and you are not.

FLAW 2: Premise 4 is belied by the history of religion, which shows that the God from which people draw their morality (for example, the God of the Bible and the Koran) did not establish what we now recognize to be morality at all. The God of the Old Testament commanded people to keep slaves, slay their enemies, execute blasphemers and homosexuals, and commit many other heinous acts. Of course, our interpretation of which aspects of biblical morality to take seriously has grown more sophisticated over time, and we read the Bible selectively and often metaphorically. But that is just the point: we must be consulting some standards of morality that do *not* come from God in order to judge which aspects of God's word to take literally and which aspects to ignore.

COMMENT: Some would question the first premise, and regard its assertion as a flaw of this argument. Slavery and torture and genocide are wrong by *our* lights, they would argue, and conflict with certain values we hold dear, such as freedom and happiness. But those are just subjective values, and it is obscure to say that statements that are consistent with those values are objectively true in the same way that mathematical or scientific statements can be true. But the argument is fatally flawed even if Premise 1 is granted.

17. The Argument from Altruism

1. People often act altruistically—namely, against their interests. They help others, at a cost to themselves, out of empathy, fairness, decency, and integrity.
2. Natural selection can never favor true altruism, because genes for selfishness will always out-compete genes for altruism (recall that altruism, by definition, exacts a cost to the actor).
3. Only a force acting outside of natural selection and intending for us to be moral could account for our ability to act altruistically (from 2).
4. God is the only force outside of natural selection that could intend us to be moral.
5. God must have implanted the moral instinct within us (from 3 and 4).
6. God exists.

FLAW 1: Theories of the evolution of altruism by natural selection have been around for decades and are now widely supported by many kinds of evidence. A gene for being kind to one's kin, even if it hurts the person doing the favor, can be favored by evolution, because that gene would be helping a copy of *itself* that is shared by the kin. And a gene for conferring a large benefit to a non-relative at a cost to oneself can evolve if the favor-doer is the beneficiary of a return favor at a later time. Both parties are better off, in the long run, from the exchange of favors.

Some defenders of religion do not consider these theories to be legitimate explanations of altruism, because a tendency to favor one's kin, or to trade favors, is ultimately just a form of selfishness for one's genes, rather than true altruism. But this is a confusion of the original phenomenon. We are trying to explain why people are sometimes altruistic, not why genes are altruistic. (We have no reason to believe that genes are ever altruistic in the first place!) Also, in a species with language—namely, humans—committed altruists develop a reputation for being altruistic, and thereby win more friends, allies, and trading partners. This can give rise to selection for true, committed, altruism, not just the tit-for-tat exchange of favors.

FLAW 2: We have evolved higher mental faculties, such as self-reflection and logic, that allow us to reason about the world, to persuade other people to form alliances with us, to learn from our mistakes, and to achieve other feats of reason. Those same faculties, when they are honed through debate, reason, and knowledge, can allow us to step outside ourselves, learn about other people's points of view, and act in a way that we can justify as maximizing everyone's well-being. We are capable of moral reasoning because we are capable of reasoning in general.

FLAW 3: In some versions of The Argument from Altruism, God succeeds in getting people to act altruistically because he promises them a divine reward and threatens them with divine retribution. People behave altruistically to gain a reward or avoid a punishment in the life to come. This argument is self-contradictory. It aims to explain how people act without regard to their self-interest, but then assumes that there could be no motive for acting altruistically other than self-interest.

18. The Argument from Free Will

1. Having *free will* means having the freedom to choose our actions, rather than having them determined by some prior cause.

2. If we don't have free will, then we are not agents, for then we are not really *acting*, but, rather, we're being acted *upon*. (That's why we don't punish people for involuntary actions—such as a teller who hands money to a bank robber at gunpoint, or a driver who injures a pedestrian after a defective tire blows out.)

3. To be a moral agent means to be held morally responsible for what one does.

4. If we can't be held morally responsible for anything we do, then the very idea of morality is meaningless.

5. Morality is not meaningless.

6. We have free will (from 2–5).

7. We, as moral agents, are not subject to the laws of nature—in particular, the neural events in a genetically and environmentally determined brain (from 1 and 6).

8. Only a being who is apart from the laws of nature and partakes of the moral sphere could explain our being moral agents (from 7).

9. Only God is a being who is apart from the laws of nature and partakes of the moral sphere.

10. Only God can explain our moral agency (from 8 and 9).

11. God exists.

FLAW 1: This argument, in order to lead to God, must ignore the paradoxical Fork of Free Will. Either my actions are predictable (from my genes, my upbringing, my brain state, my current situation, and so on), or they are not. If they are predictable, then there is no reason to deny that they are caused, and we would not have free will. So, if we are to be free, our actions must be unpredictable—in other words, random. But if our behavior is random, then in what sense can it be attributable to us at all? If it really is a random event when I give the infirm man my seat in the subway, then in what sense is it *me* to whom this good deed should be attributed? If the action isn't caused by my psychological states, which are themselves caused by other states, then in what way is it really *my* action? And what good would it do to insist on moral responsibility if our choices are random, and cannot be predicted from prior events (such as growing up in a society that holds people responsible)? This leads us back to the conclusion that we, as moral agents, *must* be parts of the natural world—the very negation of Premise 7.

FLAW 2: Premise 10 is an example of the Fallacy of Using One Mystery to Explain Another. It expresses, rather than dispels, the confusion we feel when faced with the Fork of Free Will. The paradox has not been clarified in the least by introducing God into the analysis.

COMMENT: Free will is yet another quandary that takes us to the edge of our human capacity for understanding. The concept is baffling, because our moral agency seems to demand both that our actions be determined, and also that they not be determined.

19. The Argument from Personal Purpose

1. If there is no purpose to a person's life, then that person's life is pointless.
2. Human life cannot be pointless.
3. Each human life has a purpose (from 1 and 2).
4. The purpose of each individual person's life must derive from the overall purpose of existence.

5. There is an overall purpose of existence (from 3 and 4).
6. Only a being who understands the overall purpose of existence could create each person according to the purpose that person is meant to fulfill.
7. Only God could understand the overall purpose of creation.
8. There can be a point to human existence only if God exists (from 6 and 7).
9. God exists.

FLAW 1: The first premise rests on a confusion between the purpose of an action and the purpose of a life. It is human activities that have purposes—or don't. We study for the purpose of educating and supporting ourselves. We eat right and exercise for the purpose of being healthy. We warn children not to accept rides with strangers for the purpose of keeping them safe. We donate to charity for the purpose of helping the poor (just as we would want someone to help us if we were poor). The notion of a person's entire *life* serving a purpose, above and beyond the purpose of all the person's choices, is obscure. Might it mean the purpose for which the person was born? That implies that some goal-seeking agent decided to bring our lives into being to serve some purpose. Then who is that goal-seeking agent? Parents often purposively have children, but we wouldn't want to see a parent's wishes as the purpose of the child's life. If the goal-seeking agent is God, the argument becomes circular: we make sense of the notion of "the purpose of a life" by stipulating that the purpose is whatever God had in mind when he created us, but then argue for the existence of God because he is the only one who could have designed us with a purpose in mind.

FLAW 2: Premise 2 states that human life cannot be pointless. But of course it could be pointless in the sense meant by this argument: lacking a purpose in the grand scheme of things. It could very well be that there is no grand scheme of things because there is no Grand Schemer. By assuming that there is a grand scheme of things, it assumes that there is a schemer whose scheme it is, which circularly assumes the conclusion.

COMMENT: It's important not to confuse the notion of "pointless" in Premise 2 with notions like "not worth living" or "expendable." Confusions of this sort probably give Premise 2 its appeal. But we can very well maintain that each human life is precious—is worth living, is not expendable—*without* maintaining that each human life has a purpose in the overall scheme of things.

20. The Argument from the Intolerability of Insignificance

1. In a million years, nothing that happens now will matter.
2. By the same token, anything that happens at any point in time will not matter from the point of view of a time a million years distant from it in the future.
3. No point in time can confer mattering on any other point, for each suffers from the same problem of not mattering itself (from 2).
4. It is intolerable (or inconceivable, or unacceptable) that in a million years nothing that happens now will matter.
5. What happens now will matter in a million years (from 4).
6. It is only from the point of view of eternity that what happens now will matter even in a million years (from 3).
7. Only God can inhabit the point of view of eternity.
8. God exists.

FLAW: Premise 4 is illicit: it is of the form "This argument must be correct because it is intolerable that this argument is not correct." The argument is either circular, or an example of the Fallacy of Wishful Thinking. Maybe we *won't* matter in a million years, and there's just nothing we can do about it. If that is the case, we shouldn't declare that it is intolerable—we just have to live with it. Another way of putting it is: we should take ourselves seriously (being mindful of what we do, and the world we leave our children and grandchildren), but we shouldn't take ourselves *that* seriously, arrogantly demanding that we must matter in a million years.

21. The Argument from the Consensus of Humanity

1. Every culture in every epoch has had theistic beliefs.
2. When peoples, widely separated by both space and time, hold similar beliefs, the best explanation is that those beliefs are true.
3. The best explanation for why every culture has had theistic beliefs is that those beliefs are true.
4. God exists.

FLAW: Premise 2 is false. Widely separated people could very well come up with the same *false* beliefs. Human nature is universal, and thus prone to universal illusions and shortcomings of perception, memory, reasoning, and objectivity. Also, many of the needs and terrors and dependencies of the human condition (such as the knowledge of our own mortality, and the attendant desire not to die) are universal. Our beliefs arise not only from well-evaluated reasoning, but from wishful thinking, self-deception, self-aggrandizement, gullibility, false memories, visual illusions, and other mental glitches. Well-grounded beliefs may be the exception rather than the rule when it comes to psychologically fraught beliefs, which tend to bypass rational grounding and spring instead from unexamined emotions. The fallacy of arguing that if an idea is universally held then it must be true was labeled by the ancient logicians *consensus gentium*.

22. The Argument from the Consensus of Mystics

1. Mystics go into a special state in which they seem to see aspects of reality that elude everyday experience.
2. We cannot evaluate the truth of their experiences from the viewpoint of everyday experience (from 1).
3. There is a unanimity among mystics as to what they experience.
4. When there is unanimity among observers as to what they experience, then, unless they are all deluded in the same way, the best explanation for their unanimity is that their experiences are true.
5. There is no reason to think that mystics are all deluded in the same way.
6. The best explanation for the unanimity of mystical experience is that what mystics perceive is true (from 4 and 5).
7. Mystical experiences unanimously testify to the transcendent presence of God.
8. God exists.

FLAW 1: Premise 5 is disputable. There is indeed reason to think mystics might be deluded in similar ways. The universal human nature that refuted The Argument from the Consensus of Humanity, #21, entails that the human brain can be stimulated in unusual ways that give rise to widespread (but not objectively correct) experiences. The fact that we can stimulate the temporal lobes of non-mystics and induce mystical experiences in them is evidence that mystics might be deluded in similar ways. Certain drugs can also induce feelings of transcendence, such as an enlargement of perception beyond the bounds of effability, a melting of the boundaries of the self, a joyful expansion out into an existence that seems to be all One, with all that Oneness pronouncing *Yes* upon us. Such experiences, which, as William James points out, are most easily attained by getting drunk, are of the same kind as the mystical: "The drunken consciousness is one bit of the mystic consciousness." Of course, we do not exalt the stupor and delusions of drunkenness, because we *know* what caused them. The fact that the same effects can overcome a person when we know what caused them (and hence don't call the experience "mystical") is reason to suspect that the causes of mystical experiences also lie within the brain.

FLAW 2: The struggle to put the ineffable contents of abnormal experiences into language inclines the struggler toward pre-existing religious language, which is the only language that most of us have been exposed to that overlaps with the unusual content of an altered state of consciousness. This observation casts doubt on Premise 7. See also The Argument from Sublimity, #34, below.

23. The Argument from Holy Books

1. There are holy books that reveal the word of God.
2. The word of God is necessarily true.
3. The word of God reveals the existence of God.
4. God exists.

FLAW 1: This is a circular argument if ever there was one. The first three premises cannot be maintained unless one independently knows the very conclusion to be proved—namely, that God exists.

FLAW 2: A glance at the world's religions shows that there are numerous books and scrolls and doctrines and revelations that all claim to reveal the word of God. But they are mutually incompatible. Should I believe that Jesus is my personal saviour? Or should I believe that God made a covenant with the Jews requiring every Jew to keep the commandments of the Torah? Should I believe that

Muhammad was Allah's last prophet and that Ali, the prophet's cousin and husband of his daughter Fatima, ought to have been the first caliph, or that Muhammad was Allah's last prophet and that Ali was the fourth and last caliph? Should I believe that the resurrected prophet Moroni dictated the Book of Mormon to Joseph Smith? Or that Ahura Mazda, the benevolent Creator, is at cosmic war with the malevolent Angra Mainyu? And on and on it goes. Only the most arrogant provincialism could allow someone to believe that the holy documents that happen to be held sacred by the clan he was born into are true, whereas all the documents held sacred by the clans he wasn't born into are false.

24. The Argument from Perfect Justice

1. This world provides numerous instances of imperfect justice—bad things happening to good people, and good things happening to bad people.
2. It violates our sense of justice that imperfect justice may prevail.
3. There must be a transcendent realm in which perfect justice prevails (from 1 and 2).
4. A transcendent realm in which perfect justice prevails requires the Perfect Judge.
5. The Perfect Judge is God.
6. God exists.

FLAW: This is a good example of the Fallacy of Wishful Thinking. Our wishes for how the universe should be need not be true; just because we want there to be some realm in which perfect justice applies does not mean that there is such a realm. In other words, there is no way to pass from Premise 2 to Premise 3 without the Fallacy of Wishful Thinking.

25. The Argument from Suffering

1. There is much suffering in this world.

2. Suffering must have some purpose, or existence would be intolerable.

3. Some suffering (or at least its possibility) is demanded by human moral agency: if people could not choose evil acts that cause suffering, moral choice would not exist.

4. Whatever suffering cannot be explained as the result of human moral agency must also have some purpose (from 2 and 3).

5. There are virtues—forbearance, courage, compassion, and so on—that can only develop in the presence of suffering. We may call them "the virtues of suffering."

6. Some suffering has the purpose of inducing the virtues of suffering (from 5).

7. Even taking Premises 3 and 6 into account, the amount of suffering in the world is still enormous—far more than what is required for us to benefit from suffering.

8. Moreover, some who suffer can never develop the virtues of suffering—children, animals, those who perish in their agony.

9. There is more suffering than we can explain by reference to the purposes that we can discern (from 7 and 8).

10. There are purposes for suffering that we cannot discern (from 2 and 9).

11. Only a being who has a sense of purpose beyond ours could provide the purpose of all suffering (from 10).

12. Only God could have a sense of purpose beyond ours.

13. God exists.

FLAW: This argument is a sorrowful one, since it highlights the most intolerable feature of our world, the excess of suffering. The suffering in this world is excessive in both its intensity and its prevalence, often undergone by those who can never gain anything from it. This is a powerful argument *against* the existence of a compassionate and powerful deity. It is only the Fallacy of Wishful Thinking, embodied in Premise 2, that could make us presume that what is psychologically intolerable cannot be the case.

26. The Argument from the Survival of the Jews

1. The Jews introduced the world to the idea of the one God, with his universal moral code.
2. The survival of the Jews, living for millennia without a country of their own, and facing a multitude of enemies that sought to destroy not only their religion but all remnants of the race, is a historical unlikelihood.
3. The Jews have survived against vast odds (from 2).
4. There is no natural explanation for so unlikely an event as the survival of the Jews (from 3).
5. The best explanation is that they have some transcendent purpose to play in human destiny (from 1 and 4).
6. Only God could have assigned a transcendent destiny to the Jews.
7. God exists.

FLAW: The fact that Jews, after the destruction of the Second Temple by the Romans, had no country of their own, made it *more* likely, rather than less likely, that they would survive as a people. If they had been concentrated in one country, they would surely have been conquered by one of history's great empires, as happened to other vanished tribes. But a people dispersed across a vast diaspora is more resilient, which is why other stateless peoples, like the Parsis and Roma (Gypsies), have also survived for millennia, often against harrowing odds. Moreover, the Jews encouraged cultural traits—such as literacy, urban living, specialization in middleman occupations, and an extensive legal code to govern their internal affairs—that gave them further resilience against the vicissitudes of historical change. The survival of the Jews, therefore, is not a miraculous improbability.

COMMENT: The persecution of the Jews need not be seen as part of a cosmic moral drama. The unique role that Judaism played in disseminating monotheism, mostly through the organs of its two far more popular monotheistic offshoots, Christianity and Islam, has bequeathed to its adherents an unusual amount of attention, mostly negative, from adherents of those other monotheistic religions.

27. The Argument from the Upward Curve of History

1. There is an upward moral curve to human history (tyrannies fall; the evil side loses in major wars; democracy, freedom, and civil rights spread).
2. Natural selection's favoring of those who are fittest to compete for resources and mates has bequeathed humankind selfish and aggressive traits.
3. Left to their own devices, a selfish and aggressive species could not have ascended up a moral curve over the course of history (from 2).
4. Only God has the power and the concern for us to curve history upward.
5. God exists.

FLAW: Though our species has inherited traits of selfishness and aggression, we have inherited capacities for empathy, reasoning, and learning from experience as well. We have also developed language, and with it a means to pass on the lessons we have learned from history. And so humankind has slowly reasoned its way toward a broader and more sophisticated understanding of morality, and more effective institutions for keeping peace. We make moral progress as we do scientific progress, through reasoning, experimentation, and the rejection of failed alternatives.

28. The Argument from Prodigious Genius

1. Genius is the highest level of creative capacity, the level that, by definition, defies explanation.
2. Genius does not happen by way of natural psychological processes (from 1).
3. The cause of genius must lie outside of natural psychological processes (from 2).
4. The insights of genius have helped in the cumulative progress of humankind—scientific, technological, philosophical, moral, artistic, societal, political, spiritual.
5. The cause of genius must both lie outside of natural psychological processes and be such as to care about the progress of humankind (from 3 and 4).
6. Only God could work outside of natural psychological processes and create geniuses to light the path of humankind.
7. God exists.

FLAW 1: The psychological traits that go into human accomplishment, such as intelligence and perseverance, are heritable. By the laws of probability, rare individuals will inherit a concentrated dose of those genes. Given a nurturing cultural context, these individuals will, some of the time, exercise their powers to accomplish great feats. Those are the individuals we call geniuses. We may not know enough about genetics, neuroscience, and cognition to explain exactly what makes for a Mozart or an Einstein, but exploiting this gap to argue for supernatural provenance is an example of the Fallacy of Arguing from Ignorance.

FLAW 2: Human genius is not consistently applied to human betterment. Consider weapons of mass destruction, computer viruses, Hitler's brilliantly effective rhetoric, or those criminal geniuses (for example, electronic thieves) who are so cunning that they elude detection.

29. The Argument from Human Knowledge of Infinity

1. We are finite, and everything with which we come into physical contact is finite.
2. We have a knowledge of the infinite, demonstrably so in mathematics.
3. We could not have derived this knowledge of the infinite from the finite, from anything that we are and come in contact with (from 1).
4. Only something itself infinite could have implanted knowledge of the infinite in us (from 2 and 3).
5. God would want us to have a knowledge of the infinite, both for the cognitive pleasure it affords us and because it allows us to come to know him, who is himself infinite.
6. God is the only entity that both is infinite and could have an intention of implanting the knowledge of the infinite within us (from 4 and 5).
7. God exists.

FLAW: There are certain computational procedures governed by what logicians call recursive rules. A recursive rule is one that refers to itself, and hence it can be applied to its own output ad infinitum. For example, we can define a natural number recursively: 1 is a natural number, and if you add 1 to a natural number, the result is a natural number. We can apply this rule an indefinite number of times and thereby generate an infinite series of natural numbers. Recursive rules allow a finite system (a set of rules, a computer, a brain) to reason about an infinity of objects, refuting Premise 3.

COMMENT: In 1931 the young logician Kurt Gödel published a paper proving The Incompleteness Theorem (actually there are two). Basically, what Gödel demonstrated is that recursive rules cannot capture all of mathematics. For any mathematical system rich enough to express arithmetic, we can produce a true proposition that is expressible in that system but not provable within it. So even though the flaw discussed above is sufficient to invalidate Premise 3, it should not be understood as suggesting that all of our mathematical knowledge is reducible to recursive rules.

30. The Argument from Mathematical Reality

1. Mathematical truths are necessarily true (there is no possible world in which 2 plus 2 does not equal 4).
2. The truths that describe our physical world are empirical, requiring observational evidence.
3. Truths that require empirical evidence are not necessary truths. (We require empirical evidence because there are possible worlds in which these are not truths, and we have to test that ours is not such a world.)
4. The truths of our physical world are not necessary truths (from 2 and 3).
5. The truths of our physical world cannot explain mathematical truths (from 1 and 3).
6. Mathematical truths exist on a different plane of existence from physical truths (from 5).

7. Only something which itself exists on a different plane of existence from the physical can explain mathematical truths (from 6).

8. Only God can explain the necessary truths of mathematics (from 7).

9. God exists.

Mathematics is derived through pure reason—what the philosophers call a priori reason—which means that it cannot be refuted by any empirical observations. The fundamental question in the philosophy of mathematics is, how can mathematics be true but not empirical? Is it because mathematics describes some trans-empirical reality—as mathematical realists believe—or is it because mathematics has no content at all and is a purely formal game consisting of stipulated rules and their consequences? The Argument from Mathematical Reality assumes, in its third premise, the position of mathematical realism, which isn't a fallacy in itself; many mathematicians believe it, some of them arguing that it follows from Gödel's incompleteness theorems (see the Comment in The Argument from Human Knowledge of Infinity, #29, above). This argument, however, goes further and tries to deduce God's existence from the trans-empirical existence of mathematical reality.

FLAW 1: Premise 5 presumes that something outside of mathematical reality must explain the existence of mathematical reality, but this presumption is non-obvious. Lurking within Premise 5 is the hidden premise: mathematics must be explained by reference to non-mathematical truths. But this hidden premise, when exposed, appears murky. If God can be self-explanatory, why, then, can't mathematical reality be self-explanatory—especially since the truths of mathematics are, as this argument asserts, necessarily true?

FLAW 2: Mathematical reality—if indeed it exists—is, admittedly, mysterious. Many people have trouble conceiving of where mathematical truths live, or exactly what they pertain to. But invoking God does not dispel this puzzlement; it is an instance of the Fallacy of Using One Mystery to Explain Another.

31. The Argument from Decision Theory (Pascal's Wager)

1. Either God exists or God doesn't exist.
2. A person can either believe that God exists or believe that God doesn't exist (from 1).
3. If God exists and you believe, you receive eternal salvation.
4. If God exists and you don't believe, you receive eternal damnation.
5. If God doesn't exist and you believe, you've been duped, have wasted time in religious observance, and have missed out on decadent enjoyments.
6. If God doesn't exist and you don't believe, then you have avoided a false belief.
7. You have much more to gain by believing in God than by not believing in him, and much more to lose by not believing in God than by believing in him (from, 3, 4, 5, and 6).
8. It is more rational to believe that God exists than to believe that he doesn't exist (from 7).

	God exists	God doesn't exist
Believe	Eternal salvation	You've been duped, missed out on some sins
Don't believe	Eternal damnation	You got it right

This unusual argument does not justify the conclusion that "God exists." Rather, it argues that it is rational to believe that God exists, given that we don't know whether he exists.

FLAW I: The "believe" option in Pascal's Wager can be interpreted in two ways.

One is that the wagerer genuinely has to believe, deep down, that God exists; in other words, it is not enough to mouth a creed, or merely act *as if* God exists. According to this interpretation, God, if he exists, can peer into a person's soul and discern the person's actual convictions. If so, the kind of "belief" that Pascal's Wager advises—a purely pragmatic strategy, chosen because the expected benefits exceed the expected costs—would not be enough. Indeed, it's not even clear that this option is coherent: if one *chooses* to believe something because of the consequences of holding that belief, rather than being genuinely convinced of it, is it really a belief, or just an empty vow?

The other interpretation is that it is enough to *act* in the way that traditional believers act: say prayers, go to services, recite the appropriate creed, and go through the other motions of religion.

The problem is that Pascal's Wager offers no guidance as to *which* prayers, *which* services, *which* creed to live by. Say I chose to believe in the Zoroastrian cosmic war between Ahura Mazda and Angra Mainyu to avoid the wrath of the former, but the real fact of the matter is that God gave the Torah to the Jews, and I am thereby inviting the wrath of Yahweh (or vice versa). Given all the things I could "believe" in, I am in constant danger of incurring the negative consequences of disbelief even though I choose the "belief" option. The fact that Blaise Pascal stated his wager as two stark choices, putting the outcomes in blatantly Christian terms— eternal salvation and eternal damnation—reveals more about his own upbringing than it does about the logic of belief. The wager simply codifies his particular "live options," to use William James's term for the only choices that seem possible to a given believer.

FLAW 2: Pascal's Wager assumes a petty, egotistical, and vindictive God who punishes anyone who does not believe in him. But the great monotheistic religions all declare that "mercy" is one of God's essential traits. A merciful God would surely have some understanding of why a person may not believe in him (if the evidence for God were obvious, the fancy reasoning of Pascal's Wager would not be necessary), and so would extend compassion to a non-believer. (Bertrand Russell, when asked what he would have to say to God, if, despite his reasoned atheism, he were to die and face his Creator, responded, "O Lord, why did you not provide more evidence?") The non-believer therefore should have nothing to worry about—falsifying the negative payoff in the lower-left-hand cell of the matrix.

FLAW 3: The calculations of expected value in Pascal's Wager omit a crucial part of the mathematics: the probabilities of each of the two columns, which have to be multiplied with the payoff in each cell to determine the expected value of each cell. If the probability of God's existence (ascertained by other means) is infinitesimal, then even if the cost of not believing in him is high, the overall expectation may not make it worthwhile to choose the "believe" row (after all, we take many other risks in life with severe possible costs but low probabilities, such as boarding an airplane). One can see how this invalidates Pascal's Wager by considering similar wagers. Say I told you that a fire-breathing dragon has moved into the next apartment, and that unless you set out a bowl of marshmallows for him every night he will force his way into your apartment and roast you to a crisp. According to Pascal's Wager, you should leave out the marshmallows. Of course you don't, even though you are taking a terrible risk in choosing not to believe in the dragon, because you don't assign a high enough probability to the dragon's existence to justify even the small inconvenience.

32. The Argument from Pragmatism
(William James's Leap of Faith)

1. The consequences for the believer's life of believing should be considered as part of the evidence for the truth of the belief (just as the effectiveness of a scientific theory in its practical applications is considered evidence for the truth of the theory). Call this the pragmatic evidence for the belief.
2. Certain beliefs effect a change for the better in the believer's life—the necessary condition being that they are believed.
3. The belief in God is a belief that effects a change for the better in a person's life.
4. If one tries to decide whether or not to believe in God based on the evidence available, one will never get the chance to evaluate the pragmatic evidence for the beneficial consequences of believing in God (from 2 and 3).
5. One ought to make "the leap of faith" (the term is James's) and believe in God, and only *then* evaluate the evidence (from 1 and 4).

This argument can be read out of William James's classic essay "The Will to Believe." The first premise, as presented here, is a little less radical than James's pragmatic definition of truth according to which a proposition is true if believing that it is true has a cumulative beneficial effect on the believer's life. The pragmatic definition of truth has severe problems, including possible incoherence: in evaluating the effects of the belief on the believer, we have to know the truth about what those effects are, which forces us to fall back on the old-fashioned notion of truth. To make the best case for The Argument from Pragmatism, therefore, the first premise is to be interpreted as claiming only that the pragmatic consequences of belief are a relevant *source of evidence* in ascertaining the truth, not that they can actually be *equated* with the truth.

FLAW 1: What exactly does effecting "a change for the better in the believer's life" mean? For an antebellum Southerner, there was more to be gained in believing that slavery was morally permissible than in believing it heinous. It often doesn't pay to be an iconoclast or a revolutionary thinker, no matter how much truer your ideas are than the ideas opposing you. It didn't improve Galileo's life to believe that the earth moved around the sun rather than that the sun and the heavens revolve around the earth. (Of course, you could say that it's always intrinsically better to believe something true rather than something false, but then you're just using the language of pragmatism to mask a non-pragmatic notion of truth.)

FLAW 2: The Argument from Pragmatism implies an extreme relativism regarding the truth, because the effects of belief differ for different believers. A profligate, impulsive drunkard may have to believe in a primitive retributive God who will send him to hell if he doesn't stay out of barroom fights, whereas a contemplative mensch may be better off with an abstract deistic presence who completes his deepest existential worldview. But either there is a vengeful God who sends sinners to hell or there isn't. If one allows pragmatic consequences to determine truth, then truth becomes relative to the believer, which is incoherent.

FLAW 3: Why should we only consider the pragmatic effects on the *believer's* life? What about the effects on everyone else? The history of religious intolerance, such as inquisitions, fatwas, and suicide bombers, suggests that the effects on one person's life of another person's believing in God can be pretty grim.

FLAW 4: The Argument from Pragmatism suffers from the first flaw of The Argument from Decision Theory (#31, above)—namely, the assumption that the belief in God is like a faucet that one can turn on and off as the need arises. If I make the leap of faith in order to evaluate the pragmatic consequences of belief, then, if those consequences are not so good, can I leap back to disbelief? Isn't a leap of faith a one-way maneuver? "The will to believe" is an oxymoron: beliefs are forced on a person (ideally, by logic and evidence); they are not chosen for their consequences.

33. The Argument from the Unreasonableness of Reason

1. Our belief in reason cannot be justified by reason, since that would be circular.
2. Our belief in reason must be accepted on faith (from 1).
3. Every time we exercise reason, we are exercising faith (from 2).
4. Faith provides good rational grounds for beliefs (since it is, in the final analysis, necessary even for the belief in reason—from 3).
5. We are justified in using faith for any belief that is so important to our lives that not believing it would render us incoherent (from 4).
6. We cannot avoid faith in God if we are to live coherent moral and purposeful lives.
7. We are justified in believing that God exists (from 5 and 6).
8. God exists.

Reason is a faculty of thinking, the very faculty of giving grounds for our beliefs. To justify reason would be to try to give grounds for the belief: "We ought to accept the conclusions of sound arguments." Let's say we produce a sound argument for the conclusion that "we ought to accept the conclusions of sound arguments." How could we legitimately accept the conclusion of that sound argument without independently knowing the conclusion? Any attempt to justify the very propositions that we must use in order to justify propositions is going to land us in circularity.

FLAW 1: This argument tries to generalize the inability of reason to justify itself to an abdication of reason when it comes to justifying God's existence. But the inability of reason to justify reason is a unique case in epistemology, not an illustration of a flaw of reason that can be generalized to some other kind of belief—and certainly not a belief in the existence of some entity with specific properties such as creating the world or defining morality.

Indeed, one could argue that the attempt to justify reason with reason is not circular, but, rather, unnecessary. One already is, and always will be, committed to reason by the very process one is already engaged in—namely, reasoning. Reason is non-negotiable; all sides concede it. It needs no justification, because it *is* justification. A belief in God is not like that at all.

FLAW 2: If one really took the unreasonability of reason as a license to believe things on faith, then which things should one believe in? If it is a license to believe in a single God who gave his son for our sins, why isn't it just as much a license to believe in Zeus and all the other Greek gods, or the three major gods of Hinduism, or the Angel Moroni? For that matter, why not Santa Claus and the Tooth Fairy? If one says that there are good reasons to accept some entities on faith, while rejecting others, then one is saying that it is ultimately reason, not faith, that must be invoked to justify a belief.

FLAW 3: Premise 6, which claims that a belief in God is necessary in order to have a purpose in one's life, or to be moral, has already been challenged in the discussions of The Argument from Moral Truth (#16, above) and The Argument from Personal Purpose (#19, above).

34. The Argument from Sublimity

1. There are experiences that are windows into the wholeness of existence—its grandeur, beauty, symmetry, harmony, unity, even its goodness.
2. We glimpse a benign transcendence in these moments.
3. Only God could provide us with a glimpse of benign transcendence.
4. God exists.

FLAW: An experience of sublimity is an aesthetic experience. Aesthetic experience can indeed be intense and blissful, absorbing our attention so completely, while exciting our pleasure, as to seem to lift us right out of our surroundings. Aesthetic experiences vary in their strength, and when they are overwhelming, we grope for terms like "transcendence" to describe the overwhelmingness. Yet, for all that, aesthetic experiences are still responses of the brain, as we see from the fact that ingesting recreational drugs can bring on even more intense experiences of transcendence. And the particular triggers for natural aesthetic experiences are readily explicable from the evolutionary pressures that have shaped the perceptual systems of human beings. An eye for sweeping vistas, dramatic skies, bodies of water, large animals, flowering and fruiting plants, and strong geometric patterns with repetition and symmetry was necessary to orient attention to aspects of the environment that were matters of life and death to the species as it evolved in its natural environment. The identification of a blissfully aesthetic experience with a glimpse into benign transcendence is an example of the Projection Fallacy, dramatic demonstrations of our spreading ourselves onto the world. This is most obvious when the experience gets fleshed out into the religious terms that come most naturally to the particular believer, such as a frozen waterfall being seen by a Christian as evidence for the Christian Trinity.

35. The Argument from the Intelligibility of the Universe (Spinoza's God)

1. All facts must have explanations.
2. The fact that there is a universe at all—and that it is *this* universe, with just these laws of nature—has an explanation (from 1).
3. There must, in principle, be a Theory of Everything that explains why just this universe, with these laws of nature, exists. (From 2. Note that this should not be interpreted as requiring that *we* have the capacity to come up with a Theory of Everything; it may elude the cognitive abilities we have.)
4. If the Theory of Everything explains everything, it explains why it is the Theory of Everything.
5. The only way that the Theory of Everything could explain why it is the Theory of Everything is if it is itself necessarily true (i.e., true in all possible worlds).
6. The Theory of Everything is necessarily true (from 4 and 5).
7. The universe, understood in terms of the Theory of Everything, exists necessarily and explains itself (from 6).
8. That which exists necessarily and explains itself is God (a definition of "God").
9. The universe is God (from 7 and 8).
10. God exists.

Whenever Einstein was asked whether he believed in God, he responded that he believed in "Spinoza's God." This argument presents Spinoza's God. It is one of the most elegant and subtle arguments for God's existence, demonstrating where one ends up if one rigorously eschews the Fallacy of Invoking One Mystery to Explain Another: one ends up with the universe and nothing but the universe, which itself provides all the answers to all the questions one can pose about it. A major problem with the argument, however, in addition to the flaws discussed below, is that it is not at all clear that it is *God* whose existence is being proved. Spinoza's conclusion is that the universe that itself provides all the answers about itself simply *is* God. Perhaps the conclusion should, rather, be that the universe is different from what it appears to be— no matter how arbitrary and chaotic it may appear, it is in fact perfectly lawful and necessary, and therefore worthy of our awe. But is its awe-inspiring lawfulness reason enough to regard it as God? Spinoza's God is sharply at variance with all other divine conceptions.

The argument has only one substantive premise, its first one, which, though unprovable, is not unreasonable; it is, in fact, the claim that the universe itself is thoroughly reasonable. Though this first premise can't be proved, it is the guiding faith of many physicists (including Einstein). It is the claim that everything must have an explanation; even the laws of nature, in terms of which processes are explained, must have an explanation. In other words, there has to be an explanation for why it is *these* laws of nature rather than some other, which is another way of asking why it is *this* world rather than some other.

FLAW: The first premise cannot be proved. Our world could conceivably be one in which randomness and contingency have free reign, no matter what the intuitions of some scientists are. Maybe some things just *are* ("stuff happens"), including the fundamental laws of nature. Philosophers sometimes call this just-is-ness "contingency," and if the fundamental laws of nature are contingent, then, even if everything that happens in the world is explainable by those laws, the laws themselves couldn't be explained. There is a sense in which this argument recalls The Argument from the Improbable Self, #13. Both demand explanations for *just-this*-ness, whether of *just this* universe or *just this* me.

The Argument from the Intelligibility of the Universe fleshes out the consequences of the powerful first premise, but some might regard the argument as a *reductio ad absurdum* of that premise.

COMMENT: Spinoza's argument, if sound, invalidates all the other arguments, the ones that try to establish the existence of a more traditional God—that is, a God who stands *distinct* from the world described by the laws of nature, as well as distinct from the world of human meaning, purpose, and morality. Spinoza's argument claims that any transcendent God, standing *outside* of that for which he is invoked as explanation, is invalidated by the first powerful premise, that all things are part of the same explanatory fabric. The mere coherence of The Argument from the Intelligibility of the Universe, therefore, is sufficient to reveal the invalidity of the other theistic arguments. This is why Spinoza, although he offered a proof of what he called "God," is often regarded as the most effective of all atheists.

36. The Argument from the Abundance of Arguments

1. The more arguments there are for a proposition, the more confidence we should have in it, even if every argument is imperfect. (Science itself proceeds by accumulating evidence, each piece by itself being inconclusive.)
2. There is not just one argument for the existence of God, but many—thirty-five (with additional variations) so far, in this list alone.
3. The arguments, though not flawless, are persuasive enough

that they have convinced billions of people, and for millennia have been taken seriously by history's greatest minds.

4. The probability that each one is true must be significantly greater than zero (from 3).

5. For God *not* to exist, every one of the arguments for his existence must be false, which is extremely unlikely (from 4). Imagine, for the sake of argument, that each argument has an average probability of only .2 of being true. Then the probability that all thirty-five are false is $(.8)^{35} = .0004$, an extremely low probability.

6. It is extremely probable that God exists (from 5).

FLAW 1: Premise 3 is vulnerable to the same criticisms as The Argument from the Consensus of Humanity, #21. The flaws that accompany each argument may be extremely damaging, even fatal, notwithstanding the fact that they have been taken seriously by many people throughout history. In other words, the average probability of any of the arguments' being true may be far less than .2, in which case the probability that all of them are false could be high.

FLAW 2: This argument treats all the other arguments as being on an equal footing, distributing equal probabilities to them all, and rewarding all of them, too, with the commendation of being taken seriously by history's greatest minds. Many of the arguments on this list have been completely demolished by such minds as David Hume and Baruch Spinoza: their probability is zero.

COMMENT: The Argument from the Abundance of Arguments may be the most psychologically important of the thirty-six. Few people rest their belief in God on a single, decisive logical argument. Instead, people are swept away by the sheer number of reasons that make God's existence seem plausible—holding out an explanation as to why the universe went to the bother of existing, and why it is this particular universe, with its sublime improbabilities, including us humans; and, even more particularly, explaining the existence of each one of us who know ourselves as unique conscious individuals, who make free and moral choices that grant meaning and purpose to our lives; and, even more personally, giving hope that desperate prayers may not go unheard and unanswered, and that the terrors of death can be subdued in immortality. Religions, too, do not justify themselves with a single logical argument, but minister to all of these spiritual needs and provide a space in our lives where the largest questions with which we grapple all come together, which is a space that can become among the most expansive and loving of which we are capable, or the most constricted and hating of which we are capable—in other words, a space as contradictory as human nature itself.

ACKNOWLEDGMENTS

I wish to shout out my gratitude to both the Guggenheim Foundation and the Radcliffe Institute, Harvard University, for supporting the writing of this novel. Among the wonderful fellows at the Radcliffe Institute during the year of my residence was Megan Marshall, who was one of the first of my readers. I thank her for her comments and her friendship.

Gabriel Love was another early reader who provided me with essential feedback. Elaine Pfefferblit's comments were, as always, illuminating.

I am grateful to the following people for being, I'd wager, the only ones in the world who would not respond "huh?" when sent my bizarre questions but answered them with precision and playfulness: Douglas Hofstadter, Martin Seligman, and, pivotally, Doron Zeilberger.

Readers may be surprised to learn that I did not make up the Kabbalistic musings on such Jewish delicacies as potato kugel, but learned of them from the article "Holy Kugel: The Sanctification of Ashkenazic Ethnic Foods in Hasidism," by Allan Nadler, reprinted in *Food & Judaism,* edited by Leonard Greenspoon, Creighton University Press, 2005. The puns on philosophers' names in chapter VIII come from the Web site www.philosophicallexicon.com, to which many contribute and which is edited by Daniel Dennett and Asbjørn Steglich-Petersen.

It is a gift for me to be able to avail myself of the wealth of smarts, from the most practical to the most literary, that Tina Bennett provides. Stephanie Koven has been wonderful in her efforts on behalf of this book. I thank the stars to have been able to place my work in the hands of Dan Frank, an editor with whom I have long dreamed of working.

The gratitude and love that I owe my partner, Steve Pinker, are too deep and too many for the telling. Suffice it to say that, among all the profusion of his talents, is his perfect knowledge of love.

I selfishly raised my two daughters, Yael Goldstein Love and Danielle Blau, to be astute critics, and they have never let me down. Each has become a consummate artist in her own right. This book is dedicated to Danielle, who helped me, through all the years, not to lose Azarya. It is often her voice and her purity of vision that I hear and see in him.

SUM: FORTY TALES FROM THE AFTERLIVES
David Eagleman

At once funny, wistful, and unsettling, *Sum* is a dazzling exploration of unexpected afterlives—each presented as a vignette that offers a stunning lens through which to see ourselves in the here and now. In one afterlife, you may find that God is the size of a microbe and unaware of your existence. In another version, you work as a background character in other people's dreams. Or you may find that God is a married couple, or that the universe is running backward. With a probing imagination and deep understanding of the human condition, acclaimed neuroscientist David Eagleman offers wonderfully imagined tales that shine a brilliant light on the here and now.

Fiction/978-0-307-38993-0

EINSTEIN'S DREAMS
Alan Lightman

A modern classic, *Einstein's Dreams* is a fictional collage of stories dreamed by Albert Einstein in 1905, when he worked in a patent office in Switzerland. As the defiant but sensitive young genius is creating his theory of relativity, a new conception of time, he imagines many possible worlds. Now translated into thirty languages, *Einstein's Dreams* has inspired playwrights, dancers, musicians, and painters all over the world. In poetic vignettes, it explores the connections between science and art, the process of creativity, and ultimately the fragility of human existence.

Fiction/Literature/978-1-4000-7780-9

THE INVISIBLE BRIDGE
Julie Orringer

Paris, 1937. Andras Lévi, a Hungarian-Jewish architecture student, arrives from Budapest with a scholarship, a single suitcase, and a mysterious letter he promised to deliver. But when he falls into a complicated relationship with the letter's recipient, he becomes privy to a secret that will alter the course of his—and his family's—history. From the small Hungarian town of Konyár to the grand opera houses of Budapest and Paris, from the despair of Carpathian winter to an unimaginable life in labor camps, *The Invisible Bridge* tells the story of a family shattered and remade in history's darkest hour.

Fiction/978-1-4000-3437-6

A BLIND MAN CAN SEE HOW MUCH I LOVE YOU
Amy Bloom

In *A Blind Man Can See How Much I Love You*, National Book Award nominee Amy Bloom enhances her reputation as a true artist of the short story form. Here are characters confronted with tragedy, perplexed by emotions, and challenged to endure whatever modern life may have in store. A loving mother accompanies her daughter in her journey to become a man, and discovers a new, hopeful love. A stepmother and stepson meet again after fifteen years and a devastating mistake, and rediscover their familial affection for each other. And in "The Story," a widow bent on seducing another woman's husband constructs and deconstructs her story until she has "made the best and happiest ending" possible "in this world."

Fiction/Short Stories/978-0-375-70557-1

HIS ILLEGAL SELF
Peter Carey

Seven-year-old Che Selkirk was raised in isolated privilege by his New York grandmother. The son of radical student activists at Harvard in the late sixties, Che has grown up with the hope that one day his parents will come back for him. So when a woman arrives at his front door and whisks him away to the jungles of Queensland, he is confronted with the most important questions of his life: Who is his real mother? Did he know his real father? And if all he suspects is true, what should he do? In this artful tale of a young boy's journey, *His Illegal Self* lifts your spirit in the most unexpected way.

Fiction/Literature/978-0-307-27649-0

THE PREGNANT WIDOW
Martin Amis

The year is 1970, and the youth of Europe are in the chaotic, ecstatic throes of the sexual revolution. Though blindly dedicated to the cause, its nubile foot soldiers have yet to realize this disturbing truth: that between the death of one social order and the birth of another, there exists a state of terrifying purgatory—or, as Alexander Herzen put it, a pregnant widow. Keith Nearing is stuck in an exquisite limbo. Twenty years old and on vacation from college, Keith and an assortment of his peers are spending the long, hot summer in a castle in Italy. The tragicomedy of manners that ensues will have an indelible effect on all its participants, and we witness, too, how it shapes Keith's subsequent love life for decades to come.

Fiction/Literature/978-1-4000-9598-8

ATLAS OF UNKNOWNS
Tania James

An utterly irresistible first novel: The story of two sisters, the yearning to disappear into another country, and the powerful desire to return to the known world. Linno is a gifted artist, despite a childhood accident that has left her badly maimed, and Anju is one of Kerala's most promising students. Both girls dream of coming to the United States, but it is Anju who wins a scholarship to a prestigious school in New York. She seizes it, even though it means lying and betraying her sister. When her lie is discovered, Anju disappears; when Linno learns of Anju's disappearance, Linno strikes out farther still, with a scheme to come to America to look for her sister and save them both.

Fiction/Literature/978-0-307-38901-5

EVERYMAN
Philip Roth

Everyman explores one man's lifelong skirmish with mortality in this candidly intimate yet universal story of loss, regret, and stoicism. The fate of Roth's everyman is traced from his first shocking confrontation with death on the idyllic beaches of his childhood summers, through the family trials and professional achievements of his vigorous adulthood, and into his old age. The terrain of this powerful novel is the human body. Its subject is the common experience that terrifies us all.

Fiction/Literature/978-0-307-28036-7

HOTEL DU LAC
Anita Brookner

In the novel that won her the Booker Prize and established her international reputation, Anita Brookner finds a new vocabulary for framing the eternal question "Why love?" It tells the story of Edith Hope, who writes romance novels under a pseudonym. When her life begins to resemble the plots of her own novels, however, Edith flees to Switzerland, where the quiet luxury of the Hotel du Lac promises to restore her to her senses. But instead of peace and rest, Edith finds herself sequestered at the hotel with an assortment of love's casualties and exiles. Beautifully observed, witheringly funny, *Hotel du Lac* is Brookner at her most stylish and potently subversive.

Fiction/978-0-679-75932-4

VINTAGE BOOKS
Available at your local bookstore, or visit
www.randomhouse.com

Meet with Interesting People
Enjoy Stimulating Conversation
Discover Wonderful Books

Visit ReadingGroupCenter.com where you'll find great reading choices—award winners, bestsellers, beloved classics, and many more—and extensive resources for reading groups such as:

Author Chats
Exciting contests offer reading groups the chance to win one-on-one phone conversations with Vintage and Anchor Books authors.

Extensive Discussion Guides
Guides for over 450 titles as well as non–title specific discussion questions by category for fiction, nonfiction, memoir, poetry, and mystery.

Personal Advice and Ideas
Reading groups nationwide share ideas, suggestions, helpful tips, and anecdotal information. Participate in the discussion and share your group's experiences.

Behind the Book Features
Specially designed pages which can include photographs, videos, original essays, notes from the author and editor, and book-related information.

Reading Planner
Plan ahead by browsing upcoming titles, finding author event schedules, and more.

Special for Spanish-language reading groups
www.grupodelectura.com
A dedicated Spanish-language content area complete with recommended titles from Vintage Español.

A selection of some favorite reading group titles from our list

Atonement by Ian McEwan
Balzac and the Little Chinese Seamstress by Dai Sijie
The Blind Assassin by Margaret Atwood
The Devil in the White City by Erik Larson
Empire Falls by Richard Russo
The English Patient by Michael Ondaatje
A Heartbreaking Work of Staggering Genius by Dave Eggers
The House of Sand and Fog by Andre Dubus III
A Lesson Before Dying by Ernest J. Gaines

Lolita by Vladimir Nabokov
Memoirs of a Geisha by Arthur Golden
Midnight in the Garden of Good and Evil by John Berendt
Midwives by Chris Bohjalian
Push by Sapphire
The Reader by Bernhard Schlink
Snow by Orhan Pamuk
An Unquiet Mind by Kay Redfield Jamison
Waiting by Ha Jin
A Year in Provence by Peter Mayle